WICKED

"THE DOROTHY PARKER MURDER CASE is a lute delight from the opening quip to the parting shot . . . . An enormous cast of real-life personalities . . . seem[s] to come alive on virtually every page, not all of them in too pleasant a light, which makes this a very wicked read. Luckily for Baxt, you can't libel the dead."

—Tom and Enid Schantz
Denver Post

"An entertaining and surprisingly touching read."
The Detroit News

"One delightful mystery."

—Herbert L. Carson
Grand Rapids Press

"Characterization by wisecrack . . . But it's a very high class of wisecrack, and that makes this book a bright and diverting entertainment."

—Bob Wiemer
Newsday

"A delight . . . The book's best feature is the intelligent banter between Mrs. Parker and her fellow wit Alexander Woollcott. Be prepared for puns, and don't be too hard on Woollcott if he recycles some old jokes. After all, as Mrs. Parker explains, her friend has a 'one-crack mind.' "

—Keith Graham
Atlanta Journal Constitution

BY GEORGE BAXT:

The Pharoah Love Trilogy

A QUEER KIND OF DEATH*
SWING LOW, SWEET HARRIET*
TOPSY AND EVIL*

The Van Larsen/Plotkin Series

A PARADE OF COCKEYED CREATURES*
"I!" SAID THE DEMON*
SATAN IS A WOMAN*

The Celebrity Series

THE DOROTHY PARKER MURDER CASE*
THE ALFRED HITCHCOCK MURDER CASE*
THE TALLULAH BANKHEAD MYSTERY CASE*

Non-Series Novels

THE AFFAIR AT ROYALTIES*
BURNING SAPHO
THE NEON GRAVEYARD*
PROCESS OF ELIMINATION
WHO'S NEXT*

now available in a Crime Classics® edition.

THE DOROTHY PARKER MURDER CASE

GEORGE BAXT

INTERNATIONAL POLYGONICS, LTD.
NEW YORK CITY

For the Brickels—Gail, Steve, Elise, and Matthew

THE DOROTHY PARKER MURDER CASE

Copyright © 1984 by George Baxt.
Originally published by St. Martin's Press.
Reprinted with permission.

Cover: Copyright © 1989 by Nicky Zann.

Library of Congress Card Catalog No. 86-80384
ISBN 1-55882-056-6

Printed and manufactured in the United States
of America.
First IPL printing April 1986. New edition November 1989.
10 9 8 7 6 5 4 3 2 1

The following information appeared in the original
hardcover edition:
Library of Congress Cataloging in Publication Data
Baxt, George
The Dorothy Parker murder case.
1. Parker, Dorothy, 1893 - 1967,
in fiction, etc. I. Title
PS3552.A8478D6 1984 813'.54 84-13271
ISBN 0-312-21791-9

After slitting her wrists, Dorothy Parker sat in the bathroom patiently waiting to be rescued. Her delicate hands were submerged in the washbasin, which was filled almost to the brim with warm water. Her previous attempts at slitting her wrists had been messy and painful, and a kindly nurse at St. Luke's had suggested the submersion in warm water for future reference. She recognized suicide in Mrs. Parker as a chronic condition. The nurse had confided to a trainee impressed by Mrs. Parker's growing celebrity, "They're all alike, these halfway suicides. Just looking for sympathy. A kind word. Or just blackmailing the poor son of a bitch what threw them over. The idea is to fill the bastard with guilt once he gets wind of the news she tried to pass over with a straightedge razor. This one didn't really cut deep enough. It's all superficial. If she'd really meant to go, she'd have jumped off the roof."

"I'm afraid of heights," said Mrs. Parker to the nurse, who blushed. She'd thought the patient was unconscious.

"There there, my dear," said the nurse, swiftly recovering from her embarrassment. "Mr. Woollcott's in the waiting room."

"Waiting for what?"

"Waiting to take you home."

That scene had played two years ago, and here she was again, taking center stage in the revival. Waiting to be rescued by Alexander Woollcott, who should have called for her fifteen minutes ago to take her to lunch at the Algonquin. She stared at her watch, which was propped up on the basin against the wall, under the mirror in which Mrs. Parker had just turned away from her reflection abashedly. Alec was late, and the water in the basin was turning an alarming color, fiery, topaz red. I'm losing a lot of blood, thought Mrs. Parker, albeit not yet alarmed. This could be fatal. Mrs. Parker sighed. The blood of a poet. Dead before her time. Such a small body of work to show for her thirty-odd years on earth. She thought of *Enough Rope,* her first collection of poetry soon to be issued by Boni and Liveright, and of the Pulitzer Prize she'd be awarded posthumously. She thought of Harold Ross, editor and publisher of *The New Yorker* magazine, and her column of book reviews now two days overdue. The hell with Ross and the hell with book reviews and the hell with all creative writing. I need to be in love.

Feeling about to nod off, she roused herself. She stifled a yawn. She looked at the watch. Woollcott was now twenty minutes late. The porcine oaf. If she'd try being honest with herself, she'd admit to not really liking the critic. Androgynous people repelled her, and Alec in her eyes was repulsive. As a critic, she found his preferences deplorable and his prejudices despicable. As to his writing in general, she often wished the alphabet hadn't been invented. As to trading smart talk with him, she frequently accused him of shooting from the quip. But then there was his avuncular side. Her face softened at the thought of it. He could be kind and thoughtful. He could be warm and merry. He could be, but not often. Like now. I'm dying, you son of a bitch, where are you? She stifled another yawn, shook her head to keep herself awake, and thought about changing the water in the basin.

Her head rolled back. She stared at the ceiling. There she saw the face of her most recent lover, Richman Seward Collins. Oh, go away, Richman, go away. You're out of my life, stay out of my life. Just wait until you've heard I tried to commit suicide. You egotistical mutt. You'll be crowing all over Europe that you drove me to it.

"How can you fall in love so often?"

Sara Murphy's face replaced that of the recent lover. It was Sara as she remembered her that warm afternoon just a few months ago, seated across from her on the outdoor terrace of a café in Cap d'Antibes. She was Sara and her husband Gerald's houseguest while still deeply involved with Richman Collins. "Well, Dottie, I'm waiting. How *can* you fall in love so often?"

"I have no taste." Mrs. Parker sipped her apéritif while waiting for Sara to remonstrate. Sara didn't. Mrs. Parker tried to mask her annoyance as she settled back in the cane chair with her arms folded. "Actually, Richman's swell. There's plenty of gals who think he's the cat's pajamas."

"Oh, he's quite attractive," said Sara agreeably. "But you just don't get along with each other. You're temperamentally unsuited. Those arguments!"

"Have we been terribly noisy?" She looked like a naughty child, and Sara resisted the urge to reach across the table and embrace her friend.

"Romance is never very easy for you, is it, Dottie?"

"Is it for anyone, after the initial rash of passion fades away?"

"Gerald and I still love each other deeply."

"Yes, I know. How do you put up with it?" The Murphys also had three children and were terribly rich. But so was Richman. "I wonder if his name is eponymous."

"Whose name?" asked Sara, somewhat perplexed by the non sequitur.

"Richman's. Rich man, get it?"

"Got it. Now take it back."

"He's so terribly rich. All those tobacco shops his family owns." She folded her hands in her lap. "He gives me money. He's paid all my debts. Does that make me a whore?"

"No, that just makes you kept."

"From what?"

"From writing."

"I don't like writing."

"What else are you equipped for?"

"I've often thought of going into police work," Mrs. Parker said. Sara shifted in her chair. "Well, why not?"

"If you go into police work, you ought to start by investigating why you fall in love with so many rotters. Take your husband . . ."

"You take him, I can't stand him. I haven't seen him in six years."

"He's an alcoholic. Didn't you know he was an alcoholic when you married him?"

"There wasn't time. He went from the altar to the army. He came home a morphine addict. Poor Ed."

"Why don't you divorce him?"

"Oh, I'll get around to it one of these years."

"What about Charley MacArthur?"

"What about him?" Mrs. Parker looked uncomfortable.

"He drove you to attempt suicide."

Mrs. Parker was staring at the sailboats on the Mediterranean. "Charley was something special."

"Another drunkard."

"All newspapermen are drunkards. There isn't one of the Algonquin bunch who ever draws a sober breath except for about thirty minutes after they arise in the morning."

"George S. Kaufman doesn't drink."

"We'll get him yet."

"And then there was Ring Lardner."

Mrs. Parker suddenly bristled with indignation. "Who told you about Ring and me?"

"You did. All that winter."

Mrs. Parker fussed with the hem of her dress. "My life is an open book. But it's not a best-seller. Let's order another drink."

The bathroom was stifling. Mrs. Parker thought, Who but a damned fool like me would attempt suicide on one of the hottest days in August? Her brow was damp, and her eyes were moist as she thought of MacArthur and Lardner and her unrequited love for Bob Benchley. She thought of Edwin Parker and faced the truth that she had never been in love with him, that she married him because she was tired of being Miss Rothschild. She wanted to be Mrs. Anybody and prove to her despised stepmother that she was perfectly capable of attracting and winning a man of her own. Some prize. Sleep began to overtake her again. She lowered her head and dozed.

It was the previous Friday at the Algonquin. Some of the regulars were with Mrs. Parker at the Round Table in the Rose Room. Franklin P. Adams, looking like a mustached gopher, entered the room commenting, "There must be life on Mars. There's certainly none here." As he sat, he acknowledged Mrs. Parker. "When did you get back from Europe?"

"Last night."

"And dare one ask what has become of Mr. Collins?"

"Look behind me. I've thrown him over."

"All that wealth." He stared at Robert Benchley, who sat next to Mrs. Parker. Benchley shrugged. George S. Kaufman, who was studying the menu, asked Mrs. Parker what she was thinking of eating.

"My young."

"Is it just the four of us for lunch?" asked F.P.A. as he signaled a waiter for a drink.

"If we're lucky," said Kaufman. Then he saw Alexander Woollcott arriving. "We're not lucky."

Woollcott espied Mrs. Parker and stopped in his tracks. "My God!" he exclaimed in a voice loud enough to arouse the attention of the entire room. "It's the orphan of the storm! My dear, my dear, welcome home." Mrs. Parker sat stiffly as he reached her and kissed her cheek. "Where's the boyfriend?"

"He is now consigned to a position in my history." Mrs. Parker gently raised her teacup and sipped her gin. F.P.A.'s drink arrived, and he raised his teacup in salute to Mrs. Parker. Woollcott lowered his ample body onto a chair next to Mrs. Parker. He patted her hand gently.

"I'm glad you're back. If you're free, you can accompany me tonight to one of the summer concerts at Aeolian Hall."

"Is Toscanini conducting?" she asked softly.

"I wouldn't baton it," replied Woollcott swiftly.

Mrs. Parker groaned. She heard Woollcott shouting her

name. The front door was opening, and there stood the building janitor, shoved to one side by Woollcott as he came hurrying into her small studio. "Dottie! *Dottie!* Where the hell are you?"

"The phone's off the hook," offered the janitor as he sniffed the stale air in the room. Woollcott found Mrs. Parker.

"Oh, Christ, not again!" He grabbed hand towels and ministered swiftly to Mrs. Parker, attending to her wounded wrists with the alacrity he had displayed as a hospital attendant during the late Great War.

"I knew you'd rescue me," said Mrs. Parker in a pathetic voice that reminded Woollcott of Maude Adams's impassioned plea to her audience at *Peter Pan* to believe in fairies.

"Of course you did," snapped Woollcott. "You remembered we had a date for lunch." The bathroom was a mess, and the janitor stood in the doorway clucking his tongue. From the unattended condition of the studio and the mess in the bathroom, he had come to the decision Mrs. Parker was as big a slob as his wife. Woollcott turned to the man and peremptorily ordered him out of the apartment. "Thank you for the use of your passkey. As you can see, Mrs. Parker has cut herself while giving herself a manicure." The janitor shook his head back and forth while clucking his way out. Woollcott regarded Mrs. Parker sternly as he bandaged a wrist with a roll of gauze he found in the medicine chest. "Why don't you get zippers for your wrists?"

"Don't be cruel." Her voice was so soft he had to strain to hear her. "I really meant it this time. I really want to die."

Woollcott's owlish face reshaped itself into a look of compassion. "No man is worth this. Besides, you haven't given yourself enough time to get over Collins." With the left hand bandaged, Woollcott now concentrated his attention on the right wrist. "This is really nasty."

"So was our last fight in Paris. I got so mad, I threw the wristwatch he gave me out the window and do you know what the son of a bitch does? He goes running out into the street to reclaim it. Can you imagine? He leaves me standing in the middle of the room without so much as an apology or a by your leave to go running after some expensive fucking wristwatch. He could buy dozens of the goddamn things and never notice the dent in his bankroll!"

"I suppose it is cruel to find yourself taking a back seat to a piece of jewelry, but then, we all have different priorities. I suppose I should get you to a doctor, but there's no time."

"What's the rush? I certainly don't have an appetite."

He helped her out of the bathroom. In the studio, Woollcott looked around with an undisguised expression of distaste. "How can you live in all this filth and disorder? When was the last time you had this room cleaned?"

"I think it was New Year's Day." She lowered herself into an easy chair and stared at her bandaged wrists. "Alec, will you be a dear and look in the top drawer of my dressing table? You'll find some lovely velvet bracelets I had designed especially for these occasions." Woollcott lumbered across the room, found the bracelets, and then watched as she camouflaged the bandages. "There!" she cried, displaying her handiwork with pride. "Don't they look lovely?" Woollcott looked at his wristwatch and then sat across from Mrs. Parker.

"Kaufman's in trouble." He watched as she applied a kitchen match to the cigarette in her mouth.

"Bea found out about a new sweetheart?" She well knew Beatrice Kaufman couldn't care less about her husband's affairs. Their marriage had ceased to be a sexual one by mutual consent, and now all their energies were concentrated on the welfare of their recently adopted daughter, Anne. Kaufman maintained a small apartment of his own in a building on West Seventy-second Street as the setting for his frequent assignations, mostly with prostitutes.

"Something's happened that Beatrice must never find out about." The gravity of his voice captured Mrs. Parker's complete attention. She was even kind enough to exhale smoke away from his face. "There's a dead woman in Kaufman's pied-à-terre."

Mrs. Parker's mouth was open with shock. "You're not telling me he's murdered her."

"He found the body shortly before noon. She was supposed to have been out of there by then."

"If there's a beginning to this story, I wish you'd start there." She stubbed the cigarette out in an ashtray and then leaned forward with her hands clasped between her well-shaped legs.

"Last night, George loaned the apartment to Ilona Mercury." Mrs. Parker screwed up her face. The name rang no bell. "Ilona Mercury is that exotic beauty Flo Ziegfeld imported from Hungary for last year's production of the *Follies*."

"Oh, yes. That one. Her face was plastered all over the newspapers."

"So was her body."

"Has George been to bed with her?"

"Not last night."

"Doesn't she have an apartment of her own?"

"She lives in a hotel in the West Thirties."

"Then why did she have to borrow George's place?"

"There are several gentlemen who have keys to her hotel apartment."

"I see. She was afraid the traffic would get too heavy."

"One of the gentlemen is a celebrated gangster with a lethal right fist."

"I see. So this time Ilona had someone special on the string and needed someplace neutral for the big moment. And good old George came through with his private sex salon. And now Ilona is dead and George is the most likely suspect."

"Who's supposed to be telling this story?"

"Where's George now?"

"With the body, waiting for us to join him."

Mrs. Parker had left the chair and was staring out an

opened window. "Does George know the name of last night's big moment?"

"He swears he doesn't. He's always been very fond of Ilona, so he just gave her a set of keys to the place and she promised to be out before noon today."

"Well, she's certainly out. Do you believe Kaufman's story?"

"Why would he lie?"

"To protect himself."

"Are you insinuating Kaufman's killed her and is lying to us? I thought you liked George!"

"I adore George. I can't understand why I've never had an affair with him." She was now sitting at her dressing table fixing her hair. Her look of concentration made Woollcott think of himself as a child trying to sew an eye back into his wounded teddy bear.

"Dottie, I wish you'd hurry. It can't be pleasant for George sitting there with a corpse."

"Especially in this weather. I hope he's had the sense to open the windows."

Five minutes later they were in a Checker taxicab slowly snaking their way from Dorothy's building on West Fifty-seventh Street. "Do you know if any of the other boys at the Algonquin have received a share of Miss Mercury's favors?" Woollcott sank deep into thought. "Marc Connelly? Bobby Sherwood?"

"Not Bobby. He's very faithful to that dreary wife of his."

Mrs. Parker recited the roll call. F.P.A.? Donald Ogden Stewart? Harold Ross? Benchley? Harpo Marx? Heywood Broun? Woollcott's face lit up. "Possibly Broun." Mrs. Parker momentarily had a vision of the ursine Broun wrestling in bed with the Hungarian beauty and then dismissed the scene from her mind as highly unlikely.

"She sounds like a perfect diversion for Charley MacArthur," he said.

"He's out of town."

"What about Ben Hecht?"

"He's out of touch."

"Certainly not you."

"Certainly not, and this is hardly the time for whimsy. Driver, what is all that awful traffic congestion ahead of us?" They had turned right into Broadway heading uptown, and traffic heading in both directions was jammed up. Trolley cars were stalled with passengers hanging out the windows trading japes with passengers in stalled autos. A beer wagon fronted by a team of horses adjoined an elegant Minerva Landaulet imported from Belgium, the driver of the beer wagon making lewd suggestions to the ladies seated in the back seat of the town car. Mounted policemen and foot patrols were trying vainly to unsnarl the bottlenecks.

"Is it a parade?" asked Mrs. Parker.

"Lady, it's a funeral," the driver told her. "Dincha know Rudolph Valentino died yesterday?"

Along with my will to live, thought Dorothy. "No, I didn't know. Did you know, Alec?"

"Of course I knew. It was in all the bulldog editions. The poor bastard. And only thirty-one years old."

The driver worried his klaxon for a while until Woollcott demanded he desist. "Exercising that ugly horn of yours will hardly alleviate the situation. Will you look at that crowd, Dottie, it's unbelievable. Why, for crying out loud, almost all the women are dressed in black. It's *unbelievable.*"

The driver laughed. "Some broad committed suicide this morning. She left a note saying she was going to join Rudy. Can you beat that? Even my missus hung the laundry at half-mast. Y'know the rumor's around he was poisoned." He pronounced it "perzonned."

Woollcott was making notes in a pocket pad. "What's the date?"

"August twenty-fourth, nineteen hundred and twenty-six," contributed Mrs. Parker.

"How clever you are."

"August twenty-second was my birthday."

"Aha," said Woollcott, "which precipitated this morning's

unfortunate decision to do yourself the injuries."

"The decision was made two days ago. It took that long for me to get moving. Do you suppose we ought to get out and walk?"

"It's too hot to walk."

"It's stifling in this cab."

"We're only at West Sixty-sixth Street. It's six blocks more." They stared out the window at Frank Campbell's funeral parlor where Valentino's body was on view. There was a line that stretched out of sight of people waiting to view the remains. Newspaper photographers swarmed wildly like locusts in heat, and Woollcott and Mrs. Parker recognized several of the reporters milling around the entrance of Campbell's.

Woollcott was writing feverishly. "Why would they suspect he might have been murdered?"

"It was in all the papers," the cabby told him. "He was at this here private party on the night of August fourteenth given by that there rich guy somebody Van Weber."

"Lacey Van Weber," Mrs. Parker contributed.

Woollcott blinked his owl eyes. *"Lacey Van Weber?* Sounds like a name only Edna could conjure up for one of her novels. Gaylord Ravenal. Magnolia Hawkes." Mrs. Parker wrinkled her nose. She wasn't a fan of Edna Ferber's and barely tolerated her presence at the Algonquin Round Table. She knew Woollcott's eyes were riveted to her face.

"Where did *you* ever hear about Lacey Van Weber?" he asked.

"There was an article about him in the *Daily Graphic* on Monday."

"I didn't know you read that rotten scandal sheet."

"As a rule I don't. But Neysa does." Neysa McMein, the artist, and her husband, John Baragwanath, were Mrs. Parker's neighbors. "I found a copy lying outside Neysa's door, so I copped it. Mr. Van Weber sounds absolutely fascinating. And he's a real good looker."

"Obviously, the article was illustrated."

"Obviously."

"Well?"

"Well, what?"

"Well, what about Lacey Van Weber?"

"What do you want to know? And why do you care?"

"Because Mr. Valentino took ill at Van Weber's party."

"So?"

"The lady he escorted to the party was Ilona Mercury."

Mrs. Parker rearranged herself so that she faced Woollcott. "Now how the hell do you know *that?*"

"Kaufman told me earlier. Stop looking so perplexed. I haven't told you everything that went on with George because there hasn't been time. The Mercury thing was terribly upset when she asked George for the use of his place. One of the things upsetting her was Valentino's death. That's when she told him she had been with him at the party."

"Continue. I'm fascinated."

"That's about as much as I know. Well, there wasn't all that much time to palaver on the phone. George was upset and needed help right away. There was no reaching you by phone because you had yours off the hook. And for all I know, since it seems to be taking us an eternity to arrive for his rescue, he's probably turned himself in to the police and the devil take the hindmost."

"We're clear," sang out the cabdriver. "You realize what we just drove through was history."

"Young man. I have been through the Great War. *That* was history."

The driver stared at Woollcott through his rear-view mirror. "Listen, mister. There'll be lotsa wars. But there'll only be one Valentino."

Mrs. Parker leaned back in her seat with a sly smile. "And Henry Mencken dares revile the likes of him as the booboisie."

"Where the hell have you been?" George S. Kaufman held the door slightly ajar. His friends could see he was under a severe strain. As Mrs. Parker was later to explain, the bags under his eyes could have accommodated a week's laundry. His hair, an oversized bird's nest when properly looked after, now gave him the appearance of a Zulu warrior fighting a high wind.

"You'll have to open the door wider," snapped Woollcott. "I could never pass through the space you're allowing me." Kaufman moved away from the door and Woollcott pushed it open. Mrs. Parker followed him into the apartment, gently closing the door behind her. The living room was simply furnished. The windows were wide open. They looked out on the street. "Where's the stiff?" asked Woollcott.

"In the bedroom, of course," Kaufman told him sullenly, "where she's most at home." Mrs. Parker decided the door straight ahead would lead to the bedroom, and the men followed her. Kaufman recognized the velvet bracelets disguising Mrs. Parker's bandaged wrists. "For Christ's sake, Dottie, you didn't try it again."

"For want of anything grimmer to do." She pushed the bedroom door open and was grateful Kaufman had been thoughtful enough to open both windows. "She's beginning to decompose."

Kaufman remained in the doorway with his hands on his hips. "I wish people would have the decency to decompose in their own apartments."

In death, Ilona Mercury looked nowhere near as alluring as Mrs. Parker imagined she must have looked in life. Her face was bloated. Her tongue protruded from between bulbous lips. The color of her skin was a bluish-gray. Her honey-colored bobbed hair was a mess, hanging over her forehead and almost masking the eyes which were half open. Her sleeveless blue sheath was hiked over her knees, and Mrs. Parker briefly considered the decorum of readjusting the dress until she realized the hemline would reach just above the knees anyway. "I think she's been strangled."

"Let me have a go at her," said Woollcott.

"That's Alec's standing offer, after they're dead." Woollcott glared at Kaufman.

"Innuendo, and out the other. And let's spare each other the smart-ass repartee. This is serious business." Woollcott devoted his attention to the corpse. Kaufman walked slowly into the room until he was standing next to Mrs. Parker. "She's been strangled, of course. Looks to me as though she died sometime last night."

"She left me a little after ten," Kaufman told them. "I met her at Gino's, that's a little joint over on West Seventy-third, for dinner around eight and to give her the set of keys to the apartment. That's when she told me about the party at Van Weber's."

"I want to hear about that," said Mrs. Parker as she led the men back to the living room. She shared the couch with Kaufman while Woollcott sank into a morris chair and after three attempts to cross his legs, settled for legs outstretched, one ankle across the other.

"I liked Ilona," said Kaufman.

"Obviously." Woollcott sounded smug, and it was at a time like this that Mrs. Parker had to resist the urge to excoriate him.

"She had a great sense of humor."

"George, tell us what she told you about the party."

"Oh, the hell with the party!" He leaped to his feet, running his hands through his hair. "What do I do about this? I can't afford a scandal. They might take Anne away from us and that would kill Bea. How do I get out of this?"

"I'll get you out of this," said Mrs. Parker confidently. "My friend Jacob Singer will come to the rescue. He owes me a few." Both Woollcott and Kaufman knew detective Jacob Singer, the legendary Manhattan lawman. Big Jake with the beefy fists, the scourge of the underworld, the terror of the Chinatown tongs and Little Italy's Black Hand. He'd even been known to take on a ferocious rabbi he suspected of bottling illegal sacramental wines. Jacob Singer had one lamentable shortcoming. He was incorruptible. He played everything straight, his career, his private life and stud poker. Mrs. Parker had often wished he'd make a pass at her, but to a man like Singer a celebrity like Mrs. Parker

-14-

was an untouchable. "Now tell me what Miss Mercury told you about the party."

Kaufman sat down. "Ziegfeld introduced her to Valentino, who invited her to be his date. Ilona knew Van Weber and seemed annoyed she didn't have an invitation of her own. She wasn't particularly fascinated by Valentino or of the prospect of spending an evening with him . . ."

". . . because, dollink, I've been told he's such a *bore.*" Ilona was ignoring the plate of spaghetti she'd been served and instead sipped red wine from the coffee cup in which it had been served. Prohibition was no match for the clever restaurateurs determined to hold onto their drinking clientele. Kaufman was just as little interested in the chicken cacciatore congealing on the plate set before him. He sat with his arms folded and resting on the table, enjoying his stunning companion, as were several other gentlemen in the restaurant who were sneaking looks at her. "Besides, how dare Lacey Van Weber not invite me to his party? I who have introduced him to many of Ziegfeld's most gawjuss girls!"

Kaufman laughed. "You mean you weren't even looking forward to Valentino making a pass at you?"

"Valentino making a *pass* at a *voman?* Are you *mad,* dollink? Are you sniffink somet'ink?" She knew Kaufman neither took drugs nor drank nor smoked, but she enjoyed teasing him.

"Now you're not going to tell me those stories about him being a pink powder puff are true."

"I don't know vat color is the puff, but vomen are not on Valentino's diet."

"But he's been married twice."

"Hoo ha ha ha ha." She slapped the table and the silverware trembled. "First vife, Jean Acker. Lesbian."

"Aw, go on."

"I vill. Second and present vife, Natacha Rambova. Lesbian."

"I don't believe it."

"Is true. Even her name is phony. She is from the cosmetic family, the Hudnuts. Her real name is Vinifred . . ." meaning Winifred, ". . . Hudnut."

"You mean she's a Hudnut to crack."

"Rambova and Acker vere all part of Nazimova's harem in Hollywood."

"Alla Nazimova?"

"How many Nazimovas have you heard of? Is also said Valentino's true love is Ramon Novarro."

"Oh, now stop that and for God's sake lower your voice, we're the center of attention."

"That is because I am so stonning."

"You are so loud."

"So I am so loud and stonning. Vere vuss I? Oh, yes. Valentino is focking Ramon Novarro. But then, since he starred in *Ben Hur,* is very fashionable to fock Ramon Novarro. Anyway, the party is at Lacey's penthouse on Central Park Souse. *Everybody* is there. Lacey greet me like long-lost lover."

"Are you?"

"I call him naughty bastard not to invite me, and he say, 'But you are here, no, dollink?' Then he sees I am with Valentino, and this he doesn't like."

"Aha. He's jealous of Valentino."

"Is not important. Valentino is very sweet to him. From the moment they meet you would think they are longtime friends from the way Valentino acts. But then, Valentino is surrounded and I am left with ziss strange man. You perhaps know Joseph Force Crater?"

"Judge Crater? Oh, sure. I've met him a couple of times."

"At the party he is with Vera DeLee, one of Polly Adler's girls."

"I've met Vera. Sweet kid."

"Oh, sure. Judge Crater calls her the cat's meow. The judge, by the way, isn't very happy at the party. I remember he says to me, 'Someday, my dear young woman, life will catch up vit me and I just might have to disappear.' Kvaint, no?"

"Very quaint."

"Was also there your friend the playwright."

"I have lots of friends the playwright."

"The little bald one."

"Marc Connelly."

"Right!"

"Was also there Flo Ziegfeld, of course, who is having terrible time these days with money and also his wife."

"Billie Burke puts up with an awful lot from Flo. He's not very discreet about his affairs."

"Is lousy lay, Flo."

"Who was Connelly with?"

Ilona stared into her wine, and apparently that's where the name of Connelly's date for that night materialized. "Lily Robson." Ilona could tell from the blank look on Kaufman's face the name didn't ring a bell. "Lily is one of Texas Guinan's girls. She dances at the Club Guinan. Flaming red hair. She always looks as though her head's on fire. Anyway, was also movie stars, like Nita Naldi, who was in *Blood and Sand* with Valentino. She's a great gal, Naldi. She tells me Mae Murray likes to fock Cubans. Is cute, yes? And then"— her face darkened—"is there a man I detest."

"Don't tell me there's actually a man you don't like."

"Is many men I don't like, but not like I don't like Bela Horathy."

This name Kaufman recognized. "Dr. Bliss. It figures he'd be at a party with those high fliers."

"Dr. Bliss," repeated Ilona with a sneer. "Better his name is Dr. Caligari. I can see Valentino does not like him. Is very obvious. He knows, we all know, Bela Horathy is a drug pusher. How many lives, I wonder, has he destroyed."

"The cops have never been able to get a thing on him."

"Very clever man, Horathy. I remember stories from the old country."

"Which old country?"

"Hungary, you dear sweet man, what other old country could I *possibly* mean? They still remember him there. And Valentino remembers him from Hollywood. Oh, how he is

-17-

angry and scowling when he see Bela Horathy. He is like Vesuvius, vich is also Italian. How Valentino explodes! 'Murderer!' he screams wid his awful wop accent, pointing a manicured finger at Horathy. 'You destroy Wally Reid and Barbara LaMarr and Mabel Normand and you hook poor little Alma Rubens . . .' and he mentions all these Hollywood stars who either die from drugs or soon will and it is a terrible scene. Lacey tries to calm him. 'I say, old sport, let's get out on the terrace for a breath of fresh air.'" Ilona was playing every role in the melodrama she was describing, and the entire restaurant was mesmerized. "Judge Crater says, 'He needs a drink,' and gets him one. Then later, Rudy clutches his stomach and screams, 'Oh, my God! The pain! The pain!'"

"The *Times* said he suffered from ulcers.

Ilona leaned across the table conspiratorially and at last lowered her voice. "I think he was *poisoned*. Now may I have the keys? I do not vish to be late." She favored him with her dazzling smile. "Tonight is a most important night for Ilona."

"The ultimate night of importance for Ilona," appended Kaufman with a weary sigh. "I walked her here and then I took a cab home. When I got here shortly before noon, intending to do some work on my new play, I found her dead."

Mrs. Parker fixed him with her brown, fawnlike eyes. "You didn't touch the body? You didn't touch anything?"

"Just the phone to call Alec."

Woollcott had been making notes throughout Kaufman's discourse. Some of his best articles were dissertations on true life crime stories. He scented another beauty now. "I like this murder. I like this murder very much." Mrs. Parker expected him to smack his lips, but he disappointed her. "I'm going to stay with it. My instincts tell me this is the beginning of one of the most fascinating crime stories of this era. Don't you agree, Dottie?"

"I think it's more fascinating than making an inside

straight. I'd love to know who was Ilona's appointment in Samarra."

Kaufman began raging again. "Will you for God's sake get hold of Jacob Singer and get me out of this mess?"

"Always remember, George," said Mrs. Parker as she crossed to the telephone, "in defeat there is also triumph."

Woollcott, perplexed, screwed up his face as he asked, "Now who said *that?*"

Replied Mrs. Parker, "Why, I just did."

2

While Mrs. Parker was at the telephone tracking down detective Jacob Singer, Woollcott studied the notes in his pocket pad, mopping away at his forehead and neck with a large blue handkerchief. Kaufman was slumped in a straight-back chair, hands clasped and staring at the floor with the woebegone expression of a dyspeptic bassett hound. "Jake?" they heard Mrs. Parker trill. "I've found Jake," she announced. Her conversation with the detective was brief and to the point. In less than two minutes, she was finished with the telephone and seated on the couch. "He's on his way and in his own car. There'll be no police sirens, no hullabaloo, no inquisitive crowds gathered on the sidewalk. It'll all be as discreet and private as ladies' night at a Turkish bath. I wish one of you would try to look cheerful."

"Tell us about Lacey Van Weber." Woollcott's pince-nez dropped from the crown of his nose, dangling beneath his double chins from the chain around his neck. He leaned back and wiped his eyes with his handkerchief.

Kaufman said to Mrs. Parker, "I didn't know you knew Lacey Van Weber."

"I don't. I just happened to read an article about him in

the *Graphic*. It was illustrated. He's quite good-looking, with kind of movie star looks. Now, let me see . . . ," she said, pursing her lips and adjusting the velvet bracelets, ". . . he seems to be unmarried and available, apparently quite wealthy, knows everybody who's anybody, and there was a soupçon of a hint that he could have connections with the mob."

"Which mob?" asked Woollcott.

"I haven't the vaguest idea. There are so many of them. I suppose you just take your pick. For example, we know one of Texas Guinan's girls was at his party and everybody knows Larry Fay's behind Texas."

"They're lovers," said Kaufman.

"There you go," said Mrs. Parker agreeably, "so he's more than just behind her. And one of Polly Adler's girls was there, so whoever she's linked to . . . well, is she linked to anyone?"

"Polly insists she hasn't any mob connections. She runs a good house and without any outside interference." Kaufman was standing at a mirror trying to tame his hair.

"What else about Van Weber?" prodded Woollcott. "Anything juicy, scandalous, where does he come from?"

"The article hinted he was from a titled British family, although Van Weber strikes me as more Germanic than English."

"Maybe it's not his real name," said Kaufman.

"That's a thought. Jot that down, Alec." Alec dutifully made a note while Mrs. Parker continued. "In addition to his penthouse on Central Park South, he lives in a mansion in East Cove out on Long Island. He has a swimming pool, tennis courts, a golf course, a landing field. It seems he's also a licensed pilot . . . something like two dozen in help not counting additional servants hired for his parties. He maintains an office on Fifth Avenue in the mid-Thirties where presumably he waxes wealthy. There seems to be no particular light of love in his life, and until about a year ago, nobody had ever heard of him."

"You're kidding," said Kaufman.

"Oh, not at all. It's what's written in the article, not that you can ever believe or trust much of what is printed in the *Graphic*. But from what I can gather, Mr. Lacey Van Weber, like Mrs. Stowe's Topsy, 'jes' growed.' Don't you get the feeling that, by some miracle, he's the figment of someone's imagination who just happened to take human form? I think he's fascinating.

"Oh, dear," said Woollcott, "Dottie is in danger of falling in love in absentia."

"I'd love to meet him. I'd love to meet anyone who's sexy and sinister. In fact, I'd just love to meet anyone. I can't stand it when my emotions are gathering dust. That house in East Cove has twenty bedrooms."

Queried Woollcott, "Is that a statement or a challenge?" Kaufman was at one of the windows, standing forlornly like a derelict ship waiting to be claimed for salvage.

"Just think about him," persisted Mrs. Parker. "A man arrives in the city from out of nowhere and in the brief course of a year captures the imagination of the populace. He claims no major accomplishments, he hasn't discovered fire or invented the wheel, he's not a lionized hero . . ."

"Except perhaps to his butler," interjected Woollcott.

". . . and yet now when he snaps his fingers, just about anybody who's anybody jumps."

"Gangsters, whores, showgirls, crooked judges, that's anybody who's anybody?" Kaufman shook his head sadly and plunged his hands into his trouser pockets.

"That could be the tip of the iceberg." Mrs. Parker was beaming. In the brief course of an hour she had run the emotional gamut from deep tragedy to titillating melodrama. She was enjoying herself enormously. "After all, out there in East Cove you've got the elite of society. La crème de la crème. I'll bet every society matron and submatron including their virginal daughters wearing their most expensive deflowered prints are giving bloody battle to see who can fill their dance cards with Mr. Van Weber's name. You know, East Cove is not too far from Great Neck. The Lardners have a home in Great Neck. We could get ourselves invited out to the Lardners' this weekend, Alec. Then by some subterfuge or other, drive over to East Cove and invade Van Weber's kingdom."

"What *are* you carrying on about?" huffed Woollcott.

"It's necessary to meet the man if we're to solve the murder of that poor creature decomposing in the bedroom. You have to be interested—why else take those copious notes?"

"Well, of course I'm interested. But actual *physical* participation?"

"We're in a position to accomplish a hell of a lot more than the police. We're celebrities. Van Weber devours celebrities. After a steady diet of whores, gangsters and the perversely corrupt, I'm sure he's starving for a rich helping of culture. I'm sure he's thirsting to meet people like us and our peers. I'll bet he'd adore to swap funnies with Benchley and Broun, share his opinion of the Barrymores in *The Jest* . . ."

"I don't think I'd give a damn to hear what he thinks of them in *The Jest*," exploded Woollcott.

"I think Dottie's right," Kaufman interrupted softly but distinctly. "I think the guy's a direct line to Ilona's murder."

"And Valentino?" Mrs. Parker was trilling again.

"*If* he was murdered," responded Kaufman.

There was a knock at the door. Mrs. Parker leaped to her feet and admitted Jacob Singer. "Jacob, you're a dear. Are you alone?" She looked past him but saw no one else in the hallway.

"I got a couple of men in the car downstairs. I figured I'd get the lay of the land first and then decide what's needed. You cut your wrists again?"

"Just keeping in practice," she replied while shutting the door. "You know Woollcott and Kaufman."

"How do you do, gents." The trace of the Gowanus Canal in the detective's voice was about as much of Brooklyn as still clung to him. After ten years on the Manhattan police force (five of them in the elite group of detectives), Singer sought to improve himself both cosmetically and intellectually. He spent money on clothes and general good grooming and forced himself to read Dickens, Henry James, and on one brief depressing occasion, Tolstoy. He attended the theater and concerts as often as possible, but the opera only under the threat of death. Mrs. Parker's admiration for the man was honest and limitless. "Okay, Mr. Kaufman, what's the problem?"

"I've got a dead woman in the bedroom."

"I've had lots of those, but usually they get dressed and go home."

They followed him into the bedroom. "Oh boy, oh boy. That is one ugly stiff."

"She used to be quite beautiful," said Kaufman. "Ilona Mercury."

Singer pierced the air with a shrill whistle of astonishment. "I'd never guess. Would you believe just the other night I saw her in Ziegfeld's revue, *No Foolin'.*"

"We believe you," said Mrs. Parker.

Singer shot her a look. *"No Foolin'* is the name of the show. It's at the Globe."

"Oh. I've been away."

"Let's get back to the other room. This is too depressing. Imagine a beautiful broad like that turning into such an ugly slab of meat. That's life."

"That's death," corrected Mrs. Parker.

In the living room, the foursome sat facing one another, while Singer heard Kaufman's story. After Kaufman finished, the detective sat back and contemplated Mrs. Parker. "You want me to fix a cover-up."

"Well, George certainly didn't kill her. That body in there is just the unfortunate result of George's misplaced generosity."

"And if it turns out he did kill her, what then?"

"Why, he goes to the chair!" she shot back gaily.

"I did not kill her," insisted Kaufman. "What I've told you, Mr. Singer, is the truth."

Singer rubbed his chin with the palm of a hand. "So you think maybe there's some connection to this shindig where Valentino took sick. Boy, am I not looking forward to this investigation."

Mrs. Parker sat up like an eager lapdog. "Why not?"

"Ahhhh, already there's talk that there's a cover-up going on in Valentino's death. Like maybe he was poisoned, who the hell knows. He seemed healthy enough the day of the party." He was on his feet and pacing the room. "So Ilona was his date that night. And Valentino lets go a blast at Dr. Horathy."

"And Van Weber told somebody to get him a drink," reminded Mrs. Parker.

Singer stared at her. "That could have been the poison, eh?"

"Why not?" interjected Woollcott. "At a crowded party like that, there must be countless opportunities to commit murder without being apprehended."

Mrs. Parker snapped her fingers. "I've got it! Ilona Mercury saw whoever slipped Valentino the mickey and was blackmailing him!"

"Nice shot, Mrs. Parker," said Singer affably, "but why bring him here? She could have shaken him down in her own place or some restaurant or some gin mill or a bench in Central Park."

"Jacob, this apartment is something special," said Mrs. Parker. "It certainly is to Mr. Kaufman."

"Not any longer," said Kaufman with an agonized groan.

"Don't interrupt me, please. Ilona knows Mr. Kaufman well and therefore knows how special this apartment is. Whomever she brought here last night was someone special in her life. Obviously the feeling was one-sided. She may have been special to this person at one time, but no longer. For reasons we have to find out, she needed to be murdered."

"It could have been accidental," ventured Woollcott, "murder at the heat of passion."

"At the heat of passion, dear," said Mrs. Parker knowledgeably, "it may sometimes seem like murder, but it's rarely fatal, unless one or the other partner suffers from a weak heart. Miss Mercury's heart did not fail her, it was her trust in another human being. Now, Jacob, I think you're in for a difficult time with this case." Singer didn't deny her prescience. He continued studying her with subdued admiration, wondering, if only briefly, if at some future time he might suggest she share with him a tumble in the hay. "You know how people in high places clam up before the police."

"They do it in low places, too," said Singer.

"Well, my dear, these people are more accessible to people like Alec and myself. We intend to investigate, you know, like ambassadors without portfolio. Of course everything we learn we'll turn over to you."

"Mrs. Parker," said Singer, "we are all too familiar with your death wish. I don't think you're equipped to tackle the big boys."

"The trouble with you, Mr. Detective, is that you overestimate you and underestimate me."

"Maybe so, but I'm not underestimating people like Dr. Bela Horathy. He's not exactly known for being conducive to good health and a long life."

"So why haven't you pulled him in?" asked Kaufman.

"On what charges? He's a doctor. He's licensed. Nobody's caught him with his foot outside the law. And he's got big connections."

"Valentino accused him of being a drug pusher," said Woollcott.

"Do you know any doctors who don't prescribe drugs?" asked Singer. "Exactly. So it's a Mexican standoff."

"Horathy's a Hungarian," Mrs. Parker reminded them.

"You're so sure?" asked Singer.

"Oh. I see. There's some doubt." Mrs. Parker smiled at the three men. "Wouldn't the Immigration Department have something on him?"

"Sure. But that can be fixed, too. Mrs. Parker, we live in a world and in an era where everything can be fixed except the inevitable, which is death. Now let me tell you, if you and Mr. Woollcott want to stick your noses into this case, there's nothing I can do to stop you, unless you get caught breaking and entering, something ignoble like that." *Ignoble,* thought Mrs. Parker, he must be reading Victor Hugo. "But I want you to use excessive caution. I mean be really careful."

"You know more than you're telling us," said a somewhat nervous Woollcott.

"No, I don't. I just suspect more than I'm telling you." He pointed to the bedroom. "That unfortunate lady ain't the first to come to an untimely end from knowing all the wrong people. I'll give you a tip. Find out who she was."

"She was a Ziegfeld girl," persisted Kaufman.

"But besides that, Mr. Kaufman, besides that. What else was she? She was also a Hungarian, right? Or so she says."

"You could have cut her accent with a butter knife," countered Kaufman.

"So what? Anybody can fake an accent. There was a lot of publicity about Ziegfeld importing her from Europe. I'll see what I can find out there."

"The poor thing," interrupted Mrs. Parker, "surely she must have a family somewhere."

"Probably peasants herding goats somewhere in the heights of the Carpathian Mountains," suggested Woollcott.

"Or dirt farmers growing potatoes somewhere in the wilds of Idaho," said Singer with a faint trace of a smile.

"So much for hyperbole," said Mrs. Parker. "Alec and I will know what to do. Now then, how do you dispose of Miss Mercury's body?"

"Well, first of all, my boys bring up a laundry hamper we got on the back seat of the car. We dump the lady in the hamper. Then we take her for a drive out to the wilds of Canarsie. For your general edification, that is a little village out in Brooklyn on the shores of Jamaica bay. I was born near there. It is not densely populated. The gangs drop most of their stiffs out there. It's very convenient. Eventually, some innocent citizen of that venue will come across the body and hopefully yell for the cops. We then go through the tedious process of making an identification, then the tabloids cry 'Murder,' and then the investigation begins. Mrs. Parker, Mr. Woollcott, please don't jump the gun and ask around who has murdered Miss Mercury until Miss Mercury's body has been discovered and identified."

"Oh, we wouldn't dream of jumping the gun," Mrs. Parker assured him.

"I would prefer to do nothing with guns at all," added Woollcott.

"Come now, Alec. Guns didn't frighten you in the war."

"I had nothing to do with guns in the war, my dear Mrs. Parker." Woollcott's eyes were ablaze with indignation.

"Ah, guns are just phallic symbols," advised Singer with a slightly superior look.

"Which is why Mr. Woollcott had nothing to do with them in the war," said Mrs. Parker.

"Mr. Singer, what do I have to do? asked Kaufman.

"Mr. Kaufman, I suggest you go home or go to a movie or do whatever you were planning to do. Me and the boys have a lot of work to do here before we remove the body. The apartment has to be dusted for prints and I would prefer you take nothing with you, but leave it in its pristine purity. I noticed there's a handbag on the dressing table in the bedroom. I assume that's the lady's?"

"I suppose so," said Kaufman.

Singer got the handbag from the bedroom and examined its contents in front of the others. He emptied them out on the dining room table. "Handkerchief."

"Pretty pattern," said Mrs. Parker. "That looks like an Alençon lace trimming. Expensive."

"Compact case. Powder, lipstick, rouge, eyebrow pencil. Two sets of keys."

"One of them belongs to this apartment," Kaufman told him.

"Right. Take your pick, they're no use to me." Kaufman pocketed the keys. "Coin purse. Eighty-five cents. Bills." He whistled. "There's close to two G's here."

"Two thousand dollars?" asked Kaufman incredulously. "And I picked up the dinner check?"

"Men are such fools," said Mrs. Parker, and nobody took the trouble to disagree with her.

"Two thousand smackers indeed," repeated Singer. "Well, who knows, maybe there's something to your blackmail theory, Mrs. Parker." She tried not to look smug. He enumerated the remaining contents of the dead woman's handbag. "Powder puff."

"Pink." Mrs. Parker batted her eyelashes. "Isn't that what someone called Valentino? The pink powder puff? And didn't Valentino challenge the man to a duel?"

"What were the weapons to be?" asked Woollcott. "Salad forks at twenty paces?"

"You know, folks, about a week before Valentino died, he was operated on at Polyclinic Hospital for gastric ulcers and a ruptured appendix."

"He didn't do things by halves, did he?"

"Well, I'll tell you Mrs. Parker, if he had been poisoned the night before at Van Weber's party, the doctors would certainly have found some sign of it."

"Maybe they did and were bought off." Singer was almost mesmerized by her eyes, they burned into him so intensely. "Well, you said just about anyone can be bought off in this town. I'm sure doctors can. Certainly Bela Horathy is an example of that. Which of course boils their Hippocratic oath down to just another recitation piece."

"I'm going," announced Kaufman.

"How do I find you when I need you?" asked Singer.

Kaufman gave him his home phone number. "They'll always know where I am. But how do I explain you to my wife when she starts wondering why the police are calling?"

"The same way you explain your strange absences," suggested Mrs. Parker.

"Thanks," said Kaufman to the three, "I really appreciate what you're doing."

After Kaufman left, Singer said, "Okay, folks. There's no need for you to hang around. Let's get downstairs so I can get my boys working."

"The staff won't suspect anything?"

"No, Mrs. Parker, we know them and they know us. Kaufman isn't the only unhappy husband with a hideaway. Let's go."

Mrs. Parker put her arm through Singer's. "You're a good man, Jacob Singer. I'm glad we're friends."

Keep holding onto me like that, thought Singer, and we just might graduate beyond a mere friendship.

A few minutes later, Mrs. Parker was guiding Woollcott toward Central Park West. Woollcott, not having had his lunch, was feeling both peckish and cranky. "Where are we going?" he demanded.

"I thought we might drop in on Marc Connelly."

"He loathes being dropped in on, especially when he's working."

"How do you know he's working?"

"He mentioned at lunch yesterday he was starting work on a new play. *The Wisdom Tooth* didn't do too badly for him this season, considering he wrote it on his own and without Kaufman." In 1921, Kaufman and Connelly had collaborated on *Dulcy,* which, with Lynn Fontanne in the title role, became a smash hit and started the writers on the road to fame and fortune. "And talk about lunch, I'd like some right now." He referred to his pocket watch. "Good God, it's almost three o'clock. I must be famished."

"Connelly will make you a sandwich."

"I don't want a sandwich! And supposing he's not in?"

"Connelly wouldn't lie about working. He's so dedicated. It makes me ill just thinking about it." Mrs. Parker's own inclination to avoid working at any cost was a familiar aberration to her friends and employers. "I don't understand disciplined people, or the compulsion to be creative. I did so enjoy being kept by Richman. He was so generous, but such an obstinate ass. God knows I'm well rid of him." She turned on Woollcott angrily. "Why did you have to bring it up?"

"What the hell are you angry at me for? You're the one who's running off at the mouth. How far are we from Connelly's anyway? I'm ravished!"

Marc Connelly's apartment house faced Central Park. The doorman announced the intruders over the intercom, and both got the feeling they were being welcomed up with reservations. When Connelly opened the door to them, they could tell by the look on his face that their first instinct was correct. "We just happened to be in the neighborhood and thought you'd be glad if we dropped in," said Woollcott suavely as he led the way into Connelly's comfortable living room. The French windows had been thrown open to greet any trace of a breeze. Connelly was mopping his bald head with a handkerchief.

"And exactly what are you doing in this neighborhood?"

"We thought we'd pop in for a look at Valentino, but all the performances are sold out. Woollcott's not had any lunch, sweetheart; can you offer him anything substantial?"

"Unlike your recent play," added Woollcott.

"I can offer you hemlock," said Connelly, trying hard not to clench his teeth. "The kitchen is this way." They followed him into the kitchen where the sink was piled high with unwashed dishes.

"This is as bad as my place," commented Mrs. Parker. Then espying the pile of dishes asked, "What in God's name is *that?*"

"A challenge." Connelly was rummaging in the icebox. "There's some cold chicken." He squinted. "At least it looks like cold chicken."

"Let me have a look." Mrs. Parker gently pushed Connelly to one side. Connelly fought hard to control his temper.

Woollcott glared at Connelly, who stood staring at Mrs. Parker's backside while clenching and unclenching his fists. "Instead of standing around resembling an infected hangnail, you might busy yourself with a shaker of martinis."

"Why don't you both go to hell!" Connelly exploded as he stormed back to the living room.

"He's got to learn to control that temper," said Mrs.

Parker as she carried plates of leftovers to a table.

Ten minutes later in the living room, the atmosphere was friendlier as they toasted each other's health, and Connelly sank into an overstuffed armchair to watch the other two gorging themselves on chicken and salad. While chewing, Mrs. Parker asked the playwright, "How well do you know Lacey Van Weber?"

"Van Weber? Don't know him well at all. Met him once about ten days ago. I was taken to a party at his penthouse on Central Park South." He shifted in his seat. "As a matter of fact, Valentino was there with that Hungarian beauty of Ziegfeld's. There was an unfortunate ruckus. Valentino took umbrage at Dr. Horathy. Can't say I didn't blame him. Unctuous creature, Horathy. Valentino accused him of all sorts of awful things involving the illegal prescribing of narcotics. And sadly enough, that's where Valentino took ill." Then suspiciously, "Why this interest in Van Weber?"

"Well," said Mrs. Parker, "I read this article about him in the *Graphic.*"

"How could you read that nasty sheet?"

"A minor vice. Anyway, he interested me as a character. There's something terribly familiar about the reporter's description of his life style."

"Tippecanoe and déjà vu."

"Alec, that's contemptible." She returned her attention to Connelly. "Familiar in the sense that I seem to have seen his mansion in East Cove described in a similar context. Marc, am I getting through to you?"

"Like a saber thrust. It was Lily Robson who took me to the party."

Mrs. Parker feigned innocence. "Lily Robson?"

"She's one of Texas Guinan's girls."

"I didn't know you went for that kind of thing."

"She isn't a 'thing'; she's a terribly lovely, terribly charming young woman. She has a delicious sense of humor and laughs at all my jokes. Yes, I go for that kind of thing. I'll go for anything that doesn't slip through my fingers and says 'yes' often enough. Are you finished eating? Good. Now do you mind clearing up after yourselves. My housekeeper's on vacation."

"I get the feeling you want us to leave," said Woollcott peevishly.

"I didn't want you to arrive."

Mrs. Parker took the tray of soiled dishes and silverware to the kitchen.

Connelly fixed Woollcott with the look of a hanging judge. "What are you two after?"

"Why are you always so suspicious?"

"Why do you always answer a question with a question?"

Mrs. Parker returned. "You have roaches."

Connelly got to his feet and bowed deeply. "Good afternoon, good friends. I have an assignation with my writing desk." Mrs. Parker went to him and held his head between her hands, kissing him lightly on his bald pate.

"Thank you for being such a deadly dull host, and for the new martinis and the old chicken. Now we owe you one. Come, Alec, enough of this intrusion." Woollcott followed her out of the apartment.

At the elevator he asked her, "What did all that gain us other than a perfectly horrendous lunch?"

"He corroborated Ilona Mercury's story of the Valentino fracas."

"Had you thought she was lying."

"That sort frequently does. They have to. They lead so many lives. Their own and that of the men who go for them. Well, at least we know Kaufman got the story straight from the hussy's mouth." In the street, she said to Woollcott, "Is it difficult to get tickets to *No Foolin'?*"

"In August it isn't difficult to get tickets to anything. And anyway, the show's been doing only so-so since its opening in June. I panned the hell out of it."

"Maybe you'll like it better a second time."

"I have absolutely no intention of attending that rubbish again. On the street they call it 'Ziegfeld's Folly.'"

"Ilona Mercury was in the show. She shared a dressing room with the other showgirls. Showgirls talk a lot. Often indiscreetly."

Woollcott stopped walking, put his hands on his hips and peppered Mrs. Parker with some verbal buckshot. "Didn't that detective person tell us to lay off until the body's found and positively identified?"

"He most certainly did and we have been laying off."

"Bearding Connelly about the party, tickets for *No Foolin'*, that's laying off?"

"Connelly is a dear intimate friend and we just happened to drop in on him. Actually, I was hoping he did know Van Weber personally and might bring us together. But isn't that what detecting work is all about? A blind alley here, a bum steer there. And as for the show, I didn't intend us to see it tonight. Tomorrow night, though. By tomorrow night I should think Canarsie will have revealed its sordid secret and the poor thing will be properly identified in blazing tabloid headlines. Oh, Alec, I'm having such a good time and I need a good time so badly. I've had so many bad times and I'm only thirty-three. And look at all the material you're gathering for your article. It'll be such a swell article, too. You'll have Harold Ross begging you to let him have it for *The New Yorker*. Or something."

"I'm such a softhearted, sentimental old fool," snapped Woollcott. "Indulging you is like making love to a cobra. All right. Tomorrow night. *No Foolin'*."

"And by then we'll have thought of some clever reason to go backstage and cross-examine the showgirls. Oh, before I forget. How well do you know Polly Adler?"

Woollcott drew himself up haughtily. "How dare you suggest I would consort with the madam of a whorehouse?"

"I've been told she's quite petite, just like me. Actually, I've been thinking of doing a study of prostitutes and what better place to start than at Polly's house. She might introduce me to Vera DeLee."

-33-

"Who?"

"Vera DeLee. The one who was at Van Weber's party with Judge Crater."

"You're moving too fast," Woollcott cautioned her.

"I'm just going out to scout the territory."

"Well, I'll be damned," said Woollcott with a change of tone of voice. "Here we are at Columbus Circle, practically at your doorstep. I've walked a distance without realizing it."

"See how some things can creep up on you. Want to come up for a drink?"

"No, thank you. I shall hail a taxi and head home to West Forty-seventh Street." Woollcott shared a brownstone with Harold Ross and his wife, Jane Grant. They were an incompatible threesome, but Woollcott chose to ignore all unsubtle hints he seek other quarters until a change was convenient for him. "I'll phone you later. We'll plan to dine after the theater tomorrow night."

"Perhaps we can ask one of the girls along."

"Which one?"

"The one who can tell us the most about Ilona Mercury." She blew him a kiss and hurried towards Fifty-seventh Street, leaving him waving frantically for a taxi.

The phone began ringing as she inserted the key in the lock. The ringing persisted until she had the door open, removed the key, kicked the door shut and almost stumbled on a scatter rug getting to the instrument.

"Hello?"

"Dorothy Parker!" raged the voice at the other end. She recognized Harold Ross.

"You don't have to shout, Harold. I know my name."

"Your copy is two days overdue. You have been no-where near this office for days since you got back from Europe."

"That's not true. I was there just the other morning, but somebody was sitting on the chair."

"I'm cutting off your drawing account!"

"Harold, do you enjoy going through life abusing

women? I've just gotten home. I'm hot and tired. I need a bath and a drink in no particular order. I've had a very trying day and if you'll leave me alone, I'll finish the copy tonight and drop it off at the office in the morning.

"I don't believe you."

"I don't blame you." She heard something rude from the other end of the wire and then they hung up simultaneously. She removed the suffocating cloche from her head and flung it onto a table. She entered the bathroom to run the bath. Once the taps were opened, she stared at her decorated wrists, sat on the throne and burst into tears.

An hour later, Horace Liveright of the publishing firm of Boni and Liveright, who were preparing to issue Dorothy Parker's collection of verse, *Enough Rope,* was delighted when his secretary told him Mrs. Parker was in the office wondering if she could see him. Liveright personally went to the outer office to escort Mrs. Parker into the inner sanctum. He greeted her with outstretched hands. "Dear, dear Dorothy, how good to see you."

"My, don't you look well, Horace!" exclaimed Mrs. Parker as she selected one of the outstretched hands and shook it gently. She preceded him into his office and sat in the easy chair facing his desk. Once he was settled he asked her if she wanted a drink. "In a few minutes."

"Now to what do I owe this pleasure?"

"Well, I'll tell you, Horace. A little while ago I was soaking in my tub wondering how to get an introduction to someone who must certainly be a very sought after man about town, when it suddenly occurred to me . . . Horace Liveright!"

"You already know me."

Wit, Mrs. Parker reminded herself, was never Liveright's strong point. "I know I know you, Horace, but I don't know Lacey Van Weber, and that's the man I want to meet."

All trace of joviality left Liveright's face. "Why?"

"Why what?"

"Why do you want to meet him?"

"Why do you sound so somber?"

"Why did you think I'd know him?"

"Because you seem to know everybody. You travel in the best circles. You're the scion of one of our best families."

"Van Weber isn't."

"Oh, come on now, Horace, stop acting like a curmudgeon."

"Why are you interested in him?"

Mrs. Parker gave him her story about the article in the *Graphic*. "The story fascinated me more for what it didn't tell than for what was printed."

"And what do you think it didn't tell?"

"That's what I want to find out. I kept missing too much between the lines. There's a good story in that man, and I've convinced Harold Ross that *The New Yorker* ought to run an in-depth piece on him. After all, that's what the magazine's supposed to be all about, New York and New Yorkers, and he's a New Yorker, right?" She knew Liveright and Ross knew each other slightly, and any likelihood of Liveright's uncovering her lie was remote. "And frankly, I need the money."

"I'll be glad to lend you whatever you need."

"Oh, no, Horace, you've already been more than generous with your advance on *Enough Rope*. Now I'd like to earn some money honestly."

"I don't like Lacey Van Weber."

"There's a lot of people I don't like, but if friends want to meet them, then what the hell, I'll do them the courtesy."

"You're too persuasive." He signaled for his secretary. When she entered, he told her to try to reach Lacey Van Weber. He looked at his wristwatch. It was almost five o'clock. "You'll probably find him at the Athletic Club." A few minutes later, Liveright was speaking on the phone with Lacey Van Weber.

"Well, old sport," said Van Weber, "what a surprise. I just dropped in for a massage."

Liveright got straight to the point. "I'm sure you've

heard of Dorothy Parker. She's in my office right now. She read about you in the *Graphic*."

"Tell her that's not me at all."

"That's what she suspects. She'd love to meet you. Wait a minute." He put his hand over the mouthpiece. "Drinks at Jack and Charlie's in half an hour?"

"Perfect. I love Jack and Charlie's." The speakeasy was on West Fifty-second Street just off Fifth Avenue.

Liveright was saying into the phone, "You'll know her easily enough."

"Aren't you coming, too?" asked Mrs. Parker.

Liveright shook his head no as he described Mrs. Parker and what she was wearing.

"And if that isn't enough," said Mrs. Parker, "tell him I'll be wearing a rose in my teeth. Anyway, I'll recognize him. I've seen his picture."

After hanging up the phone, Liveright said to her with concern, "Be very careful, Dorothy. You're treading where angels fear."

She flashed him a beguiling smile. "I'm your slave, Horace."

At five-thirty, she was hurrying along Fifth Avenue toward West Fifty-second Street and Jack and Charlie's. She didn't feel her feet on the pavement or suffer the intense humidity that seemed intent on suffocating the city. She felt lightheaded and eighteen years old. It had been months since she had last trod where angels feared.

3

While Mrs. Parker was sailing lightheartedly along Fifth Avenue to her appointment with Lacey Van Weber, New York City's most notorious madam, the diminutive Polly Adler, was sitting on the piano stool in her carefully appointed apartment, watching her maid, Gloria, arranging flowers in an expensive, cut-glass Tiffany vase. The grand piano at which Mrs. Adler sat had been especially selected for her by the great musician Leopold Godowski, who had also supervised its tuning. The magnificent Spanish shawl artfully draped across the piano had been a gift from the celebrated cellist Pablo Casals. As she idly ran her fingers along the keyboard, she studied the photograph of her parents which the piano supported, the photograph contained in a platinum frame donated by the great Broadway star Holbrook Blinn. A dozen times a day she studied the couple, her father handsomely attired, wearing a white yarmulke, her mother small and dignified, a beautiful lace shawl protecting her *sheitel*, the wig all orthodox Jewish wives were required to wear. If they knew what I do for a living, thought Polly, they'd convert. The phone rang. "Get it, Gloria," ordered Polly in the rasping growl that was known to make walls tremble, especially within the confines of an assortment of police precincts after her premises had been raided.

"It's Mr. Liveright," said Gloria. Gloria had been with Mrs. Adler for less than a year. She had been interviewed as a prospective prostitute, but her inherent talents for housekeeping soon outpointed her values between bedcovers. It was a satisfactory compromise for both parties. A good maid was hard to find. Good whores could be found in rich abundance.

"What can I do for you, Horace?" She didn't much like Liveright, but he was a steady and lucrative client.

In his office, Liveright sat with his feet on the desk, his

swivel chair tilted back. At his elbow was a glass of Scotch, none of that bootleg hooch, but the real thing off a yacht recently arrived from England. "I could use a half-dozen long-stemmed American beauty roses. I'd like them delivered at midnight. The usual place."

Polly's eyes widened with disbelief. "*Six?* I only maintain four for the regulars and tonight's gonna be a busy night. I mean I already got over fifteen bookings. I'll need to job the rest and you ain't giving me much time to round them up. I mean, some of my girls are respectable wives and mothers. They need time to feed the kids, get them to bed, and wait for the man of the house to pass out from the exhaustion of everyday living. What do you think I am?"

"A very clever businesswoman," said Liveright. "Maybe you can borrow a few girls from Belle Livingston."

"Ain'tcha heard? Belle's on Rikers. They raided her last night and she got a new judge what's a dummy. He don't take bribes. Can y'imagine, a Jimmy Walker appointee what don't take bribes?" Mayor James J. Walker was one of Polly's most respected clients. "Let me see what I can do in the next couple of hours. Where can I reach you?" She jotted down the telephone number he gave her in the booking ledger on the desk.

Liveright swung his feet off the desk. "Is there any chance Miss DeLee might be available?"

Polly studied her face in the mirror presented to the establishment by film star Wallace Beery. What she saw still looked good to her. Prostitution had treated her kindly. She was still on the better side of middle age, and when the time came she knew she'd be smart enough to retire. Polly harbored a secret desire to get a higher education. She wanted to go to college. New York University gave night courses that interested her. She wanted to learn languages and study economics so she could look after her investments without worrying about being cheated by some snake of a stockbroker. The market was soaring, and Polly was soaring with it.

"Polly?"

"I'm here, Mr. Liveright, I'm here. I was just thinking. Vera ain't been feeling so hot lately. I mean last night she fainted in the arms of a very important client. It frightened the shit outta him, and let me tell you, this one's got plenty to spare. As a matter of fact, she's got an appointment with her doctor right now I think. If he gives her the nod, I'll see she's part of your package. And Mr. Liveright"—he recognized the advent of an admonition—"none of that rough stuff, you hear me? I mean where I come from, chains is for slaves. Is that kinky Frank Tinney on your guest list?" Frank Tinney was a celebrated comedian who was known for his sadistic treatment of women.

"He is. Don't worry. I'll keep him in line."

"You damn well better. Cigar burns on their tits put my girls out of action for too long. It also puts them off cigars. What about Crater?"

"I hadn't thought of asking the judge."

"Well, it's just that Vera is one of his favorites. Okay, Mr. Liveright. Or should I pronounce that Live Right. You sure know how."

"Don't hang up yet. Polly, how well do you know Lacey Van Weber?"

Polly replied cautiously. "We've never socialized."

"Your girls have been at some of his parties. Vera De-Lee was at the one where Valentino took sick."

"So what about it?"

"Well, it's like this, dear. I suspect that someone who means a great deal to me is on the verge of getting very dangerously involved with him."

"Mr. Liveright, you publish too many romances. There's no such thing as dangerously involved unless you're stepping into a lion's cage without a whip and a pistol."

"Obviously, you're very fond of Van Weber."

"It's like I said, Mr. Liveright, I've never socialized with him. Now let me get on with the roundup." She hung up while glaring at the phone.

"Can I get you something?" asked Gloria.

"Yeah. You can get me a new head, a new stomach and a new past."

Mrs. Parker was early. If members of her luncheon circle heard of this, somebody would have raised a flag. Jack Kreindler led her to a quiet table in the back room when she introduced herself and told him she was waiting for Van Weber. "This is Mr. Van Weber's favorite table," explained Kreindler. "Can I get you something while you're waiting?"

For a second, Mrs. Parker thought of asking for a copy of *War and Peace,* but decided this was no time for frivolity. She asked for a Jack Rose, and Kreindler relayed the order to a waiter who had placed a small bowl of salted nuts on the table. When Kreindler and the waiter left, Mrs. Parker opened her handbag, found a pocket mirror and checked herself out. It's about as good as it'll ever get, she decided. Mirror back in place, clasp snapped shut, Mrs. Parker put her elbows on the table, interlaced her fingers and rested her chin on the framework. She wasn't wearing her spectacles, and so her range of vision was limited. The room was crowded with celebrities and just plain rich people, the congestion at the long bar being certainly fifty deep. She would later compare it to a colony of worker ants. The waiter brought her drink and then departed after being told she didn't require anything else. She knew the liquor would be excellent because Jack Kreindler and his brother Charlie were celebrated for running a top-grade saloon. This wasn't your ordinary peephole-in-the-door, sawdust-on-the-floor, plug-ugly-ex-prizefighter-bouncer checking the would-be clientele place. Jack and Charlie's was a class operation, paying classy sums to the corrupt police department to keep it that way. It was also one of the mayor's favorite midtown spas, and nobody high in officialdom cared to displease the mayor.

"Mrs. Parker?"

The voice was like an exquisite balm applied to a superficial wound. She looked up and suppressed a gasp of sexual excitement. He was almost six feet tall with the physique of an athlete. His eyes were a cobalt blue, and she knew they hid the secrets of the pharaohs. She would later describe his nose to Woollcott as "excruciatingly perfect." She could tell he had been poured into his Palm Beach suit. There wasn't a crease or wrinkle in evidence. He held his Panama hat lightly in his right hand. His smile filled her with fairy-tale enchantment. His teeth were of a Steinway grand quality, and the texture of his skin was enough to make a six-month-old enfant scream with envy. He was too perfect and destroying her metabolism.

"I do so hope I'm Mrs. Parker," she said softly and girlishly, one hand at her chest because she was finding breathing difficult. He sat down next to her, his smile widening and more dazzling, and she wondered if this was how you felt when you're about to suffer a stroke.

"That looks like bourbon. Is it good?"

"I haven't tasted it yet." She knew her mouth had moved. She hoped she had said something. She could only hear the ringing in her ears.

"May I?" Without waiting for her consent, he tasted the drink. "It's lovely." The waiter arrived, and Van Weber ordered the same for himself.

"I'm a great admirer of your writing, Mrs. Parker."

"So am I." She felt her cheeks redden. "That was not meant to sound egotistical."

"You have every right to be."

"I really don't. What I meant to say is that I admire finishing a piece of work. I find writing terribly difficult. I mean, if I was hired to write some of those Nancy Drew mysteries, we'd all be in terrible trouble. I know the women who write them just tear them off about one a month. A simple quatrain can take me a week." She caught her breath. "We're not here to talk about me. We're here to talk about you."

He leaned forward seductively. "Are we in any rush?"

"Why, no," she replied graciously, "not unless there are

tumbrels waiting for us at the door."

"I understand Liveright is publishing your collection of verse." The waiter served his drink and left.

"Yes, he's terribly brave. Poetry has never been known to make anyone rich."

"I was under the impression you made a great deal of money."

"Good heavens, no. I'm a free-lance writer. A free lance is someone who starves at his own discretion."

"But you contribute regularly to F.P.A.'s column in the *World*."

"That's for free and for ego. Frank doesn't pay. But he has a large readership and it's good to be published by him."

"What about *The New Yorker?*"

"City postal clerks do better. May I ask? You have such a strange accent. Are you British or affected?"

He laughed and it made her spine tingle. There was nothing wrong with this man. He was absolutely perfect. Nonpareil. One of a kind. She kept her hands under the table because they were trembling. "There are all sorts of rumors about my origins. Which would you prefer me to repeat?"

"The one I like is that you're a descendant of British aristocracy. Except how could that be with a name like Van Weber?"

"There's lots of German blood in the royal house of Britain. Did that piece in the *Graphic* really interest you that much?"

"Yes. I love a mystery." Now her hands were clasped atop the table. He covered them and she winced.

"I'm sorry. I didn't mean to hurt you."

"Oh, it's just my wrists. I cut them while peeling an onion."

"So, domestic, too."

"No, domestic three. One, I'm a hedonist, two, I'm a creative artist, and three, when I'm desperately hungry, I feed myself." She sipped her drink and then fixed him with her captivating eyes. "Who are you, Lacey Van Weber?"

His face betrayed nothing. "What do you mean?"

"Everything about you is too perfect. You're like the place setting at a state dinner. Too carefully arranged. The mansion in East Cove. The penthouse in the city. An office on Fifth Avenue. You seem to have captured the imagination and trust of the who's who of the city. You're an absolute smasher in the looks department." He smiled, and she wondered if pinning that verbal medal on him made him expect to be kissed on both cheeks. "But what exactly is it that you do? Are you a stockbroker? An international financier? Or are you a clever hoaxer?"

"I'm everything and I'm nothing. I'm what people want me to be. I'm malleable. I can be shaped and reshaped to satisfy anybody's fantasy of what I am or should be."

"You're also a superb double talker. I'm amazed Marc Connelly had so little to tell us about you."

"Marc Connelly?"

Mrs. Parker was somewhat astonished. "You don't know Marc Connelly, the playwright? He was at your party the night Valentino took ill."

"Mrs. Parker, there were so many people at that party. There are so many people at all my parties. I sometimes think there's a secret organization located somewhere in the bowels of this city created solely to breed pests who crash my parties."

"Marc didn't crash. His date brought him. Lily Robson." She didn't miss the subtle change that came over his face. "I believe she's a Guinan girl. Don't you know her?"

"Oh, I certainly know Lily. Once you meet Lily, you never forget her. She has flaming red hair."

"So I've heard. It's been described to me as resembling a house ablaze." She added with demure archness, "Unlike mousy little me."

"If there were more mice like you, I'd pay less attention to flaming redheads. You're a good friend of Mr. Connelly's?"

"Oh, yes. Alec Woollcott and I had lunch at his place

today. That's when he told us about your party. Isn't it sad about Valentino? Only thirty-one. Did you know him well?"

"Um . . . not really all that well."

"Surely you've been to Hollywood."

"I've been all over the world."

And she was beginning to wonder if the world had been all over him. He was a queer duck, all right. Beautiful but strange. Affable but guarded. "I get the feeling, Mr. Van Weber, that you live under a terrible strain."

"Why is that?"

"It must be exhausting to choose every word as though it needs first to be examined and appraised under a jeweler's loupe."

"That's my upbringing."

"And what was that?"

"Very strict."

That sounded very Prussian to her. "Are you married?"

"Do I look like the marrying type?"

"You'd love Marc Connelly."

"Why?"

"He always answers a question with a question."

"Mrs. Parker—" he leaned forward, his eyes blinding hers—"when you get to know me better, you'll get to know me."

She knew the blood was bubbling in her veins. "And do you plan for me to get to know you better?"

"We could start by having dinner tomorrow night."

"Tomorrow night? Oh." She was crestfallen.

"Tomorrow night's no good?"

"Not for dinner, no. Mr. Woollcott has invited me to see Flo Ziegfeld's show, *No Foolin'.*"

"Oh, yes. I saw it opening night."

"Did you like it?"

"I've seen better, I've seen worse."

"I hear the girls in it are Flo's most gorgeous. I'm sure they didn't escape you."

"They're quite lovely."

"Do you know any of them?"

"Why?"

"I thought they'd be good to know to help decorate your parties. I mean their good looks would help decorate your party."

He was playing with her, and he knew she knew it. Smart lady. Very smart lady. The façade all little girl and helpless. The interior all clever and calculating. She intrigued him. She didn't frighten him. "I've met Paulette Goddard and Claire Luce."

"Oh, are they in the show?"

"Yes, indeed. They're two beautiful kids. In fact, they're all beautiful kids. Polly Walker, Peggy Fears, Greta Nissen . . ."

"Ilona Mercury . . ."

"Oh, of course. The lady from Hungary. The other names were all unfamiliar to you, yet you knew Miss Mercury's. How's that?"

Mrs. Parker was warming up. She was treading where angels fear. Liveright's warning was flashing before her eyes. Detective Jacob Singer's warning not to pursue an investigation until the murdered woman's body had been found and recognized was forgotten. "Why, she's a friend of a friend. George S. Kaufman? You *must* have heard of George S. Kaufman."

"Yes. Yes, I know about most of the people who meet regularly at the Algonquin. I read Mr. Adams's column religiously. And he chronicles you religiously. I was pulling your leg when you asked about Marc Connelly. We had a long talk at my party." Yet Connelly had told her and Alec he barely knew Van Weber. "I should lunch more often at the Algonquin. With any luck, I might sit at an adjoining table and be dazzled by all the smart conversation."

"It isn't always all that smart. Lots of times we have hangovers. Too often we snarl and backbite, then they're less luncheons than they are holy wars. Sometimes, when we're all in a good mood, and that isn't too often, we're even warm and affectionate and say a kind word for Frank Case who's the boniface of the establishment. Yes, you must drop by. Everyone's heard about you and wonders about you. It would be a great feather in my cap."

"Well, hello there, Lacey Van Weber!" Judge Crater loomed above them with his hand outstretched.

"Hello, Joe. What a nice surprise." Van Weber shook his hand. "Do you know Dorothy Parker?"

"I've certainly heard of her."

"Mrs. Parker, this is Judge Crater."

"How do you do, Judge. It's so nice to meet a judge sociably for a change."

Crater favored Van Weber. "Will I be seeing you later tonight at the . . . um . . . meeting?"

"I didn't know there was one scheduled."

"Oh, sure. At midnight as usual."

Mrs. Parker was fascinated by the cryptic interchange. She wondered if she had missed the key word that would decipher it.

"Perhaps there's a message waiting at my apartment. But if I'm not there, have fun."

Judge Crater smiled a crooked smile. "Try to be there. It's always such a pleasure to see you at the meetings." His head swiveled and focused on Mrs. Parker. "Stella, that's my wife, is a great admirer of yours."

"Oh, how nice. Say hello to Stella for me. We must take tea together sometime."

"I'm sure she'll like that. Nice to see you both."

When he was well out of earshot, Mrs. Parker said, "So that's Judge Crater. There are all sorts of rumors about him, too. Taking bribes. Working with the mobs. About as crooked as a bobby pin."

"This city's a hotbed of rumors. There are those about you, you know."

"I do know, and some of it's true. I'm sorry about to-morrow night."

"Where will you be after the theater?"

"I'm not sure. We haven't decided where to dine. Have you a suggestion?"

"Tony's on West Forty-sixth Street is quite good. It's

just around the corner from the Globe Theater. That's where *No Foolin'* is playing. I can have my secretary phone for a reservation. They know me at Tony's."

Lucky Tony's, thought Mrs. Parker. I wish I could say I knew you. Is there anyone that does? "I'm sure Tony's will be just fine by Alec. He's always looking forward to new experiences. And a short walk from the theater is even more appealing. Mr. Woollcott doesn't do too much walking. He discourages most forms of physical exertion. Getting out of bed in the morning requires a half-hour's rest."

Jack Kreindler had returned. "Everything satisfactory, Mr. Van Weber?"

"Just perfect, old sport. Couldn't be better."

"Can I get you anything, Mrs. Parker?"

"Out of here. I'm a bit tired and I'm sure Mr. Van Weber is about to be late for another engagement."

"You're reading my mind," said Van Weber.

"If I am, it's the first time this evening."

Van Weber walked her to Sixth Avenue where he hailed a cab for her. "How can I reach you, Mrs. Parker?"

"I'm in the phone book, Mr. Van Weber. How long do we continue the formalities, Lacey?"

"Do you prefer Dottie or Dorothy?"

"I prefer a good relationship." He held open the cab door for her. "Dottie is usual." She got into the back seat. He closed the door and she poked her head out the open window. "Oops. Almost forgot my manners. Thanks for the drink. It was just lovely." The cab pulled away from the curb as Mrs. Parker gave the driver her address. She looked out the rear window. Van Weber hadn't moved. Without seeing him clearly, she knew his face would be a study. She sat back and crossed her legs. She was reviewing the conversation with Van Weber. The evasions. The contradictions. The charm. The subtle sexuality. The party at the penthouse. Valentino. Lily Robson and Vera DeLee. Ilona Mercury. Her intuition told her Lacey Van Weber would be looming large in her future. She might have overplayed her hand, but he seemed to have bought it. What was that he had said to Jack Kreindler? "Just perfect, old sport."

Old sport.

She uncrossed her legs and stared out the window. The streets were crowded. It was almost seven o'clock. Overhead an El train roared by. The driver was about to turn off Sixth into West Fifty-seventh. She hated riding under El trains. She always feared there'd be a slip-up and one would come plunging down into the street. They left Sixth Avenue and she breathed easier.

Old sport.

She hated the sound of the El. She could hear the Ninth Avenue El from her studio, and for some reason, the sound of it filled her with melancholy. All sounds of movement filled her with melancholy, reminding her that she wasn't moving often enough or fast enough. Dorothy Parker was in a state of stasis and needed to be prodded into action. She must go home and write the copy she had promised to deliver to Harold Ross the following morning.

"We're here, lady."

"Oh, that's nice." She rummaged in the purse and gave him the fare and a good tip. He thanked her. She said, "My pleasure, old sport." There it goes again. *Old sport.*

Vera DeLee lay on the couch staring at the ceiling. At least she thought it was a ceiling. Her eyes weren't quite focused. Her mind didn't feel much in focus either. Her mouth was dry, and her tongue tasted as though it were covered with rust. Someone was bending over her, staring into her face. Vera wet her lips and said, "What do you want?"

"Feeling better, Miss DeLee?"

The voice was familiar. She'd heard it before. It was a highfalutin voice. Phony as a three-dollar bill.

"Miss DeLee?"

"Wha'?"

"Feeling better?"

"Am I sick?"

"You passed out."

"Where?"

"Here."

"Where's here?"

"The doctor's office."

The doctor's office. Now she could put a name to the voice. Nurse Gallagher. Nurse Cora Gallagher. Dr. Bliss's Cora. Dr. Blissful Bela Horathy's nurse Cora Gallagher.

"Why'd I pass out?"

"Hypertension."

"Did he fuck me?"

"Not in the office, dear. Never in the office."

"How long have I been out?"

"It's almost two hours. It's after seven o'clock."

"Oh, shit. I gotta call Polly. Help me up." Nurse Gallagher got her into a sitting position. "My feet feel like rubber. My head's spinning. My mouth feels like it's been filled with ashes. What did he do to me?"

"What he always does."

"I've never reacted like this before." She was frightened. "You don't remember me reacting like this before, do you?"

"It's not uncommon, after a while."

"What do you mean, after a while?"

"Well, dear, you've been receiving these injections for quite a long time. After a while, the body system builds up a resistance. The dosage has to be increased. Sometimes the body overreacts, and you pass out. There are some who pass away," she added cheerfully. "That's better in the long run."

Vera's eyes were beginning to focus. Nurse Gallagher had a big red face with a big red nose and two big brown eyes. There was a mole on the left side of her chin, just like Gloria Swanson's, and there the resemblance to Gloria Swanson ended. She had frizzy yellow hair and big hips and looked big enough to win a wrestling championship if the opportunity ever presented itself to a woman. And there was her highfalutin voice.

"Where's Dr. Horathy?"

"The doctor's with another patient."

"After seven o'clock?"

"He takes special late appointments. You know that. You've been special. You've been late."

"Where's my purse? I have to pay him."

"It's over here on the table. Shall I help myself?"

"Yeah. Help yourself. Only don't help yourself too much. I know what I got and I know what I owe."

"You can trust me, dear," she said, clipping each word, as she helped herself to the doctor's fee.

"I gotta use the phone. Was Polly trying to find me?"

"Not yet."

"I gotta tell Polly where I am. Help me to the phone."

"*Please.*"

"Please." She was helped to the phone. She gave Central Polly Adler's private number. "Hello, Gloria. It's me. Vera. Tell Polly. Well, interrupt her fuckin' bridge game!"

Polly scowled and excused herself from the table. Into the phone she growled, "Where the hell you been?"

"I'm at Horathy's. I don't feel good."

"I thought he was supposed to make you feel better."

"I don't feel good. I can't work tonight."

"There's a party on at Liveright's at midnight. He asked for you special."

"Please, Polly. Be my friend. I don't feel good."

Polly had a warm spot in her heart for Vera DeLee, who was the illegitimate daughter of a laundress and a Catholic priest. "I'm your friend, Vera darling. Go home. Will you get home okay? Is that snotty nurse still there?"

"Yeah."

"Tell her to help you to a taxi and maybe I'll help her get laid one of these days."

"Sure." After hanging up on Polly, she relayed her message to nurse Gallagher. Gallagher slapped Vera's face.

"I don't need any help from any whores. Now here's your hat and your purse and get out of here."

"The least you can do is point me to the door."

The reception room was empty. Vera was alone. She fumbled in her purse for her compact. She examined her face in the mirror and groaned. While replacing the mirror in the purse, the door to Dr. Horathy's office opened and a man emerged, shutting the door behind him. He didn't notice Vera immediately. He was massaging his temples with his fingers. Then he lowered his hands, shook his head, and from under his arm took his hat which he elaborately went about bringing back into shape. Vera smiled.

"Hello, big boy. Don't you recognize me? I'm one of Polly's girls. Vera. Vera DeLee. We met a couple of weeks ago. Imagine us both using Dr. Bliss. Small world, ain't it?"

Jacob Singer's office in his precinct headquarters on West Fifty-fourth Street was a little bigger than a jail cell. Its solitary window overlooked a back alley and hadn't been washed in five years, the length of Singer's tenure. There was a desk with a phone and an office intercom. Behind the desk was a swivel chair, now occupied by Singer reading Nathaniel Hawthorne's *The Scarlet Letter*. With difficulty. His lips moved as he read and he squinted. The print was very small. It was a special reprint edition where the paper was shoddy, the binding inadequate and the print was squeezed together to conserve space. It was the only kind of edition that agreed with his limited budget. Albeit a bachelor without the responsibilities of a wife, children and mortgage, Singer kept a very charming one-bedroom apartment on Lexington Avenue near Grand Central Station and put the rest of his money into wine, food and the clothes on his back. Occasionally, he would press a button on the intercom and ask impatiently, "They find the stiff yet?" The answer was still in the negative. Singer referred to his wall clock. It was almost eight o'clock. It was finally dark outside. The summer was coming to an end, and not a day too soon for Singer. He was a cold weather man. In cold you can always manage to stay warm. But in warm, you can't always manage to keep cool. Like his office. It was stifling. Even with the fan going on top of the filing cabinet, it was equatorial. True, he kept the window closed, but that was to avoid the stench of garbage and dead animals in the alley two floors below. He was thirsty. He was hungry. He was growing more impatient by the minute. The intercom buzzed, and he selected a button and pressed.

"What?"

"A stiff has been found in an empty lot in Canarsie, lot located at the corner of Remsen Avenue and Avenue M."

"It's about time."

"It is a woman. White. She has been strangled."

"Come on, Cassidy, stop the comic strip stuff. I want my dinner."

"There was a purse but no identification in the purse." The two thousand dollars was safely locked away in a tin box in the bottom right-hand drawer of Singer's desk. Its fate would be decided at a more advantageous time.

"Take her to the morgue."

"Brooklyn's claiming her," Cassidy protested. He sounded strangely uneasy.

"Fuck them!" yelled Singer. "They know she's ours! Finders keepers! You bring her uptown where she belongs and move fast on the ident. Get her prints and get them to Immigration and fast." He clicked off, simmering. He pressed another button.

"Sherman."

"Sherm, what's with Immigration? They got anything on Mercury?"

"For Chrissakes, Jake, it's after eight. They're shut."

"Ahhh, you can never get anything done around this fucking place. They finally found the stiff. They're bringing her in. Stay with it. I'm going over to the chink's for some chop suey." He leaned back in his chair. He blinked his eyes. He thought about Mrs. Parker. He wondered did he dare. He had her phone number in his little black book. He looked it up and gave it to Central. Her phone rang once, twice, a third time. He was about to hang up.

"Hello?" She sounded anxious.

"It's Jacob Singer. Am I interrupting you at anything?"

"Oh, no. As a matter of fact, I'm glad you called."

"I'm glad you're glad." He took a deep breath and then

-53-

plunged. "Mrs. Parker, if you have not had your dinner yet, there's a nice little Chinese joint on Eighth Avenue just a couple of blocks from your place and they know me so we can get booze and . . ."

"I know the place. I'll meet you there in fifteen minutes. If you get there first, order me a bourbon sour, easy on the sugar." She hung up. He exhaled.

Mrs. Parker smiled at Neysa McMein. "That was Jacob Singer. He's a detective."

Neysa's eyes narrowed. "What have you been up to?"

"Nothing illegal." She moved to the dressing table where she began repairing her face.

"Are you going out?"

"Yes. He's invited me to a Chinese dinner."

Neysa was not usually inquisitive. She was one of the brighter lights of the Algonquin's Round Table because she neither obtruded nor attempted to compete. Unlike the novelist Edna Ferber, who tended to bulldoze her opinions into a discussion, Neysa chose to sit back and wait for the occasional lull in the conversation and then dip her intelligence in. She was one of the two women Mrs. Parker either admired or confided in (Sara Murphy in France being the other), and it was she who had located the tiny studio Mrs. Parker now occupied. Her own apartment across the hall was many times larger and held as many as over a hundred guests at the parties she and her husband, John Baragwanath, frequently hosted. She was an excellent artist, successful and respected by her peers. Her marriage was a comfortable one, not terribly passionate as far as Mrs. Parker could discern, and her husband was sufficiently intelligent to remain in the background, which territory he had all to himself. "I'm not being a scold, Dottie, but five minutes ago you said you were too tired to eat when I invited you to dinner."

"I only intend to nibble. I have to see Mr. Singer. He's being very helpful with a project of mine."

"Is he attractive?"

"He's a detective."

"Is he an attractive detective?"

"Yes, I suppose you'd say he is."

"Wouldn't you say he is?"

Mrs. Parker left the dressing table and faced her friend. "Neysa, must we carry on the kind of clipped conversation we find so deplorable in the plays of Miss Rachel Crothers?"

"How are your wrists?"

"They feel fine. Have you seen my handbag? Oh, there it is."

"What about the copy you promised Ross?"

"I'll write it when I get home. Are you feeling abandoned?"

"Hell, no. I've got an illustration to do for *Harper's.* I was just hanging around to keep you from attempting anything foolish again."

"Oh, no fear of that. It's out of my system. Come on." She held the door open for Neysa, who preceded her out. She switched off the lights, locked the door and then crossed to the elevator. Neysa stood in the doorway to her apartment.

"Have a good time."

"I'll try." The elevator arrived, and she said good evening to Martin the night operator as she stepped in. She was humming "One Alone" or at least she hoped she was humming "One Alone" because she didn't have much of an ear for music.

"It's nice to hear you humming again, Mrs. Parker," said Martin.

"Haven't I been humming?"

"Not since you got back from Europe."

"There was nothing much to hum about when I got back from Europe."

"Ain't it awful about Rudolph Valentino?"

"Nothing much to hum about there either."

When they arrived at the lobby, Martin asked, "Do you need a cab?"

"No thanks, Martin, my date's waiting for me just a

-55-

couple of blocks away." As she hurried out of the building, she thought, my date. That makes two dates in one evening. My cup runneth over.

Old sport.

The Fan Tan Gardens on Eighth Avenue was not only a short and convenient walk from Mrs. Parker's apartment house, it was a bargain hunter's paradise. A combination dinner could be had for a dollar; the servings were generous and the food above passable. There was also a four-piece orchestra, the Fortune Cookies, consisting of piano, drums, bass fiddle and banjo.

"The banjo player is cross-eyed," observed Mrs. Parker. Singer squinted into the semidarkness and corroborated her observation. "Do you suppose it's good luck to spot a cross-eyed Chinese banjo player? You know, like finding a four-leaf clover or rubbing a hunchback's hump?"

"Do I make you nervous?" Mrs. Parker was fussing with the velvet bracelets which were beginning to fray at the edges. So were Mrs. Parker's nerves. Detective Singer was quite astute.

"You don't make me nervous. I make me nervous."

"You haven't tasted your drink. The hooch is hot off a sampan."

She sipped her bourbon sour. "Nice. It's sour. Not too much sugar."

"I ordered us two specials. I hope that's okay."

"Oh, it's just fine. I'm not fussy. I don't eat much. It's too hot to eat much anyway." Her conversation was underlined by the hum of the overhead ceiling fans and the buzzing of a fly impatient to share their dinner. The Fortune

Cookies were trying to get together on a weird interpretation of "Alexander's Ragtime Band" which Mrs. Parker thought was "Rule Britannia."

"Ilona Mercury's body was found an hour ago. No identity's been made yet, but that'll be taken care of by tomorrow morning." The food arrived, and it looked and smelled appetizing. Singer dug in immediately like a dues-paying trencherman. Mrs. Parker examined every item on the plate as though looking for a counterfeit gem in a diadem. "She should be in the morgue by now. They'll do an autopsy tomorrow." Mrs. Parker gently placed her fork down and sipped her sour. She no longer had a trace of an appetite. What little she had possessed now rested alongside Ilona Mercury in the New York City morgue. She knew she had to tell him about her encounter with Lacey Van Weber, but she dreaded the possible scolding with which he might reward her. Seeing she wasn't eating, he asked, "Would you prefer to order something else?"

"Oh, no, it's just that I'm really not hungry. When you phoned, I was having a cup of tea and a biscuit with my friend Neysa McMein. I'm sure you can handle my plate, too."

"I can. Would you like another drink?"

"I wouldn't say no."

He signaled the waiter for a fresh round and then asked Mrs. Parker, "What's bothering you?" He was thinking she had decided she'd made a mistake in accepting his offer for dinner.

She decided to come clean. "I've done something today you're absolutely going to disapprove of."

"Who'd you murder?"

"Nothing that colorful. I had drinks with Lacey Van Weber."

Singer didn't bat an eyelash. "What did you get out of him?"

"Not much. He's a very cool character." It took her less than fifteen minutes to unwind the litany that took her from bearding Horace Liveright in his office to Van Weber hail-ing her a cab. In the course of this, Singer demolished his serving of food and was now digging into Mrs. Parker's dinner. A third round of drinks was ordered, and the Fortune Cookies had thrown down the gauntlet to Victor Herbert by demolishing "Stout-Hearted Men."

"I think you handled him okay." Mrs. Parker beamed. Now she was hungry but didn't dare tell him. He was pouring himself a cup of tea while trying desperately not to suck his teeth. He didn't want her to think him uncouth and a lout. He swished the tea around in his mouth, but it dislodged nothing. "So Liveright gets you to Van Weber and Judge Crater gets thrown in as a bonus."

"Don't you think it's strange, people holding meetings at midnight?"

"Mrs. Parker, don't be naïve. I know you travel in a fast crowd. You know what them midnight meetings mean."

Mrs. Parker was annoyed. She drew herself up and folded her arms. "You don't find many instructors in fast crowds. I don't know what these midnight meetings mean." Pause. "Well? What are they?"

"Orgies. Hosted by Liveright."

Her eyes widened as she leaned forward, her interest piqued, trying hard not to salivate. "Horace Liveright holds orgies?"

"Boy, does he hold orgies. From what we've learned, those orgies get so hot and heavy and involved you need a scorecard to tell one participant from another. Believe me, I dread the day the *Graphic* or the *Daily News* or the *Mirror* or any of them other scandal sheets get wind of it."

"*My* Horace Liveright? *My* publisher?"

"He's a pervert."

"I need another drink."

"You sure you can handle it?"

"Can Horace handle an orgy?" The Fortune Cookies were showing little mercy to "A Pretty Girl Is Like a Melody." A new round of drinks was requested. Mrs. Parker dwelled unhappily on the prospect of Lacey Van Weber as a participant in orgies.

"You look like somebody just stole your candy." Singer had succumbed to the necessity of a toothpick.

"I never get invited to orgies. It's just as well. I wouldn't know which way to turn. What do you think of Mr. Van Weber?"

"Haven't met him yet."

"From what I've told you, what do you think?"

"Suave, smooth and sophisticated. Smart. With his kind of fancy footwork, he could probably score a dozen touchdowns a game. And I don't think he's real."

"Oh, he's real, all right. He has lovely manners."

"Mrs. Parker, what you saw was an excellent performance. We ain't got nothing on this guy, and when we ain't got nothing on a guy, I'm doubly suspicious."

"You've been investigating him."

"Sure, I've been investigating him. A long time before you got interested in him." She couldn't understand why she was blushing. Singer did. "We came across him long before the party where Valentino took sick. From almost the first time we got wind of him, a little over a year ago, when he began to make Walter Winchell's column. A guy hits town from nowhere, makes a big splash, flashes a big roll of green, gives lavish parties, gets to know the mayor and the more suspect members of the municipality such as Judge Joseph Force Crater, hangs around Tex Guinan's and Helen Morgan's place, bends elbows with Flo Ziegfeld and at least two of the Shubert brothers, suddenly buys one of East Cove's most notorious white elephants . . ."

"It sounded perfectly glorious to me. Like Versailles."

"Well, maybe Van Weber took a lesson in how to waste from the late Marie Antoinette. That place in East Cove had been barren, moldy, overgrown with weeds and rat-infested for over twenty years until Van Weber quietly took it over, repaired it, overhauled it and announced an open house. Oh, yeah. It's everything they tell you it is today. It's also got a big new dock, big enough to accommodate a gunboat if one wanted to sail in. I've been there." He broke the toothpick in two and dropped it in the ashtray. Mrs. Parker now sat with her hands primly folded on the table. She was dying for an egg roll but too shy to ask. "I was there a couple of months ago. Some business involving an illegal alien." Her mouth formed a moue. "Little Italian kid we found murdered in an alley down in Little Italy. Throat slashed. Couldn't have been more than maybe eighteen or nineteen years old. No identity, no nothing. But then like sometimes happens, we run lucky. Somebody turns in a missing persons report. A cute kid, Italian, Rosie something. We take her to the morgue, she identifies him, and then she tells us while sobbing her guts out he worked out in East Cove for Van Weber. So I went out there. Nothing. Not a clue. Not a line. Nobody knew the kid. Rosie something says his name was Angelo d'Amati. Brought in illegal. Want to know what I suspect?"

"I'm fascinated."

"He was brought in with some other illegals and docked at Van Weber's. Probably on a boat carrying bootleg hooch. Maybe Angelo wasn't meant to get off the boat. Maybe he was supposed to head back for Europe or from wherever they originated. But I think he got hungry to stay in this country. You can guess his origins. Poverty, no indoor plumbing . . ."

"How awful . . ."

"With the mansion in East Cove as a yardstick, the United States looks real promising. He runs away. But they catch up with him. He knows too much. Throat slashed." He made an ugly gesture across his own throat. She lost her appetite again. "So far nobody's come after Rosie. Maybe they don't know she exists. But what I'm telling you, I got from Rosie, who naturally got it all from Angelo. In Italian, of course. *Kapish?* . . . old sport?"

Singer had reacted with both amusement and interest when she told him Lacey Van Weber's favorite expression seemed to be "old sport." Her fourth bourbon sour was beginning to get results. Mrs. Parker's face was flushed, and she felt a slight disassociation from her head.

"You feeling all right, Mrs. Parker?"

"Why, of course. Why shouldn't I?"

"You look like the drinks are beginning to hit you."

The devil take the hindmost. "They are. Can I have an egg roll?"

He ordered the egg roll. The Fortune Cookies attacked "Give My Regards to Broadway." Singer urged some hot tea on Mrs. Parker. "What's troubling you, Mrs. Parker?"

"Lacey Van Weber. I'm such a romantic, Mr. Singer, and Mr. Van Weber cuts such a romantic figure, I hate to think of him as being anything less than top drawer."

"Mrs. Parker, I thought Scott Fitzgerald was a good friend of yours. You know, travels in your set, literary, wise-cracks, the whole *shmeer.*"

"I had dinner with Scott and Zelda in Cap d'Antibes last month. Would you like to meet them? I think they're still abroad."

"Sure, I'd like to meet them. You know I'm impressed by writers. You, Woollcott, Kaufman. That's a big deal for a guy like me. I've told you how hard I work to improve my mind. I try to read the classics, even when I don't under-stand them, I don't give up. I plow ahead. Nice words please me."

She smiled. "That's lovely. That's very lovely. Fitzgerald writes nice words."

"Oh, yeah. He's right up there with the best. Like you and this new guy Hemingway."

"Thanks for the flattery. My sagging ego can use a fresh prop every now and then."

"What I'm getting at, Mrs. Parker, is Van Weber and him calling every guy he meets 'old sport.' Didn't you read Fitzgerald's *The Great Gatsby?*"

"Twice. I told Woollcott I planned to read it a third time very soon, and he's accused me of trying to build up an immunity."

"What's Jay Gatsby's favorite expression?"

Her chin dropped as the egg roll was set on the table before her. *"Old sport!"*

"You got it. Now where did Gatsby live?"

"Out on the island. In West Egg. In a huge mansion. My God. For West Egg, read East Cove. For Jay Gatsby"— she paused and then stared at the detective in astonishment, not knowing whether to laugh or cry—"for Jay Gatsby, read *Lacey Van Weber*."

"It's pretty good casting, you have to admit."

"Well, I'll be damned."

"Eat your egg roll."

"I've lost my appetite." She pushed the plate to one side. Singer shrugged and proceeded to demolish the egg roll. "That was very good, Jacob Singer. That was a brilliant example of your superb detective work. Can you imagine that? Jay Gatsby. I wonder if anyone else has caught the analogy. I can't wait to tell Woollcott. He'll never forgive himself for not having recognized it." She paused while thinking about something. "Mr. Van Weber, I think, intends to . . . um . . . pursue my friendship."

"Does that frighten you?"

"To be perfectly frank, Mr. Singer, I find Mr. Van Weber deadly attractive. And if he doesn't come chasing after me, I shall be bitterly disappointed."

"So will I," replied Singer. Their eyes locked. Mrs. Parker was no innocent. She knew Singer was interested in her beyond a superficial acquaintance. From the time they had first met, two years earlier, during a speakeasy raid, and he overheard Mrs. Parker referring to her escort, a wealthy septuagenarian, as "an old gloat," Singer knew he had someone special in the paddy wagon. When she identified herself, and this was at a time when fame was first beginning to brush her skirt, Singer was overwhelmed. He was also not blind to her petite beauty, later describing her to a fellow officer as "a nice box of candy." He interceded with the judge, explaining that in his opinion Mrs. Parker's attacking an arresting officer with an unopened bottle of champagne was a clear case of self-defense. From that moment, Mrs. Parker declared him a friend for life. She invited him to lunch at the Algonquin, and he was promptly adopted by the Round Table. They promised to make his name as celebrated as that of another famous and feared detective, Johnny Broderick. Mrs. Parker would never forget the first time Franklin P. Adams mentioned Jacob Singer in his column, "The Conning Tower." Singer sent a dozen roses to her and a bottle of champagne confiscated in a raid the night before to Adams.

"It wouldn't worry you if Van Weber and I began to see more of each other?"

"That's what an investigation is all about, isn't it? When you volunteered to help today, you said it was because you and Woollcott have easier access to a certain kind of person than I do. You've already proven that. You've met Van Weber. Fast work. Now you've met Crater. Even better. You already know Liveright."

"You couldn't possibly think he could be tied to Ilona Mercury's murder."

"I will if we find out she did a guest turn at one of his orgies."

"If you know about these goings-on, why haven't you raided them?"

"In the first place, there's been no complaints filed. And in the second place, we've been told to lay off."

"I see. Doesn't that bother you? I mean, I know you're so moral, so upstanding, so . . ."

"Cut the eulogy, Mrs. Parker. We're in a chink joint, not at my memorial." She wished they were at the Fortune Cookies' memorial. They were now lacerating "Roses of Picardy."

"Don't those boys ever take a break?"

"The band? Hell, no. Not coolie labor. Now, by the way, Mrs. Parker, don't let me find you trying to get Woollcott or one of your other buddies into one of them orgies."

"Woollcott at an orgy? Why, that would be as fascinating as meeting a son of Gertrude Stein. On the other hand, where does Liveright get his female participants? I mean, I'm sure he doesn't declare open season on shopgirls in Woolworth's."

"Polly Adler supplies him." He shrugged. "What the

hell, that's why she's in business. They get a fair share of showgirls looking to make a better score in life. There's still them what's dumb enough to think they got an even chance of snaring a rich lover at one of these penis parties. Oh, sorry if I've offended you."

"How can I be offended when I'm numb? Those poor girls. Those poor, poor exploited women."

"It's like I said before, nobody's made a complaint."

Mrs. Parker shook her head sadly. "It sounds as bad as white slavery."

"Lady, I could tell you plenty about *that*. Be glad I don't."

"Will you let me know the minute the poor Mercury girl's been officially identified. I mean, I'm rarin' to go, if you can stand a cliché. Woollcott's got seats for us for *No Foolin'* tomorrow night. I'd like to go backstage and get friendly with any of the girls who might have been close to the Hungarian lady."

"Go right ahead. She'll probably be headlines in the afternoon sheets. Complete with pictures."

"Then somehow I'd like to meet Mrs. Adler. I already know Texas Guinan." She was drumming her fingers on the tabletop. "Of course, if Mr. Van Weber decides *not* to pursue me . . ."

"My money's on you. You'll be hearing from him. I'll give you another tip. For free. A couple of hundred feet from the Globe Theater stage door, there's a filthy little crib called the Harlequin. It's a hole in the wall. We don't even bother raiding it. But mostly that's because a lot of singers hang out there."

"Opera or musical comedy?"

"My kind of singers, Mrs. Parker. Informers. The kind of rats who'd steal the flowers off of their mother's grave. There's one in particular you might get to know, should maybe you and Mr. Woollcott think of dropping in there for a drink tomorrow night."

"Mr. Van Weber recommended we have an after-theater dinner at Tony's."

"Nice place. Good wop food. The booze won't burn your lining. Very convenient to the Harlequin. You could drop in after dinner. Sid's usually there. Sid Curley. Small-time grifter, but a big-time snoop. He feeds Winchell stuff for his column. He feeds us plenty for a price. I don't go in there because I'm known, I could be recognized and that could put Sid on the hot seat. You and Woollcott go in, you're a couple of swells slumming. You're both quick on the uptake."

"Of course. We're always interested in meeting new people. How will we know Mr. Curley? I mean, we just couldn't ask the bartender or a waiter to introduce us. That would be stupidly suspicious."

"Indeed. But leave the action up to Sid. If he's there, he'll find a way to introduce himself. You can also hear him. All the time he goes 'sniff sniff sniff.' He used to be on cocaine, but he's clean now. But he can't get out of the habit of making believe he's sniffing it. So he goes 'sniff sniff sniff.' Got it?"

"It's written on my brain with lightning."

"If you get to meet him, bring the conversation around to the show you just saw and what a shame that poor show-girl got the finger. He'll pick up on you. Eventually, if you like, you sort of subtly drop it that we're acquainted. He'll get the message. And then maybe he'll give you a message."

Mrs. Parker sat back and sighed. "My, haven't I had quite a day. And my, isn't there tomorrow to look forward to."

"Tired?"

"Yes. I'm tired. And good God! Listen! Don't you hear it?"

"Hear what?"

"The silence!" The Fortune Cookies were gone.

"I've got to get back to drinking straight Jack Rose," announced Mrs. Parker to George, the headwaiter, in the Rose Room of the Algonquin Hotel where the members of the Round Table convened. "I've been drinking fancy stuff like bourbon sours, and I think they're upsetting my system."

"That's a very grave decision you've come to," said Robert Benchley, who sat next to her, wondering how long it would take her to complete the process of removing her gloves which she had set into operation when she sat down five minutes before.

"I'm a hotbed of grave decisions this morning, Mr. Benchley. We seem to be the only ones here. Woollcott's late as usual. He's taking me to the theater tonight." She returned her attention to the headwaiter. "I'll have a Jack Rose over a piece of ice. Mr. Benchley?" He asked for a Manhattan with three cherries. George left them. "How's Gertrude, Mr. Benchley?"

"Oh, Gertrude's all right, if you like Gertrude."

"I think your wife is just peachy."

"No, you don't. You can't stomach her."

"Don't raise your voice."

"I never raise my voice. It's too heavy." She was still working on her gloves. "Peggy Hopkins got married again." Miss Hopkins was a celebrated showgirl, a gold digger supreme, said to be the inspiration for Anita Loos's delightful *Gentlemen Prefer Blondes.*

"And who gave the bride away?"

"Everybody." He gently rubbed the tip of his nose. "I see you've been arguing with your wrists again."

"A slight lapse of discipline on my part. I hear you're going to Hollywood."

"Yes, I need the money. Gertrude needs the money. Something about feeding the family and paying off the mortgage. I should have married you. We'd have led a very merry devil-may-care bohemian existence."

"But we do, Mr. Benchley, we do."

"I wish you'd stop falling in love with the wrong men."

"Stop policing my emotions. Oh, dear, here comes Ross. Hello, Harold. I'm sorry about not delivering the copy as promised. I really began to work away at it diligently last night, but then my quill broke." Ross took a seat opposite them wordlessly. His massive pompadour quivered as he sat, and since there wasn't a strong wind in the Rose Room, Mrs. Parker suggested sweetly it might be the nesting ground of a family of field mice.

"I won't be needing your copy after all, Dottie."

"Oh, dear. Now I'm being punished." A waiter brought Mrs. Parker and Benchley their drinks and promised to be quick about Ross's gin martini.

"I've got some wonderful stuff from Janet Flanner in Paris this morning."

"Are you telling me my contributions will no longer be eagerly awaited?" Benchley was making a production of studying the three cherries in his Manhattan. Internecine strife embarrassed him. Mrs. Parker and Ross were the perennial combatants in a never-ending battle in the arena known as *The New Yorker* magazine. Neither would be the victor. Mrs. Parker would soon set herself adrift from Mr. Ross's patronage, and Mr. Ross would begrudgingly realize the lady's gifts were not readily replaceable.

"Your contributions will always be eagerly awaited, Dottie, although they always will not arrive."

Benchley sipped his drink and then inquired of neither of them in particular, "Give me a sentence with 'testosterone.'"

After giving the word some serious thought for a moment Mrs. Parker said with a wicked twinkle in her eye, "At lunch, the waiter tossed salads for Lily and Elsie, but Tess tossed 'er own."

It was while Benchley and Ross were groaning that Woollcott arrived. He was carrying the early editions of several of the afternoon newspapers. "Good afternoon, my cherubs!" He took one of Mrs. Parker's hands and kissed it, making ugly smacking noises. "You have such a lovely hand."

As he lowered himself into a chair, Benchley commented, "It took her the better part of fifteen minutes to display it."

Mrs. Parker announced lugubriously, "We are losing Mr. Benchley to the fleshpots of Hollywood."

"When do you leave?" Ross asked Benchley.

"Saturday morning."

"Are you taking Gertrude with you?"

"Which Gertrude?"

Woollcott placed the newspapers in front of Mrs. Parker. "Another murdered showgirl, my dear, if such trash interests you."

"Anything about murder interests me," trilled Mrs. Parker gaily, "as long as I'm not the illustration." Ilona Mercury had made it big at last. She was headlines splashed across the front page of the three newspapers. Mrs. Parker began reading in her softly modulated voice: "'The brutally strangled body of Ziegfeld showgirl Ilona Mercury was found early last evening in a vacant lot in the Canarsie section of Brooklyn.'"

"Nobody should be found strangled in Brooklyn," said Benchley.

"Nobody should be found in Brooklyn, strangled or not," added Woollcott.

"'An autopsy, performed this morning, ruled out alcohol or narcotics.'" She looked up and her eyes locked with Woollcott's. "Dear Alec, have we good seats for tonight?"

"Fifth row center, my dear. I haven't booked for dinner yet. Have you any preference?"

"Oh, I should have phoned and told you last night."

"I wasn't home last night. What should you have phoned and told me?"

"We're booked at Tony's for after theater, it's just around the corner from the Globe Theater."

"The Globe. That's where Ziegfeld's revue's playing." Ross wrinkled his nose with distaste.

"Didn't you like it, Harold?" asked Mrs. Parker.

"Not my cup of tea. Haven't you seen it already, Woollcott?"

"Yes. Now I shall examine it as a social study." He directed his mouth at Mrs. Parker. "Who booked us at Tony's? Put down that newspaper and answer me, and you, Benchley, signal a waiter. I need a drink."

Mrs. Parker dutifully folded the newspaper and let it fall to the floor. "I met and had drinks with a friend of the management late yesterday afternoon. A very charming gentleman named Lacey Van Weber." Woollcott's pince-nez dropped.

"Now how the hell did you get to meet him?" asked Ross.

"Horace Liveright fixed it. Say, Harold, I've got a hell of an idea. Van Weber has really captured the imagination of the city . . ."

"Among other things," interjected Woollcott.

"Wouldn't he make a hell of a subject for a *New Yorker* profile?"

"Not a bad idea," chipped in Benchley. "Gertrude can't get to read enough about him. She says he reminds her of Jay Gatsby."

Mrs. Parker blanched slightly. "What do you say, Harold? He's really hot and up to the minute." And sexy and handsome and I want a really good excuse to try to get to know him better in case he doesn't call for a date within the next crucial twenty-four hours.

"I'll think it over," said Ross, without enthusiasm.

Woollcott piped up. "I think it's a brilliant idea. You mustn't ignore brilliant ideas, Harold, just because they're not your own. And will you just look at our Mrs. Parker's face? How many months has it been since we've seen such enthusiasm brightening her cheeks and lighting up her eyes like exploding Roman candles?"

"Gentlemen," said Mrs. Parker with a slightly trembling voice, "speak of the devil, here he is."

Lacey Van Weber entered the Rose Room as though he were in the center of a theatrical spotlight. Ten feet into the room, he paused, waited for the effect to sink in, doffed his homburg and smiled in Mrs. Parker's direction. He shifted his walking stick and gloves from his right hand to his left and smartly stepped forward with his right hand out-stretched. "Mrs. Parker, how nice to see you again, and so soon."

Mrs. Parker hoped somebody had smelling salts but dreaded the thought of the need for them. She shook hands with Van Weber and introduced him to the others. "Won't you join us?" asked Mrs. Parker.

"Just for a moment," said Van Weber. "I've two business associates waiting in the other dining room. I had a feeling you might be lunching here today, so I popped in for a look. You look lovely." Somebody grunted. Mrs. Parker suspected it was Benchley. Van Weber sat down.

Woollcott picked up the ball. "I gather you've recommended we dine at Tony's tonight. Is it a sincere recommendation, or do you own a piece of the place?"

Van Weber smiled. Mrs. Parker clutched her stomach. "It's a sincere recommendation, and I own a piece of the place."

"I'll bet you own a piece of a lot of places," suggested Benchley.

"My investments are indeed diverse and scattered. They have to be. It's all a crap shoot."

"It's quite a coincidence, your entrance, Mr. Van Weber, just when I was suggesting to Mr. Ross you might make an interesting subject for a *New Yorker* profile," said Mrs. Parker.

"That's very flattering," responded Van Weber. "Would you write it?"

"When I suggest it, I write it."

Ross was crumbling a bread roll. "Might be worth a go. You interested, Van Weber? Would you cooperate?"

"Let me think it over. You're moving a little too fast for me."

"Oh, my!" said Mrs. Parker suddenly, punctuating with a slight gasp, "I'll bet you haven't seen the afternoon papers."

"Not yet. No."

Mrs. Parker took one of the papers from Benchley's hands and spread it on the table in front of Van Weber. "Isn't it awful?"

Woollcott, looking about as innocent as Jack the Ripper, asked, "Did you know the victim?"

"Slightly. Rudolph Valentino brought her to a party at my penthouse a week or so ago."

"Was that the night he took ill?" pursued Woollcott.

"Sadly enough, that was the night. Poor girl. Strangled. How sad."

"And dumped in Brooklyn," mused Benchley. "That's adding insult to injury."

Van Weber got to his feet. "You must excuse me. I promised my associates I'd only be a few minutes."

"You'll let me know about the profile?" asked Mrs. Parker.

Van Weber smiled and took her hand. "You'll hear from me very soon." He left as the waiter finally brought Woollcott a drink. Woollcott glowered at the waiter and then focused on Mrs. Parker.

"Dorothy," he said, "you look like Lillian Gish with a stomachache."

Mrs. Parker said nothing. She lifted her Jack Rose and drank. She had a feeling she was sailing into a stormy sea.

"Good afternoon, fellow Philistines." Woollcott and Mrs. Parker were surprised to see Kaufman. He had a newspaper under his arm.

"Where've you been keeping yourself, George? Haven't seen you in weeks." Ross was fond of Kaufman, if only because his own mountain of hair towered over the other man's.

"No place special, Harold. Been catching up on the new movies." A waiter approached, and Kaufman ordered iced tea. Benchley shuddered. "Saw the new Barrymore yesterday, *Don Juan*. It has music and sound effects. I suppose soon they'll be talking. There's a pretty little actress in it, Mary Astor. A real good looker."

"What've you got there?" asked Woollcott, referring to Kaufman's newspaper.

"The *Journal.*"

"We've seen the *Journal*," said Mrs. Parker. Then as though suddenly stricken, she exclaimed, "Oh, George! That poor thing who was strangled and dumped in Brooklyn. Ilona what?"

"Mercury," growled Woollcott.

"Didn't you know her, George?" Mrs. Parker resembled Little Eva on the verge of running amok.

"I'd met her." He opened the paper and stared at the revolting photograph of the strangled woman. "Some girls' looks fade fast." He folded the paper and shoved it under his seat. "What else is new?"

"I had dinner last night with our detective protégé, Mr. Singer." She paused dramatically to let the news take effect where she was hoping it would take effect. Kaufman was constructing a pyramid of sugar cubes, Woollcott was studying the menu. Benchley and Ross were participating in a game of cat's cradle with a string Benchley had produced. "He's really a fine example of self-improvement."

"You mean he was able to pronounce the dishes on the menu?" asked Woollcott.

"Don't be so superior, Alec," said Mrs. Parker in a voice that recalled an old maid schoolteacher. "You could afford to learn a few things from Mr. Singer."

"And what did you learn last night?" asked Kaufman.

Mrs. Parker swept the table with a meaningful look. "That it frequently pays just to sit back and listen." She saw Edna Ferber entering. "Oh, dear. Gangrene is setting in." Her dislike of the wealthy novelist was accepted and tolerated by all at the table, including Mrs. Ferber herself, who looked upon Mrs. Parker as a parvenu in the shaky world of modern literature.

"Hello, my darlings," yodeled Mrs. Ferber as she sat down next to Kaufman, for whom she harbored what she thought was a secret passion. Unfortunately, her face was more eloquent than her novels. "Dottie, I just ran into your publisher."

"Horace?"

"Yes. He looks like a corpse they forgot to embalm."

"He looked perfectly fine when I saw him yesterday. But then," she continued with an air of perverse innocence,

"I heard him say something about holding a meeting at midnight." The men exchanged knowing glances. Mrs. Parker now knew they knew. She hated them for not having let her in on the scandalous goings-on.

"Why, Dottie, darling, what have you done to your wrists?"

"You know damn well what I've done to my wrists, Ferber."

"You should stop doing that, Dottie. It obviously doesn't work."

"*Touché*," murmured Woollcott.

"How's Beatrice?" Ferber asked Kaufman.

"We're still married. Doesn't anybody care about eating any lunch?"

"I'm starving," said Mrs. Parker. "I haven't eaten in days."

"What about your dinner last night with the detective?" asked Ross.

"He did all the eating."

"How's the *matzo brei* coming?" asked Polly Adler as she came into the kitchen where Gloria was bending over the stove carefully scrambling eggs and soggy unleavened bread. It was one of Mrs. Adler's favorite dishes.

"Almost ready."

"Any word from Vera?"

"Not a peep."

"Any complaints from any of the girls who worked for Liveright?"

"Not a peep."

"I see. My chickens aren't peeping this morning." She poured herself a cup of coffee, then sat down at the kitchen table. "How's the day shaping up?"

"There are three girls on outcalls now."

Mrs. Adler nodded. "The luncheon special."

"There are two booked for seven this evening."

"The blue-plate special."

"And Mr. Julian Eltinge"—a celebrated female impersonator—"has asked for Agnes to be at his theater for the second intermission."

"Nothing special."

The phone rang. "I'll get it. You stay with the *matzo brei.* Keep stirring. I like it hard." She paused. "No pun intended." Into the phone she growled, "Yeah?" She looked at her wristwatch. "Mr. Vanderbilt, I am chagrined and ashamed of myself. I absolutely did not mark it down in my appointment book. I am so sorry. Consider I'm groveling at your feet. I've never disappointed you before so I know you'll forgive me. It's just that Vera wasn't feeling too well last night. I didn't learn that until just a few minutes after you called. So I gave her the night off. If you still want her, I'll phone her and get her over to your mansion within an hour." Whatever Vanderbilt said made her smile. "Mr. Vanderbilt, for my money you're number one in the Four Hundred." She hung up. "That stupid cunt. She knew she was due at Vanderbilt's at one. I should have reminded her when she phoned in from Horathy's last night." She jiggled the hook on the phone. "Hello, Central, wake up for Christ's sake, the war's over."

Vera DeLee lived in an apartment hotel on West Thirty-fourth Street near Tenth Avenue. The day clerk explained to an impatient Polly Adler that as far as he knew Miss DeLee was still in her apartment. He hadn't seen her leave and he'd arrived at seven in the morning and God knows the only time he'd seen her at seven in the morning was when somebody pulled the fire alarm. "If you'll wait," he told Mrs. Adler, "I'll send one of the maids up to shake her up. Well, she's not answering the phone!" Mrs. Adler told him she'd wait.

The maid opened the door to Vera DeLee's room with her passkey. There was a terrible stench in the room. The windows were shut, and the shades were drawn. She saw Vera DeLee sprawled across the bed, face up. Drunk again, she thought. She shook her head and shuffled to the bed. "Miss DeLee!" she shouted, but the shout stuck in her throat. Her hands flew to her mouth but too late to gag the scream that welled up in her stomach, forced its way up past her lungs, out her throat and into the room and the hall outside where it brought several of the frightened tenants on the run.

Vera DeLee was not a pretty sight. Her face was bloated. Her skin was an ugly greenish-gray. Her tongue protruded from between bloated lips. Her body was stiff with rigor mortis. She had been strangled.

5

Jacob Singer sat in a straight-backed chair taking notes while the morgue boys wrapped Vera DeLee's body for removal. The maid stood with her back to the bed, her hand covering her mouth, a feather duster clenched tightly in her other fist. The desk clerk, Vincent Laurie, had opened the windows wide and stood against the wall facing Singer, arms folded, a veteran of murders, suicides and physical beatings. It was less than half an hour since the maid had found the prostitute's body, and Singer had already efficiently cross-examined the two employees, which added up to next to nothing. They had very little to tell him. Laurie explained that the night clerk might be able to add more to Singer's meager store of information on the dead woman. Singer restrained from enlightening him that he knew almost everything about the dead woman except who had murdered her.

"Can't I please go now?" pleaded the maid. "I'm getting behind on my rooms and I can't stand it in here no longer. It's giving me the heebie-jeebies." The morgue attendants were carrying the corpse out on a stretcher. Poor Vera DeLee, thought Singer, I hope there'll be somebody to claim her. If not, he knew he could rely on Polly Adler to do the right thing. After all, she was famous for guaranteeing her girls legal and medical services. Vera DeLee's was an admirable reputation in whoredom. Surely Polly would award her the bonus of a decent burial. Vera DeLee. He wondered what her real name was.

Singer dismissed the maid and the desk clerk. After they left, he went to the phone and asked the switchboard to connect him with the Algonquin Hotel. It was not yet two in the afternoon. There was every likelihood Mrs. Parker was in temporary residence in the hotel's Rose Room.

At the Round Table in the Rose Room, Harold Ross was asking George S. Kaufman, "What's the new play about, George?"

"It's about triplets. Princesses." Mrs. Parker was examining her fingernails and deciding she could use a manicure. "One's good, one's evil, and the third is undecided." Edna Ferber breathed a sigh of relief. Kaufman had promised not to reveal to anyone that he had agreed to collaborate with her on a new play, at least not until they were both satisfied with the first draft.

"Why has Marc Connelly abandoned us?" asked Benchley. "It's over a week since he's been here."

"Oh, didn't I tell you?" contributed Ferber. "I spoke to him early this morning. He's in the throes of a writer's block. The agony is unbelievable. It seems he was invaded yesterday afternoon by some uninvited guests, causing his delicate muse to flee."

"I don't think that's what caused his muse to flee," suggested Mrs. Parker. "I think it was the dreadful decor. I mean who was his interior decorator? Helen Keller?"

Woollcott swallowed the last of his lemon meringue pie and then sat back contentedly. "I composed a poem this morning." Silence descended over the table. The air was pregnant with expectation. Woollcott cleared his throat and recited, "This morning I met a pelican/ Whose stomach held more than my belly can."

"Is that it?" asked Mrs. Parker incredulously.

"That's it. I shall offer it to Mr. Adams for his column.

I should think it might enhance my celebrity."

"Why, Alec," said Mrs. Parker agreeably, "it just might make you as celebrated as Whistler's father." She saw George, the headwaiter, approaching with a phone.

"It's for you, Mrs. Parker."

Mrs. Parker's hands fluttered. She favored Lacey Van Weber as the likely caller, probably sitting in one of the bank of telephone booths in the lobby. She could see his profile as he held the telephone receiver to his ear, waiting to be excited by her bell-like tones. George placed the phone in front of her and then plugged it into the wall. Conversation stopped. Mrs. Parker stared at the phone as though it were about to develop a life of its own.

"Well, for crying out loud, answer it," said Woollcott testily.

"Hello?"

"It's me. Jake Singer. There's been another murder." He had her undivided attention. She listened placidly to the sordid details of Vera DeLee's final exit. She was wondering if the pattern of strangulations was becoming epidemic. Her eyes moved from Kaufman's hands to Ross's hands and then to Benchley's hands. Then her eyes found Woollcott's, and she wondered if he was psychic. She had a feeling he sensed it was Singer at the other end of the line and there was a new murder to consider. "I'll be calling on Polly Adler in about half an hour. Want to join me? I can pick you up in about fifteen minutes."

"Mr. Woollcott is here with me." All eyes were on Woollcott. He smiled sweetly and dropped four sugar cubes into his cup of coffee. It was really coffee.

"Oh, by all means bring Mr. Woollcott, if he isn't too sensitive for an establishment like Mrs. Adler's."

"Mr. Woollcott isn't sensitive to too much, so I wouldn't let it worry you. By the way, is this news for publication?"

"Oh, by all means."

"In fifteen minutes we'll be standing outside under the canopy." She hung up, and George removed the phone and himself. "That was our detective friend, Jacob Singer. Another woman of dubious reputation has been murdered."

"Mrs. Calvin Coolidge?" asked Benchley.

"Vera DeLee. One of Mrs. Adler's girls." She studied her companions, all but Miss Ferber. She was pretty sure it was safe to assume that Edna Ferber was not a client of Mrs. Adler's. Considering Woollcott would be as likely as Jack Dempsey prancing in a Vassar daisy chain.

"Also strangled?" asked Kaufman while Ross reread the article on Ilona Mercury in one of the newspapers.

"Brutally."

"In whose apartment?" asked Woollcott wickedly while Kaufman stared daggers across the table at him.

"Her own."

"Ah," said Kaufman with a forced smile, "a home girl."

Ross leaned forward and aimed his mouth at Mrs. Parker. "How come you're so privy to all this inside dope?"

A puckish look spread across Benchley's face. "Oh, tell me privy maiden, are there any more at home like you?"

He was ignored. Mrs. Parker was struggling with her gloves. "Last night when dining with Mr. Singer, I told him Alec and I were seriously considering collaborating on a series of articles about contemporary murders."

Ross looked dubious. "You and Alec collaborating? That's like crossing a lynx with a mastodon."

"And why not?" interjected Woollcott. "Might be fun. Where are you off to, Dottie?"

"Where are *we* off to, sweetheart. Why, we're off to Mrs. Adler's house of ill repute as Mr. Singer's companions. He's picking us up in a squad car in a few minutes. If you're a good boy, he'll let you stand on the running board with the wind in your hair."

Ferber snorted. "This could be history—Alec in a whorehouse."

"And why not?" Woollcott inquired acerbically. "Mrs. Adler is a delightful conversationalist. She's a hell of a lot more intelligent on diversified subjects than a few in my immediate vicinity. She's also one hell of a backgammon player."

"Imagine patronizing a madam for a game of backgammon."

Mrs. Parker wondered if she dare reach across the table in an attempt to strangle Ferber.

Ross was asking Woollcott, "How the hell did you get to meet her in the first place?"

"She attended one of my lectures. Afterward, she came forward to ask some incredibly intelligent questions. When I asked her to identify herself, she did. I couldn't have been more pleased if I had found myself in the presence of Queen Mary of England."

"Come on, Alec, we've got to go." Mrs. Parker was on her feet with her handbag hanging from her hand.

"You haven't paid your share of the lunch," growled Ross.

"Take care of it for now, Harold," said Woollcott imperiously. "We'll settle up with you later."

As they walked away, they heard Edna Ferber telling the others about a party she had attended the previous evening. "It was one of those star-studded affairs where the person at the piano playing Gershwin was Gershwin."

Mrs. Parker took Woollcott's arm as they walked through the lobby. "I have a feeling about all of us, Alec. I have a feeling that, very soon, we shall have outlived our need for each other."

"But we'll still be friends, won't we, darling?"

"That depends on how you review my collection of poetry." She glanced around the lobby, but there was no sign of Lacey Van Weber. She made a mental note to beard Ross later in the day about the profile.

Woollcott was testy again. "Now what about you and Van Weber? I mean, I arrived at the tail end of your exposition. You most certainly owe me an explanation."

"I most certainly do, and I have every intention of giving you one, but there's Mr. Singer waiting for us in the squad car. Mr. Singer! How did you get here so soon?"

Singer sat in the front seat next to the driver, detective Al Cassidy. "We used the siren." When Mrs. Parker and

Woollcott were lodged in the back seat, Singer introduced them to Cassidy, and they took off. "Cassidy's working with me on the case. He knows about Kaufman's connection to the Mercury stiff. DeLee's at the morgue now, and I've ordered a quick autopsy. I got a feeling she was a junkie from what the maid told me. She said she'd seen syringes on top of DeLee's dresser, stuff like that. DeLee said she was diabetic, which could be a reasonable explanation. But in our circumstances, I prefer to think she was on junk. Either of you met Mrs. Adler before?"

"I have," said Woollcott. Cassidy studied him in the rear-view mirror and suppressed a guffaw, covering his mouth with a beefy hand while his huge frame shook.

Mrs. Parker explained, "Mr. Woollcott enjoys a verisimilitude of friendships."

Singer explained to Cassidy, "That means all different kinds."

"What does?" asked Cassidy as he avoided sideswiping a beer wagon drawn by two sorry-looking horses.

"Is she expecting us?" asked Mrs. Parker.

"I called her from the hotel. She's pretty shook up. De-Lee was one of her pets, or so it sounded like over the phone."

They pulled up in front of Mrs. Adler's apartment house. The doorman paled at the sight of the squad car. "Mrs. Adler's expecting us," barked Singer. "Keep an eye on the car."

Polly Adler was wearing one of her most expensive, black Lucile creations which she had had especially designed for herself on a recent talent-scouting trip to London. It gave her some much needed height and a look of regal elegance. Lucile was a sister of the celebrated novelist, the self-styled goddess of sex, Elinor Glyn, whose steamy tale of passion in palatial pits, *Three Weeks*, had won her the eternal patronage of the moguls of Hollywood. It was there, the previous year, she had dubbed Clara Bow "The It Girl," thereby launching the young actress on a trajectory of misfortune and tragedy. She braced herself against the grand piano while Gloria, in response to the door chimes (a careful selection from Brahms), admitted Jacob Singer, Al Cassidy, Woollcott and Mrs. Parker. While the introductions were in process, Gloria discreetly withdrew to the kitchen, where she finished chopping ice in a bucket. Mrs. Adler had foreseen the need for drinks and hors d'oeuvres. Mrs. Parker was admiring Mrs. Adler's taste in interior decoration.

"You really like the place?" Mrs. Adler knew Mrs. Parker by reputation. She knew a kind word could be followed by a lethal indictment.

"I could live here myself, except I wouldn't be much use to you."

"Let's get down to business," interrupted Singer, who had a heavy day ahead of him and wasn't looking forward to it. They were all seated now in a circle around the centerpiece of a marble-topped coffee table. The marble, Mrs. Parker was positive, had been quarried in Venice. "From the condition of the body," he began authoritatively, "I guess that the woman was strangled sometime last night. I won't know for sure until I get an autopsy report, which should be in an hour or so, but still, Mrs. Adler, it would help if you could tell us about for instance the state of her health. Who were her enemies if you know of any? What was her relationship to Judge Crater? Do you know if she knew Ilona Mercury?"

"Mr. Singer," said Mrs. Adler with overstated patience, "as any good madam instructs a new girl in the business, honey, one thing at a time." Gloria entered wheeling a cart laden with drinks, glasses, ice and nosh. "Let's begin with her health while Gloria fills your orders." Gloria placed the plate of food on the coffee table and then dispensed the drinks. "Vera was a diabetic. She was what the doctors call a border-line case, so she didn't have to inject herself with insulin."

"She had hypodermics," said Singer. "So she was on junk."

"I don't know about that," said Mrs. Adler huffily? "I don't allow any of that shit . . . forgive me, Mrs. Parker . . .

on the premises." She paused. "I heard she was on morphine."

"Was she on call last night?" asked Singer.

"She was, but she begged off. She was wanted for a
midnight party." Mrs. Parker and Woollcott exchanged
a knowing glance. "But she phoned me around seven
o'clock—I think it was from her doctor's office—and said
she wasn't feeling too good. So I told her to go home and
take it easy. I don't like to supply my customers with dam-
aged goods. My girls are clean. I'll stake my reputation on
that." Mrs. Parker admired the other woman's look of fierce
pride.

"Who's her doctor?"

"Horathy. Bela Horathy."

Singer sighed. "Old Dr. Bliss himself."

Mrs. Adler shrugged. "It was Ilona Mercury who recommended him."

"You mean Mercury was hooked, too?" There was no
evidence from her autopsy report.

"I think she claimed to know him from the old country.
After all, they're both Hungarians, except Ilona was a good
deal younger."

Mrs. Parker cleared her throat, and Singer knew it was
time to turn the floor over to her. "Mrs. Adler, did Ilona
work for you, too? I mean, I know her official designation is
that of one of Mr. Ziegfeld's showgirls, but so many of these
girls have such expensive tastes, you know what I mean."

"I catch your drift. Yeah, Ilona was one of my back-up
girls. But very choosy. You couldn't just offer her anything,
like some fat butter and egg man from the Midwest. Ilona
went in for big money and big names."

"Like Rudolph Valentino?" To Mrs. Adler, Woollcott
looked like an evil cherub, but he played one hell of a game
of backgammon.

"Valentino was her own score, Alec. She said they were
old friends."

It was Singer's turn again. "I thought she'd only been
here a year and spent all that time here in the city. I didn't

-82-

know she'd done a tour of the West Coast."

"I wouldn't know that either," responded Mrs. Adler. "I never had a hen session with Ilona. Girl to girl talk wasn't her specialty. Vera was about the only one of my kids that Ilona socialized with occasionally."

Mrs. Parker asked Singer, "Isn't Immigration investigating Miss Mercury's background for you?"

"They are, but they're very slow. Damned administration is overworked and understaffed."

"So's my place," said Mrs. Adler sadly. "With Vera and Ilona gone, I gotta start holding auditions again." She smiled affably at Mrs. Parker, who wondered if she was being friendly or propositioning. "Nobody's eating nothing. Come on folks, help yourselves. I made that pâté myself from genuine Long Island goose livers." Woollcott dived in.

"What about enemies? Vera ever tell you she'd been threatened?"

"Sure. Lots of times. Some of my clients have kinky notions. Some of the girls ain't interested. It makes for bad feelings on both sides. Now I make sure I choose the girl to suit the client's taste." She favored Mrs. Parker again. "Every day in my business, you learn something new."

"Ain't it the truth," agreed Mrs. Parker. Woollcott had a coughing fit. Gloria brought him a glass of water. Cassidy slapped him on the back. Woollcott waved him away. Singer resumed questioning.

"What about Judge Crater?"

"What about him?"

"Was he seeing a lot of her? I mean, we know he took her to Lacey Van Weber's penthouse party."

"Well, you know how it is with Joe. He's always fooling around with one chippie or another. I mean, Stella, his wife, ain't exactly passion's pet."

"So what about Vera?"

"So what about her?"

"Were they steady?"

Mrs. Adler gave the question some deeper concentration. "Well, I'll tell you, Mr. Singer, to my knowledge, he did see more of her than he did of my other girls. But I wouldn't call it steady. There were other of my kids he took a shine to from time to time. And listen, you gotta keep in mind I ain't the only exotic establishment in town. By the way, they still holding Belle Livingston on Rikers?"

"Naw, she got sprung this morning," Cassidy informed her.

"Poor Belle. She shouldn't be in this line of business. She should settle in Italy and indulge her supreme passion."

"And what is that?" inquired the fascinated Mrs. Parker.

"Fuckin' wops. Say, how are you two involved in this?" She was referring to Mrs. Parker and Woollcott. Woollcott explained their collaboration. "Weird," was Mrs. Adler's only comment.

"Vera have any family?"

"Someplace upstate, I think. But don't worry. I'm taking care of the funeral. I own a plot out in Montefiore." She explained to Mrs. Parker and Woollcott, "That's a very sweet cemetery out on Long Island. I keep it for emergencies. I've already planted three of my kids there. I guess some girls are just doomed from birth." Woollcott thought he heard Mrs. Parker stifling a sob. Mrs. Parker was stifling laughter. Somewhere there had to be a delicious short story in a madam who kept a cemetery plot exclusively to accommodate her deceased employees. She would have to try to remember if Guy de Maupassant hadn't already covered that territory. "Was there anything in her room about her family?"

"There was not much information there. There was an address book, but that was mostly filled with local stuff. My boys are still looking. If anything good turns up, I'll let you know. If she's got a family, they ought to know."

"Her murder'll be in the papers?" Singer assured her the tabloids would be feasting on it. "So if they can read, they'll know. Who's for a refill?" She had no takers. "When can I claim the body?"

"Maybe sometime this afternoon. For sure by tomorrow morning."

Mrs. Adler was standing as the others prepared to leave. "I'm giving her a nice send-off. She's going from Campbell's, same as Valentino. I hear that polack Opal Engri's in from Hollywood laying all over Valentino's coffin. Them polacks'll lay over anything. Say, Singer, anything in the rumor he was poisoned?"

"We got no proof."

"So what? He still could've been poisoned. Well, Mrs. Parker, it is a delight to meet you at last. We been reading you in my literature class at City College. Why are you so cynical and tear-stained?"

Mrs. Parker was startled, but soon recovered. "I guess that's just my style."

Mrs. Adler took Woollcott's arm as she led the party to the door. "When are you coming up for some backgammon? We ain't faced each other across the board in a long time."

"Very soon, I promise you, very very soon."

"And Mrs. Parker, I'd be happy to see a lot more of you, too. I mean, now that you know the way, don't be a stranger." Gloria held the door open. "And Mr. Detective, when you find the bastard that strangled her, turn him over to me. I'll cut off his balls and *gardemff* them." She explained to Mrs. Parker, "That's a style of Yiddish roasting."

"I know," said Mrs. Parker, "my father was Jewish. So nice to meet you, Mrs. Adler."

Later, Cassidy steered the squad car in the direction of Mrs. Parker's apartment house on West Fifty-seventh Street.

"What do you think?" Singer asked the others in the back seat.

"I think she's lovely," said Mrs. Parker. "Imagine attending a class in literature." She resisted a comment on Mrs. Adler's analyzing her work as cynical and tear-stained. She would have to reexamine the direction of her gift. Cynical was fine, but tear-stained?

Woollcott was speaking. "Do you think both murders are the work of the same person?"

"You got any better ideas?" asked Singer.

"Too soon to formulate them. But still, both strangled. The girls knew each other. They shared the same doctor."

Mrs. Parker sat up straight. "Why are we driving me home?"

"Because you asked me to," said Cassidy.

"Shouldn't we be calling on Dr. Horathy?"

"I was going to wait until after the autopsy report," explained Singer.

"Surely that report must be in by now. Let's find a phone booth and you call the morgue, Mr. Singer. I mean, why waste time? Mr. Woollcott and I have hours before we go to the theater."

"Has it occurred to you I might have other and more pressing matters to attend to?" raged Woollcott.

"Such as?"

Woollcott folded his arms and glumly stared out the window. Cassidy pulled up at a candy store where a bank of phone booths was evident through the plate-glass window. Singer borrowed a nickel from Cassidy and then spent five minutes in a phone booth. Settled back in the front seat of the squad car, he told the others, "She was shot through with morphine. There were tracks all over her backside. She's obviously been under a long-term treatment. I looked up Horathy's address in the phone book." He recited it to Cassidy. They were soon pulling up at Horathy's office in a building on lower Park Avenue. A newsboy was peddling the latest edition of the afternoon *Journal.* He was enticing buyers with the news of Vera DeLee's sordid murder in a powerful voice that deserved to graduate to Grand Central Station. Woollcott splurged two cents and bought a copy. A photo of DeLee's body in the morgue was plastered across the front page. Mrs. Parker grimaced and followed the detectives into the building.

* * *

Nurse Cora Gallagher sat behind her desk reading the newspaper. She sat so still, she looked like the finished product of a taxidermist. The door to the doctor's office opened, and she quickly became animated. She folded the newspaper and put it to one side. She smiled at the patient who emerged from the doctor's office, an incredibly beautiful young woman with flaming red hair. Dr. Horathy followed Lily Robson into Nurse Gallagher's domain and then put his arm around Lily's shoulder.

"If there is continued pain, double the dosage. And if it gets worse, you will phone me, okay?" Bela Horathy was not quite six feet tall. He had aquiline features with a head of jet-black hair through which there ran an inch-wide streak of white. He had an athlete's slimness with fingers that tapered artistically. His voice was buttered and mellifluous. His accent was slight, almost unnoticeable.

"I don't want to get hooked on this stuff," said Lily Robson in her slum-cultivated voice.

"Surely you are making a joke." He couldn't see the look on Cora Gallagher's face. Lily Robson was obstructing his view.

"Surely I ain't. Tex Guinan don't want nobody on the premises what's hooked. You're sure this stuff's safe?"

"You'll love it. As soon as it's finished, you'll be back for more." He took one of her hands and kissed it.

Lily smiled. "Ain't you somethin'?" Horathy saw her to the door. After she left, Cora Gallagher showed him the newspaper.

"God," he muttered, taking the newspaper back into the office with him.

As Lily Robson got on an elevator, the second elevator reached the floor, from which marched Mrs. Parker, Woollcott, Singer and Cassidy. In the vanguard, Singer led the way to Horathy's office. Cora Gallagher stood up when the foursome entered, and Singer and Cassidy flashed their badges. "We'd like to talk to the doctor," said Singer.

"You don't have an appointment," said Nurse Gallagher.

"Girlie, we don't need one," said Cassidy.

"I'll see if he's in." She went swiftly into Horathy's office.

"No diplomas," commented Mrs. Parker.

"What do you mean?" asked Woollcott.

"There are no framed diplomas hanging on the walls. All doctors show off their diplomas. Where they graduated from. What degrees in medicine they've received. My doctor's walls are absolutely dripping with diplomas."

Nurse Gallagher returned. "The doctor will see you." She stood to one side as they entered Horathy's office. It was beautifully furnished in soft brown and white. A door led to an examining room and another door led to a laboratory. The doctor's windows overlooked Park Avenue. Here, Mrs. Parker noticed with satisfaction, there were framed diplomas on the walls. They were in a foreign language which she presumed was Hungarian. The doctor stood behind the desk as they trooped in and Singer identified himself and the others. Horathy made charming noises about how pleased he was to meet Mrs. Parker and Woollcott as he offered them seats. Singer wasted no time in getting down to his inquiry. The doctor admitted Vera DeLee had been a patient and yes, he had just read about her tragic death; he indicated the folded newspaper on his desk. Yes, he had seen her last night around five o'clock when she came for a booster shot. She hadn't felt well and fainted. He and the nurse assisted her to the couch in the waiting room and soon revived her. She left shortly after that.

"Was she your last patient of the day?" asked Singer.

"Yes, she was," replied Horathy.

"What's in this booster shot you gave her?"

"I'm sorry, but that's privileged information."

"I could subpoena your records." He was bluffing, and the doctor knew he was bluffing. By the time he got the court order, Horathy could have destroyed every record in his office.

"Our autopsy shows she was on morphine. A lot of morphine and for a long long time, according to the coroner. There are enough tracks on her backside to make the Baltimore and Ohio envious."

Horathy blithely asked Mrs. Parker if she and Woollcott were friends of the deceased. She explained her collaboration with Woollcott. She briefly entertained the thought of having cards printed with the explanation in case the investigation proved to be prolonged.

"What about them tracks?" persisted Singer.

"I administer booster shots in the buttocks because Miss DeLee's body was essential to her profession. It would not look good if her arms looked as though they had been repositories for needles."

"What about the morphine?"

"I know nothing about morphine."

"That's not the way we hear it."

"What you hear is slander."

Mrs. Parker interjected blithely, "But, Dr. Horathy, Rudolph Valentino accused you of being a dope pusher at Lacey Van Weber's party, and to my knowledge, you haven't instigated a suit for slander against him."

"It is pointless to sue the dead," said Horathy, as though he were faced with a congenital idiot.

"You could sue his estate." She wasn't sure if she knew what she was talking about. She pleaded with Singer, "Can't he?"

Singer went off on another tack. "Ilona Mercury was your patient, too, wasn't she?"

"Not really. We were merely acquainted."

"Acquainted enough for her to introduce Vera DeLee to you."

"I do not recall how Miss DeLee came to me."

"Polly Adler says it was Mercury that introduced DeLee to you. We trust Mrs. Adler." The inference that Horathy wasn't trusted didn't escape the doctor.

"You have no right to harass me!" raged Horathy. "I will not put up with this!"

Singer asked Mrs. Parker and Woollcott, "Do you see

any signs of harassment around here?"

"I think you're being perfectly charming," said Woollcott, who really meant it. He was thoroughly fascinated with Jacob Singer and decided he would later compliment Mrs. Parker for her rare good judgment in introducing the detective to their circle.

"I must ask you people to leave." Horathy stood firm and dignified. Mrs. Parker wondered if he'd ever been a hussar in the Hungarian army. She thought he would fit the part well.

"If you insist, then you insist," said Singer. "But it would help if you'd decide in the future to be a bit more cooperative."

"I can assure you, sir, there will be no 'in the future.'"

"I wouldn't bet on that." He said to the others, "Let's go." After they left the office, Cassidy slamming the door shut behind them, Horathy barked a number into the telephone.

At the elevator, Woollcott said grimly, "I really didn't like that man. There's something terribly sinister about people with white streaks in their hair."

"The guy was lying," said Cassidy. "We should look into him."

"The minute we get back to the precinct." The elevator arrived. As they got in and the operator closed the doors, Singer asked Mrs. Parker what she thought of Bela Horathy.

"Well, quite frankly," she said in a voice heavy with whimsy, "he rather struck me as a typographical error. If I were you, Mr. Singer, I'd look into him with the American Medical Association. I mean, perhaps he doesn't really have a license to practice in this country." She could see the elevator operator was all ears. "Young man, what you've heard here is strictly between us," she admonished him while suddenly mesmerized by his cowlick which seemed to rise from his head like the periscope of a submarine, "or my law officer friends here will haul you into the precinct for a grilling, or something equivalent."

In his office, Horathy raged into the telephone. There were attempts to pacify him from the other end. Horathy continued to rage. Then the voice at the other end became ominous and dangerous. Horathy's rage abated. After replacing the receiver on the hook, he shouted for nurse Gallagher. She heard him through the door and hurried to him.

"Vera DeLee was the last patient I saw yesterday."

"But what about . . ."

He interrupted her abruptly, his voice harsh and threatening. "Vera DeLee was the last patient I saw yesterday."

"Certainly, doctor."

When she returned to her desk, she sat staring into space, wondering if she dared quit and look for another job.

In the squad car, Mrs. Parker was serenely silent. The others traded small talk until Woollcott finally said to Mrs. Parker, "Your silence is maddening. What are you hatching in that perplexing mind of yours?"

"Just contemplating the perplexities of others. You know what I'd try to find out, Mr. Singer? I'd try to find out if Dr. Horathy saw another patient while Miss DeLee was stretched out recovering from her fainting spell. Sometimes I'm like other women, I have spells of intuition. Somehow, I felt the doctor was protecting someone. Am I making any sense?"

"You're making a lot of sense, Mrs. Parker. I'm beginning to understand you when you go quiet all of a sudden. I used to have an aunt who would do that at times. It used to drive my uncle nuts. Then she'd come up with one hell of a recipe."

Woollcott smiled at Singer, feeling cozy and Christmassy, even in the stifling heat of August. He understood aunts and uncles and recipes and didn't care how sentimental a fool his contemporaries considered him; he still treasured the old values of family and hearth and homestead. He looked as though he was about to wipe a tear from his eye, but didn't. Instead, he speared Mrs. Parker with his tongue.

"You there, Tess of the Storm Country." The abrasiveness of his voice didn't escape her. "What was that look you flashed me when Mrs. Adler mentioned DeLee being excused from a midnight party?"

"It was so arcane a reference, I was wondering if you knew what she was talking about. I only found out last night from Mr. Singer."

Woollcott folded his hands over his stomach, a very superior expression on his face. "She was alluding to Horace Liveright's orgies. The only person who thinks they're a secret is Horace Liveright on the rare occasions when he thinks."

"Don't be harsh on Horace," said Mrs. Parker. "There's obviously some psychological flaw in him that compels him to indulge in an occasional moral lapse, and God knows I dread ever knowing what it is. I just deplore the damage he's doing to a lot of innocent kids."

"Innocent kids don't participate in orgies," said Singer.

Mrs. Parker favored him with a tiny smile. "I always knew I wasn't cut out to be a philosopher. What are you going to do about Dr. Horathy?"

Singer shifted around on the front seat and now faced Mrs. Parker and Woollcott. "Tonight, I assign Yudel Sherman, who is a very good detective, when his mind isn't on baseball, to interview the night elevator operators in Horathy's building. They'll know if there was someone in Horathy's office at the same time as DeLee. I also send a long telegram to my buddy out in Los Angeles, the chief of police, and ask him for everything he can give me on Dr. Bela Horathy.

"Don't forget Ilona Mercury," cautioned Mrs. Parker,

-92-

fidgeting with her fingers, wishing she had thought to bring along her knitting.

"L.A. got the word on Mercury yesterday."

"Oh. Aren't you clever?"

"Of course he's clever!" boomed Woollcott, who had now decided to officially adopt Jacob Singer as his own. "He's an amazingly intelligent young man."

"Mr. Singer," said Mrs. Parker softly, "you have just been knighted." Singer's expression was neutral. He was educated in the excesses and eccentricities of the Algonquin set. He knew that each of them lived in a world of his own, ruled and governed by the self, yet still feeding off each other's egos and intellect, occasionally allowing access to wife, husband or lover, who felt in turn like illegal trespassers. He didn't know of a single happy marriage or romantic relationship among them. They were doomed and they were blessed and he had learned to accept, just as they had probably learned to accept that it couldn't be any other way for them. Singer, a dedicated cop without any entanglements, had even less than they did.

"Where are we going?" asked Woollcott testily.

"Just cruising around waiting for a decision," explained Cassidy.

"I'd like to have a chat with Judge Crater." Singer pulled out his pocket watch. "It's not yet four o'clock. He might still be in his office. Cassidy, find a phone."

Cassidy found a phone in a cigar store at the corner of Twenty-third Street and Fifth Avenue. Mrs. Parker studied the wooden Indian with his hand upraised wielding a tomahawk which stood next to the entrance. "It looks like Ring Lardner."

"What does?" asked Woollcott.

"The wooden Indian."

"Yes, it does, when he's sober."

Jacob Singer got Crater's number from Central and asked to be connected. They could see him chatting through the window. "It's really dangerous placing phone booths against storefront windows, isn't it?"

"Why's that?" asked Cassidy.

"It makes a person so vulnerable. One is so exposed. I suppose that's why so many gangsters get bumped off in telephone booths."

Singer returned and told Cassidy to head downtown to City Hall. "Crater's expecting us."

"I'm feeling shanghaied," grumbled Woollcott.

Mrs. Parker riposted with irritation, "I'm sure Mr. Cassidy could drop you at the corner if you'd prefer to go home. I'll meet you at the theater just before curtain time."

"Oh, the hell with it! In for a penny, in for a pound." He settled back, tried to cross one leg over the other, gave up the effort as Cassidy rounded a corner on two wheels, almost dumping Woollcott in Mrs. Parker's lap.

"Alec, please stop fidgeting," admonished Mrs. Parker, annoyed at being interrupted while contemplating Lacey Van Weber. It was obvious he had arranged his luncheon at the Algonquin just to run into her. Run into her, hell; he'd come looking for her. He didn't nail a lid on her suggestion she do a profile on him for *The New Yorker*. He said he'd be in touch. Maybe we'll run into him tonight. He knows what show we're seeing. He knows where we're taking supper after the show. She felt Woollcott's elbow nudging her ribs.

"Wake up, sleeping beauty, we're here."

There were no unnecessary preliminaries. Crater was expecting them, and his secretary ushered them into his office immediately. Chairs had already been placed facing Crater's desk. Somebody around here is very efficient, thought Mrs. Parker as introductions were exchanged. Crater was at least six feet tall, heavyset, with gray hair and beautiful blue, piercing eyes. She recognized false teeth and also noticed later his right index finger was mangled. He wore a choker collar and white spats, and she couldn't for the life of her understand how any woman could find him attractive. For example, he had a broad nose, and Mrs. Parker found broad noses suspect in a man. Her husband had one and so did the object of her most recent unpleasantness.

"May I offer you anything?" asked Crater in his judicial voice as he settled behind his desk.

"Some information," replied Singer. Good lad, thought Woollcott, gets right to the point. No pointless pleasantries. A good warrior. Mrs. Parker wished Woollcott would erase that stupid look from his face.

"How can I help you?" asked Crater, leaning forward while forming a pyramid with his hands.

"When was the last time you saw Vera DeLee?"

Crater pursed his lips, sat back, crossed his legs, folded his arms, and looked past Singer's head to the wall behind. Superb performance, thought Mrs. Parker. I'd love to be there on one of those occasions when he tells Mrs. Crater he's been out all night with the boys exchanging legal briefs. "Now that's a good question," said Crater.

"I've got even better ones," said Singer.

Crater smiled. His false teeth were ugly with stains. Mrs. Parker wanted to cringe, but managed not to. She hadn't noticed his ugliness the previous evening when Van Weber had introduced them at Jack and Charlie's. "If I recall correctly, the last time I saw Vera was at a party given by a mutual acquaintance . . ." He riffled the pages of his desk calendar. "Ah, yes, here it is, the night of August fourteenth. At Lacey Van Weber's." He directed his stained smile at Mrs. Parker. "Your escort yesterday at Jack and Charlie's. You're not involved in Vera's death, are you, Mrs. Parker?" Mrs. Parker explained the collaboration with Woollcott, and Crater didn't question the impropriety of their accompanying a police officer in an official investigation.

"Not since then?" asked Singer.

"No, not since then."

"Got any ideas why anybody would want to murder her?"

"A crime of passion, perhaps?"

"You weren't very passionate about her?"

Crater wasn't fazed either by the question or by the presence of Mrs. Parker and Woollcott. "I've been to bed with her. That's quite obvious. I'm sure you're aware she's one of Polly's girls. I only sleep with them. I don't kill them."

Mrs. Parker intervened smoothly. "That was quite a dust-up at the party between Valentino and Horathy, wasn't it?"

"Horathy?"

"Dr. Bela Horathy. The one they call Dr. Bliss. Valentino accused him of pushing dope in Hollywood, ruining the lives of some of his dearest friends. Wallace Reid, Barbara LaMarr, Mabel Normand . . ."

"Of course. *That* altercation."

"And then suddenly Valentino took ill," continued Mrs. Parker. Singer let Mrs. Parker have her head. He knew she was after something, and with any luck she'd trip Crater and get it.

"Yes, the poor lad. I was standing on the terrace just near him when suddenly I heard his outcry, and he clutched his stomach crying something in Italian, I think it was. Shortly afterward, he was helped from the party by the young woman he was with . . ."

"Ilona Mercury," interjected Mrs. Parker.

"Yes, that's right, a delightful creature."

"Also murdered."

"Good God, yes, how tragic."

"He was helped from the party, you were saying . . .?"

"By Miss Mercury and Lacey Van Weber."

Mrs. Parker felt her stomach doing a somersault. "You're sure it was Mr. Van Weber?"

"Yes. I heard Miss Mercury shouting for him."

"She didn't shout for the doctor?"

"As I recall, Valentino was having no part of that doctor or any doctor. It was definitely Van Weber who helped Valentino to the elevator and out of the building."

"Did Vera DeLee have anything to say about that?"

"What do you mean?"

"Didn't she comment on Valentino's sudden illness?"

"She might have said something like 'Oh, gee whiz' or possibly 'Aw, shit' which is one of . . . was one of her favorite expressions."

"Don't you find it odd that since that party three of the guests are dead under mysterious circumstances? Valentino, Ilona Mercury, Vera DeLee."

"A sad coincidence."

"Murder isn't a coincidence, Judge Crater," said Mrs. Parker. "Murder, especially premeditated murder, is brutal and obscene. You've been a solon in these parts for many a year; surely you've had some previous experience with murder."

"You seem to believe the gossip that Valentino was poisoned," said Crater, now beginning to wonder why detective Singer had surrendered the spotlight to Mrs. Parker.

Singer might have been reading Crater's mind, because now he spoke. "No poison turned up in his autopsy."

"And an autopsy report can't be doctored," said Crater.

"We hope not, but we can't always be sure, can we?" The judge was glad Cassidy had a voice.

Now Woollcott piped up. "How well do you know Lacey Van Weber?"

"Such a good sport, Lacey is."

"How well do you know him?" repeated Woollcott.

"We've run into each other quite a bit over the past year," said Crater.

"Have you been to his mansion in East Cove?" continued Woollcott.

"Stella and I have driven there on a few occasions for lunch."

"Do you have any business dealings with him?" Woollcott was nagging away like a dentist's drill.

"I find that question irrelevant. It hasn't anything to do with Vera DeLee. I thought that was what brought you here, Vera DeLee. Now you're being impertinent, sir."

"I meant no disrespect, your honor," said Woollcott,

wondering if Crater was under the idiotic misapprehension that his office was a courtroom and a trial was in session.

Singer decided it was time to step in. "I think what Mr. Woollcott's getting at is that there is some reason to harbor suspicions about the connection of the party to the murder victims."

"I don't know anything about that. I had a very good time at that party, and as far as I recall, so did Vera. It was a very crowded party and at times we lost sight of each other. But I brought her there, I spent time with her and then I took her home to her apartment, where, if it will nourish your prurient hunger, I spent the night with her."

Mrs. Parker couldn't resist. "Was she any good?"

"Really, Mrs. Parker!"

"Sorry. Every so often I get a bit anthropological. One more question, Judge. You know Horace Liveright, don't you?"

The judge huffed and then puffed. "We belong to the same club."

"Did you ever run into either of the victims at one of his orgies?"

Crater's chin dropped. Woollcott's knuckles whitened. Singer was madly in love with Mrs. Parker.

"Well, did you?"

"Mrs. Parker, you are out of order."

"I'm also out of questions. Mr. Singer."

"I guess we've learned about as much as we'll ever learn." Singer arose, and it was the signal for the others to join him. "Thank you very much, Judge. I appreciate your cooperation." There was enough irony in his voice to sink a battleship.

When they were back in the squad car heading uptown, Mrs. Parker said to Singer, "After your Yudel Sherman questions the elevator operators in Horathy's building, I'm sure it's occurred to you he ought to pay the same courtesy to the gentlemen who man the elevators in Vera DeLee's place. I'm sure someone is about to remember if she came home accompanied last night. There seems to be such heavy traffic in the direction of her apartment." She then clucked her tongue with the rapidity of castanets. "How do those girls do it? I mean, night after night after night."

"And frequently at matinees," added Woollcott.

"Just like theater critics," concluded Mrs. Parker.

"Where to," asked Cassidy, with a side glance at Singer.

"Home, James," said Mrs. Parker with feigned haughtiness, "and don't spare the horses." She smiled at Singer. "We've accomplished about as much as we can, haven't we, Mr. Singer?"

"We've done damn well, all things considered. I'm proud of both of you." Woollcott beamed as though he'd been kissed by an angel. "Of course if Crater gives it some thought, he can make a complaint over my head at letting you two accompany me on official business. And on the other hand he may decide to play it smart until he begins to feel some uncomfortable pressure."

Mrs. Parker was startled. "I thought we'd given him a great deal of uncomfortable pressure."

"Mrs. Parker, that was nothing. He sidestepped skillfully. You didn't get too much out of him."

"Oh, yes, she did," snapped Woollcott. "She found out Van Weber helped Valentino out of the party with the Mercury creature. There could have been some colloquy between them vital to this case."

"If there was, we'll never know it from Valentino or Mercury," said Singer.

"We could try and find out from Mr. Van Weber," suggested Mrs. Parker.

"That's your department," said Singer. She said nothing. She stared out the window, lost in thought, lost in a whirlpool labeled "Lacey Van Weber."

Then she felt the squad car pulling up at the curb and turned to Woollcott as he told her, "I'll pick you up in a taxi promptly at eight o'clock."

"Are you sure you'd rather not meet in front of the

Globe? I don't mind getting there on my own steam."

"Well, *I* do. I have no intention of cooling my heels under a theater marquee while you're still deciding on which frock to wear. In time you will find, Mr. Singer, should you survive this relationship with Mrs. Parker, that promptness is a word of little meaning and little importance in her vocabulary. Eight o'clock sharp," he boomed.

Detective Yudel Sherman's boyhood ambition had been to become a prizefighter. A star athlete in high school, Thomas Jefferson in the Brownsville section of Brooklyn where he was born and raised, Sherman had been taken under the wing of a small-time promoter who saw a potential in the young man at some amateur exhibitions. A year later, after three victories and fourteen defeats, Yudel was convinced by his older brother, a lawyer, that he ought to find another profession, one that assured him of a greater longevity than seemed apparent in fisticuffs. Yudel took a civil service examination and became a policeman. He was a very good policeman. He enjoyed collaring hoods, bashing skulls, chasing burglars, and beating up small-time chiselers. He was swiftly upgraded to detective and now enjoyed the company of Jacob Singer and Al Cassidy.

He was not enjoying the company of one of the elevator operators in Horathy's building. He had shown him a photograph of Vera DeLee, one from the department file when she had been booked after one of their infrequent raids on Mrs. Adler's establishment. He recognized Vera. Yes, he did transport her from Horathy's floor to the lobby last night. It was sometime around seven o'clock. He recalled that, too. She didn't seem to steady on her feet. He called them "pins." "Her pins wasn't too steady, y'know?"

"Who was she with?" asked Sherman.

"Now let me t'ink."

"Think hard. Take your time."

"I'm not so sure, now."

"I want you to be sure."

"I'm t'inkin'."

"Would it be easier to do your thinking at the precinct?"

"Oh, no. I can t'ink real good here. Now let me see."

"Don't see. Think." It was obvious to Sherman, Vera DeLee had not descended in the elevator alone. "Was it Dr. Horathy?"

"Oh, no. He and his nurse they come down later."

"Let's go to the precinct."

"It was a guy."

"What did he look like?"

"I couldn't tell real good. He was wearing cheaters with dark glasses that hid most of his face. An' he had a hat pulled down over his head. He also kept wiping his nose with his handkerchief like maybe he had a summer cold."

"Did they do any talking?"

"She did all the talking."

"Did you remember what she said?"

"Not much. It's a short haul from the doctor's to the lobby. Oh, yeah. She asked him if he was going to the midnight party. I didn't hear him answer her."

"That's it?"

"That's all I can give you. Kin I git back to work now?"

In his book-cluttered study, Woollcott held the telephone receiver to his ear, listening to a blistering peroration from George S. Kaufman. Woollcott tried to interrupt from time to time, but then sighed and let the stream of vituperation flow undammed. Finally he managed to say, "But really, George, it was just my little joke."

"Little joke! 'And in whose apartment was her body found!' What the hell are you trying to do? Assassinate me? I thought you were my friend."

"I am your friend. I am up to my hips in your friendship. Your friendship has completely rearranged my life which is no longer my own. It is now a murder investigation. It is eating into my precious life and my precious time, all in the guise of friendship. We are doing this to protect you and if every so often I care to indulge in a bit of whimsy for my own amusement, I shall do exactly that without seeking the permission of a fatheaded satyr!" He slammed the phone down.

In Kaufman's living room, his wife asked, "Who was that you were yelling at?"

"Huckleberry Fink."

The elevator operator in Vera DeLee's apartment hotel was young, eager and stupid. He sure did know Vera DeLee. Some hot number, right? With a lascivious wink and a lewd leer for emphasis.

"You carted her up to her place last night?"

"Yessiree indeedy, it was yours truly." He did a quick time-step for emphasis.

"This was around half-past seven or so last night."

"Or so and so and so, if you read me."

Sherman wanted to hit him. "Who was she with?"

"She was always with somebody. She was one real hot busy chick. There wasn't no grass growin' under her."

No, thought Sherman, it'll soon be growing over her. "Who was she with last night? It was some guy, right."

"It was some bozo, okay."

"What did he look like?"

The boy screwed up his face. "Can't much remember. Real hard to tell." He snapped the fingers of both hands. "Hat pulled down to his ear. Dark glasses. Kept a hand-kerchief to his face. That's it. Okay?"

"Okay," responded Sherman wearily. But at least he knew there was someone with Vera DeLee that night, someone whom she had met in either Bela Horathy's office or in the hallway while waiting for the elevator. He phoned the information in to Singer, who was waiting at the precinct. Singer relayed the information to Mrs. Parker, who was dressing for the theater. The information, said Singer, required another confrontation with Horathy.

"He'll lie," said Mrs. Parker. "He'll continue to protect whoever he's protecting."

"Then I'll go after his nurse."

"That's more like it," agreed Mrs. Parker. "Let's hope she's not in love with him. In the cheap fiction I occasionally read to bolster my morale, nurses are always in love with their doctors. If she's in love with him, she won't betray his confidence."

"I'll cross that bridge when I get to it. Have a good time tonight."

"I'll try."

Woollcott arrived promptly at eight. She managed to get down to the lobby by eight-fifteen. He was fuming with impatience. The taxi meter was ticking away, and Woollcott was notoriously frugal. Traffic was heavy in the theater district, even for a midweek evening in August. Woollcott recounted his unpleasant argument with Kaufman. "Oh, God," he began wailing, "will I never attain a state of perfect bliss! Bring me to Nirvana!"

"Is that in Cuba?" asked Mrs. Parker. The cabdriver winced. "Who's in the show?"

Woollcott was mopping his perspiring brow. "It's a very good company Ziegfeld's rounded up, as a matter of fact. He tried the show out earlier this year in Florida when it was called *The Palm Beach Girl*. It was a great success there, which is why he transferred it to New York. Of course Florida is one thing and Broadway is another."

"Who's in the show?" repeated Mrs. Parker.

"There's James Barton, who's quite a good comic. And there's Moran and Mack. They work in blackface. Not too offensive. Audiences love them. There's Ray Dooley."

"I adore Ray Dooley. She doing her kid bit?"

"That's about all she can do. Charles King is the tenor and Claire Luce is absolutely dazzling."

"Then why is it so mediocre?"

"The sketches are rotten. The songs are so-so. But the decor is absolutely gorgeous. No expense spared. You know Flo."

"I don't really. We don't move in the same circles."

"Jacob Singer is a delightful chap, isn't he?"

She was wondering when he'd get around to Jacob

Singer. Protégés and the unattainable had a fatal fascination for Woollcott. It was Heywood Broun who said Woollcott warmed himself at the fires he helped to light for other people. First there was his limitless passion for the young actress Ruth Gordon. Then they suffered through his passion for Helen Hayes. Mrs. Parker had lost Charles MacArthur to her, and good riddance. Thank God Woollcott had passed swiftly through his F. Scott Fitzgerald phase. Now he spoke of Scott and Zelda only with loathing. Poor Scott, thought Mrs. Parker; *The Great Gatsby* was such a disappointment to so many of his peers. *Old sport.* Lacey Van Weber. Jacob Singer.

"Yes, Mr. Singer is an original. Are you thinking of adopting him?"

"Don't be vulgar."

"I'm not being vulgar, I'm being pragmatic. In Mr. Singer you see a potential protégé. You thrive on protégés. To quote Mr. Bernard Shaw, protégés are like mother's milk to you. Perhaps if treated gently and with kindness and understanding, Mr. Singer could become a friend, possibly an intimate friend. I happen not to think so."

Woollcott bristled. "Why not?"

"He's a very self-contained young man. He lives for his work. What little impression I get from him is that there's nothing else in his life but his work."

"He took you to dinner last night, didn't he?"

"That's because I suspect he would like to lay me."

"You do give yourself the best of it, don't you?"

"I'm not giving myself the best of anything. You know as well as anybody else does that in affairs of the heart I'm always ending up with the short end of the stick . . . and why does that sound dirty? Anyway, last night I could tell from his phone call he would have been absolutely devastated if I had turned down his invitation. I like Mr. Singer. In fact, there are times when I absolutely adore Mr. Singer."

"And you'd like to go to bed with him."

"If my sexual drought continues, I'll even bed down with Judge Crater, God have mercy on my soul."

"Well, I do like Mr. Singer. I think I shall invite him to lunch."

"Make sure it's someplace like Dinty Moore's. He's a steak and potato man. He's two-fisted, a he-man."

"Not to worry, I'm reading you correctly. By the way, having infiltrated ourselves into this somewhat mordant investigation, do you suppose we might be placing ourselves in danger?"

"Why, Alec darling, what took you so long to catch up? From the very first questions we asked a suspect, I assumed we were on the spot. Oh, thank God, there's the Globe Theater. I was beginning to think we'd be spending the rest of our lives together in this conveyance."

"What a grisly thought," snapped Woollcott as he paid the fare. The taxi driver silently agreed with Woollcott.

The overture was half over as they were led down the aisle to their seats. Once seated, Mrs. Parker looked around and commented, "There's hardly any audience."

"There's hardly any show," said Woollcott.

An hour later, Mrs. Parker agreed. The theater was like an oven. The show was indeed lavish and Claire Luce made a spectacular entrance from a shimmering egg that parted to reveal her, provocatively posed and eager to go into her dance. This was her first show since she had captivated Paris a year earlier. The comics were amusing, and the singers were on key, but like this August night, they were over heated and listless. The showgirls were stunning. Woollcott in a series of asides identified Greta Nissen ("Scandinavian. She has a Hollywood contract. Going to Fox") and Louise Brooks ("She's filming for Paramount at Astoria. Look at those legs").

Those legs, thought Mrs. Parker, and her beautiful Dutch bob, and her flashing teeth. I feel like a frump.

Woollcott continued, "Now that beauty on the right is Paulette Goddard. She's just a child."

"She'll mature soon enough."

"Next to her is Susan Fleming, and next to Fleming is Kay English."

"Who's the sullen-looking blonde at the head of the staircase?"

"I haven't the vaguest idea. That used to be Ilona Mercury's spot. This girl must be her replacement." He opened his program and then lit a match to read by. "They've still got Mercury listed. I guess there's been no time to alter the program."

The second act was blissfully short. There was an embarrassing paucity of curtain calls. Woollcott nudged Mrs. Parker. "The far aisle, going through the safety door to backstage, that's Flo Ziegfeld. Let's follow him."

Woollcott was amazingly agile as he led the way through a row of seats to the safety door. Once they were through the door, there was no minion to challenge them. Woollcott marched to the dressing room area like a fire marshal doing a safety check. Mrs. Parker followed obediently like a Chinese wife.

"Woollcott!" Mr. Woollcott recognized Ziegfeld's voice. He was standing in the doorway to the showgirls' dressing room. Obviously someone in there was one of the lucky chosen. "What the hell are you doing here? You hated it when you saw it opening night."

"My opinion hasn't changed. It's perfectly awful. But the girls are simply beautiful."

From inside he heard a mouse squeak, "Get *him*."

Woollcott introduced Mrs. Parker, and Ziegfeld's smile broadened. "Now *you* are a writer," said Ziegfeld magnanimously.

"As opposed to what?" demanded Woollcott.

"A critic," replied Ziegfeld.

Woollcott's tongue lashed back, "And how's your wife, Flo?"

"Billie's fine. Say, you know something, it's providence you two turning up here tonight. I'm beginning to put together next year's *Follies*. Benchley and Kaufman and Lardner have already promised to contribute some sketches. Now what about Parker and Woollcott?"

"I'll give it some thought," said Woollcott.

"Mrs. Parker?" She could see why women found the producer attractive. He pronounced her name as though it was something special, invented solely for her use and identity.

"I've never written revue sketches."

"I pay handsomely."

"I'll give it a try."

There was an explosion of laughter from the dressing room. Woollcott clucked his tongue. "Such levity and poor Ilona Mercury lying dead in her coffin. Isn't there any respect for the dead in the theater?"

Ziegfeld shouted into the room, "Girls! A little more respect for the dead!"

"Oh, are we closing?" asked a voice pitched so high that Mrs. Parker thought, another decibel and only birds and dogs can hear it.

"Who was Miss Mercury's replacement?" asked Mrs. Parker. "Was that the blond girl who stood at the top of the staircase?"

"That was indeed. She understudies all the girls."

"She's terribly beautiful."

"Would you care to meet her?"

"Why, I'd love to meet them all." Ziegfeld catered to her whim and introduced Mrs. Parker and Woollcott to the girls.

"And this is Charlotte Royce." It was the blonde who had replaced Ilona Mercury. At close inspection, she seemed smaller and more fragile than she had appeared on stage. In fact, Mrs. Parker realized, it was the clever costume designs, the lighting and the decor that gave the girls their statuesque appearance.

"So tragic about poor Miss Mercury," said Mrs. Parker.

"Yeah."

"Did you know her?"

"Yeah."

"Were you close friends?"

"Why d'y'ask?"

"Because we understand the other young lady who was murdered, Vera DeLee, was also a friend of Miss Mercury's."

"The cops send you here?" Charlotte Royce, Mrs. Parker decided, might act and sound like one, but she was nobody's fool. From the look on Ziegfeld's face, she could tell his mind was beginning to work along the same lines. Mrs. Parker explained about her collaboration with Woollcott. "Oh, I see," said the girl, "literature."

"Miss Mercury was also a friend of a friend of ours," explained Woollcott, "which is why we're also concerned."

"Kaufman," said the girl, and Mrs. Parker almost trembled.

"You know Mr. Kaufman?" she asked.

"I met him a couple of times. Ilona brought him around for drinks once. And once he took us to a couple of gin joints. Nice guy."

Mrs. Parker decided to jump in with both feet. "You were Miss Mercury's roommate?"

"Yeah. Now I need a replacement. I can't carry the rent myself." She studied Mrs. Parker from head to toe. "Any suggestions?"

Mrs. Parker sidestepped the question. "We'd like to talk to you about Ilona, if we may."

"Not tonight. I gotta date." It was obvious the date was with Ziegfeld.

"I'd like to call you tomorrow."

"Sure. I'm at the Wilfred Arms. Don't call me too early, huh?"

"About noon?"

"Yeah, that's good."

Mrs. Parker and Woollcott said goodbye to Ziegfeld, and when they said goodbye to Charlotte Royce, the girl finally smiled, winked her right eye and said, "So long. Abyssinia!"

Woollcott took Mrs. Parker by the arm and hurried her out of the theater. "The Wilfred Arms. Don't forget it," he cautioned.

"How can I?" asked Mrs. Parker. "That's where Vera DeLee was murdered."

Jacob Singer was working late. Paperwork was catching up on him. There were also the Ilona Mercury and Vera De-Lee autopsy reports to be read and reread until thoroughly digested and memorized. Los Angeles had wired him pages of information on Ilona Mercury and Bela Horathy. It was better than pulp fiction. There was an Alice in Wonderland quality in the file on Ilona Mercury, as though she had stepped through a looking glass into an unbelievable world of her own design that could easily have colored Lewis Carroll's face green with envy.

The report read:

Our files on Ilona Mercury go back to 1919 when the subject first came to our attention. She was eighteen years old, known as Bessie Landau, when booked for vagrancy and indecent behavior. She was bailed out by a man named Sands who identified himself as being in the employ of the movie director, William Desmond Taylor. Taylor was murdered on the night of February 1, 1922. Assailant is still at large, unknown to us; the file on the case stays open. Suspects included movie stars Mary Miles Minter, now retired, Mabel Normand, also inactive but planning a return, Minter's mother, Charlotte Selby, and Sands, the butler, who disappeared and is still at large. It's rumored Sands may have actually been Desmond Taylor's younger brother, Dennis Deane Tanner, Deane Tanner being Desmond Taylor's real name. In 1919, the assumption is that Mercury and Sands were lovers. In 1920, thanks to Desmond Taylor, Mercury got some bit parts in films and it seemed she might have a future. She ran with a wild crowd that included Wallace Reid, since dead of narcotics, Barbara LaMarr, deceased this year of narcotics, Olive Thomas and her husband, Jack Pickford, Mary's younger brother. Thomas was found dead September 10, 1920, in the posh Crillon Hotel in Paris. She'd been trying to make a heroin score for herself and Pickford. It is still debatable if she was murdered or a suicide. She was thirty-two years old. She'd been a Ziegfeld girl. Pickford family was powerful enough to cover up for baby brother. We suspect he's still on it, as is Mabel Normand, actress Alma Rubens, and a few others we don't dare mention for fear of studio backlash. After the death of Thomas, followed by that of Wally Reid, Mercury seemed to hit a bad patch in pictures and started working as a singing hostess at the Bluebird Club in Hollywood. The place is under constant surveillance as a dope drop. When the Desmond Taylor scandal blew the town wide open, Mercury disappeared. We think she acted as a go-between peddling drugs to the stars, or helping them make a score. Desmond Taylor and Sands were suspected of being part of a dope ring here. They frequented the Bluebird Club. One story we had here was that Charlotte Selby murdered Desmond Taylor because she suspected he was trying to hook her daughter, Miles Minter. Ilona Mercury was also very friendly with a chiropractor named Hans Javor. Javor was a pusher. He tried to get close to the Nazimova–Natacha Rambova–Rudolph Valentino set, but Valentino would have none of him. Javor is also suspected of spreading the word that Valentino was in on some sexual hanky-panky with Desmond Taylor, a suspected bisexual, and Sands the butler (or brother). Javor said he was Hungarian. See further in the report on Bela Horathy.

Here the report on Ilona Mercury ended. Singer stretched and yawned. They sure know how to burn out fast out there, he thought as he crossed to the window looking out on his bleak alley. There was a cat fight going on, and the noise bothered him. He opened the window, almost keeling over backward from the stench, shouted some clearly pronounced epithets, then shut the window and returned to his desk, where he reread the report on Bela Horathy.

Now, Jake, this one is a little sketchier than the Ilona Mercury because we're not too sure about some of our facts, and you know how far hearsay evidence will get you in, a court of law. We go back to Hans Javor and 1923, when he was brought in and arraigned on charges of peddling dope. He seemed to have no papers on him that we found satisfactory, so we shipped him to Mexico as an undesirable alien. Six months later or thereabouts, a Dr. Bela Horathy hangs out his shingle in a house behind the Hollywood Hotel. In no time at all, he's getting heavy traffic, especially from such celebrities as Barbara LaMarr and Alma Rubens. LaMarr's boyfriend then was a big power at the Metro studios, Paul Bern. Bern, in an attempt to rescue LaMarr from the habit, started a campaign to get rid of Horathy. Horathy at this time had a mistress, Magda Moreno, who bore a strong physical resemblance to Ilona Mercury. Our assumption is Mercury hotfooted it to Mexico to wait for the Desmond Taylor scandal to cool off, and somehow there hooked up with old buddy Hans Javor. It figures they then got back into the States, probably by way of Arizona where it's always easier to get in illegally, renewed their drug connections and set up house as Horathy and Moreno. That is, until Bern blew the whistle on the operation about two years ago. So now Mercury is a murder victim and Horathy's operating in your bailiwick. If Horathy is continuing heavy in drugs, be very careful. He fronts a very powerful syndicate originating in Sicily. He is not alone. They come through here by way of South America and Mexico, and we've found a lot of strange bodies floating off the pier at Venice. Sometimes you can't tell the fish from the stiffs. As to your third inquiry, we have nothing on Lacey Van Weber.

Singer looked at his wristwatch. It was almost eleven-thirty. He was tempted to bring the reports to Mrs. Parker and Woollcott at Tony's, but then decided it could wait until morning. He was hungry and thirsty. And there was that old, familiar nagging feeling in his loins. He wondered what the action might be like at Texas Guinan's.

After they entered Tony's restaurant and mentioned Lacey Van Weber's name, Tony himself greeted Mrs. Parker and Woollcott as though they were presenting diplomatic credentials. He bowed and scraped them to a comfortable table away from the kitchen and promptly ordered a bottle of wine. "Just off the boat," he confided, Mrs. Parker assuming he meant the Staten Island Ferry. "The wine is with my compliments," said Tony effusively, and Woollcott was tempted to ask him how large was his weekly payoff to the local gendarmerie. He didn't ask because corruption and police made him think of Jacob Singer, and Singer couldn't possibly be corrupt. He could probably be mean and dangerous when angry, but never corrupt.

"Stop furrowing your brows," said Mrs. Parker as Tony

gave them menus. "It makes you look like an obscene teddy bear."

"May I recommend the osso buco?" asked Tony.

"You may," said Woollcott, "to that noisy party across the room." He studied the menu carefully. "I think I've read this before." He asked Mrs. Parker, "Some pasta to begin with?"

"Nothing messy," she replied. "Actually, I'll have an antipasto. I'm not very hungry."

"Well, I am." Woollcott ordered spaghetti followed by a veal piccata.

"I'm glad you didn't order breaded veal cutlet." Tony was replaced by the sommelier with the bottle of wine.

"I never eat breaded veal cutlet," insisted Woollcott while polishing his pince-nez with an end of the tablecloth.

"Good. Breaded veal cutlet is how I'd describe the texture of Judge Crater's skin."

Woollcott sampled the wine. "Absolutely poisonous, but I suppose it'll do." The sommelier filled their glasses and departed.

Mrs. Parker sipped her wine. "You're absolutely right, Alec. Undoubtedly made of grapes from the Medici vineyards. What did you think of Charlotte Royce?"

"I think she's expecting a great deal from Mr. Ziegfeld."

"I think she's going to get it. Probably not stardom, but whatever she's going to get from him, she's going to get a great deal. She didn't bat an eyelash at the mention of Mercury and DeLee."

"I did adore the way she slipped in Kaufman. Anyway, I suppose being neighbors, the girls knew each other fairly well."

"Oh, sure. Probably dropping in on each other every so often to borrow a cup of a new cure for a social disease."

"Now, now. Don't be too hard on these ladies. Theirs is not an easy life."

"I'd swap it for mine. They don't have to meet deadlines." A waiter brought the antipasto and the spaghetti. Both began to eat, Mrs. Parker sparingly.

"Your Mr. Van Weber is quite right. The vongole sauce is exquisite." Woollcott broke off a piece of Italian bread and began sopping up the sauce.

"Mr. Van Weber's taste is exquisite."

Woollcott paused in his sopping up to study Mrs. Parker as she tried to spear a black olive. "You're quite taken with him, aren't you?"

"You saw him. You saw how he behaved toward me. He's impeccable."

"And much too enigmatic."

"Therein lies his fascination. Jacob Singer put his finger on something which for the life of me I cannot understand how it escaped my observation."

"And that is?"

"His use of the expression 'old sport.'"

Woollcott dabbed at some sauce dribbling down his chin. "Lots of people use the expression. I believe it originated in Britain. 'Hello, old sport,' 'Hello, old bean,' things like that. Fitzgerald gives it to Gatsby. Gatsby is 'old sporting' all over that wretched book." He had demolished the spaghetti. He was looking around ravenously for his dish of veal. "What's that wild gleam in your eyes?"

Mrs. Parker laughed lightly. "It's gone right past you. So much for your deductive powers. 'Old sport.' Gatsby. Lacey Van Weber."

Woollcott's mouth formed an O. "Well, I'll be damned. That mansion out in East Cove. The setting, the performance, the dialogue, it's all out of the book. And Singer spotted it immediately?"

"Oh, yes. He's quite literate, our Mr. Singer. I think he's even read *Moby Dick*."

"I tried to read *Moby Dick*, but I had to give it up. It made me seasick. Ah, here's my veal!" He tore into the food as though he had just emerged from a hunger strike. "Mighty fine this, absolutely lovely."

"Jacob Singer recommended a speakeasy just a few feet from here."

"Oh? Are you in the mood for a speakeasy?"

"I'm always in the mood for a speakeasy. I'm especially in a mood for this one." She told him about Singer's tip regarding Sid Curley, the informant.

"How will we know him? We just can't ask for him."

"He'll go 'sniff sniff sniff.'" Woollcott's look of confusion was amusing. She wondered if he ever considered acting as a second career. But then, Woollcott was always giving a performance. She had long ago decided his life was a starring vehicle created by himself, for himself, and no understudy needed because nobody else could fill the master's shoes. She explained Curley's erstwhile cocaine addiction now replaced by a talent for sniffing out celebrities and information the police might treasure and reward handsomely.

"I must say, this investigation is certainly bringing us in touch with a fascinating class of people." He ran down the list concluding with a eulogy to prostitutes.

"The only difference between them and us," said Mrs. Parker, "is that they admit they're prostitutes." She was repairing her face while Woollcott signaled for the bill.

"The Harlequin, did you say?"

"The Harlequin."

"Is there a secret password, like 'Joe sent us' or 'we're friends of Abie's'?"

"I haven't the vaguest idea. I suppose we'll have to charm our way in."

The orchestra in the Kit Kat Club was blasting away at the "Black Bottom." The dance floor was crowded with revelers acting as though the end of the world were imminent. They danced under a huge revolving crystal ball suspended from the ceiling while waiters crossing the dance area deftly dodged between them. Florenz Ziegfeld lit a cigar and sat back in his chair, contemplating the dancers while looking like an Oriental potentate. Charlotte Royce was digging into a piece of apple pie wondering why there were always these long silences between herself and Ziegfeld. How often had she complained, "It's always eat, drink and fuck, eat, drink and fuck. We never talk about nothing. Just eat, drink and fuck." She pushed the plate to one side and diverted her attention to a tall glass of undiluted Scotch. She took a long swig and then sat back smacking her lips.

"You're going to make yourself sick," said Ziegfeld.

"Listen, Flo, what's with us?"

"What do you mean, what's with us? Aren't you having a good time?"

"Sure. Swell." She sounded as though there'd be greater hilarity in a mass burial. "But where's it getting us?"

"I told you you have a spot in next year's *Follies*."

"Is that why you think I'm here?" Ziegfeld looked into her little girl's face. She was such a sweet-looking child, but yet, a child. There was none of the sophistication of his wife, Billie Burke, or the wit of some of his former show-girls such as Ina Claire and Lilyan Tashman. He supposed some alienist could explain why he cheated on Billie with these show kids, but it was something he had long ago decided to stop examining. It was a game he played, Who Does the Boss Fuck Next? "I'd like you to talk to me sometimes. I got things to talk about."

"Such as?"

"Lots of things. Like how come you don't talk about Ilona Mercury?"

"I don't talk about Ilona Mercury."

"Why not?" She giggled. "You sure know plenty about her."

Ziegfeld casually flicked some cigar ash into a tray. "You must learn, my little pixie, to keep your trap shut."

"Oh, I ain't going to talk about her."

"Mrs. Parker will certainly be phoning you tomorrow."

"Good. And if she asks me to, I'll see her. I like to be with famous people who are smart. And I'll answer all her questions."

Ziegfeld's face looked saturnine in the reflections from the revolving crystal ball. His eyes narrowed, and his voice was sharp and heavily underlined. "You put a button on your lips."

"Oh, ha ha ha, I'm laughing up my sleeve. You know I'll feed her a line of double talk. I'm *real* smart. And every day I get smarter. You got some real smart ones in this show. That Paulette Goddard, boy, does she know what she wants!"

"She'll probably get it, too."

"And that snotty Louise Brooks. Oh, my"—she struck an artificial pose—"but ain't we grand. Still, I like to listen to her, that is, when she decides to talk."

"Louise and Paulette and most of the others are too smart to get mixed up in drugs. Just remember, kitten, there's no vaccine for drug addiction."

"What are you feeding me that line of apple sauce for? I ain't on the hook."

"I hope you're not. I've found myself wondering, you rooming with Ilona, real neighborly with Vera DeLee."

"Vera was nuts. I didn't like her. Ilona was okay, though. What a rotten way to die. And dumped all the way out in Brooklyn, for crying out loud. Sayyyy, who's going to bury her? I mean what with her family and all back there in Hungary. D'y'think they'll ship her back to Hungary?"

"I can't think why," responded Ziegfeld suavely. "There's certainly nobody there to claim the body, unless it's shipped to a medical school."

All of a sudden her face brightened. "Hey, Flo, guess what?"

"What?"

She said with delight, "We've been talking."

The Harlequin Club was situated in the basement of a brownstone. There was a blue light casting an eerie pall over the cement stairs leading to the door, which was painted black. There was an eyehole in the door. Woollcott gingerly led Mrs. Parker down the stairs and then knocked hard on the door. After a moment, the eyehole opened and a voice that apparently belonged to the eye examined them and asked, "Whaddyawant?"

Mrs. Parker piped up immediately. "We're friends of Lacey Van Weber."

The eye disappeared. The eyehole was shut. They heard a bar sliding back. Woollcott gently pinched Mrs. Parker's cheek. "You clever girl."

"I had an idea that would work," she said with the pride of an Olympics winner. The door opened for them and they entered. Their ears were attacked by the rinky-tink music of a mechanical piano. Mrs. Parker asked Woollcott, "Do you have a machete?"

"What for?" inquired a startled Woollcott.

"To hack our way through the smoke."

The man at the door looked as though he had just been rescued from a head-on collision. "Yawannatable?" Mrs. Parker was fascinated by the way he ran words together, like a seamstress gone berserk.

"I think we'd adore a table," replied Mrs. Parker. The man raised his arm and pointed into the room, but at nothing in particular. Mrs. Parker, with Girl Scout instinct, led the way to a table near the end of the bar. The other tables were mostly occupied, and they recognized some celebrities. A waiter took their order, bourbon neat for Mrs. Parker, gin and orange juice for Woollcott.

"I don't hear any sniffing," said Woollcott.

"How can you hear anything with the racket that player piano's making?" The wall behind the bar was hung with framed photographs of athletes and showgirls. Mrs. Parker thought that made good sense. Showgirls, in their way, were athletes of a sort. There were about a dozen people at the bar, most of the women fanning themselves with their hands. The ventilation at best was inadequate, with a few overhead revolving fans stirring up an occasional trace of a breeze. The waiter served their drinks, made a notation on a little pad and then went elsewhere. Mrs. Parker sipped her drink. "This is pure, unadulterated lye."

"Don't insult our hosts. Why, hello!"

There was a tall, raven-haired, sultry-looking beauty newly arrived at their table, smiling at Mrs. Parker. "Don't you remember me, Mrs. Parker? We met in Cap d'Antibes a couple of months ago. I had just arrived from Germany."

Woollcott recognized her immediately. "Don't be such a fool, Dottie, this is Nita Naldi!"

"Oh, my God, of course!" exclaimed Mrs. Parker. "I'm not sure who anybody is with all this smoke. Please sit down."

"Just for a bit," said Naldi as she sat. "I'm with a movie producer and I can't leave him alone for too long. They run out of things to say to themselves." Woollcott introduced himself. "What are you two doing in a dive like this?"

"I dote on dives," said Mrs. Parker swiftly.

"I don't, but whither he goeth"—Naldi jerked a thumb over her shoulder in the general direction of her escort—"I goeth."

"How long will you be in town?" asked Mrs. Parker politely. She didn't dare admit not recalling meeting the glamorous movie vamp in France. At the time she was in a dazed state of crumbling romance. At a time like that she couldn't remember her telephone number.

"Christ knows," replied Naldi. "There's a slump in the market for movie vamps. I haven't worked since those two pictures I did abroad."

"Ah, you've worked in Europe? With Fritz Lang? F. W. Murnau?"

"Please, Mr. Woollcott, nothing so fancy. I worked for a porker named Alfred Hitchcock. Two disasters. *The Pleasure Garden* and *The Mountain Eagle*. They're so awful I'm sure they'll never be released. The producers will probably turn their backs on them and let them escape. As for the director, he didn't know shit from shingles. But still, these days you go where the work is, and like I said, there's not much open for fading vamps these days." She spoke with great good humor, and Mrs. Parker liked her. "The number I'm with says he's going to be doing some films here in New

York. So, you know, you have to play along until he either makes the right or the wrong proposition." She looked at her wristwatch. "Midnight, and he hasn't even put his hand on my knee yet." She turned around in her chair and waved at the man. He raised his glass in a silent, admiring toast. "I can relax. He's pickled." She roared with laughter. Then she asked, "Where you been tonight?" Woollcott told her they'd seen *No Foolin'*. "No kidding! So did we! I didn't see you there."

"Why didn't you come backstage?" asked Mrs. Parker.

"Oh, no." Her voice was now a different color. "I saw Flo. You know I was one of his discoveries a couple of centuries ago. I'm one of the girls who got away. I don't like him, never have. You read about this Ilona Mercury kid? He's not raised a finger about helping to bury her. Tomorrow I start passing the hat. In fact, maybe I'll start tonight with my sousled Romeo." Mrs. Parker made a mental note to mention the matter to George S. Kaufman.

"Were you a good friend of hers?" asked Woollcott.

"There's good and there's good. I knew her years back in Hollywood under a lot of other names, I can't remember which. She was a nut, that Ilona. I kept my distance when I found out she traveled in that drug set out there. A mean bunch they are." Mrs. Parker and Woollcott were delighted and exchanged a glance. They had struck pay dirt.

"Did she get into trouble there?" asked Mrs. Parker.

"Well, after William Desmond Taylor's murder, she disappeared." Naldi told them much of what Jacob Singer had in his report from the Los Angeles police.

"And the butler has never resurfaced?" asked Woollcott.

Naldi shrugged. "Maybe he's dead. I never saw him. I never knew Desmond Taylor. Listen, my best friend's laying in a coffin over at Campbell's. Poor Rudy. Poor bastard. I was one of the few people who listened when he talked."

"Would you like a drink?" asked Mrs. Parker, wondering if she could palm off hers on the actress.

"No, thanks. I don't much. I don't look it, but I'm a

good girl." She let loose with another burst of laughter that spoke of health and energy. "Rudy wasn't much for hooch either. Jeezus, what good times we had. *Blood and Sand, Cobra, The Sainted Devil.*"

"You were lovely in *Blood and Sand*," said Woollcott. Then he added quickly, "Do you believe these rumors Valentino might have been poisoned?"

"Who the hell knows? There sure were some who would want him out of the way. He had Sicilian connections. Some said Rudy did the Black Hand some errand a couple of years back when he was so broke. He walked out on a contract with Paramount and they blacklisted him. He had so little money to begin with. Rambova, that's the wife, was bleeding him dry with her extravagances. Ah, who knows what you do when you're up against it? All I know is, there were a lot of people at a certain party a couple of weeks ago who heard Rudy laying it into a certain Dr. Horathy, and they wouldn't have liked what Rudy knew to be noised about." She looked over her shoulder. Her escort was at the piano player feeding it coins. "I better get back to him. Quiet types like him usually have a short fuse."

Mrs. Parker was loath to lose her. She pressed her with a question. "Did you know Dr. Horathy?"

"Oh, sure. Back on the Coast." Mrs. Parker and Woollcott sat up. "He was Dr. Bliss back there, too. Rudy was right. The son of a bitch did help hook a lot of nice people. Let's hope he gets his very soon." She stood up. "It was just lovely talking to you two."

"The feeling's mutual," said Mrs. Parker. Woollcott, in a rare display of courtliness, got to his feet, took Miss Naldi's hand and kissed it.

Said Miss Naldi, "I'll bet that's about as much action as I get tonight." With another tremendous roar of laughter, she made her way back to her escort. Woollcott sat down.

"Now wasn't that a bit of a bonus?" he said.

"Yes, things are starting to fall into place. I'm beginning to feel better about our investigation."

Sniff sniff sniff.

Sid Curley must have come to their table on little cat feet. It was quite possible because he was a little man wearing a loud, checkered suit and a loud purple tie, which, Mrs. Parker later thought, was worn to blend with the color of his past. On his head he wore a black derby which was now perched somewhat precariously at the back of his head.

Sniff sniff sniff.

Mrs. Parker nudged Woollcott's knee under the table.

"I see you know my friend Nita," said Sid Curley to Mrs. Parker.

"How observant you are," replied Mrs. Parker.

"Are you somebody special?" he continued, head cocked to one side like an inquisitive sparrow.

Mrs. Parker tried to assume a pose of modesty. "Well, my name is Dorothy Parker. Have you heard of me?"

"Yeah. I think I heard of you." He pivoted his eyes until they focused on Woollcott. "And who is this?"

"My governess," said Mrs. Parker.

"My name is Woollcott, my good man," said Woollcott somewhat testily, never understanding how there could still be anyone at large who didn't recognize him since his face had been reproduced in numerous periodicals for one reason or another. "Alexander Woollcott."

"Oh yeah," said Sid Curley, as uninvited he took charge of the seat recently vacated by Nita Naldi. "It's still warm."

"Yes, it's terribly warm," agreed Mrs. Parker.

"I mean the chair. Nita's got a hot butt."

Mrs. Parker restrained herself from saying "The better to eat you with, my dear" because it really didn't pertain. "It's so nice of you to join us. Not many people join us when we're out together. There are nights when we sit at a table, staring into our drinks, wondering when did it all go wrong, when did the magic go out of our lives."

"You talk good," said Curley.

"Would you like a drink?" asked Woollcott.

"I wouldn't mind. On you?"

"On me."

He shouted at the bar, "Hey, Maxie, send me a beer.

Their tab!" At the bar, Maxie drew the beer in a glass schooner while Curley folded his arms and rested them on the table. Mrs. Parker thought he needed a toothpick in his mouth to complete the tableau. "So you're a friend of Lacey Van Weber's."

Mrs. Parker looked at him, somewhat bemused. "Now how did you know that?"

"I got good ears. I pick up lots of stuff."

"I see. You heard me announce that through the door."

"Smart chick." The beer arrived, and Curley leaned back, making room for it.

"Does he come here often?" asked Mrs. Parker.

"He don't come here never, least not while I been around." he slurped a good mouthful of beer which left a mustache of foam on his upper lip. This he wiped away with the sleeve of his jacket.

"So how do you know him?" asked Woollcott.

"I got connections." He looked cautiously over both his shoulders and then leaned forward conspiratorially. Mrs. Parker wondered if they looked like a trio of Bolsheviks plotting the coming revolution. "You here looking for anything special?"

Mrs. Parker decided to take the plunge as Woollcott was looking a bit nonplussed. "Actually, a very dear friend of ours recommended this place to us. You see, Mr. Woollcott and I are doing an article about these two girls who were murdered."

"I read about them," said Curley. Somehow it did Mrs. Parker good to know the little man could read. She also wondered if he could tap dance. With the outfit he was wearing, she thought all he needed was a cane and a choreographer to go over big with this crowd. Over Curley's derby, she saw Nita Naldi and her escort leaving. Nita pausing in the doorway to wave at them. Mrs. Parker waved back. Curley turned in his seat and also waved. Mrs. Parker was positive Nita Naldi had never met the little man in her life. *Sniff sniff sniff.* "Where was I?"

"You had read about the girls," prompted Mrs. Parker.

"Who's the friend what sent you here?"

"Lean closer," said Mrs. Parker, thoroughly enjoying herself and the game as being played to Sid Curley's slightly demented rules, "and I'll whisper his name." Curley obeyed and she whispered, "Jacob Singer."

"Sssssh!" hissed Curley, behaving as though he'd been singed by a hot poker, "don't whisper so loud!"

Mrs. Parker apologized. "Sometimes a girl doesn't know her own strength."

Curley finished his beer, and Woollcott signaled the bartender to send another one. Mrs. Parker hoped the session with Mr. Curley would not be protracted. She didn't know how long she could sustain the meeting without saying or doing something that would blow their cover, whatever that meant. She remembered reading something like that in a detective story. Curley had lowered his head and seemed to be talking into his beer. As they listened, Mrs. Parker hoped he wasn't talking through his hat. "What I'm gonna tell you is worth twenty. You got twenty?"

"Twenty?" repeated Woollcott. "You mean dollars?"

"I sure don't mean zlotys," replied the little man, somewhat exasperated. Mrs. Parker nudged Woollcott's knee under the table again.

"Yes, I most certainly have twenty dollars."

"Slip it to me under the table. Be careful! Don't let nobody see you reaching for your wallet."

"I have a money clip." Mrs. Parker wished he hadn't sounded so haughty. Somehow, Woollcott managed to maneuver his bulk, extract a twenty dollar bill from the clip in his jacket pocket, and slip it under the table to Sid Curley.

"Now listen and listen good because I do not chew my fat twice. I gotta talk low because I don't want nobody to overhear me. The walls have ears." Mrs. Parker thought if anybody could hear them over the din in this place, they were in possession of something that deserved to be patented. "Them girls . . ." pronounced *goils* ". . . just mighta known too much about what's goin' on in the private life of a certain party in this town who happened to have entertained them along with about a hundred others . . ." pronounced *udders* ". . . a couple'a weeks ago in his penthouse. . . ."

Mrs. Parker felt her hands beginning to tremble and interlaced them.

"There is talk in important circles that he keeps this here mansion out on the island so it is a drop-off place for a bootlegging operation that comes down here by way of Canada. There are them what says at times it gets even dirtier . . ." pronounced *doitier* ". . . and certain other kinds of stuff gets dropped off there. There's a lot of protection behind this guy, protection I am told that reaches as high up as Washington letter D and letter C."

Good God, thought Woollcott, not another Teapot Dome scandal simmering.

"And you know the person . . ." pronounced *poison* ". . . of which I am speaking."

"Yes, I do," said Mrs. Parker, "he's just arrived with a gorgeous redhead."

Lacey Van Weber had entered with Lily Robson, who was very unsteady on her feet and leaning heavily on his arm. Sid Curley saw them, and Mrs. Parker heard his pained intake of breath. He started to leave the table, but not before being seen by Van Weber. The little man scurried away from them and disappeared through a door at the back of the speakeasy that probably led to a back alley. Van Weber guided Lily Robson to Mrs. Parker and Woollcott's table.

"What luck running into you here," he said with his hypnotic smile and treacly voice. Mrs. Parker could feel her knees go weak. "This is Lily Robson and she's just been taken ill."

"Oh, God," whimpered Lily Robson as her eyes rolled back in her head.

"Mrs. Parker, could I prevail on you to assist her to the ladies' room?"

"Do you think they have one here?" asked Mrs. Parker as she found the strength to stand up and put her arm around Lily Robson's waist.

"Ladies' room!" Woollcott shouted at the bartender.

"For you?"

"For them," snapped Woollcott, indicating the ladies.

"In the back," advised the bartender.

"Let me help you there." Van Weber's arm also went around Lily Robson's waist, and its warmth made Mrs. Parker wish they were alone, she and Lacey Van Weber, heading into a boudoir in his penthouse. Penthouses, as far as Mrs. Parker concerned, were too elegant for bedrooms. They had boudoirs, which were high class and elegant, like penthouses.

"Was it something she ate?" asked Mrs. Parker.

"I really don't know," answered Van Weber. "It came over her on the street a few minutes ago. I was escorting her to Texas Guinan's where she works . . ."

"Oh, God," moaned Lily Robson as her legs began to give way.

". . . when she suddenly gasped and said 'I don't feel too good.' So I saw this place, I'd heard of it and brought her in. Providential, don't you think?"

Mrs. Parker hurried Lily Robson into the ladies' room where the redhead threw up. Five minutes later, Mrs. Parker wiped her face with a paper towel dampened with cold water. The color was coming back to the girl's face. "Feeling better? You're looking better."

The girl burped and then said, "That son of a bitch. I knew them pills would make me sick."

Mrs. Parker looked interested. "Ah. You took a pill."

"For my nerves. I was feeling nervous in the restaurant we were eating in up the block. So I took this pill my doctor prescribed. I knew it would make me sick."

"Your doctor wouldn't by any chance be Bela Horathy?"

"How'dja guess? He trying to get you hooked, too?"

8

Lacey Van Weber pounded on the ladies' room door. "Are you all right?"

"We're just dandy," replied Mrs. Parker. "We'll be out in a few minutes." Satisfied, Van Weber rejoined Woollcott at the table. Mrs. Parker leaned against a wall of the squalid little room while Lily Robson stared at herself in the mirror and then began painting her cheeks with heavy layers of rouge. Mrs. Parker wanted to tell her the camouflage was unnecessary, that there was breathtaking beauty in her ivory skin framed by her blazing red hair, but she recognized that beauty was in the eye of the beholder, and Lily Robson beheld herself beautiful with heavily painted cheeks and lips. "If you know Horathy's reputation, why do you go to him?"

"Because Ilona Mercury assured me he was on the up and up in his general practice. I trusted Ilona so I trusted Horathy."

"Have you got any more of those pills on you?"

"Sure. In my purse. Help yourself. You ain't gonna try one, are you?" Mrs. Parker was daintily probing the inside of Lily's beaded bag. She found a vial of green pills. "You suicidal or something?"

Mrs. Parker managed to sound amenable. "I sometimes get depressed, but I'm feeling quite fit at the moment. I just thought I'd borrow one of your pills and have a friend of mine get it tested."

Lily moved away from the mirror and reached for the beaded bag. "I don't want to get into any trouble. Give me back those pills."

Mrs. Parker had already dislodged one and was wrapping it in toilet paper. "Would you rather be dead? I won't get you in any trouble. But if your doctor is a menace at large, then steps must be taken against him."

"Listen, lady, I don't hardly know you."

"My name is Dorothy Parker. I write short stories, poems, articles and poison-pen letters. I am frequently quoted, though most of the time incorrectly. All sorts of supposedly witty bitcheries are attributed to me, but I can assure you, most of them are apocryphal." The girl seemed perplexed by "apocryphal." Mrs. Parker couldn't resist what followed. "Surely you've heard of the four horsemen of the apocryphal."

"Oh, yeah. I saw the movie."

"You can trust me. In fact, you have to trust me. How many people do you know you can go to for help when you're in trouble?"

"Now?" Mrs. Parker could read the fear and confusion. She wanted to reach out and take the girl's hand and reassure her, but reaching out to another person was generally as alien to her as believing in an oath of undying love from a man's lips. "I could go to Tex, she'd help me."

"That's all?"

"There was Ilona and Vera, but now they're gone."

"Lacey Van Weber?"

"I hardly know him. I was at a party of his a couple of weeks ago, and I put the make on. He called me for a date, and Texas said, sure go out with him, he's a real good Joe, so here I am."

"You also know my friend Marc Connelly."

Lily brightened. "Oh, sure, I took him to the party. He hangs around the club sometimes. When he finally asked Tex to introduce us, Tex offered him a medal for bravery. Nice man. So he's a friend of yours, huh? Say, you part of that Algonquin gang?"

Mrs. Parker was powdering her face. "They let me hang around every so often."

Lily said wistfully, "I'll bet some of them are your real good friends."

Mrs. Parker replied acidly, "With that gang of bandits, a real good friend is somebody sitting on the sidelines waiting for you to fall flat on your face. Did Ilona take dope?"

"Hell, no!"

"But Vera did." Silence. "Didn't she?"

"She was on morphine. She had bad kidneys. She'd gotten beaten up bad once by some gorilla in Harlem. She needed the morphine bad, real bad."

"She got it bad, all right. She's dead. Don't tell anyone I've got one of your pills."

"I don't dare."

"You can trust me. You have to trust me." She smiled a sincere smile. "I'm your friend now."

"Oh, yeah?" She eyed Mrs. Parker suspiciously. "What's the catch?"

"The catch is that we always tell each other the truth. Do you know if Mr. Van Weber is mixed up in drugs?"

"I told you I hardly know him."

"But you could know about him. How'd you get to his party?"

"I was on Tex Guinan's list. She's always getting us asked to parties. It's fun. We go to some real good ones. We get to meet a lot of swells." She thought for a moment. "I'm making the most of it while I'm young. Pretty soon I'll be yesterday's fried potatoes. I see some of them back numbers that come into the club, still trying to look irresistible. That ain't gonna be me. I'm saving my money. I'm gonna open a beauty parlor. I go to hairdressing school. I can give a pretty good manicure already." She winked. "I know how to take care of myself."

Sure you do, thought Mrs. Parker, like putting yourself into the hands of Bela Horathy. "If you really know how to take care of yourself, then find yourself another doctor."

Lily Robson's face turned grim. "First thing tomorrow afternoon when I wake up." She looked at her wristwatch. "Oh, Christ, I got to get to the club. I already missed the first show. Tex'll skin me alive!" Mrs. Parker followed her back to the table where Woollcott looked annoyed and Van Weber looked anxious. The men stood up as the ladies arrived.

"Well, you certainly look a hell of a lot better," commented Van Weber warmly.

"Oh, thanks. I really thought my number was up."

"I'm Alexander Woollcott." He pointed at Mrs. Parker. "I'm with her, for my sins."

"Now don't be such an old curmudgeon, Alec." She explained to Lily, "If you get to know him better, you find out Mr. Woollcott is mostly *kitsch* . . . and tell. Guess what, Alec? We're really going to make a night of it. My new friend Lily Robson has invited us to Texas Guinan's to see her perform. What do you do, dear?"

Lily Robson sounded vague. "A little bit of this, a little bit of that, with a lot of the old moxie."

"In other words," interpreted Woollcott, "a maximum of energy expended on a minimum of talent."

"When Lily enters, she lights up the room. That's all that matters." Van Weber had his arm around Lily's shoulder. "She's incandescent. You can't take your eyes off her." Mrs. Parker couldn't take her eyes off Van Weber. He was no prize you might find at the bottom of a box of Cracker Jacks. He was strictly from a glass case at Van Cleef & Arpels. That's what she saw, and her eyes never lied. But something was wrong with her portrait of Lacey Van Weber. Somewhere there was a flaw, a dangerous flaw. She sensed it, her intuition cried out that it existed. But she didn't care. She had to have him. She wanted to feel his arm around her shoulder, his lips on her lips, his body interlocked with hers.

"For crying out loud, Dottie, why the hell are you blushing?" Woollcott was paying the waiter, who suspected there'd be a meager tip, and there was.

"It's very hot in here. Can we be on our way?" Smiling gently, Van Weber took her arm, leaving Lily Robson to Woollcott. "Well, Mr. Van Weber, what a pleasant surprise running into you like this. Are we destined to meet accidentally, or can I pin you down to some time to discuss the profile I'd like to write for *The New Yorker?*"

"Are you free tomorrow?" Mrs. Parker almost tripped

on the stairs leading to the sidewalk. "I have to drive out to my estate in East Cove to attend to some matters. I'd love you to see the place."

"We have a date, Mr. Van Weber."

"If I pick you up at eleven, we could be out there in time for lunch. I know that doesn't allow for much sleep tonight . . ."

Mrs. Parker laughed gaily. "Sleep? What is sleep? Who was it that said sleep was a little death?"

"Jack the Ripper," snapped Woollcott from behind her. Lily Robson hailed a taxi. In the taxi, Woollcott told Van Weber there was a shortage of funds for Ilona Mercury's funeral.

"I've already heard," replied Van Weber. "I can assure you, Ilona will have a decent funeral."

"Real bang-up," added Lily, "with a blanket of tea roses for her coffin and a crucifix twined around her fingers, just like she always wanted."

"You don't know if she had any family?" asked Mrs. Parker.

"If I did, don'tcha think I'd have got in touch?" Lily nibbled at a fingernail. "Mine live in Youngstown, Ohio, and Lily Robson is my real name. My father's Frank Robson, and he owns a feed and grain store. Now should anything happen to me, there's three of you what knows where I come from." Mrs. Parker patted her hand. "Sorry I took sick, Lacey. I hope it didn't spoil your evening."

"The evening's just beginning, sweetheart. It all happens at Texas Guinan's." He spoke to Woollcott and Mrs. Parker. "Have you ever been to Tex's before?"

"A few times," said Mrs. Parker. "I find it a bit too frenetic. Me for peace and quiet."

"Peace and quiet is very unlikely at Texas Guinan's."

Commented Woollcott, "About as unlikely as a victim being murdered in warm blood." He sniffed imperiously, and then asked, "Where's she located this week?" Texas Guinan was constantly being victimized by the police. But every time her establishment was raided and padlocked, she surfaced at another location within twenty-four hours. Her talent for survival was a source of admiration, even to her most ferocious competitors. It was an open secret that she was bankrolled by gangsters, usually Larry Fay, who was also her sometime lover. Few people remembered that a decade earlier Texas Guinan had starred as a cowgirl in a series of two-reel Westerns.

"We're on West Fifty-eighth between Seventh and Eighth. Been there almost a whole month now," Lily Robson told them. Mrs. Parker was thinking cozily the location was just a short hop to the building in which she resided. "It's real splashy. Lots of wild colors. There's balloons on the ceilings and paper bags filled with confetti, and when the place is really getting steamed up, the balloons and the confetti drop, and wow, it's like New Year's Eve, only better!"

Mrs. Parker was wondering if Frank Robson and his wife had ever given their daughter a birthday party when she was a child.

Woollcott asked Van Weber, "Wasn't that sad about Vera DeLee?"

"What? Oh, yes, very sad."

"I hope there's someone to bury Vera DeLee." Mrs. Parker wondered if Woollcott had forgotten she was to occupy a portion of Mrs. Adler's lot at Montefiore, or was he just fishing?

"Polly Adler's picking up the tab," volunteered Lily.

"Did you know the deceased?" Woollcott asked Lily.

"You mean both of them? Sure, I knew both of them. I'm gonna miss them. I mean, they were real good friends."

"Then you know Miss Mercury's roommate, Charlotte Royce."

"Yeah, I know Charlotte. She's Flo's girl . . . lately."

"Wouldn't you want to be a Ziegfeld girl?" asked Mrs. Parker.

"Ziegfeld girl, Guinan girl, any of the others like George White or Earl Carroll, what's the difference? It's all a show of skin. They all pay about the same, the difference at Tex's being you can pick up big tips."

Mrs. Parker told Woollcott Lily was saving her money to open a beauty salon. Woollcott nodded. Mrs. Parker wasn't sure if he was silently acknowledging Lily's wisdom or falling asleep. He wasn't asleep. "One of these days," Woollcott said to Lily, "you might write a book about your experiences."

"Who'd want to read about me?" she asked shyly, though it was obvious she was flattered by the suggestion.

"I know I would," said Woollcott. "Young girl afloat in a sea of show business, the underworld of gangsters and murders, surrounded by the debauchery of dirty old men and filthy dope peddlers. I'll bet you've got a lot to tell."

"I sure do!" She had leaned forward to tell him that, but then suddenly she sank back and in a small voice said, "But I won't."

"Here we are," announced Van Weber. They got out of the cab and Van Weber paid the driver. He explained to Mrs. Parker as they crossed to the entrance of the club, "Sorry I'm without my limousine and chauffeur tonight, but my man's wife was taken seriously ill and there was no time to hire a substitute."

"It doesn't bother me," said Mrs. Parker. "I dote on slumming in taxis."

At the door, Lily Robson identified herself. The doorman recognized Lacey Van Weber and tipped his cap. The door opened, and they were greeted by a blast of bedlam, a cacophony of saxophones, clarinets, drums and piano. There was the sound of dozens of pairs of feet punishing the dance floor. "Charleston! Charleston!" What presumably was a headwaiter recognized Van Weber and snapped his fingers, and soon waiters appeared carrying a table and chairs which were set up for them at the edge of the dance floor. Lily Robson hugged Mrs. Parker and then disappeared backstage. A waiter appeared at their table carrying a cooler containing a bottle of genuine French champagne. Woollcott looked at his pocket watch and sighed. Mrs. Parker hoped she looked sufficiently urbane and sophisticated as the cork popped and the wine was poured. She expected Woollcott to be grumpy and grouchy and completely out of sorts. But amazingly enough, he wasn't. He was smiling at someone behind her, smiling like a good deed in a naughty world. "Why, will you look who's here!" he exclaimed in a voice that belonged to Tiny Tim on Christmas morning. "It's Jacob Singer! What are you doing here? Are we being raided or rescued?"

"Hello, Mr. Singer. Aren't you a nice surprise?" Mrs. Parker meant it. She introduced him to Van Weber, who invited Singer to join them. The detective accepted with alacrity and didn't refuse a glass of champagne. Woollcott explained to Van Weber that Singer was the detective investigating the two murders. Van Weber showed surprise followed by pleasure followed by a request he be excused while he went looking for the men's room.

When the three were alone, Singer commented, "He's a good-looking guy."

"I'm spending the day with him tomorrow." She seemed rather pleased with herself.

Woollcott scowled. "Red Riding Hood's very words."

"He's a hell of an improvement on anybody's grandmother." Mrs. Parker was determined to enjoy herself and would have none of Woollcott's or anybody else's putdowns.

Singer won their attention by telling them about the reports from Los Angeles. Mrs. Parker explained some of that information had been given them by Nita Naldi at the Harlequin. Singer told them Naldi was here somewhere, but in this mob her location was anybody's guess. He recited from memory the autopsy reports on Mercury and DeLee. "Mercury was clean. DeLee was drowning in morphine. She'd have died soon of kidney disease anyway." Singer then told them about Yudel Sherman's success with the elevator operators. There was a man with DeLee when she left Horathy's, and the same man accompanied her to the apartment at the Wilfred Arms. "Did you connect with Sid Curley?" Mrs. Parker told him about that eccentric incident and repeated she was spending the next day with Van

Weber and hoped it would prove to be fruitful, fruitful in which direction she hesitated to elucidate. Then she told him about Lily Robson's sudden illness and her colloquy with the girl in the ladies' room of the Harlequin.

"She's not a stupid girl; in fact, she's rather bright considering her environment. But I get the feeling she's frightened—frightened, I think, about something she *might* know."

This rankled Woollcott. "When you're being oblique, Dottie, you are at your most unpleasant. And kindly speak up; it's almost impossible to understand either of you in this place. They should supply ear trumpets for those of us who care to converse."

Mrs. Parker strained to raise her voice. "I think she heard things from Ilona and Vera that meant nothing to her at the time, hearing them out of context, so to speak. But now with both of them murdered, she probably feels someone thinks she knows more than she admits to knowing or even understanding and could be a threat." She repeated to Singer Woollcott's suggestion that Lily consider writing a book, a suggestion Mrs. Parker was sure had been made in unkindly jest (Woollcott remained placid) and Lily's initial enthusiasm suddenly covered and suffocated by a blanket of obvious fear.

Woollcott interrupted. "Jacob"—his tongue caressing the name—"do you really think those drug deaths in Hollywood have any connection with those here?"

"There has to be. Ilona and Horathy are the links. As far as I'm concerned, the incidents are chained together." He could see Van Weber returning and spoke hastily to Mrs. Parker. "Now you watch your step with Van Weber. Men of mystery are glamorous, but they can also be dangerous. Desmond Taylor was a man of mystery and look at the rotten can of garbage his murder opened. You hear me? You be careful."

"I will be, too," said Woollcott in a childish voice, not wanting to be left out.

"We'd better all be careful," murmured Singer.

"Careful of what?" asked Van Weber as he sat down.

"Too much champagne," gurgled Mrs. Parker as she raised her empty glass for a refill. "We were beginning to think you weren't coming back."

"I phoned East Cove to prepare a proper lunch for us tomorrow." He refilled her glass, his own and the others, and signaled for another bottle.

"At *this* hour?" Mrs. Parker had a look of disbelief on her face.

"I keep a staff around the clock." She was amazed at the amount of modesty with which he was able to make that statement. Woollcott couldn't wait for lunch at the Algonquin the next day to paraphrase the statement with his own brand of deadly mockery. Singer was wondering if he could ever afford someone to clean his tiny apartment perhaps once a week. "I was also waylaid by Opal Engri for a few moments."

"My God, don't tell me *she's* here." Mrs. Parker was aching for a good look at the supposedly exotic movie star. "I mean Nita Naldi and Opal Engri in one evening. It's a cornucopia of something or another."

"She's here to accompany Valentino's body back to the West Coast."

"What a morbid assignment," commented Woollcott darkly.

"She insists they were engaged to be married." Mrs. Parker found the wicked smile on his face enchanting. Obviously everybody knew the rumors about Valentino and his nonrelationships with women. "Rudy, of course, is not around to deny it. The publicity is worth a fortune to her. I hear she's packed about two dozen varieties of widow's weeds to parade around in on the back platform of the train when they pull in at the scheduled whistle stops."

"What a disgusting circus," said Mrs. Parker. "I want to be cremated and my ashes poured all over the Rose Room of the Algonquin so all my beloved friends can continue to walk all over me."

She saw Woollcott zeroing in on Van Weber. "You were

a friend of Valentino's, what was he like?"

"He was a doomed innocent."

"So much for Mr. Valentino," said Mrs. Parker, hoping she wouldn't be posthumously dismissed with five words.

"You met him in Hollywood?" asked Woollcott, elbow on table, chin resting on his hand.

"I met him . . ." He paused, and then continued the flow, ". . . here."

"Of course everyone's heard how he laid Horathy to filth at your party. How can you associate with a man of such dubious repute?" Woollcott was enjoying himself. Jacob Singer was enjoying Woollcott. Mrs. Parker wanted desperately to get very drunk. She wanted Woollcott to cease and desist, leave Lacey Van Weber to her. He was hers by squatter's rights; she'd seen him first and staked out the territory. What the hell did he think tomorrow was all about? Ideally, Mrs. Parker planned to win Van Weber and his confidence and by late afternoon was positive he'd spill all, whatever "all" there was to spill.

"I don't associate with Dr. Horathy. We have mutual friends. I frankly don't remember what he was doing at my party or who brought him. Ah! Here comes Texas!"

Saved by the bell, thought Jacob Singer.

"Hello, suckers!" Texas Guinan was vainly fighting encroaching middle age. Her hair was bleached-blond and frizzled. She wore a red satin gown dotted with multicolored sequins that sparkled and glittered, thereby emphasizing the falseness of her own forced ebullience. Her red slippers sparkled with rhinestones, and diamond buckles and bracelets were shackled to her wrists. The variety of rings she sported looked like amethysts and rubies until Mrs. Parker spotted one lonesome diamond and decided the whole lot was paste. "Well, Jacob Singer, does your presence mean I'm in for another raid?"

Singer raised his hands in a pantomime of innocence. "Tonight I come as a friend, Tex."

"Okay, friend." She recognized Mrs. Parker and Woollcott. "It's nice to have the literati here tonight, it adds a little class to the joint. The Lord knows my joints can always use a little class." Mrs. Parker thought the woman was pushing too hard, and it bored her. She suspected her own face was a dead giveaway, but she was too tired to recompose it. "Must be a full moon bringing out all you celebrities tonight. We sure got a passel of them at this watering hole. Why, hell, here's Al Jolson. I hope the son of a bitch remembers to pay the check. Hello, sucker!"

"Hello, m'little Texas baby, m'little bright spot of sunshine after midnight." He gave her a bear hug and then ran his tongue over her lips lasciviously.

She pushed him aside and bellowed, "You all know Jolie, don't yuh?"

"Only on one knee," said Mrs. Parker.

Texas clapped her hand on Mrs. Parker's shoulder. Mrs. Parker felt her skin shrivel. "Great little kidder, our Dottie. Your gang's over there near the bar, Jolie." Jolson went looking for his gang. "He's off to Hollywood to do a flick for the Warners. Sounds like a real stinker to me." A waiter whispered something to her. "Right you are, McGillicuddy. It's showtime!" She signaled the orchestra leader who cued the drummer. The drummer tattooed a long roll, and the dancers left the floor. Texas took center stage on the dance floor bathed in a blinding pink light. "Hello, suckers!" she bellowed again. "Welcome, you sheiks and flappers and all you butter and egg men in from the boondocks just looking to get rolled." Large peals of laughter. Mrs. Parker thought it sounded rehearsed. "We got a great little show for you tonight and a real big surprise. But first, let me bring on the girls." The room was filled with piercing whistles, and the floor shook from stomping feet.

"Dear God," gasped Woollcott.

"It's a ritual here, old sport," explained Van Weber. "Texas is the high priestess. An evangelist without portfolio. She directs the flock, the bellwether of hedonists. This is nothing, tonight. Try it on a weekend when it's absolutely Hogarthian."

"Now here's that redheaded vixen you all been waiting

for! The flaming bombshell herself, Lily Robson. Come on, you suckers! Give the little girl a great big hand!" Guinan left the spotlight, which expanded as Lily Robson, wearing what Mrs. Parker assumed was an oversized handkerchief bordered with blue baguettes, came dancing out onto the floor with six other girls. For about five minutes, Lily did exactly what she had told them she did, a little bit of this, a little bit of that with a lot of the old moxie. She was magnificently untalented and wonderful to look at. The line of girls behind her danced as though they were being pelted with buckshot. One cute young brunette kept winking at Al Jolson. Van Weber explained she was Jolson's new heart-throb, Ruby Keeler.

"She's a long way from Mammy," commented Mrs. Parker.

Lily Robson and the girls left the stage to a thunderous ovation, causing Mrs. Parker to wonder if the roof would have caved in had there been a truly talented performance. Texas was introducing a dance team, "Hot from Madrid. That's from over there in Spain where they grow lemons and olives and these two great flamingo dancers." Van Weber explained she meant "flamenco," and Jacob Singer watched for a reaction from Mrs. Parker but saw none. Woollcott was pouring himself another glass of champagne, and Mrs. Parker decided he looked as though he was resigned to an early death. "Let's give a great big hand to Juan and Juanita!" With an explosion of castanets, Juan and Juanita came rushing onstage from either side of the band-stand. They waved their hands and stomped their feet and made ugly guttural noises as they chased each other around the stage. The scene was bizarre and madly out of syn-chronization, as either the dancers were ten beats ahead of the orchestra or the orchestra was ten beats behind the dancers.

Mrs. Parker whispered to Woollcott, "I suppose there are people who come here nightly?"

"Masochists. How much more of this must we endure?"

Mrs. Parker couldn't answer. Texas Guinan was center

stage again, this time bathed in a stomach-churning blue light. "And now, folks, I have a special treat for you. It's a real sad special treat. You know the world is mourning the death of that great lover, that great actor, that great old pal of mine, Rudy Valentino." There was a smattering of applause.

Mrs. Parker asked Jacob Singer, "Do you suppose they're for or against?"

"We ain't never gonna see the likes of Rudy again, folks. When they made Rudy, they threw away the mold." Mrs. Parker expected the orchestra to back her up with a rendition of "Hearts and Flowers," but realized it wouldn't work without violins. There were never string instruments in a Texas Guinan jazz band. "Let's hope that our sheik of sheiks, Monsoor Beaucaire himself, the son of the desert, is up there before the cameras in that great movie studio in the sky." She had her right hand upraised, index finger pointing at the ceiling. The effect was interesting, and the reaction was tumultuous. "With us tonight is a great little lady whose suffering is worse than any of ours. Rudy's fiancée."

"Balls!" shouted a woman, and Mrs. Parker recognized Nita Naldi's voice. She identified Naldi to the group, and for the first time in minutes, Woollcott grinned from ear to ear.

Guinan glared nastily in the direction of the vulgarity and then remembered there was an audience out there hanging hopefully on her coming words. "Like I said, Rudy's fiancée is with us tonight. In memory of Rudy, she has consented to dance his favorite 'Tango d'Amour'. Dancing with her is our own favorite, Georgie Raft." Applause. "Ladies and gentlemen! Let's give one hell of a great big hand to the one, the only, the great . . . Opal Engri!" The place exploded. Raft, a short man with sleek, shiny, patent-leather hair, entered as Guinan left. He adjusted his tight bolero jacket and then stretched out his hand. Opal Engri slowly walked onto the stage. She wore on her hair a black mantilla. Her dress was trimmed in black Chantilly lace, which Mrs. Parker didn't think was quite the ruching for black satin. She wore black pumps, black bracelets, a string of black pearls around her neck, and Mrs. Parker was disappointed that neither of her eyes was blackened. The orchestra struck up the tango, and the uproar settled down to a minor din. Raft deftly whisked Miss Engri through the intricate steps while the audience was treated to a fresh vulgarity from Nita Naldi.

"Horseshit!"

Woollcott said to the table, "I'm entertaining the thought of falling in love with that woman."

"Has Engri no shame?" inquired Mrs. Parker.

"None," Van Weber said.

"She's one hell of a looker," contributed Jacob Singer.

"She's not one hell of a dancer," said Woollcott.

"Her partner's pretty good, if a bit too oily," said Mrs. Parker.

"He's Guinan's latest," said Singer.

"Oh? And where does that leave Larry Fay?" asked Woollcott.

"He knows what's going on," said Singer. "But Raft's useful. He's a bagman for the gang. Fay will send him out to Hollywood soon. It's what Raft's after anyway. He's local, you know. Hell's kitchen. George Ranft was his real name."

Woollcott inquired loudly, "Does anyone else but me feel he's in the center of the decline of Western civilization?"

The dance was drawing to a close. Raft had Engri pressed against his body, her back to him, his arms around her waist, his right hand clasping her right hand, her eyes smoldering with repressed sexuality, his eyes indicating he was counting out the beat.

"You polack bitch!"

The dance came to an end. The applause swelled. Flowers were thrown at Engri. A whisky bottle missed her by inches, thrown, they later learned, by Nita Naldi. Raft kissed Engri's hand, and she rewarded him with a flower. Then, suddenly remembering she was in mourning, she burst into tears as Raft led her offstage. Now Mrs. Parker saw Nita Naldi. She had lifted a chair and was being restrained by her escort. Guinan sent two bouncers over to remedy the situation. Naldi conceded the chair but not her contempt. She drew herself up with a sneer and a loud raspberry that penetrated through the din, and majestically marched out of the club followed by her gentleman friend.

"Poor Nita," said Van Weber. "She's having a rough time. There's no more work for her in pictures. Imagine being washed up at twenty-seven."

"My God, is that all she is?" asked Mrs. Parker. "Hollywood must be a very cruel place."

"It certainly is," said Van Weber.

And that, thought Mrs. Parker, has *got* to be a clue.

Jacob Singer couldn't believe his ears. Mrs. Parker had asked him to dance. The orchestra had slipped smoothly into "Somebody Loves Me," a ballad both could cope with. Despite the cacophony in the overcrowded speakeasy, they could hear the orchestra and each other.

"I had to get you alone because there's something I've been trying to give you all evening." She had palmed the pill she had taken from Lily Robson before asking Singer to dance and now gave it to him. "Horathy gave those pills to Lily Robson this afternoon. We must have just missed her. She took one at dinner with Van Weber. They're for her nerves."

"Van Weber made her nervous?"

"I think everything makes her nervous. I get the feeling the simple act of opening a door could be a prelude to hysteria."

"You think one of these pills made her sick?"

"Something made her sick. She was quite ill at the Harlequin."

"Lots of people get ill at the Harlequin. I'll put the lab to work on this the first thing in the morning." The pill was transferred to his pocket with the deftness of a magician. "How'd you make out with Sid Curley?"

Three minutes and the new accompaniment of "Somebody Stole My Gal" later, Singer had heard the entire adventure at the Harlequin. At Mrs. Parker's suggestion, he kept a smile on his face throughout her dissertation, the better to give the impression he was being amused rather than provided with information. "I hope I'll know more tomorrow, after he's shown me around his estate at East Cove."

"Don't be too smart tomorrow." There was as much concern as caution in his voice.

"Good heavens, no. I shall be terribly girlish and all fluttery hands and make all the correct, appreciative noises."

"The guy with Opal Engri is trying to attract your attention. Or else he's making a pass at me."

"Why, heaven help us, it's Horace Liveright. He's publishing my poetry. And now he's brave enough to escort Miss Engri. My God, her black stockings have fleurs-de-lis embroidered on them. I'm dying to meet her, aren't you? Hello, Horace! What a surprise meeting you here."

Liveright stood and kissed Mrs. Parker lightly on the cheek. Engri acknowledged the introductions dolefully and gave what Mrs. Parker later described as some sort of Polish grunt when the couple agreed to sit down with them for a quick drink. Liveright had additional glasses brought immediately and poured champagne. Mrs. Parker, feeling no pain and quite gay, asked the screen temptress, "I suppose you prefer this stuff drunk from your slipper."

"Very unsanitary." Engri's voice seemed to come rumbling from the bowels of her body, a voice seductively husky, heavily accented, and it seemed to have grabbed

Singer by the throat. He was hypnotized.

"How tragic, Mr. Valentino's death." Mrs. Parker wondered if Miss Engri might have attended Liveright's midnight party the previous evening.

"I sit before you in ruins." Miss Engri was not too ruined to down a glass of champagne.

"Oh, come, come, dear," trilled Mrs. Parker, "from the ashes the phoenix shall arise again."

"I am in ruins, not in ashes." Liveright refilled her glass. "We were going to star together in Tolstoy's *Resurrection*. Now posterity has been robbed of this great epic masterpiece. Films will never be the same again."

Mrs. Parker rejoined, "I suppose neither will Tolstoy. Well, Horace, you certainly do get around, and with some of the most fascinating people. Imagine knowing Opal Engri."

Liveright tried hard not to preen too much and didn't succeed. "Opal and I go back quite a few years." Engri's eyes smoldered at the "quite a few years." "We met in Germany when she was filming *Bovary*."

"I was child. Very young child." Engri's eyes zeroed in on Singer. "Why are you so silent?"

"I guess I'm in awe of the great Opal Engri."

"Yes, I understand. Who are you? What do you do?" She was running her tongue around the rim of her glass, and Singer crossed his legs as though preparing to ward off an attack.

"I'm a detective."

Mrs. Parker thought Liveright's face colored, but she couldn't be too sure under the erratic lighting system. She plunged deeper. "Mr. Singer is investigating the murders of Ilona Mercury and Vera DeLee. You know of course Miss Mercury was Mr. Valentino's date at the party where he took ill."

Engri leaned back in her chair, found her cigarette holder on the table somewhere between her gold metal evening purse and a package of Turkish cigarettes, squeezed a cigarette into the holder, then raised the holder as Liveright struck a match on cue, applying it to the cigarette. Engri inhaled, nostrils flaring just as Mrs. Parker remembered they had flared in most of her films. She sent a perfect smoke ring in orbit toward the ceiling and then impaled Mrs. Parker with her eyes. "Rudy and I had no secrets except those we shared with each other. I was the only woman in Rudy's life." She brought a black handkerchief to her eyes with her other hand. Mrs. Parker could detect no sign of a tear, but the dramatic effect was breathtaking. "Other women were walk-ons, extras, bit players. Engri was the queen sharing his throne!" The handkerchief hand was strikingly raised above her head, the eyes were shut, the breast heaved (somewhat threateningly, thought Mrs. Parker), the nostrils quivered, and Mrs. Parker resisted the temptation to shout "Cut!" Singer softly suggested it was time they return to their table, and Mrs. Parker agreed, albeit reluctantly. She was in a wicked mood thanks to too much champagne and wanted to ask Liveright about his orgies and Miss Engri about Valentino's frigid wives, but Singer was gallantly helping her to her feet while she made cooing noises which the others interpreted as "This has been absolutely memorable."

Singer led Mrs. Parker around the perimeter of the dance floor. Their table had now expanded to two tables. They'd been joined by Florenz Ziegfeld and Charlotte Royce. "Oh, look, Mr. Singer, it's just like the Mad Hatter's tea party!" Woollcott looked surprisingly unruffled by the company, the hour, and the abandonment by Mrs. Parker and Jacob Singer. He was smoking a cigarette and chatting amiably, it seemed, with Miss Royce, who was sipping from what looked like a tall glass of straight gin. Mrs. Parker apologized for herself and Mr. Singer, explaining they'd had a drink with Horace Liveright and the inimitable and never-to-be-forgotten Opal Engri.

"Why, you lucky children," gushed Woollcott insincerely, "and what is Miss Engri like?"

"Like nothing real," commented Mrs. Parker, tapping Van Weber's hand for his attention. She needed more champagne and got it.

"Flo's been telling us about his big season coming up," explained Van Weber as he replenished Mrs. Parker's and Singer's glasses.

"A big season. Probably the biggest of my career." Ziegfeld was staring at the smoldering end of his cigar as though it were a crystal ball and his big season was therein predicted. "I've got *Show Boat* to open my new theater on Sixth Avenue."

Mrs. Parker clapped her hands together, looking like an evil waif. "A new theater! Oh, goodie! Just what New York needs. What's it called?"

Ziegfeld's chest expanded. "The Ziegfeld."

"That figures."

Woollcott piped up, "You can't exactly expect him to name it after a competitor."

"Lucky Edna," said Mrs. Parker, thinking of Miss Ferber, whose best-selling novel was the basis for the musical version of *Show Boat*. "This should undoubtedly make her a millionaire."

"Let's hope it makes us all millionaires," said Ziegfeld.

Woollcott announced, "Miss Royce is reading Proust."

"How?" inquired Mrs. Parker. Singer had a coughing fit, and Charlotte Royce stared at the sleek-haired man approaching the table with a big smile on his face.

"Why, hiya, Lacey, I thought I spotted you when I was dancing with Opal." George Raft didn't wait to be invited to join the table. He kidnapped a chair from an adjoining group and wedged himself between Van Weber and Mrs. Parker. Van Weber looked less than overjoyed and Mrs. Parker wondered who had dared manufacture the cologne the dancer was wearing. Raft didn't seem interested in introductions. "Lacey and I are old buddies, ain't we, old buddy?" He made a fist and then feinted an old-buddy jab at Van Weber's arm. Van Weber was uncomfortable and did not offer Raft a drink. Raft seemed impervious to anything but himself.

Mrs. Parker wanted to hear more about the old buddies. "How long old buddies are you old buddies, old buddy?"

Mrs. Parker didn't like Raft's smile but managed to look agreeable while waiting for his answer. "I was at Lacey's party a couple of weeks ago," he said.

"It seems there was everybody at that party but the schola cantorum," commented Woollcott.

"I guess they weren't asked," said Raft. Jacob Singer stifled a groan.

"Did you know Rudolph Valentino?" continued Mrs. Parker.

"Did I *know* Rudy Valentino?"

"That's what I asked you."

"Do you know how far back him and me *go?*"

"I give up. How far back?"

Raft roared with laughter while punishing the table with his fist. Near the orchestra, under an arch that led to the dressing rooms, Texas Guinan was keeping an eye on Raft, an angry expression on her face, both hands on her hips and her right foot tapping an ominous staccato beat. "I'm gonna tell you how far back Rudy and I go."

"I'm all ears, Mr. Raft." She was glad he was all mouth.

"I met Rudy just after he got off the boat. He was a greenhorn. A dumb wop kid what couldn't even speak our lingo. But, baby, could he dance."

"You were his dancing partner?" Mrs. Parker took a gentle sip of champagne or whatever it was.

"Ha ha ha! Dancing partner, she asks!" Raft's chair was tilted back, and the others were waiting for him to spill, but God was on his side. "Listen, lady, Rudy and I were dancing partners, all right, but not the way you think. We were paid to truck the old broads around at tea dances."

"Oh, taxi dancers," said Mrs. Parker.

"That's it. The dames paid us to dance with them. And,

baby, that's one lingo Rudy could converse in. He'd shove his legs between their thighs and then jolly them around the floor crooning some wop love songs in their ears, and, baby, what tips they gave him. That's how he became Joan Sawyer's dancing partner."

"And what became of you, Mr. Raft?" asked Woollcott.

Raft's skin was thick enough to protect a fortress. "Here I am, kiddo, alive and kicking. Let me tell you, there was a lot of us kids taxi dancing back in the old days. Besides Rudy and me there was Denn—" And suddenly he caught himself.

"Yes?" Mrs. Parker's eyes couldn't leave Raft's face.

Van Weber suddenly found his voice. "Tell us, George, what's this news you may be going to Hollywood?"

"I don't know who's spreading them rumors," replied Raft jauntily. "But the Warners are gonna test me out at their Brooklyn studio next week. But you know, you can't count your chickens before they're hatched."

"But you can count them while they're laying eggs," said Woollcott, his voice dripping icicles.

"I think you're fascinating, Mr. Raft," complimented Mrs. Parker, hoping a bolt of lightning wouldn't strike her. "I mean, here you sit, an actor manqué, who knew Rudy Valentino, has danced with Opal Engri, is an intimate of Texas Guinan's—or is that a secret?"

"Hell, no, Tex and I are good buddies."

"Why, Mr. Raft, I just think you've got one hell of a future ahead of you."

"Gee, thank you, lady, that's real nice of you." A waiter arrived and knelt beside Raft, saying something they couldn't hear, but causing Raft's mood to alter. "Guess I gotta get going. My master's voice." Surely he meant "mistress," thought Mrs. Parker. Raft pushed his chair back and got up. "Well, it was nice meeting you all." But he's met no one, thought Mrs. Parker; he's barely said a dozen words to Lacey Van Weber. She watched him strut away like a bantam cock.

"What an absolutely strange young man," said Mrs.

Parker. Then she turned to Van Weber. "Ostensibly he came to say hello to you and then proceeded to ignore you almost totally."

"George is a pushy son of a bitch." They'd almost forgotten Charlotte Royce had a voice.

"Then you know him well," observed Woollcott.

"Everybody knows him around town. He tried to get me to do a dance act with him a couple of months ago."

"He didn't even say hello to you!" Mrs. Parker seemed appalled. She wasn't. She was tired and bored and frustrated. She knew there was something important about this night; there were clues to be heard between the lines and the innuendos. To be heard from Engri and Liveright and Van Weber and from Raft, especially from Raft who had been stopped in midname. *Denn* . . . Denn what? Denn who?

"Sure, he didn't say hello. Why should he? There's bigger fish for him to try and fry. There's Flo here. He's dying to get into a *Follies.*"

"He's a very good dancer," acknowledged Ziegfeld, "but I don't like his reputation."

"And what reputation is that?" inquired Woollcott, not having forgotten he'd been told Raft was an errand boy for the mob.

"His underworld associations."

"Don't you have underworld associations?" Woollcott spoke evenly and without embarrassment. Mrs. Parker thought he was being terribly brave and would tell him so at the first opportunity. She was liking him tonight. He was being a good sport. It was long past his bedtime but not long past his bitch time. She had a suspicion he was catching his second wind and didn't even demur as Van Weber refilled his glass. She didn't dare look at her wristwatch. She didn't want to know what hour it was. She didn't want to suffer Cinderella's fate and go fleeing from the ballroom leaving behind a champagne glass. She wanted to stay up all night until Lacey Van Weber came to call for her at eleven A.M.; she wanted to be in her early twenties again, flirtatious and outrageous and romantic. The rasp in Ziegfeld's voice shattered her mood.

"What do you mean, Mr. Woollcott?"

"What I mean is don't you need the underworld's financial support for your productions? We all know that's where George White finds money for his *Scandals* and Earl Carroll procures his for his *Vanities.*"

"That's where they got the dough for my show," said Mrs. Parker from out of nowhere.

"And what show was that?" asked Ziegfeld, grateful for the temporary reprieve.

"What? You never heard of the show I wrote with Elmer Rice? Shame on you, Mr. Ziegfeld. It ran four weeks or so. *Close Harmony.* I wanted to call it *Close Call.* That was two years ago. A very depressing experience."

"I'm investing in Mr. Ziegfeld's productions." All eyes were on Lacey Van Weber. "My money is in *Showboat, Rio Rita* and next year's *Follies.* I think it's going to be a banner year for all of us."

"Do you have underworld connections, Mr. Van Weber?" Woollcott was cool, without a trace of champagne in his voice. He had lit a cigarette and was holding it with the devil-may-care flair of a man of the world.

"I have all sorts of connections, Mr. Woollcott. I know a great many people with links to the underworld. Who doesn't? I invest in the stock market, and we all know what a shadowy enterprise that is. Look around you, Mr. Woollcott, and what do you see? You see a cross section of the wealthy, the near-wealthy, and the wish-to-hell they were wealthy. Everyone's cheek by jowl here. The crooked and the legitimate and the illegitimate." Good heavens, thought Mrs. Parker, when he articulates he really articulates. Jacob Singer sat with his arms folded, listening and absorbing. He was admiring Woollcott. "Does that answer your question?"

"Well, it's a lot of words," replied Woollcott.

"The *Times* ran their review of *Close Harmony* with the obituaries." Mrs. Parker shook her head sadly while Woollcott glared daggers at the interruption.

Ziegfeld said to Charlotte Royce, "I think it's time we left."

"Oh, sure, Flo."

"Miss Royce?"

"Yes, Miss Parker?"

"I'm supposed to call you at twelve noon tomorrow."

"Oh, yeah. I'm glad you reminded me."

"I'm afraid I'll have to try you later in the day. Something's come up." She smiled at Van Weber, who smiled back. Oh, good, she thought, he still cares. "When will it be convenient later in the day?" She pronounced each word carefully, trying not to slur them.

"Any time around six or so. I always rest for an hour or so before I leave for the theater."

"That's just dandy."

Suddenly a roar went up from the crowd, and Mrs. Parker wondered if somewhere unseen by her Christians were being thrown to the lions. From the ceiling came a downpour of balloons and confetti.

"Whee!" yelled Charlotte Royce. Mrs. Parker was unsurprised that she was the "whee" type. The orchestra was blaring away, "There'll Be a Hot Time in the Old Town Tonight." Singer said something to Woollcott that made his entire being come close to bursting with pride. Mrs. Parker saw the look and would later describe it as something akin to a sixteen-year-old girl receiving her first kiss.

"By God, what chaos!" shouted Van Weber.

Mrs. Parker drew herself up regally and told him, "Henry Brooks Adams wrote 'chaos often breeds life.'"

"Who was Henry Brooks Adams?"

"Oh, don't be such a spoilsport."

At which moment, all hell broke loose. Police came pouring into the speakeasy, some bearing arms, other wielding axes. "Oh, shit!" said Singer, not hearing Texas Guinan making the same statement because she was standing near the orchestra.

"What joy!" exclaimed Woollcott; "my first raid! Isn't it glorious! Do you suppose it was like this at the decline and fall of the Roman Empire?"

Singer shouted to his group, "Follow me!" He grabbed Mrs. Parker by a wrist and pulled her toward the arch that led to the dressing rooms. Mrs. Parker wondered if there was a mouse on her left until she realized it was Miss Royce who was making squealing noises. Ziegfeld had grabbed the girl by both arms and was pushing her ahead of him. Mrs. Parker saw Horace Liveright straining under the weight of Opal Engri, who had apparently fainted or decided she wanted to be carried in somebody's arms. Mrs. Parker doubted Liveright was man enough to survive the ordeal. One of the detectives in charge of the raid stood in the archway. He recognized Singer and wigwagged an index finger at him signifying "naughty naughty," and Singer told him to do something to himself which is a physical impossibility.

Backstage, a policeman caught George Raft trying to hide himself in a foul-smelling bathroom. Raft offered him ten dollars to forget he was there. They settled on twenty. Lily Robson was struggling in the arms of a massive police matron. "Stop groping me, you fucking old lez," shrieked Lily Robson.

"Wait here," said Singer to Mrs. Parker as he hastened to run interference for Lily Robson.

Singer said something to the police matron, who said, "Says who?"

"Says me," snapped Singer as he showed her his badge. The woman was slavering, and Singer thought of punching her, which would have meant a demotion to foot patrolman and an assignment to the wilds of Staten Island.

"Oh, gee whiz, pal, thanks!" cried Lily Robson as Singer now propelled her and Mrs. Parker through a back door.

"You certainly know your way around here!" cried Mrs. Parker with admiration.

"This place has been raided under a dozen different names," Singer told her. "Here we go. Turn left." The alley led them to West Fifty-seventh Street."

"Oh, good," announced Mrs. Parker, "I live just down the street. Who's for a nightcap?"

Woollcott, out of breath, leaned against a storefront. Ziegfeld hurried Charlotte Royce into a taxicab and they sped away. Singer offered Lily Robson, who was half naked, the use of his jacket, but she settled for a loan of five dollars and a taxicab. Van Weber said to Singer and Woollcott, "I'll see Mrs. Parker home." Mrs. Parker happily accepted the arm he offered her, sending her goodnights over her shoulder at Woollcott and Singer and promising to be in touch with them late the next day. She next wondered if Mr. Van Weber was expecting her hospitality for the remainder of the night. If he was, then he was a winner.

Texas Guinan had eluded the raiders. She was at the desk in her office above the club that was reached by a secret staircase, shouting into the telephone at her sleepy lawyer viciously underlined instructions to get his fat ass downtown and spring her kids. Five minutes later she had the ear of a very sleepy police commissioner, telling him in language that would have made even a longshoreman blush that she expected a refund of all the under-the-table thousands she had paid him and his minions to keep her latest enterprise raid-free. He countered with numerous apologies and explanations, claiming total confusion at the foul-up and assuring her she could open again tomorrow night.

"The place is a wreck!" she screamed into the phone. "Your gorillas went at it with axes and crowbars!"

The commissioner assured her a police department work gang would arrive first thing in the morning.

"They'd better!" threatened Guinan as she slammed the receiver on the hook. She stalked down the stairs to assess the damage and in the backstage hallway saw George Raft sneaking out of the bathroom. "You miserable son of a bitch!" she shouted, hurling herself at him, pulling at his hair and scratching at his face.

"Lay off, Tex, lay off," shouted Raft while attempting to save himself from serious damage.

"I told you to stay away from Lacey Van Weber! He can't stand the sight of you!"

"That's a load of shit! We're old buddies!"

"You're such old buddies that he warned me to keep you away from him!"

"Oh, yeah? Why'd he invite me to his party?"

"You *crashed* his party, you pushy Hungarian lounge lizard! You took Valentino and Mercury and crashed it because you knew with Valentino in tow you wouldn't be stopped at the door! And then look what happened!"

"How'd I know Horathy would be there? Stop scratching me, you fucking whore, or I'll bust your fucking jaw!" He now managed to grab her wrists, but it didn't control her feet. Her volcanic rage would not spend itself. She kicked his shins and tried to knee him in the groin.

"You miserable little hunkie greaseball, you're finished around here, y'hear me? *You're finished!*"

Sid Curley was pleading with his eyes. He couldn't plead with his mouth because it was sealed tight with masking tape. His hands were bound tightly behind him, and his feet were damp. They were being held firmly in a bucket of setting cement by two gentlemen of dubious origins. One had a knife scar down his right cheek running from his ear to his mouth. From that mouth there hung a dead cigar. His grip on Sid Curley's left leg was like an iron vise. The man holding Curley's right leg was bald due to a metal plate in his head, a souvenir of the late war. He was missing part of his right ear, and although not yet thirty years old, he had a full set of ill-fitting false teeth. Sid Curley started to struggle again. He'd been struggling ever since the two goons had caught up with him at his boardinghouse on Eleventh Avenue near Forty-third Street, convenient to Times Square and also, unhappily for Sid Curley, the Hudson River. A cloth dampened with ether had rendered Curley harmless in the hallway outside his room, and the goons were able to carry him out to their waiting sedan without incident. The proprietress of the boardinghouse, a reformed pickpocket, was familiar with the sight of bodies being removed from the premises, alive or otherwise. She was rather sorry to see Curley go. She liked the little man. He kept his room tidy and himself never less than dapper. He paid his rent promptly every Friday morning and sometimes wrapped it around a freshly purchased American Beauty rose. But the lady had long ago recognized that sooner or later circumstances would overtake Curley and payment would be exacted. Curley knew this, too but, like other paid informants, always expected that he would be the one to survive.

When the ether-induced fog had cleared, Sid Curley's mouth was taped, his hands tied behind him, his feet tied to the legs of the chair in which he was seated, while the two evil-looking nemeses mixed the cement in the tub conveniently supplied by the captain of the garbage scow that was now sailing toward midriver. When the texture of the cement satisfied the goon with the steel plate in his head, Curley's feet were untied. He fought ferociously to keep his feet from being submerged in the deadly concoction, but to little avail. It only brought him a crack on the jaw that rendered him unconscious again, this time bringing him a rather sweet dream of his mother and sister seeing him off at the train station in Baronowitsch, a little shtetl on the Polish-Russian border.

"I'll be sending for you very soon!" he shouted in Polish, "as soon as I make my first hundred dollars in America!"

He had made many hundreds of dollars in America, but had somehow managed to overlook the promise made twenty years ago when he was but a lad of fourteen. When he awoke with an aching jaw and no future, he remembered the dream and thought wistfully of the tiny mother and the tiny sister still languishing in the old country, assuming some pogrom hadn't got them. They never wrote, because they had never been taught how to write. *Sniff sniff sniff.*

The boat stopped. They were in stygian darkness. With the assistance of the captain, Sid Curley was lifted out of his chair and slowly lowered over the side of the boat. A scream welled up in his throat, but it had nowhere to go. The cement tub carried Sid Curley very slowly to the bottom of the Hudson River. He didn't die right away. He held his breath, hoping for a miracle, moving his eyes about wildly, searching for some underwater swimmer hurrying to his rescue with a knife between his teeth, the sort of thing he remembered as Douglas Fairbanks's specialty. What he saw instead, to his surprise and almost delight, were several old friends he hadn't seen around town lately. To his left was Looey the Bum, who had ratted once too often on Arnold Rothstein, a very dangerous racketeer. And just ahead of him was Police Lieutenant Barney Fermelli, who had taken a bribe and then double-crossed the donor.

Sniff sniff sniff. Sid Curley felt better. He was among friends. He would not die alone.

Van Weber escorted Mrs. Parker to her door, and under the inquisitive eyes of the night porter she threw caution to the winds and invited him in for a nightcap. He thanked her for the offer but refused, not rejecting her charm or her company or whatever promise lurked or possibly cowered behind the invitation, simply reminding her they had a date at eleven A.M. which was only six hours away. He needed some sleep. Mrs. Parker understood. There was always tomorrow. Brazenly, she offered her lips, and delicately, he took them. She felt as though her lips had been brushed by a hummingbird in flight, or perhaps in fright. She watched as he found a cab and departed.

The night elevator man roused himself as she shook him hard and took her to her floor to an accompaniment of his foul-breathed yawns. She could hear the phone ringing in her apartment as she struggled with key and lock. Whoever was on the calling end had no intention of giving up until they reached her. Breathlessly, she asked into the mouthpiece, "Yes?"

It was Jacob Singer. He assumed he hadn't awakened her as it was little more than ten minutes since they had parted company. Mrs. Parker explained she had just gotten home and was out of breath from struggling with the lock. She sat down on the chair next to the desk which held the phone. In answer to his next question Mrs. Parker said, "Yes, it's quite safe to talk. I'm alone." Singer had discreetly not implied Van Weber might be with her.

"I wanted to catch up with you tonight in case we miss connections in the morning." He was sitting on the floor of his tiny living room holding a glass of warm beer, the receiver propped between his ear and his shoulder. "I want you to exercise a lot of caution tomorrow on this here outing with Van Weber. I mean, he was pretty good at double-talking tonight when friend Woollcott nailed him with that underworld connection bit."

"Yes, I was rather proud of Alec. I'll tell him tomorrow night when I get back."

"I repeat, don't try to be a heroine. I'm glad you're getting this chance to be alone with him because we need every piece of information you can get out of this bozo. I'm pretty convinced there's a strong connection between him and these murders." So am I, thought Mrs. Parker, but I won't say so; I won't ruin tomorrow. I'm suicidal, after all, and what a heavenly way to die. "I want to hear from you no later than six o'clock tomorrow night."

"Why?"

"Because then I'll know you're safely back in town."

Mrs. Parker sat up. "Why, Mr. Singer, you don't think any harm could befall me tomorrow, do you? Everyone at the table heard him ask me to spend the day with him."

"You could have a sudden accident."

"I hope not."

"I hope not, too. But he knows you and Woollcott are looking for information and beginning to get it. He knows you have a date to talk to Charlotte Royce. He knows you recognized Raft was about to make a slip and name somebody who Raft and Valentino whored around with in their salad days, a name I strongly got the feeling Van Weber didn't want repeated."

"And he agreed that Hollywood is a very cruel place."

"I didn't miss that one."

"I didn't think you did, Mr. Singer. I can see you don't miss very much."

"I try not to. But I repeat, Mrs. Parker, I don't want you swimming out over your head."

"I'm a very good swimmer, Mr. Singer. And I'll make sure we're back in the city by six o'clock. And Mr. Singer . . ."

"Yeah?"

"Sleep tight, don't let the bedbugs bite." She hung up, went to the bathroom and ran the tub. Slowly, she undressed, her mind deep in troubled thought. She poured salts into the bath and stirred the water with her hand, causing a small whirlpool. And in this whirlpool, she saw Lacey Van Weber's face, smiling at her. But the smile could not mask the eyes, the eyes she had studied at every opportunity at Texas Guinan's.

Blue. Cold. And cruel.

The man used his skeleton key to let himself into George Raft's hotel room. He had developed materializing from out of nowhere into a fine art. He had entered the hotel unseen, made his way up the back stairs unseen, crossed the corridor to Raft's room unseen. It was as easy as murder. The errand had been assigned him less than an hour ago. He was used to being given odd jobs at odd hours. Six in the morning was a good hour for a surprise visit. He even had time to stop off at an all-night cafeteria in Times Square for coffee and sinkers. The doughnuts were fresh and crisp, the first batch of the day. The coffee was piping hot and aromatic; it was their own brew. It didn't matter if he was recognized. His face was a familiar one in these parts at any hour of the day and night. That was part of the game, never any surprises.

He looked around the modest premises with distaste. Raft's tuxedo jacket was on the floor near the radiator. The trousers hung over a chair, his underwear discarded in the middle of the floor next to a pile of dancing slippers and black hose. Raft lay on the bed, naked. The two windows were open and the man could hear the garbage being collected in the street, which reminded him he had a job to do. An electric fan was poised on one of the windowsills directed at Raft, giving off a faint hum and little relief from the heat. The pillow was stained with the grease Raft used to plaster down his hair. There were scratches on his face and bruise marks on his legs. The man lifted a leg and kicked Raft gently. There was no response. He kicked again, increasing the pressure. A grunt from Raft. The third kick rewarded him with Raft's eyes flying open, the dancer staring about bewilderedly until the man's beefy face came into focus. Raft was confused and then, recognizing the man, frightened. The man sent his beefy right fist crashing into Raft's ribs. Raft's howl was cut short when the man smothered his face with a pillow.

"You talk too much," said the man. Raft lay still, breathing heavily, knowing the man wasn't here to kill him. His ribs ached and his heart throbbed and he knew he didn't dare try to defend himself. He waited for the man to make the next move. "You talk too much about your friend Rudy and your other dancing buddies. You're too ambitious, Georgie. You push yourself where you're not wanted, where you're not needed. You been promised your payoff. You're gonna be a big movie star. We need a big movie star out there, too many of the others are dead or dying. You gotta be patient, Georgie. Success takes time. A couple of years maybe, then *pow*." The man hit him in the ribs again. Raft groaned. "But you gotta be patient, you know? Next time, Georgie, we're gonna break your legs. Now just lay there till I get out of here. Go back to sleep. It's still early." The pressure on the pillow relaxed. He heard the man say, "Christ, but you are uncouth," and then the door opened and closed, softly. Raft flung the pillow on the floor and struggled to a sitting position, his face contorted with pain. He sat back against the brass headboard and took a series of deep breaths. Then he reached for the package of cigarettes and matchbox on his night table. After the first puff, his face screwed up like a child's, and he burst into tears. Oh, shit, he was thinking, oh, shit, I'm theirs for life. I belong to them forever. Oh, shit, this had better be worth it.

Neysa McMein couldn't believe her ears. It was ten o'clock in the morning and Dorothy Parker was scratching at the door, begging admittance. Neysa asked her husband, who was seated at the kitchen table absorbed in a plate of scrambled eggs and bacon, "Do you hear what I hear?"

"We're in the same room."

"But Dottie, at ten in the morning?" Neysa unlatched the door and Mrs. Parker swept in, a vision in cool green chiffon, a yellow straw hat dangling from a string loosely held in her left hand. Her right hand clutched a canary yellow handbag which she remembered purchasing somewhere in Spain from a pathetic urchin whose arms were dotted with scabs.

"Am I too early for you?" asked Mrs. Parker.

"No, you're too early for *you*," replied Neysa.

"Dare I beg a cup of coffee?"

"You can even get eggs and bacon if you play your cards right," replied Neysa as she poured piping black coffee into an earthenware mug. Mrs. Parker sat at the kitchen table and smiled at Baragwanath, a man she once described as wading through life trying to prove himself necessary.

"Did you have a good night, John?"

"No," he replied through a mouthful of egg, "I had a very bad night."

"You always have a very bad night," reminded Mrs. Parker.

"That's true. I haven't had a good night since the one

before the day I married Marjorie." Marjorie was Neysa's real name. She loathed it.

"What about your night, Neysa?" Neysa had brought the coffee and a mug for herself and sat down next to Mrs. Parker.

"I haven't been to bed yet," replied the artist cheerfully. "I was up all night making gin in the bathtub. I've got the gang coming over tonight. You, of course, do not require a formal invitation." She sipped the coffee. "By God, this is good stuff." Mrs. Parker agreed with her. "It's the Armagnac. Real stuff, none of that South Bronx turpentine."

"What luxury!" exclaimed Mrs. Parker.

"Stop stalling, Parker. Tell us about *your* night." Neysa McMein knew the lady well. She was her closest friend, one of the few women Mrs. Parker permitted to be a close friend. One was a writer, the other a gifted artist and illustrator, so there was no rivalry there. They had alien tastes in men, Mrs. McMein tending toward the bland, like her husband, whom Mrs. Parker saw only as an unidentifiable cipher. Mrs. Parker's taste bent toward the neurotic or the unattainable, men with weak characters or strong wives.

Mrs. Parker was delighted that Neysa was quick on her cues this morning, and eagerly took center stage. Her litany started with *No Foolin'* and concluded with the gentle goodnight kiss awarded her by Lacey Van Weber. The litany required three cups of coffee apiece, in the middle of which Mr. Baragwanath departed the apartment unnoticed, his usual exit, and Mrs. Parker still had fifteen minutes at her disposal before Van Weber's arrival. "What do you think?" asked Mrs. Parker.

"It's all so terribly glamorous and exciting," said Neysa, but that wasn't what she really thought and Mrs. Parker knew it.

Mrs. Parker came flat out with it. "What do you really think?"

"I think you're playing in the wrong ballpark and with the wrong team. I've never seen your Lacey Van Weber, I've never met him, but God knows I've read all about him in Winchell and the other dispensers of garbage I find irresistible. I think Texas Guinan is a freak and as to murdered whores, well, dear," continued Neysa as she worried a fingernail with an emery board, "prostitution isn't exactly a modern miracle. There's nothing new about murder for silence either, but when it's on your front doorstep, I say call the Department of Sanitation or move. You and Alec aren't exactly my idea of paradigms of detection. Holmes and Watson you ain't, especially since you don't have Conan Doyle around to call the shots."

"I must say, Alec was terribly impressive last night."

"He'll be terribly impressive laid out in a mortuary." She gave the idea further thought, and the canvas in her mind widened. "With Ring Lardner conducting a crap game at the foot of the catafalque. Dottie, whether you want advice or not, you're getting it. Get your head out of the noose before somebody tightens it around your neck. Shame on Jake Singer for sending you into the spider's parlor in green chiffon!"

"Don't you like the dress?"

"It's absolutely adorable." Neysa refrained from commenting she also thought it would look better on one of D. W. Griffith's simpering ingenues, but oh, what the hell. "Are you going to take my advice?"

"Of course I'm not going to take your advice." She was adjusting the green chiffon bracelets she'd hastily run up earlier for her wrists. Neysa recognized the inflection in her voice. The last time she'd heard it was when trying to dissuade Mrs. Parker from going wading in the Plaza Hotel's fountain. "What I might do is invite Mr. Van Weber to your soiree tonight. Would that be *au fait?*"

"That would be just dandy. And Dottie"—Mrs. Parker was at the door preparing to exit—"don't be too demure to scream for help should the occasion arise."

"I send you a loving kiss," said Mrs. Parker, and then closed the door behind her.

"A loving kiss, my ass," muttered Neysa as she headed into the bathroom to doctor the gin.

Back in her apartment, Mrs. Parker telephoned Woollcott. "Have I awakened you?"

"I've had no sleep whatsoever," lied Woollcott as he sank his teeth into his third prune Danish. "In fact, I've been wondering if we haven't bitten off more than we can chew." He was chewing ravenously.

Mrs. Parker sounded chagrined, but looked determined. "Alec, you can't back out on Jacob Singer now!" Hearing Jacob Singer's name, Woollcott mellowed. The movement of his jaws decelerated, and his face gave the impression he was listening to a chorus of castrati singing a Haydn oratorio.

"Of course I'm not backing out," blustered Woollcott, as he spooned five helpings of sugar into his tea, "but this isn't exactly a Boy Scout outing we've gotten ourselves into. Don't you realize we were surrounded by danger everywhere last night?"

"Wasn't it exciting?" She was staring out the window at the traffic below. There was no car waiting yet outside her building. There was still time. He wouldn't disappoint her. Not Lacey Van Weber.

"I must admit, it gave me a bigger jolt than drawing to an inside straight. I suppose you're being all girlish and alluring this morning?"

"Alec, there's something I'd like to tell you."

"And that is?"

"I thought you were just wonderful last night at Texas Guinan's."

Woollcott squirmed uneasily. A compliment from Parker usually camouflaged a descending guillotine blade.

"When you asked Ziegfeld and Mr. Van Weber if they were connected to the underworld, I just wanted to reach over and pin a *croix de guerre* on your chest. Of course I don't carry any with me, but the thought was genuine."

"And generous," conceded Woollcott, now preening before a mirror that hung on the wall next to the table where he was breakfasting. Happily, Harold Ross and his wife, Jane Grant, with whom he shared the premises, had long departed, Ross to *The New Yorker* office, his wife to wherever wives depart on occasional mornings.

"Alec, you're just about my favorite character in fiction. Oh, God, there's the downstairs buzzer. I'll see you tonight at Neysa's." She hung up.

Woollcott shrieked into the dead telephone, "What's going on at Neysa's?" He was left quivering with anxiety.

Lacey Van Weber stood on the sidewalk next to his Pierce-Arrow Runabout. He wore a blue blazer, white slacks, an ascot tied artistically around his neck, and on his head, a yellow straw hat. "Don't you look lovely," he said as Mrs. Parker came hurrying out of the building.

"And on time, too. I'm rarely prompt, but you are, aren't you? You look as fresh as a daisy." He helped her into the car. "Amazingly enough, I don't have a hangover. Do you have a hangover?"

"I never have hangovers," thereby slamming the door on the subject of hangovers. He pulled into traffic, heading for the Fifty-ninth Street Bridge.

"What an exciting night," said Mrs. Parker. "But then, you always have exciting nights, don't you?"

"I've never been caught in a raid before."

Oh, good, thought Mrs. Parker; then I'm one up on you. "I have. That's how I met Jacob Singer." She told him about Singer's rescue. "Did you like Mr. Singer?"

"The old sport is a bit of all right, I suppose. I always feel a bit clumsy in the company of the law." She wondered how often he'd been in the company of the law, clumsy or otherwise. "I'm never quite sure of saying the right thing or making the wrong move."

"I don't worry about those things. I'm always me."

"And quite fetching you are, too," he said, without taking his eyes off the traffic ahead of him. "And aren't we lucky with the weather? I phoned East Cove before picking you up. The weather's glorious there. If it holds, we might take a spin in my Jenny."

"What's your Jenny?"

"My airplane." Mrs. Parker paled. She was terrified of

heights. "Did you know I was a licensed pilot?"

"I seem to recall reading that in the *Graphic*," said Mrs. Parker, her voice losing strength.

"I love flying Jennies. They're war surplus, known as JN-4D. Today they're used mostly by barnstormers."

"You mean wing-walkers and people who hang by their legs from rope ladders, and other such unhinged creatures?"

Van Weber laughed. "They're quite safe. I once flew one cross-country."

Cross-country, thought Mrs. Parker; now we're beginning to get somewhere. "Do you spend a great deal of time in Hollywood?"

"What makes you assume I've lived in Hollywood?"

"You said you've flown cross-country."

"I could have flown to San Francisco."

Mrs. Parker inquired smoothly, "Do you spend a great deal of time in San Francisco?"

"I spend time all over the globe. Wind too strong for you? I can roll up the windows."

"Oh, no. I just love the wind in my hair. It's so Faith Baldwin.

Woollcott had George S. Kaufman trapped at the other end of the telephone, impressing him with the news that on his behalf he, Woollcott, and Mrs. Parker, were enduring almost unspeakable dangers. "What are those ghastly noises I hear, Kaufman?"

"Eva LeGallienne's here, trying to get me to write something for her Civic Repertory Company. Right now, she's running up and down the room giving little Annie a piggyback."

"How revolting."

"You really don't know how grateful I am, Alec, for what you're doing."

"I really don't know because I never hear from you."

"Don't be unfair. I tried reaching either you or Dottie several times yesterday after I read Vera DeLee was murdered, but neither of you were anywhere to be found."

"Well, you can bloody well buy me lunch today, and don't give me some lame excuse you've got a date to lay Bea Lillie or one of your other corps of quickie availabilities."

"I'll meet you at the Algonquin at one."

"Bring lots of cash. I'm very hungry." Woollcott hung up with a sigh and then, at the thought of lunch, smacked his lips. He looked at the wall clock. It was almost noon. He wondered how Mrs. Parker was faring.

"There it is," said Van Weber as his estate came into view. "You can see it just over the rise ahead."

"Oh, my," said Mrs. Parker, truly impressed. "It must cover thousands of acres."

"It was a derelict when I bought it. The restoration cost a fortune."

"Oh, but well worth it. Such a cozy little mansion for the occasional weekend. I'm sure it's more fun than necking in the balcony of the Loew's State."

They drove through massive iron gates opened by an attendant who, Mrs. Parker later insisted, touched his fore-lock as they drove through. The exquisite, tree-lined drive to the main house was over a mile long. On the way, Mrs. Parker could see stables and what she assumed was the hangar that housed his accursed Jenny.

Mrs. Parker was right. "That's the airport to your right; you can see the hangar. On the left are the stables."

"Do you breed horses?"

"I've got some pretty good ones. I haven't raced any yet, but, all in good time."

The main house was four stories high and turreted. It was painted a bright blue, with yellow shutters framing the windows. "Who looks after all those rooms?" asked Mrs. Parker, awestruck, her hand on her chest, her voice several octaves higher than normal.

"Oh, I've got dozens in help."

"How do you remember which one is which?"

"I don't have to. There's a majordomo to look after them."

Half an hour later, Mrs. Parker was still being given the grand tour. She had been led to impeccably designed tiered gardens and had appropriately admired the oversized swimming pool. His private dock boasted a cabin cruiser as well as a motorboat moored nearby. A short distance ahead stood an impressive lighthouse, constructed on a spit of land that overlooked and protected the entrance to the estate's private bay. Finally leading her back to the main house, Van Weber asked, "Hungry?"

"Famished," and she meant it.

Of course the interior was palatially furnished and decorated with immaculate taste. Mrs. Parker thought dolefully of her sad one-room studio and wondered how she would ever make do with it after this. Van Weber was explaining as he led her on the short hike to the dining room, "The interiors are mostly by Syrie Maugham and Elsie de Wolfe. The paintings are more or less eclectic, don't you agree?"

"Oh, yes, I do agree," said Mrs. Parker, having recognized some Tintorettos, a scattering of Van Goghs, some presumably shy and retiring Van Dycks and one rather magnificent portrait of a sixteenth-century dandy.

"Who did that?" asked Mrs. Parker.

"Oh, that, that was painted by Anon. Would you care to freshen up?"

Jacob Singer was looking uneasy. Al Cassidy had just reported waiting over an hour for Sid Curley to show up at a scheduled rendezvous. Singer called Curley's landlady, who in carefully worded sentences let him know Curley hadn't spent the night or been in touch and this was strange behavior for Curley. Singer knew what she was telling him. He'd learned to decipher the coded statements of the landladies of shady establishments a long time ago. Singer said to Cassidy, "It looks like Curley's been fingered."

"Shit."

"Right."

"What do you think?"

"I think Mrs. Parker and Woollcott are making certain people a little nervous."

"That's bad."

"Oh, no, that's good." Singer lit a cigarette and leaned back in the swivel chair. Cassidy sat opposite him and wiped the inside of his Stetson with a handkerchief. "Now those people will start getting clumsy. We'll get a break soon. Somebody'll get just frightened enough to make them come running to us for help and they'll talk. That'll be the hole in the dike. Then the water'll come trickling out, the hole gets bigger, soon the whole fucking dike collapses and we collar the whole buggering ring. What do you think, Al?"

"Very picturesque. How's for sending out for some sandwiches and java? I ain't had nothing since mud and sinkers early this morning."

"The trout is perfection." Mrs. Parker meant it, and the sincerity in her voice crossed the table and nibbled gently at Van Weber's ears.

"More wine?"

"Just a drop."

The flunky behind Mrs. Parker poured more wine. The flunky behind Van Weber wondered how the lady could pick the bones from her fish without removing her gloves. In the kitchen, the chef stood with his arms folded, white chef's hat trembling, waiting anxiously for the master of the house to compliment him on the cuisine.

"Oh, dear, I'm afraid I just can't eat anymore. It was all too marvelous."

Van Weber addressed a flunky. "My compliments to the chef. Tell him he outdid himself."

The message was relayed to the chef, who spread the word to his staff and signaled for their own lunch to be served, an expensive beef wellington complemented by imported hearts of artichoke and truffles. For Van Weber, fish, peas, mashed potatoes and salad constituted a banquet.

"We'll have coffee in the conservatory," said Van Weber over his shoulder as he conducted Mrs. Parker from the dining room. The walls in the hallway leading to the conservatory were decorated with paintings by the modernists. Mrs. Parker recognized Picasso, Utrillo, Modigliani and Sargent.

"These must be very heavily insured."

Van Weber shrugged. "There isn't a thief that could penetrate the estate." Mrs. Parker innocently wondered why not, having noticed the absence of moat and drawbridge. Then she recognized what had been hiding in the back of her mind. The dozens in help were all men. There were no maids, no sign of a housekeeper. This isn't an estate, it's a stronghold. "What are you thinking?" he asked her, as they made themselves comfortable in the conservatory where there was a bar and a stunning view of Long Island Sound.

"I'm thinking you have to be a multimillionaire to lay claim to a spread like this."

"Would you like a brandy?"

"No, thanks. I don't think I can handle one right now."

"Do you mind if I have one?"

"Please go right ahead."

She watched his catlike move to the bar where he poured the brandy and soon returned to the seat next to her.

"You're very beautiful, Mrs. Parker."

"Have another brandy."

He smiled. "I wanted to spend the night with you last night."

"But you didn't, did you?" She was nervous and feeling teenage-ish and twittery. He had taken her by surprise and was moving too fast for her. It was too soon after eating for romance. Give a girl's stomach a chance to settle; don't get it churning with unexpected emotions.

"I want you, Mrs. Parker."

"Oh."

They were in each other's arms, and he was kissing her passionately. Gone was the hummingbird; enter a bird of paradise.

"You haven't seen the bedrooms," he whispered. "I want to show you the bedrooms."

"I just adore bedrooms." Her voice was hoarse, and her feet were liquifying. This is it, she thought, her brain spinning; this is what it means to be swept off one's feet. It's never happened before and it's wonderful. She didn't remember being guided upstairs across plush carpets and past more paintings and expensive portieres and an arras that he said once hung at the Palace of Trianon. Now they were in the master bedroom, and he was undressing her while peppering her with exquisite little kisses. Then he undressed himself, Apollo revealed, and joined her on the bed, and oh, thought Mrs. Parker, isn't this better than dessert?

It had taken Woollcott another hour to pull himself together before joining Kaufman at the Algonquin for lunch. He remained at his desk compiling voluminous notes on the murders. He jotted down reminders to himself, reminders to ask Jacob Singer questions about the man in the elevator with Vera DeLee, first at Horathy's and then at her apartment hotel. He wrote down what he suspected was George Raft's almost slip of the tongue, *Denn . . . Denn* what? *Denn* who? He studied Lily Robson's name, which he had neatly lettered, and wondered if she was of any consequence to this case or just a nuisance of a red herring. On the next line was lettered Charlotte Royce's name. He didn't like her. He didn't like her one bit. But she couldn't be discounted. Not yet. After lunch he planned to be in touch with Singer and suggest a meeting to share in discussing and digesting his notes. Ah, Jacob Singer, the son I might have had. Who would have lain still long enough to be the mother? Woollcott sighed his special Woollcott sigh, the one reserved for foolish fantasies, and he entertained so many of them of late. It was time to leave to meet Kaufman.

*   *   *

"What's that you're reading?" Al Cassidy asked as he stirred sugar into his container of coffee.

"Lab report," replied Jacob Singer.

"What on?"

"A pill." Cassidy looked up with interest. "A pill Mrs. Parker thought might have been intended to poison Lily Robson."

"Well, is it poisonous?"

"It's not only not poisonous, it's absolutely harmless, useless, a placebo. But Robson took violently ill last night after swallowing one of these things. She was having dinner with Lacey Van Weber."

"Then it must have been plain old food poisoning. In this hot weather and the lousy refrigeration in most of the kitchens in these restaurants, I'm always expecting to get hit by some bug."

"Cassidy, you're such a fatalist."

"What else can you be when you're a cop?"

"I wonder how Parker's doing out there on the island with Van Weber?"

Mrs. Parker seemed to be doing just fine. They had had a refreshing swim in the pool, Mrs. Parker finding a lovely selection of bathing costumes in one of the pool houses. Then he drove her around the estate, overwhelming her with its lavishness, his mouth moving while her heart sang. She would one day remember his lovemaking as a Beethoven symphony compared to the ragtime renditions of her other lovers. They reached a fork in the road, and he seemed confused. Mrs. Parker wondered, Not all that familiar with your own bailiwick, Mr. Van Weber? He made a right turn, and they soon entered what looked like a compound within the compound, a huge stone structure topped by a slate chimney from which smoke poured forth. Two men came running out of the structure toward the car.

"It's all right, boys. It's me. I took a wrong turning!"

The men watched as Van Weber backed the vehicle out of the compound. Mrs. Parker suppressed a shudder. One man had an ugly scar on his right cheek running from his ear to his mouth. The other was missing part of his right ear and seemed to be having trouble with ill-fitted false teeth.

Mrs. Parker reminded herself she was supposed to be gleaning information. "What goes on in that building?"

"Oh, that? We do some agricultural testing there. I've acres of land lying fallow, and we're thinking of planting them with crops."

"You have partners?"

"What do you mean?" he asked sharply.

"You said, 'we're thinking of planting them.'"

"Oh, that. That's the royal 'we.'"

"Of course. The *Graphic* article said it was believed you were brought up in England."

"Like I said, I've traveled the globe. How's for a spin in Jenny?"

Shit, thought Mrs. Parker, I hoped he'd have forgotten about that. "I'm not very good about heights," she warned. "I get very sick if I go too high up. That's why I'm on the third floor of my building. They offered me a studio on the top floor, but I was having none of that and made it clear to them I wanted to be on one of the lower floors and . . ."

Van Weber interrupted her. "Mrs. Parker, you're babbling."

In a Childs restaurant just off Columbus Circle, Marc Connelly was gently holding Lily Robson's left hand. With her right, she was attacking a pile of pancakes drenched in maple syrup and sopping in a yellow lake of butter. Her eyes were slightly damp, and she was frightened, but it would take more than fear to curtail her appetite. She had violently lost her dinner the night before, and this was breakfast. She had awakened perspiring with the fear that she might have been poisoned, as hinted at by Mrs. Parker, which was followed by a cryptic phone call from Charlotte Royce telling her to keep her lips buttoned should that Parker snoop and her boyfriend Woollcott come sniffing around for information.

"But what do I know?" wailed Lily between mouthfuls of pancake.

"I don't know, dear," said Connelly with sympathy. "At least I don't know what you might know that would interest Dottie and Alec." The fools, he thought, what could they be up to now? Come to think of it, why had they really dropped in on him unexpectedly two days ago? What were they going on about? That party at Lacey Van Weber's, Valentino's illness, and what the hell was it all about? "Are you working tonight?"

"No, I phoned Tex before I came here to meet you. The joint's a wreck. It'll take the cops a couple of days at least before she can reopen."

"The cops?" Connelly was utterly bewildered.

"It's just too complex to explain, Mr. Connelly. I ought to go back to Youngstown and marry a miner or something. This town's getting too much for me."

Connelly sighed. "It's getting too much for a lot of us." He relinquished her hand. "How's the pancakes?"

"They're okay." Her voice was listless, in direct contradiction to her attitude.

"How would you like to come to a party with me tonight?"

She brightened visibly. "Whose party?"

"A good friend of mine. Neysa McMein. She's made a bathtub of gin and invited a whole gang of us over tonight."

"Oh, yeah? Who is she?"

"Neysa's a very talented artist. She does illustrations for the better magazines."

"And she makes bathtub gin?"

"Absolutely superb bathtub gin. Her own recipe. She's also a numerologist."

"No kidding? Well, how about her?"

"And on the seventh day," added Connelly wearily, "she rests."

*   *   *

The Jenny was soaring over Long Island Sound. Van Weber had outfitted Mrs. Parker and himself with flying goggles and then strapped her safely into her seat. She continued to protest until after the takeoff, and now she sank lower into her seat, the rear cockpit, while Van Weber gracefully maneuvered the craft. Briefly, she risked looking over the side and immediately cowered back at the sight of the water hundreds of feet below.

"Isn't this exciting?" she heard him shout. She opened her mouth to reply, but no sound emerged. "Hold tight! I'm going to do a barrel roll!" What in God's name is a barrel roll, she wondered as the plane revolved like a barrel. She found her voice and shrieked. She heard him laughing and thought to herself, The sadistic brute! "Hold on for a loop the loop!" The loop the loop was no improvement on the barrel roll.

Mrs. Parker was frightened. She knew she was safely strapped in, and yet, she'd been strapped in by Van Weber, not by herself. She tugged at the straps, and they held. Would a man do this to a woman? Lay her and then dump her out of an airplane? Maybe in a Cecil B. DeMille extravaganza but certainly not out here over the Long Island Sound. Take me down, she prayed, take me down. This isn't why I want to remember this afternoon; this isn't a side of you I want to know.

But I have to know. That's why I'm here. I have to get to the bottom of you, Mr. Van Weber, if you'll pardon the expression.

He was turning around in the front cockpit and smiling at her.

"Wheeeeeee!" yelled Mrs. Parker and then gratefully felt the craft descending.

"I have to be back in New York by six," insisted Mrs. Parker. She and Van Weber were having tea in the patio behind the house.

"Something special?" asked Van Weber.

"I promised to meet a friend of mine and then," she

suddenly remembered, "there's Neysa's party."

"Neysa McMein?"

"How nice. You've heard of her."

"I've heard of all of you. I get around and I have my sources of information."

"I'll bet you've got a theory or two about why those girls were murdered."

He didn't take the bait. "Do you?"

Fearless Parker rode forth to give battle. If Van Weber heard the rattling of sabers, he showed no sign of it. "As a matter of fact I do. I think their murders were dope-related."

"You mean they were part of some dangerous drug ring?"

"I mean Vera DeLee was addicted and Ilona Mercury knew too much."

"About what?"

"About what Valentino was yelling at your party when he attacked Dr. Horathy. He recognized Horathy from Hollywood."

Van Weber had been pouring a fresh cup of tea for himself and he sloshed some. Mrs. Parker saw this. *I've struck a nerve.* "Is this all supposition or do you know this for a fact?"

"I know it for a fact. Jacob Singer received some very pertinent information from the Los Angeles police linking Horathy and Ilona Mercury to a dope ring there." *Forgive me, Jacob Singer, if I'm spilling too much, but I've got to bring this man down from his empyrean heights, I've got to worry him and lead him into making a slip. Trust me, Jacob Singer, my intuition tells me I'm doing the right thing. True, it's thanks to my intuition I married Ed Parker and bedded down with an assortment of rogues who belong in Madame Tussaud's crime museum, but sometimes it can be trusted, like when I decided to make you my friend, Jacob Singer.*

"Mrs. Parker, you are absolutely fascinating," Van Weber said with amazing equanimity.

"Yes, on occasion I can be a bit of a sorceress. Did you know William Desmond Taylor?"

The cup and saucer were placed on the table, and his hands rested at the table's edge, the knuckles showing white. "Everyone's read about that case."

"Jacob Singer suspects there's a link between these murders here and the Desmond Taylor case in Hollywood. Isn't that fascinating?"

"Overpowering."

"Now you can understand why Alec and I are hooked. Mr. Van Weber, you're not listening."

"I'm listening. I haven't missed a word." He glanced at his pocket watch. "If you're to be back in the city by six, we'll have to get going."

"Would you like to come to Neysa's party tonight? She lives just across the hall from me. She makes her own gin. It's absolutely delicious, guaranteed not to induce blindness."

"How very kind of you."

How very formal of you, thought Mrs. Parker, after this afternoon's intimacy. Didn't it matter, she wondered.

"You were about to say something, Mrs. Parker?"

"You can call me Dottie, you know."

"Thank you, old sport, I'd be delighted."

Alexander Woollcott looked like the cock of the walk as he strutted from his West Forty-seventh Street home to the Algonquin Hotel on West Forty-fourth Street. He dutifully waited for traffic lights to change in his favor at all street corners until he reached the corner of Sixth Avenue and West Forty-fourth Street. As chance would have it, he saw George Kaufman strolling on the opposite side of Sixth Avenue toward West Forty-fourth.

"George!" Woollcott shouted as he started to cross the street. "Kaufman! Over here!"

Kaufman heard and turned and saw Woollcott. "Alec!" he shouted. "Get back! Look out!" A woman screamed. Woollcott heard an even shriller scream and realized it was his own. There was an unmarked delivery van bearing down on him.

11

"Alec was poetry in motion," said Kaufman, describing Woollcott's almost fatal brush with death. "I shouted, a woman screamed, Alec screamed, some people hurried to pull him out of the path of the delivery van, but Alec had already taken flight, soaring back onto the sidewalk with a leap that would have brought a blush of envy to Nijinsky's cheeks." Kaufman raised his cup of gin and orange, a rare occasion that he took liquor, in a sincere toast to Woollcott. "Bravo, Alec!"

Woollcott sat as still as a statue of Buddha, introspective, still shaken, wondering how soon it would be before Jacob Singer would arrive to rescue him from his friends. The Round Table was sparsely populated, with only Harold Ross and Robert Benchley at hand to make it a foursome.

"Poor Alec," commiserated Ross, "did your life flash before your eyes?"

The Buddha stirred. The eyes narrowed dangerously into slits. The tongue struck like a flash of lightning. "No, I saw only a parade of you worthless bastards, and what an ugly sight you were."

"Did you see the man behind the wheel?" asked Ross.

"I saw nothing but a brief enticing flash of the afterlife. Actually, I felt a searing surge of anger. I always planned to die on my own terms. For me, nothing less than a martyr's death."

"In the name of what cause?" asked Benchley.

"Myself. The supreme sacrifice." He turned to Kaufman. "I suppose no cool head thought of jotting down his license number?"

"The license plates were masked."

"Oh." Woollcott's voice was soft and tiny. Masked license plates. Vehicle shooting out of the side street without warning. It must have been waiting for me outside the house, thought Woollcott. It followed me here, waiting for an opportunity to strike. I'm a cautious pedestrian. I wait at street corners for the traffic light to favor me. I was safe until I reached this corner, and as fate would have it, there was Kaufman on the opposite side of the street and like a damn fool, I stepped into the gutter to hail him. Poetry in motion.

"What are you smiling at?" asked Kaufman, worrying that Woollcott might be in shock and need precautionary medical attendance.

"I was enjoying a most welcome euphoria."

"Euphoria," said Kaufman, "or against."

"George," said Woollcott solemnly, "I'm the one who should be in a state of shock." He settled back in his chair, looking like a wounded lion waiting for its thorn to be removed. Waiting for Jacob Singer to arrive and comfort him. Kaufman had phoned the detective at Woollcott's request when they arrived in the Algonquin lobby. A patrolman had taken their statements and those of the other witnesses, but that was routine. What had almost befallen Woollcott could not be a forgotten notation in a patrolman's report, Jacob Singer would see to that. He sipped his gin and stared at Kaufman. The look of concern on his face was almost touching. Woollcott knew there was hardly a sentimental bone in the man's body. He was selfish and remote, concerned only with finding the right curtain line for a third act. In any case, they couldn't really discuss the murder attempt without arousing the suspicions of Benchley and Ross, who were enjoying a facetious conversation of their own. It could only be discussed with Singer and, when she got back to the city, with Dottie.

Dottie. Dear God. Is she safe? he wondered, not knowing at this precise moment she was complimenting the condition of a broiled trout.

Kaufman, looking past Woollcott, said, "Here's Jacob Singer."

"Ah," said Woollcott, turning in his seat with an avuncular smile. Benchley and Ross remained absorbed in each other. Not even the announcement of the second coming would have impressed or interrupted them.

"I got here as soon as I could, Mr. Woollcott." He acknowledged Kaufman and ignored the other two, who obviously didn't care to be disturbed. Woollcott stood up and suggested he and Singer repair to the other dining room, which was smaller and quieter.

"I'll phone you later, George. Sorry about our lunch date. I'll take a rain check."

"Take care of yourself," were Kaufman's parting words.

"Now he tells me," snapped Woollcott peevishly as he led the detective out of the Rose Room.

Ten minutes later, seated across from each other at a secluded table, Jacob Singer eyed Woollcott with sympathy. "Somebody's getting nervous," commented Singer.

"So am I," replied Woollcott, drumming on the table with his fingers. Their cups of gin were replenished, and Woollcott said he might manage a club sandwich when Singer suggested food. The waiter took their orders and departed.

Singer smiled. "You look cool and collected, Mr. Woollcott. You handle yourself well under stress."

"Young man," said Woollcott with fire, his juices revived and bubbling, "I have endured and survived the enfilades of German Stukas, I have had more than my share of the slings and arrows of outrageous fortune, but let me tell you, I have never experienced the feeling of such total hopelessness and vulnerability as I did at that precise moment when I realized a man behind a wheel intended to kill me." He wiped his perspiring brow. "I have suffered nothing so deadly since Ethel Barrymore's Juliet. And what about poor Dottie? If an attempt is made on my life at one of the city's most crowded intersections, she's a sitting duck out there in the wilds of Long Island!"

"She's not alone."

"What do you mean 'not alone'? What do we know about Van Weber? The old sport might be a deadly killer!"

"I've had a tail on them from the minute they left her apartment house."

"Oh."

"One of my best boys. Yudel Sherman."

"Have you mentioned him before?"

"He got us the information there was a man with Vera DeLee the night she got murdered."

"Now what about that?"

"What do you want to know?"

"What do you mean what do I want to know?" Woollcott ran his hand anxiously through his hair, leaving it looking like an eroding pasture. "Have you followed up on that? Have you had Horathy or his nurse in the hot seat?"

"All in good time." Singer was buttering a roll as though he were honing a straightedge razor on a strop.

"All in *good* time? You mean all in *bad* time, don't you? I have lost all interest in the possibility of this investigation being my epitaph. You are looking at a ferociously angry man." Singer knew he was hearing a ferociously waspish one. "I resent being nominated for extermination without prior consultation. I like mysteries where you get a warning in advance giving you a fighting chance. I'd have preferred it if someone on the street had slipped me the black ace or a slip of paper with a red X, a little touch of sportsmanship, you know what I mean?"

"There's nothing sporting about hired killers." He was chewing his bread and butter, peacefully ruminating like a bull in a pasture. "The attempt on your life was obviously jobbed out. It wasn't the same bastard who strangled the girls."

"Jobbed out? You mean someone contacts someone else and says, Hey there, interested in knocking off a nuisance for twenty bucks, something like that?" Woollcott was genuinely incredulous. Singer couldn't believe his naïveté. He thought newspapermen were men of the world, sophisticated, knowing the ropes, exchanging such information with each other as who's our friendly neighborhood assassin.

"More like a hundred smackers, Mr. Woollcott. That was the going rate when last I heard."

Woollcott commented quietly, "What an evil world we cohabit in. My dear Jacob, you suddenly take on a completely different coloration. Your job places you in constant danger doesn't it? Someone could come through those drapes carrying a revolver and attempt to kill you."

"No revolver," explained Singer matter of factly, "a twenty-two. It's small enough to fit in the palm of your hand. Nobody sees it until you take aim and fire. It's very effective." Their food was served, and Singer dug into his beef stew with relish. Woollcott stared at his club sandwich with distaste for about thirty seconds, and then hunger overtook him. "Now tell me your version of the incident."

"You mean the attempt to kill me?" The incident. We live in different worlds, Woollcott was beginning to realize, with different vocabularies. The incident. Woollcott began his discourse, and when he was finished, he watched Singer's face and saw nothing of any value except for his usual manly good looks.

Singer finally spoke. "Nothing new in unmarked plates. The delivery van was probably stolen. It'll turn up sometime today abandoned in some back alley. One of the witnesses had a sort of make on the driver." Woollcott's ears perked up. "Nothing too useful, but it's better than a poke in the eye. The witness is a woman, probably the one who screamed when the truck was first seen coming at you. She said the driver wore a cap pulled down over his head to his eyes, which were covered with dark glasses. She thought he was wearing gloves. If he had any brains, he was wearing gloves. He wouldn't want to leave anything on the steering wheel that we could use. Anyway, that description could fit a couple of hundred boys in this town available for those assignments."

Woollcott was about to attack his club sandwich when a disturbing thought occurred. "There could be another attempt on my life."

"I have foreseen that possibility. You'll be having company for a while. At least until we crack this case."

"I see." Woollcott thought for a moment and then inquired with his old hauteur, "Someone presentable, I hope."

"You won't know he's there."

"Oh."

"I've had more bad news." Woollcott waited. "Sid Curley's disappeared." Woollcott remembered, *sniff sniff sniff.* "He was supposed to meet with my other partner, Al Cassidy, but he stood him up. I mean when a police informer is an hour late to a rendezvous, you got to believe he's met with an unfortunate accident. Preplanned, usually."

"Do you suppose Dottie and I talking to him last night might have triggered that?"

"Let us say it could well have been the straw that broke the camel's back. Let's understand each other. You and Mrs. Parker are now in too deep to retreat. You spent the better part of the day snooping with me yesterday, and that would get around fast. And then last night, what with connecting with Curley at the Harlequin, and later at Texas Guinan's"—Singer began chuckling—"taking on Flo Ziegfeld and Lacey Van Weber the way you did . . ."

"I was rather devilish, wasn't I . . ."

"Oh, you were terrific, absolutely terrific."

"Dottie phoned this morning and complimented me, too. Terribly sweet of her. One never knows how one really stands with our Dottie. One moment, she gives you the pat on the head, the next moment, the stiletto in the back. Still, she's rarely dull."

"Anyway, Mr. Woollcott, getting back to Curley's disappearance, let us assume that his somewhat dubious profession finally caught up with him. Now you see, there are a few others who just might be in jeopardy."

"Such as?"

"There's Lily Robson."

"The pill! Was it poisonous?"

"As innocent as a Tootsie Roll."

"Then what could have brought on such a violent attack?"

"My buddy Cassidy suggested food poisoning. My dirty mind inclines more toward a mickey planted in her drink when she wasn't looking."

"You mean by Van Weber?"

"By Van Weber or any number of people. I backtracked on where they ate. Gallagher's. Always crowded. Anybody could slip you a mickey when the house is full. Still, the girl insists she knows nothing." He ordered coffee for two while the waiter cleared the table. "But she's been in a position to hear a lot of things that could be dangerous if she was smart enough to remember them, and then begin adding it all up. I don't think she's smart enough, but somebody might decide not to take any chances. Then there's Charlotte Royce." The look of distaste on Woollcott's face required no explanation. "A snotty little two-bit bitch, but smart. Real smart. Ambitious. That'll trip her up. It usually does." He sat back while their coffee was poured. "Charlotte Royce is really something. She's been deep-sea fishing and she's hauled herself in one of the prize catches, Flo Ziegfeld."

"Do you think Ziegfeld could be seriously involved in these murders? He certainly knew Ilona Mercury."

"He's involved because of knowledge. He knows about the dope scene. Ziegfeld talks a lot. Maybe he's passed something on to the Royce kid." Singer shrugged. "Who the hell knows how people get involved in shit like this, deliberately or inadvertently? You could overhear a conversation at the bar of a gin mill and suddenly end up a marked man."

"I don't have to," said Woollcott indignantly. "I'm already a marked man!"

"Mr. Woollcott, my money's on you. You're a survivor. You'll outlive all of us."

"Well, actually, Jacob," said Woollcott with some pride, "Mrs. Parker once said she thought I'd have to be hammered into my grave."

Singer laughed and then sipped some coffee. "Now for the rest of them who might have had good reason for feeling uncomfortable lately. There's Ziegfeld himself, although I don't think there's any danger of a rubout where he's concerned. There's Bela Horathy, whose very being makes my mouth water at the information I'm sure he's got."

"Then why don't you bring him in for questioning?" demanded Woollcott impatiently.

"Because on the surface he's clean."

"Does he have a license to practice medicine?"

"He sure has. Don't ask me who fixed it up for him, but he's got one. This coffee's lousy."

"It always is. Drown it in cream. What about Horathy's nurse?"

"That's the baby I'm going after. Cora Gallagher. She'll take delicate handling, but I think I smelled her fear when we were in the office yesterday. She can identify who was in Horathy's office when Vera DeLee was there. But you have to go easy with these things. You can't put a scare into a potential witness. I get her nervous, Gallagher might decide to visit her sister in Oregon."

"I had no idea she had one."

"Neither do I. But in an emergency, some distant relative always manages to materialize. Oregon, Manitoba, Passaic, New Jersey, it never fails. Most distracting, but challenging."

"What about that greasy dancer we met last night?"

"George Raft?"

"Yes, Raft."

Singer was lost in thought for a moment. "Raft's a real strange one. The mob uses him as an errand boy. He, by the way, is also of Hungarian extraction."

"Would that be a link to Horathy and Mercury?"

"Just coincidental, I should think. Anyway, I have my

doubts as to whether Ilona Mercury was Hungarian or some other nationality."

"A phony, just as I suspected."

"Probably. In Hollywood for a while she called herself Magda Moreno; God knows what or who she started out in life as. It'll come out in the wash sooner or later. But Raft's got a big mouth. You saw the way he hustled his way into our table last night without an invitation."

"I didn't think Van Weber was too pleased by his presence."

"Van Weber." Singer shook his head as though trying to clear it. "I wish I could get a fix on that guy."

"We'll have to wait until Dottie gets back to town tonight."

"She'll be back by six. I made her promise. Just a precaution. I didn't want her succumbing to Van Weber's charms and spending more time there than she ought to."

"What about Van Weber?"

"You mean as a potential victim?"

"He gets around. He knows a lot of people. He hears things."

"You know what I think, Mr. Woollcott, I think Van Weber is definitely a victim."

"Ah!"

"But not the kind of victim you're thinking. I can't put my finger on it. But I'll say this, he ain't real, you know what I mean? Like I told Mrs. Parker and like I'm sure she told you, he's seemed to have patterned himself on somebody else's creation. Here we have Lacey Van Weber as Jay Gatsby. Now why would he choose to pattern himself on a small-time gangster with lofty pretensions? Why not someone in the grand manner, you know what I mean?"

"Perhaps like me," said Woollcott with a twinkle. "Mrs. Parker told me I'm her favorite character in fiction. Do you suppose she was telling me she finds me unreal?"

"Well, to the naked eye and the uninitiated, you might strike people as a little far out."

"I rather like that," said Woollcott, his old irascible self once again. "I like being far out. I wish I was far out enough to be out of reach." He was bristling again at the thought of his recent brush with death.

"Well, we'll know better about Van Weber, we hope, when Mrs. Parker gets back to town."

"My, my." Woollcott was almost bouncing. "Wait until she hears what I've experienced. Won't that knock her for a loop? By the way, what are you doing tonight?"

"Who knows?"

"Neysa McMein's having a party. Her own bathtub gin. Take it from me, it's vintage. It'll be a madhouse. Everyone will be there. Knowing Mrs. Parker, she'll probably invite Van Weber. That could be helpful."

"Where does McMein live?"

"Just across the hall from Mrs. Parker!" announced Woollcott in a voice that should have been accompanied by a blast of trumpets.

"That's also helpful. I'll be calling on Mrs. Parker to get her report on her day in the country. Why don't you join me? Say I make arrangements with her for eight o'clock? How's that suit you, Mr. Woollcott?"

"It seems to me that would suit me just fine. And by the way, Jacob, I don't think there's that much difference in our ages, do you? I find it awkward being addressed as Mr. Woollcott. Mrs. Parker does because with her it's an affectation. It began when she and Benchley worked together on *Vanity Fair* several years ago. They addressed themselves formally then, and, as you may have noticed, continue to do so. You will find, in time, Mrs. Parker has a variety of quaint affectations, one or two of them at times mind-boggling. So if you don't mind, Jacob, I'd like you to call me Alec. Not Alex, which I loathe, but Alec. Do you think you could manage that?"

"I can manage it, Alec."

"I hope I'm not interrupting." George S. Kaufman sounded concerned.

"Sit down," commanded Woollcott, "and since you owe

me a lunch, you can sign this check."

Kaufman squeezed onto the banquette next to Singer. "Now look, you two, I appreciate what you've been doing for me, but the attempted murder of Alec puts a different perspective on the situation. Mr. Singer, I think I should admit the truth about where Ilona was killed and get Alec off the hook."

"Why, Georgie Kaufman," said Woollcott with a distinct trace of malevolence, "there does breathe a soul under that iceberg exterior. Well, it's too late, fathead. As the priest said to the sailor, I'm in too deep. And I'm sure Jacob agrees with me that for the nonce, you keep both your counsel and your head. There's nothing to be gained by involving you in this mess. You do agree, don't you, Jacob?"

"Absolutely. Just go about your business, Mr. Kaufman, and leave us to go about ours."

"I can't stand having this thing on my conscience," persisted Kaufman.

"George, why don't you go make love to Ferber?" suggested Woollcott.

"I'd rather have this thing on my conscience."

"Exactly. I suppose you succeeded in arousing the suspicions of Harold Ross and Robert Benchley?"

"Not at all. The minute you left the room with Mr. Singer, they forgot you had been there. We played three-handed poker. I lost thirty dollars to Benchley."

"Aren't my friends wonderful?" Woollcott asked Singer, each word dipped in venom. "They're all heart. Kaufman, will I see you and Beatrice at Neysa's tonight?"

"Probably. You've been invited?"

"I will be the moment I phone her. Waiter! Give Mr. Kaufman the check!"

Mrs. Parker felt as though the Pierce-Arrow's wheels were barely touching the asphalt. She and Van Weber might have been back in the Jenny, flying back to the city. She was grateful they weren't. She looked at her wristwatch. They would reach west Fifty-seventh Street with time to spare before six o'clock. Van Weber was strangely silent. He kept looking into his rear-view mirror, and she wondered if it reflected anything special.

"Nothing too special," he said with a gentle smile when she finally asked the question. "We're being followed."

"Oh, my! By anyone interesting?"

"I can't tell. He's keeping a respectable distance. He followed us out from New York."

"Well, then," said Mrs. Parker amiably, "I'm sure he's glad to be getting back to the city at a reasonable hour."

Van Weber roared with laughter.

The laugh is all wrong, Mrs. Parker was thinking. It's out of character. Too loud, too boisterous. It doesn't belong to Lacey Van Weber. She remembered how he laughed because she had memorized all his peculiar traits and movements in the brief time she had known him. Lacey's laugh would be small and introspective, a charming chuckle. The way he chuckled in the garden when she gravely informed him his sundial was slow. She hadn't realized he'd spoken. "Who do you suppose would want to follow us from New York and back?"

"An adventurer?" she suggested.

"A policeman."

"Oh, really? That hadn't occurred to me." It was a feeble rejoinder, and she knew he recognized it as such.

"You're being protected, Mrs. Parker. I'm not trusted. If I'm not to be trusted, why did you spend the day with me?"

"Because I wanted to. Really, Mr. Van Weber, you can't be as ye olde worlde as all that. We've been to bed together. In some parts of this country, that would mean we were practically engaged, if not socially ostracized. You are a most peculiar man, Mr. Van Weber. I am a very curious woman. You fascinate me. I want to know you better. You want me and anyone else to know so much, and no more."

His eyes were glued to the road ahead of him. She hadn't a clue as to what he might be thinking. As far as she was concerned, the devil take the hindmost. She continued chipping away at him, beginning to think this would probably be her only opportunity. She was unhappy at the realization she was falling in love with him. It was all wrong; it couldn't work. It was always all wrong, and it never worked. Somebody said hell is other people. Like hell. Hell is Dorothy Parker's lovers. Well, if so, be it, then she was determined to make capital of this one. After a brief silence, she continued. "People don't like it when someone has something to hide. It's a form of immorality. Looked down upon but highly provocative. What's the secret? Who are you? Where do you come from? Have you any family? How'd you accumulate all that mammon?" Pause. "As in 'I'd walk a million miles for one of your smiles, my mammon.'"

"I don't like to talk about myself," he said in a voice she didn't recognize and didn't like. "The only life I like is the one I have now. What you see is what there is."

"Scott Fitzgerald would be terribly flattered and fascinated to know you've patterned this new life on Jay Gatsby."

"It does seem a bit like him, doesn't it? But Gatsby's a petty racketeer. Do you think I'm a petty racketeer?"

"Mr. Van Weber, I am not naïve. And I don't think you're petty. You're one smart cookie. You have to be to have accumulated all this wealth." She was about to say, If it is all your wealth, but then instinct told her to hold her mouth.

"I've been lucky."

"Is our shadow still with us?"

"Oh, yes, he's back there. Persistent little cuss. We're almost home."

We are, but I'm not, thought Mrs. Parker ruefully. I'm getting nowhere with this man, but I've got a pretty good idea of what he is and what he isn't. It sounds as if I'm thinking in circles, but I'm not. I need so badly to talk this over with Jacob Singer and Woollcott; I need their heads to help me sift and winnow and examine. Because I'm positive this man is *not* his own creation. And there's still time for some idle chitchat. "Whereabouts in Britain do you come from?"

"I was born in London." That didn't come easily, but here it was.

"And then?"

"I grew up."

"I think while still a young man you migrated to this country, and after a stay in New York, where nothing much happened to stimulate you financially, you headed west and settled in Los Angeles."

"That's an interesting scenario."

"You were somehow involved with movie people and met Bela Horathy and Ilona Mercury. Did you ever meet a woman named Magda Moreno?" His jaw went slack.

"I don't recall a Magda Moreno." Chalk one up for Parker. She was very pleased with herself. She was beginning to master the fine art of police interrogation. Smacking him with "Magda Moreno" did it. It proved he had lived in Los Angeles. She was convinced her scenario was right. London to New York to Los Angeles. She had to move fast. They had come over the bridge and were now on East Fifty-seventh Street heading west to her apartment house. It was ten minutes to six.

"Did you meet Valentino there or did you know him when he and Raft were dancing for dollars?"

"My dear, my dear," he said with a doleful sigh. "I can see where you could be a terribly nagging wife."

Here it is, she thought, momentarily dejected, the kiss-off. The final fadeout. Music up and audience out. "I'm a very poor wife," she said. "I haven't the vaguest idea where my husband is, and if anybody tells me, I shall sink into a subterranean dejection, not even emerging to cast my shadow. I never told you about Ed, did I? But how could I? There hasn't been time. Ed was an alcoholic. A quart a day man. Then he graduated to narcotics. Morphine mostly. Occasionally a puff of opium, with a smart dash of cocaine every now and then. When last heard from, he was promising to commit himself to a sanitarium for a drying-out or whatever it is addicts do to sidestep a swipe from the grim reaper. I hope he makes it. He's really a nice guy. Deadly dull, but nice."

They were parked in front of her building. "Thank you for a very interesting day, Mr. Van Weber."

"Isn't it about time you called me Lacey and I called you Dottie?"

"Well, quite frankly, I've had the sinking feeling you might not be calling me again."

"Tut, young woman. You must learn to have more faith in yourself. I'm used to questions and people trying to pry into my background. I was delighted to give the interview to the *Graphic* though I had been strongly advised not to." By whom, wondered Mrs. Parker. "I gave the interview in order to put paid to any further inquiries about myself."

"You didn't know there was tenacious old me creeping up from the backfield."

"A charming turn of events. You're gracious company, I enjoy your wit, and it was marvelous making love to you."

"I'm so glad you said that," she said somewhat capriciously. "I'm usually not at my best at matinees."

"As to our question and answer sessions"—he smiled his catnip smile, letting her know he was once again in total control of the situation—"I found them amusing. Did you learn what you wanted to know?"

Audacious bastard, she thought as she started to get out of the car. "Lacey, old sport, I think I hit a couple of bull's-eyes."

"Am I still invited to join you at Neysa McMein's tonight?"

"If you're game, we're on. The festivities usually don't hot up until about ten. Why don't you tap on my door about then, and then arm in arm we can go gaily skipping across the corridor into Neysa's."

"I'll see you then." He pulled away into traffic, leaving her on the sidewalk in a cloud of exhaust fumes.

At ten minutes to six, from a phone booth in a cigar store down the street from the building housing Bela Horathy's office, Jacob Singer phoned the doctor and, as he hoped, was intercepted by Cora Gallagher. Earlier he had the desk sergeant at the precinct phone and double check on the doctor's office hours. Two to six in the afternoons, mornings by appointment. He was sure she wouldn't recognize his voice, having exchanged but a few sentences with him the previous day. He asked if it was possible to see the doctor within the next ten minutes, and she curtly informed him the office was closing. Would he care to make an appointment for the following day? Singer said he'd let her know and hung up. He left the cigar store, crossed the street and positioned himself in a doorway where he could watch for Cora Gallagher without arousing suspicion. After a fifteen-minute wait, Cora Gallagher came striding out of the building. Out of nurse's uniform and in street clothes, she looked like a local housewife out for some last-minute shopping. She passed Singer without a flicker of recognition and walked purposefully toward a subway entrance at the end of the street. There, Singer caught up with her and gently held her by the elbow. Startled, she stopped walking and looked from his hand holding her elbow to his face, which favored her with a friendly smile. He did look familiar to her, but she couldn't place him. "What do you want?" she asked brusquely.

"I want to talk to you. We met yesterday in your office. I was there with Dorothy Parker and Alexander Woollcott."

Her face was ashen. "I remember. You're the detective. Well, what do you want?"

"I'd like an ice cream soda. How about you? There's an ice cream parlor on Lexington I like."

"I'm late. I have to get home."

"You'll get home sooner if you just give me some of your time. And if we don't move away from this entrance, we're in danger of being trampled to death. How's about it? A strawberry soda with vanilla cream. Just the dish to top off a scorcher like today."

"You've got no right to bother me like this."

"I thought an ice cream parlor would be much more pleasant than my office in my precinct. That's dull, dingy, hot and it smells. Be nice and maybe I'll invite you to the policeman's ball."

Bela Horathy stood under the canopy of his building. He adjusted a monocle in his right eye and gave his gray derby a dapper pat. He adjusted the walking stick that hung from his left hand and then took a harder look toward the subway entrance where he recognized his nurse talking to a man. It was after the two went around the corner out of sight toward Lexington Avenue that he remembered the man with Cora was Detective Jacob Singer. Horathy hurried back to his office.

Lacey Van Weber was secluded in the study of his penthouse apartment on Central Park South. He wore his favorite dressing gown designed for him by Paul Poiret of Paris. One of the windows of the study opened onto the terrace which overlooked Central Park. In his hand he held a tall glass of Scotch and water with just a small piece of ice, the perfect picture of the perfect gentleman enjoying the twilight in his perfect setting. Everything about him was perfect except his state of mind. His butler had given him a message received during his absence. He was to expect an important phone call from a very important gentleman with a particular gift for creating other important gentlemen. Van Weber sipped his drink and watched the strollers in the park. Above the hum of traffic from the streets below, he could hear the distant strains of the orchestra playing for tea dancing in the park casino. From another direction he heard the hurdy-gurdy refrains of the carousel and, from a terrace below, a woman's seductive laugh. Behind him he heard the telephone and hurried to answer it. It was a private line, unavailable to his staff. Seated at the desk, he spoke into the phone. A voice at the other end was cordial and melodious, bespeaking good breeding and perfect manners. It asked a question, and Van Weber described his day with Mrs. Parker, leaving nothing out. He was precise and businesslike, sounding as though he were delivering the minutes of the previous meeting of the board members of a respectable business organization. Yes, Mrs. Parker did a great deal of prying. Yes, he sidestepped her questions with the precision of the senior half of a ballroom team. Yes, she's quite a clever woman, and yes, she is deeply involved with Jacob Singer in matters pertaining to murder and narcotics and he did agree she could be dangerous. His face was noncommittal at the news an attempt on Woollcott's life had failed. There was nothing in the evening paper he had purchased. He agreed that it was wiser to stay with Mrs. Parker and continue to misdirect her until the weekend and do his best to avoid any slip-ups. Jacob Singer was something else. He had no control there. He was told none was necessary on his part. When asked if he was developing a soft spot in his heart for Mrs. Parker, he refrained from shouting "Certainly not." He said she was charming and witty and remarkably gifted in bed and being with her was no strain. He said he would be with her at Neysa McMein's party in just a few hours and was severely cautioned to be on his guard there; that bunch played rough. He also learned Bela Horathy was a bit unhappy with his nurse, Cora Gallagher, having seen her in the company of Jacob Singer. Van Weber made no comment and waited.

There was more to be told. Raft had been cautioned by the "man," and there was hope that this time the cocky little bastard had learned a lesson. Furthermore, the biggest shipment the enterprise had ever attempted would be smuggled in on Saturday night. Would it be possible to plan an impromptu weekend at East Cove inviting Mrs. Parker and Woollcott and several others, thus bringing to a climax the magnificent venture that had required years of preparation and could now safely be closed down? Van Weber's mouth was dry, his voice husky. He would do his best about the weekend. These people were like quicksilver. The voice at the other end was polite but firm. The impromptu weekend was a necessity, a cover for the arrival of the shipment. There was the promise that Van Weber would now be a very wealthy man, wealthy enough to return to Europe and there create a final identity for himself. Did Van Weber understand? Van Weber understood.

There was a gentle knock at the door, and his valet announced his bath was drawn. Van Weber shouted he'd be there in a few minutes. Into the phone he said goodbye, until later, and after hanging up, took a very deep draught of the drink and stared out the window toward the park.

Mrs. Parker. What to do about Mrs. Parker? What to do? What to do? I haven't felt this way about a woman since . . . well, what does it matter? But Mrs. Parker is something else, and I don't dare tell her. I don't ever dare tell her. I must not care this much about Dorothy Parker.

Cora Gallagher's lemon phosphate was growing warm. She hadn't even sampled it. It just sat there on the table in front of her, ignored, unwanted, an orphan without prospects. She and Jacob Singer were sharing a quiet booth in the rear of the ice cream parlor, and after placing their order, Jacob hadn't wasted words.

"Miss Gallagher, you have a record."

"That's not news to me. Is it news to you?"

She was prepared to brazen it out. Singer liked that. He wanted her to have courage because by the time he got through with her, she would need it. "Miss Gallagher, I stopped being surprised the day I found out me and girls were built different. I know you're in a hurry and so am I, so let's not waste each other's time and get right down to it. Who was Horathy's last patient the day before yesterday?"

"Vera DeLee."

"I said let's not waste time. There was a man. The elevator operator put a fix on him. He came down the elevator with DeLee. They left together. They went to her place. Elevator operator there corroborates man went up to DeLee's apartment." The phosphate and the ice cream soda had arrived, and impatiently, Singer told the waitress not to fuss. She stopped fussing and vanished. Cora Gallagher wished she could vanish, but she knew she couldn't; she worked for a doctor, not a magician. Singer spooned some ice cream into his mouth and decided she'd had enough time to think. "Don't make me lean on you, Miss Gallagher. This man is suspected of murdering DeLee." He waited twenty seconds. "When was the last time you saw your parole officer?"

"I don't know the man's name and that's the truth. He's one of the patients Horathy sees after office hours, like DeLee. He gives them their booster shots."

"Give me a booster, Miss Gallagher. Describe him."

She leaned forward. "Will you please believe me when I tell you I've never had a good look at his face? Will you, please?"

"Why not?"

"He's always got a handkerchief to his nose. He holds it so that it covers most of his face. Another thing, I'm not always there after six o'clock. Some nights I go and Horathy stays on and I don't know what goes on then, that's the truth, so help me Hannah!"

"I believe you, I believe you. Don't you like your drink?"

"I'm not thirsty. Can I go now?"

"Not yet. I'm still lonely. How big's this guy?"

"Well, he's about your height." Singer nodded and sucked on his straw. "Broad shouldered, I mean for real, not padded; I can tell those things." Singer made gurgling noises with the straw. He'd made gurgling noises with soda straws since he'd first learned what ice cream sodas were all about. "No paunch. I'd guess he was your age."

"What's he on?"

"I don't know."

"Horathy keeps records, doesn't he?"

"There's a locked file I never get to see. He keeps the key. There's only one key."

"Didn't the man give you a name the other night?"

"He said something like the man or Mr. Man. I swear, I couldn't really tell what he was saying with that rag covering his mouth."

"What his voice like?"

"Hoarse. Unpleasant. Honest to God, I was really in a state because I had DeLee passed out in the small office and I was afraid she was going to croak on me."

"Does Horathy usually overshoot?"

"What do you mean?"

"Overdose."

"God, no! He's very careful. He doesn't want a stiff on his hands. He . . ." She sat back, crestfallen. Singer had gotten what he was after. She'd talked too much. He was very pleased with himself and thought of adopting her lemon phosphate, but he was already feeling a slight discomfort from his ice cream soda. "Give me a break, Mr. Detective. If Horathy knows I'm with you, I could be singing the bye-bye blues."

"Sister, you soon won't have to be worrying about Horathy. Let's get back to DeLee. The autopsy report says she was doped up past her ears."

"We think she'd taken something before she came to the office. She's done it before. Horathy warned her. But she had this kidney disease. I think it was killing her. She was in terrible pain."

"What was Horathy's relation to Rudolph Valentino?"

"I'm only guessing. I think they knew each other in Hollywood some years back. Horathy didn't like him."

"What about Ilona Mercury?"

"She was Horathy's girlfriend then."

"When she was Magda Moreno?"

"I don't know anything about that. Ilona was a phony. She lived in some other world. She had lots of worlds. Some Hungarian. Some Russian. Once French. She was good with accents."

"And imagination."

"And imagination. We were surprised when she landed in a Ziegfeld show. I mean, she was at least ten years older than his other showgirls. But she had a magnificent body."

"It didn't look all that magnificent on a slab."

"I don't know anything about how she died, I swear on my mother's grave."

"Your mother lives out in Bensonhurst." She had the decency to blush. "Swear on your husband's grave."

"I spit on that."

"That's what I like about some of you broads. All heart. What about Mercury and Horathy? Why was he paying her? Was it simple blackmail or something a little more sophisticated?"

"A tablespoon of each. She steered him patients."

"Meaning dopers."

"I suppose."

"Do I have to say 'pretty please'?"

"Aw, Christ, yes." She slumped in her seat. "Will you believe me when I tell you I've been looking to get out? Will you?"

"I believe you, Miss Gallagher. I honestly do believe you. So why don't you?"

"I'm afraid." She looked around as though for the first time it occurred to her they might be overheard.

"Why'd you link up with Horathy in the first place?"

"Ever been on parole, Mr. Detective? Ever looked for a decent job when you got a record? Prostitution, petty larceny, what am I offered, the mangle in a steam laundry. I had enough of that in stir. I knew Sid Curley. You know him?"

"Knew him. He's on the missing persons bulletin."

"My God," she whispered.

"We think he's been planted in the middle of the Hudson. I wish they'd stop. It's scaring the fish away, they tell me. So Curley fixed you up with Horathy."

"Yes."

"Who fixed you your nurse's registration?"

"Somebody with a direct line to City Hall."

"Like maybe Judge Crater?"

"Maybe." She looked tired and spent. Singer didn't peg

her at being more than just a trace past thirty. Now she looked fifty.

"Do you know Lacey Van Weber?"

"Horathy's mentioned his name."

"Is he a patient?"

"No."

"But they're friendly."

"I think so."

Singer was growing impatient. "What do you mean, you think so? Horathy was at Van Weber's party the night Valentino took the mickey. Valentino laid him to filth, your good doctor."

"They didn't like Valentino."

"I'll bet they didn't. He knew too much about shoot-up parties back in Hollywood. He probably knew just as much about what's going on here. Do you know if Van Weber's a good dancer?"

She snorted. "What a dumb question. You been doing just great until now. How would I know if he's a good dancer? He ain't never invited me to any tea parties at the Plaza."

"Maybe someday somebody will."

"Sure. Cora Gallagher. The queen of the ball. What else do you want to know?"

"Beginning to enjoy yourself?"

"I'm out so far in the deep, I may as well keep swimming."

"Tell me who he's feeding dope to. I want big names." She reeled off several names. "That's real good, Miss Gallagher. Go to the head of the class. Who does he deal with in the police department?"

"That, I really swear to you, I do not know."

"But there's somebody."

"There has to be, right?"

"Yeah. That's the punch in the belly. There has to be. Cora, you've been a good girl. It's a shame you wasted your lemon phosphate, but you did me good." He told her how to contact him if she needed him. She hoped she wouldn't need him, but they both knew better. "Now leave here by yourself. You can go home now."

"I'm not going home. I'm going to see Gloria Swanson's new movie. She makes me feel better. She gets into worse trouble than I do. So long. Thanks for the buggy ride."

Tell him the man is here. Or Mr. Man. Or maybe Mr. Mann. I wonder.

Mrs. Parker, fresh from her cooling bath, finally got through to Woollcott. "Your line has been engaged for almost an hour," she scolded. "There was enough time there for me to have conceived and aborted."

"And did you?" rasped Woollcott.

"I've had quite a day."

"Nothing to compare with mine!" He impaled her ear with a dramatic recital of the attempt on his life which Mrs. Parker on her end punctuated with an occasional "oh, no!" or "dear me, no!" or "oh, poor Alec." Finished, she heard Woollcott gasping for air and thought he certainly deserved a thunderous round of applause. She realized it was an opportunity to get her own oar in.

"I'm glad Jacob has assigned you protection."

"Protection! I don't even know what he looks like. I have a fear I'll be spending the rest of my life looking over my shoulder!"

"Well, Alec, at last you're a hero. And heaven knows we seriously lack for heroes. Have you any idea where Jacob is? I dutifully called him at the precinct at six, but he wasn't there. He's had me shadowed all day, too, by the way."

"Well, I should think so, now that both our heads are on the chopping block."

"I don't quite see myself as Anne Boleyn, but I'm digressing." She was also wondering if the man assigned to trail her had by some miracle managed to detect what had gone on in Lacey Van Weber's bedroom. "I must see you both before Neysa's shindig."

"You are. At eight o'clock sharp, in your digs. Jacob arranged that with me at lunch."

"Oh, how nice, you lunched."

"It was very kind and thoughtful of him to rush to my side in my hour of need. Anyway, my tarnished tulip, it's past seven now and I haven't quite finished my toilette. Release me and I'll see you at eight."

"Be very careful."

"Now she tells me." They hung up simultaneously. In a rare state of efficiency, Mrs. Parker phoned Charlotte Royce and just missed her. She had left for the theater. Mrs. Parker left a message and then asked the operator to locate a number for Lily Robson. The number was located, but Miss Robson was not at home either.

In a bedroom in the employees' barracks of Van Weber's estate in East Cove, the man with the steel plate in his head and part of his earlobe missing asked his roommate, the man with the scar on his right cheek running from his ear to his mouth, if he wanted to drive into Great Neck to see a movie.

"What movie?"

"I'm thinkin' of *The Black Pirate.*"

"Who's in it?"

"Douglas Fairbanks."

"That fag."

"He ain't no fag. He's married to Mary Pickford."

"Lotsa fags get married."

"Not to Mary Pickford. Y'comin' or y'ain't comin'?"

"I ain't comin'. I'm too tired. Last night on the river knocked me out. Where do y'get your energy? Y'run around too much. Take it easy. Y'new around here, you'll soon learn to take it easy. Like y'know we got a big Saturday night comin' up. Lotsa kilos to unload. Did y'know?"

"I heard."

"Y'still goin' to the movies?"

"Sure I'm still goin'. It's early, ain't it?"

"Y'll need a pass."

"I already got one."

"Okay. Don't make no noise when y'come home."

Yudel Sherman was exhausted. Tailing somebody in the city was one thing, peaches and cream easy, lots of doorways to duck into when you think the tail is getting suspicious. But out in the open there are no doorways, maybe a tree to hide behind, but not when you're behind the wheel of a Ford with a rattling rumble seat. The only thing he enjoyed was the powerful pair of binoculars with which he had been provided. He managed to see a few things he didn't expect to see, and enjoyed seeing Jacob Singer's cheeks redden when he apprised him of what he happened to see in somebody's bedroom in East Cove. "I guess they thought they didn't have to pull down the window shades all the way out there."

"Ain't you got no respect for people's privacy?" asked Al Cassidy.

"I saw them by accident," explained Yudel.

"Don't sound to me like no accident," said Cassidy.

"It was a head-on collision."

Singer was typing up his notes on his interview with Cora Gallagher. Occasionally, Cassidy looked over his shoulder. Singer asked him to stop breathing down his neck.

"Is there anything special on for tonight?" asked Cassidy.

"No. But keep in touch with the precinct."

"Where will you be, Jake?" asked Yudel.

"I'm going to a party with Woollcott."

"You two going steady?" asked Cassidy.

"No," replied Singer, "he hasn't asked me."

"How come, I wonder," pressed Cassidy.

"I think he's just shy. Now why don't you go get your dinner or go fuck yourself, whichever is the most pressing."

"Okay. See you later." Cassidy left.

"You want to hear more," asked Yudel, "or have I told you enough?"

"You ain't told me anything about that place we don't already know."

"It's real pretty. Lotsa marble fauns and things like that

there. A real shame it ain't used for anything real useful."

"By them it's useful. Yudel, you don't have to hang around."

"I got no place to go."

"Go home to your wife!"

"Oh, yeah, I forgot about her."

"Why don't you try calling her up? Maybe it's still the same number."

"Very funny."

Texas Guinan's apartment in Greenwich Village was a monument to bad taste. Instead of doors, there were beaded drapes, which an old beau had suggested were probably inspired by her beady eyes. The furniture was frayed old plush, with oranges, reds and browns predominating. Strewn around the room was a variegated collection of Kewpie dolls and teddy bears. The grand piano groaned under the weight of numerous framed photographs of celebrities and relatives (she adored her brother, Tommy Guinan, a small-time hood in Larry Fay's employ), some autographed, some bogus, such as one of President Calvin Coolidge wearing an Indian headdress. The windows were draped with velvet green materials artfully run up for her by two reformed prostitutes she had financed with sewing machines (actually conned out of a scion of the Singer family who owed her a favor). The carpet covering the living room floor was interwoven with fauns and satyrs, uninhibited, and Texas was now reclining on a chaise longue wishing George Raft would stop wearing a path in her favorite floor covering.

"So whaddya want me to do?" snarled Guinan as she reached for a bottle of gin to refill the glass she was holding.

"I want you to tell them to lay offa me. The son of a bitch almost bust my ribs! Supposing I had to dance tonight, just supposing!"

"Well, you don't gotta dance tonight, and for Chrissakes will you light someplace, you're making me nauseous with that pacing up and down. You want to pace up and down, go over to Roosevelt Hospital and wait for some sucker to give birth."

Raft sank morosely into a morris chair. "Van Weber promised me. He promised me a lotta things."

"Oh, sure. Like Valentino promised you."

"Rudy was setting me up a screen test, wasn't he?"

"Was he?"

"He said he was."

"You'll never know now."

He was back on his feet again. "I gotta get out of this town, I tell you."

"Why don't you go to Chi for a couple of months?"

"You trying to get rid of me?"

"For crying out loud, you're the one who's bellyaching about getting out of town!" She took a long gulp of gin, winked one eye with pleasure and smacked her lips with gusto. "What a way to die!"

"They better lay offa me, Tex, they really better lay offa me."

"Or . . .?"

"They'll see."

"They better not see. Or you won't see. Now sit down and tell me I'm gorgeous. Then maybe if you're a good boy, I'll take you to a real wild party. You see, Georgie, it's like I keep telling you. You're too anxious. You push yourself where you're not wanted. They told you to relax and hold your water. They told you if you ran their errands like a good boy, they'd spend the money and groom you for the big time. But you can't rush them. You got to let them do it in their own good time. Look at me. Look at where they put me. And look at Van Weber. They sure made him look good." He started to speak, but she waved him not to interrupt. "I wasn't impatient, and Van Weber wasn't impatient. So you mustn't be impatient. You should also learn to look before you speak."

"Whaddya mean?"

"You don't think. You just start running off at the mouth. Half the times you sound as though you don't know what you're saying. And just too often you say the wrong thing. Little things, but the wrong little things. I heard about that slip-up you almost made on Denny."

"That's all it was! A slip-up!"

She swung her legs off the chaise and sat up with anger. "A damn dangerous slip-up! That's why they sent the man up to your room."

"You knew he was sent and you didn't warn me?"

"Tex Guinan looks out for number one and only number one. I told you that when we first hooked up. I ain't no spring chicken, kiddo. In any other society I'm a back number, yesterday's news. With these guys, God bless every one of the murdering bastards, I'm the one and only Texas Guinan! The Queen of the Nightclubs!" She waved the bottle of gin imperially, her sceptre. "And someday the whole world will know about Georgie Raft. But in the meantime, while they're waiting for the news, come crawl over here and give me a big fat nasty old wet kiss."

Mrs. Parker had thoughtfully provided Chinese food for her guests. Neysa McMein rarely catered her parties with other than peanuts and other nibbles, not wishing to detract from the main attraction, her homemade gin. Woollcott was not a partisan of Chinese food, but the delicious aroma soon lured and entrapped him and he piled his plate high. Jacob Singer was a Chinese food enthusiast, he could eat it every night of the week, and this week it seemed that was exactly what he was doing. Mrs. Parker nibbled daintily at a spare-rib when she remembered there was food on her plate. While the men ate, Mrs. Parker described the estate, the impressive boat dock, the magnificent landscaping, at one point Woollcott testily commenting her discourse belonged in an edition of *Vanity Fair*. She then told them of the automobile tour with Lacey Van Weber and the wrong turning that brought them to the compound within the compound and the imposing stone building with smoke pouring from the slate chimney.

"That's their lab," said Singer.

"How do you know?" asked Woollcott.

"I know. I know a lot of things. I know what they do to morphine there. You know anything about morphine?" He put his plate aside. "It's odorless, tasteless. It takes great skill and patience to convert it into cocaine."

"Why do they bother," asked Woollcott. "Isn't morphine effective as just morphine?"

"Bigger bucks in cocaine. The chemist who does the converting has to really know his job. Because to produce the powder, you run the risk of deadly toxic fumes and an explosion."

"No wonder the building's isolated," realized Mrs. Parker.

"Exactly," corroborated Singer. "Continue, please, Mrs. Parker."

He resumed eating while she picked up the thread of her narrative. "I saw two incredibly ugly men at the lab. Quite ugly and I'm sure quite threatening." She described the scar on the cheek and the partially missing ear. Woollcott grimaced with distaste. Singer continued eating, now picking in the chop suey for pieces of shrimp.

"Tell us about Van Weber," prodded Singer. "What did you get out of him?"

"Not too much, but I think what I got is choice. You won't like this, Mr. Singer, but I told him just about everything you told us was in the reports from Los Angeles."

"That's okay. Sometimes you got to feed them carrots to get their jaws moving."

"At one point I asked him about his life and I got this much, or at least I suspect this much and I'm pretty sure I'm right. He was born in London, came to New York while a youngster where I think he first met Valentino . . ."

". . . and Raft," contributed Singer.

Woollcott snapped his fingers. "Of course! They were probably dance floor hustlers together."

"By all means," said Singer matter of factly, "which is why Van Weber was probably not all that happy when Valentino showed up at his party that night with Ilona Mercury. I have a feeling it was Raft that brought the two of them to the party. I'll have to ask him, but it's not all that important. We know they were there and set off a little explosion."

"Van Weber has probably changed a great deal since those days," suggested Mrs. Parker. "I mean physically."

"Oh, sure," agreed Singer, "he's got a different look because he's got more class." He smiled at Mrs. Parker. "Go on. From New York to where, Hollywood?"

"Yes."

"Try to get into the movies? He's got the looks."

"I think he went there to look up someone he knew quite well, someone in with that whole doping crowd. Desmond Taylor, Mabel Normand, that fun bunch."

"Okay. Sounds good. Out there he meets Horathy and Mercury under whatever alias she's using at the time, and then where?"

"I think big trouble sent him to earth." Woollcott was fascinated with Mrs. Parker's deductions.

"What big trouble?"

"Well, the only big trouble I can think of is Desmond Taylor's murder. That sent an awful lot of them scurrying for cover."

"Mrs. Parker, if I wasn't chewing on some lo mein, I'd give you a big kiss."

"That's all right," said Mrs. Parker with an unusually sweet smile, "it's the thought that counts."

"So what else you got to tell us?" asked Singer.

"Did he make a pass at you?" asked Woollcott.

"Alec," said Mrs. Parker softly, "this is my apartment, not a china shop."

"Well, if he made a pass at you and you responded, it's one way to loosen his lips." He thought for a moment. "I'm sure I didn't mean to say that that way."

"Any way you say it, Alec, would be the wrong way." She examined a fingernail. "Yes, he made a pass at me, and yes, I responded, and no, it didn't loosen his lips, it loosened mine." Singer kept his eyes on his food. She hoped she hadn't embarrassed him. After all, they were adults, and what's a roll in the hay in this day and age. "We are now in his car driving back to town, me anxious to make my six o'clock deadline."

"One of the few you've ever made," said Woollcott while trying to cross a leg.

"I laid it on the line," not caring whether "laid it" was the right choice of words or not. "I asked him how come he patterned himself on a petty racketeer like Jay Gatsby."

"Weren't you the brave one," commented Woollcott.

"Well, our boy is not exactly a babbling brook. There's a rather dear, sweet sadness about him if you ignore his rather cruel eyes, but in the conversation department, he's just about a barrel of laugh. Anyway, he made rather light of the suggestion, but I could tell I'd struck a nerve. Like the way he reacted when I asked him had he ever met a Magda Moreno in Hollywood."

Singer looked up. "You didn't tell us you'd asked him that."

"Didn't I?" She looked as though she'd been caught with her hand in a cookie jar. "I could have sworn I did, but I guess I've been skipping all over the place. I didn't dare take notes, it's just all in my head, somewhere. Well, I asked him that, and I thought he had a momentary difficulty steadying the wheel." She looked at her friends gravely. "We're not kidding him, you realize. He's wise to what we're up to."

"It's no secret," said Singer, finally finished eating. "I want him to know. I want them all to know. I want them nervous, worried . . ."

"Or just plain angry and gunning for me," snapped Woollcott petulantly. "Dear God, do you realize Neysa's party might have been my wake?"

"What a sweet thought," said Mrs. Parker.

Singer reclaimed center stage. "Your boyfriend seems pretty sure he can outsmart us, doesn't he?"

"Yes, he does. He's coming to the party."

"Nice. I like that," complimented Singer.

"It is a nice touch, isn't it," said Mrs. Parker amiably. "I think he's quite smitten with me."

"I think you're quite smitten with him," countered Woollcott.

"It could be easy, you know. Oh, dear, I can see Mr. Singer disapproves of this trend in our conversation. So let me tell you my theory." She had their attention. "I don't think any of this wealth Mr. Van Weber displays is his."

"Really?" Woollcott was gazing out the window while digesting what Mrs. Parker was feeding them.

"I think he's a front for an organization. He was created by them to be Lacey Van Weber, wealthy man about town, man of mystery, landed gentry, though God knows where he's landed, a seductive celebrity who gets to know everybody who's anybody." She added somewhat sadly, "I think one day they'll be finished with him, and he'll be discarded."

"How sad," said Woollcott wryly, "just when I was beginning to like him."

"What are you thinking, Mr. Singer?" One couldn't ignore the wistfulness in her voice.

"I'm thinking if the two of you ever decide to give up writing, you'd make one hell of a pair of detectives."

"Isn't that sweet. Alec, that is sweet, isn't it?"

"Don't overdo it, Dottie. The role of Little Eva ill suits you."

Singer steered the conversation to Cora Gallagher and the man who hid his face with a handkerchief. He shaded his information with an occasional nuance, theorizing on what Ilona Mercury's part had been in this misbegotten melodrama.

"I think she knew Lacey Van Weber in Hollywood," said Mrs. Parker.

"More than likely," agreed Singer. He thought for a moment, and then said, "There's some hot action scheduled out at East Cove this Saturday night."

Mrs. Parker's eyes were again wide with surprise. "You have an informant out there!" They heard no denial. "I'll bet you knew everything I had to tell you before I told you."

"I'm not that good, Mrs. Parker."

"You're certainly trying to be," she replied.

"I hope I still have my guardian angel following in my wake," said Woollcott grouchily.

"Indeed you do. And there's one for you, Mrs. Parker."

"Why, Mr. Singer, are you telling me you think I'm— how does gangland put it—on the spot?"

"You may be in for a little more action than you planned on."

"How funny. I'm not the least bit afraid," she said.

"Well, why should you be!" exploded Woollcott. "As often as you've placed yourself at death's door!"

"Well, darling man, we both know there are two things in life that are completely unavoidable, death and taxes!" She went to a floor-length mirror to examine her dress for wrinkles. "Do you like my dress? I bought it in Paris. It's by Edward Molyneux."

"It's a knockout," said Singer.

"I'm so glad you like it."

"I'm sure he'll like it, too," said Woollcott.

"Who?" she asked.

"Mr. Van Weber."

"Oh. Yes. I'm sure he'll like it. He's picking me up at ten."

"It's almost that now," said Singer, rising and speaking to Woollcott. "Is it too early for us to join the party?"

Woollcott had arisen and was preening at Mrs. Parker's mirror. "It's never too early to join a party. It shall undoubtedly be Neysa's usual madhouse. Utter bedlam. A tower of babel. But I shall look after you, Jacob, I'll most certainly look after you."

Mrs. Parker was at the window. If he came in his car, Van Weber would have trouble finding a parking space. A cab had pulled up at the canopy disgorging what looked like Franklin P. Adams and his wife, Esther. "I think Frank Adams is here. I can't really tell without my glasses." She said with a smile to Singer, "I'm so nearsighted. Oh, come now, Alec, why such a dour expression? What are you thinking about?"

"Zippers," replied Mr. Woollcott.

The man. Mr. Man. Mr. Mann. My man?

Mrs. Parker was reviewing Singer's interrogation of Cora Gallagher in her mind as she hurried to the kitchen to dump the remnants of the Chinese dinner. It was a rare sight, Dorothy Parker tidying up her apartment, and she thought it was too bad there was no resident movie camera to record the historic occasion. She opened the windows and with her flowing silk handkerchief, which she waved like a sailor gone berserk making semaphores, tried to whisk the stale odor of food out of the room. For good measure, she attacked the air with an atomizer, the odor of which reminded her of a French whorehouse the Murphys had taken her to one larkish night in Cap d'Antibes. She drew the screen that separated the tiny kitchen from the studio and then decided to rearrange the furniture. There was not much furniture to rearrange, so that chore was completed in under five minutes.

She was uneasy. She sat down. Her heart was pounding. She fluttered the handkerchief under her nose. This was worse than trying to compose a poem or outline a short story. This anxiety now enveloping her was born of fear. It had finally sunk in. It was no longer a lark. An attempt had been made on Woollcott's life; an attempt might be made on hers. Indirectly, she thought it had. She had been taken to bed by Lacey Van Weber. Was it genuine emotion on his part or a move to lull her into a sense of false security, to give her the feeling she was safe because he was falling in love with her? Love, nepenthe, it was all the same. She looked at her wrists.

What are you thinking about?

Zippers.

Dottie's declared war on her wrists again. Big joke. Ross laughs at Dottie and Benchley laughs at Dottie and Ferber laughs at Dottie. Ferber with her head like a bison. She belongs on a nickel. Ferber doesn't slit her wrists for the loss of love; she writes another best-seller and fattens her bank balance. She's not just rich, she's RICH. And what do I do when the guy walks out? I write a sad little poem with a cute little twist in its tail, and most everyone chortles and says "Dear little Dottie, she's so cute and clever."

Oh, Christ. Her eyes were misting up. She hurried to her dressing table to repair them. There was a knock at the door. Oh, Christ. "Just a minute," she yodeled, while in the hallway Lacey Van Weber could hear the party hotting up from behind the door of the Baragwanath ménage. Mrs. Parker opened her door wide and smiled, "Well, here you are."

"Not too early, I hope?" he asked as he walked in and she closed the door ever so gently. He was dressed in Palm Beach blue and wore smart white and blue oxfords. His shirt was open at the collar, and she wished he'd take her right then and there. But no, one mustn't look too messy when making an entrance at Neysa's.

"Not at all. Don't you look cool? Would you like a drink, or should we go straight on in to Neysa's?"

"I want to talk to you first." He took her hand and led her to the couch, where they sat down, his grip on her hand tightening.

"I may be going away soon."

"Oh?"

"For quite a long time."

"Well, I guess there goes the profile I wanted to write on you. Shot down in flames."

"Come with me."

She was jolted by those three words. It was always like

-212-

that when under the siege of a surprise attack. It was an occasion when she wished she had a delicate pink lace fan which, with the practiced dexterity of an antebellum Southern belle, she could pop open and flutter under her chin while making delicate little movements with her eyes, half-shaded demurely by their lids. Even what she said matched the banality of what she was thinking: "Why, Lacey, this is so sudden."

"Something's come up and I've decided to get away."

Get away. What he means is, he's lamming out. "Lacey, we hardly know each other. You can't be serious. To go away together we have to be in love, we have to . . . I don't know, I'm not thinking straight."

"We could go somewhere where nobody would know us."

"Not know us?" Dorothy Parker eternally condemn herself to *anonymity*? Is he madly in love or is he just plain mad? "I don't know what to say. It's not a decision I can make on the spur of the moment. You can't expect me to throw over my life, my friends, and for God's sake there's my husband . . ." She knew someday he'd come in handy. "Supposing he falls in love with somebody else and wants a divorce and there's no means of locating me and oh my heavens he goes back on the booze and narcotics and even worse, whatever that could be." She pulled her hand away from his, got up and walked to a window. There was a murmur of a breeze, and, from Broadway, the buzzing of taxis with klaxons squawking and the heartwarming clanging of a trolley. From the open window of an apartment above her, someone was strumming a ukulele and softly crooning "Somebody Loves Me," she hoped to someone who loved him. Give up all this for an unknown quantity, anonymity, a life on the run?

She hadn't heard him come up behind her. His hands were pressing on her shoulders. Her heart was pounding like a dynamo. It would be so easy now, she realized. Just a gentle shove and over the sill and into the void . . . *to grandmother's house we go.*

"What's that you're humming?" he asked.

"I always hum when I'm thinking." Lie. I always hum when I'm frightened. I hum when I come home alone at night to a dark and empty studio and it's usually something jazzy like "Yes, We Have No Bananas."

"Don't think. Say 'yes. Come away with me."

"'Come fly with me and be my bride.'" She quoted someone she couldn't identify readily in her state of bewilderment. "I couldn't even be a bride. There'd be no way to serve Ed with papers." He moved away from her, and she gave a small, tiny, very tiny sigh of relief. She followed him to the middle of the room. "I need time to think."

"I don't have that much time."

"Why is it so urgent?"

"I can't explain it to you." A statement to be placed atop the stockpile of all the other things he wouldn't explain.

"I need time, Lacey. It's like I said, we barely know each other. Give me a few days."

There was no describable expression on his face. It was as though in that moment he'd been transformed into marble, the perfectly sculptured face to be admired though cold and inanimate. "All right," he said. "Shall we go to the party?"

"Oh, yes! A party is just what's called for!"

Opening the door to Neysa McMein's huge studio was like being greeted by a blast from Vesuvius. From the Victrola they could hear the tinny rhythms of "Black Bottom," and surprisingly enough, George Raft was in the center of the room, the rug having been rolled back, doing a voluptuous shimmy, circled by a group of admiring flappers clapping their hands, snapping their fingers, urging him on to increasingly lewd movements of his midriff. Texas Guinan was in a corner of the studio deep in what appeared to be a serious conversation with Horace Liveright until he bellowed a laugh Mrs. Parker realized was detonated by the punch line of one of Guinan's notoriously filthy anecdotes. In another part of the room, Marc Connelly had an admiring audience of his own, captivated by his perennial party piece, the "Death of Cleopatra." As he pressed an imaginary asp to his breast, Connelly screamed "Jeeeeee . . . zussssss!" and tore his section of the room down. Mrs. Parker wished he'd find himself another party piece. This one was frayed by familiarity. She recognized Franklin P. Adams with his wife, Esther, and they exchanged loud hellos across the room. There were cries of "There's Dottie!" and "Oh, it's Lacey Van Weber!" and from their respective positions in some quarters of the room, Woollcott and Jacob Singer acknowledged the new arrivals. Singer was pinned to a chair by a fresh-faced pugnosed girl who appeared to be riveted to his lap. She was spooning gin into his mouth from a mug she held somewhat loosely, Singer expecting it any moment to be dumped into his crotch. On the balcony overlooking the studio, couples were necking and drinking and John Baragwanath looked silly wearing one of Neysa's hats. Neysa came out of the bathroom holding a pitcher of gin over her head and yelled at Mrs. Parker, "Where the hell have you been?" Mrs. Parker introduced her to Van Weber, who thanked her politely for letting him come to her party, and Neysa suggested he also thank her husband as nobody ever seemed to thank her husband for anything but his impending departure. Mrs. Parker was hoping for an opportunity to capture the ears of Woollcott and Singer and report the latest startling turn of events. Someone put a glass of gin in her hands, and when she turned to Van Weber, she saw him with glass of gin in hand, making his way across the room to someone he apparently knew. Abandoned so soon, she thought forlornly; men just can't be trusted, the dogs. I'm tired of them vandalizing my emotions.

She heard a familiar voice above the din saying, "I got your message, but I didn't have no time to call you back." Charlotte Royce looked like a five-and-dime trinket in her beaded dress.

"How'd you get here so soon from the theater?" asked Mrs. Parker.

"I skipped the second act." She winked. "The boss is a pal of mine. See y'around." She slithered away, and Mrs. Parker tried to get across the room to Woollcott. She was stopped by a cadaverous-looking man who complimented her on a recent contribution to F.P.A.'s column, "The Conning Tower." Staring at the man gave her the feeling she was looking into an open coffin.

An arm grabbed her elbow, and she turned and looked into Robert Benchley's smiling face. He said into her ear, "Abandon hope, all ye who enter here."

"I thought you were going to Hollywood."

"This is my farewell appearance."

"You make more farewell appearances than Sarah Bernhardt."

The Victrola was now blaring "The Sheik of Araby." Mrs. Parker wondered who was being cute, the song having been inspired by Rudolph Valentino. To her right she heard Liveright saying to a girl, "I'd love to beat you!"

"At what?" demurely inquired his intended victim.

Mrs. Parker was looking past Benchley, not hearing his conversation, to Woollcott, whom she was eager to reach. Woollcott was being asked by Neysa, "What can I get you?"

"An enema."

From the babble of voices Mrs. Parker heard someone ask someone, "Do you really know Texas Guinan?"

"I knew her years ago when she was young and almost pretty."

From behind her, Mrs. Parker felt herself pulled into the embrace of a pair of beefy arms. She turned her head and recognized the ursine Heywood Broun. She was delighted. She liked Broun and especially the fine column he wrote for the *New York World,* "It Seems to Me." "Broun, where the hell have you been keeping yourself?"

"I've been trying to put a revue together for Broadway. Why aren't you home writing me some sketches? The bastard next to you"—indicating Benchley—"is abandoning us for the fleshpots of the Babylon of the West."

"We need the money," said Benchley defensively.

"Where's the wife?" Mrs. Parker asked Broun.

"Cringing somewhere in the midst of these walls of putrefying flesh. I told her to send up a flare if she gets into trouble."

"Ruth never gets into trouble," said George S. Kaufman, who took them by surprise.

"And where's *your* wife, Kaufman?" asked Broun.

"Somewhere getting into trouble," replied Kaufman morosely. They pointed him toward a table where he could find a soft drink and perhaps a warm body, and he pushed his way in that direction.

A flapper grabbed Kaufman by his lapel and screeched, "Hey, cutie, where are you going?"

"Into cardiac arrest."

"Can I come with you?"

Kaufman shrugged and assumed the role of Pied Piper although only luring one tiny little mouse.

Broun, looking over their heads, announced Woollcott now had himself a sizable audience. "He's conducting himself like the papal nuncio at the college of cardinals."

"You must be kind to Alec," said Mrs. Parker; "he's had a dreadful shock."

"So I've heard," said Broun.

"So we've all heard," said Benchley with a bored expression and voice to match.

"Don't be unkind, Mr. Benchley, it was a traumatic experience. The poor boy might have been killed."

"Nothing can kill Woollcott," said Broun, "not even a silver bullet."

Two girls were pushing past them. One said, "He's such a bore! He's telling the same joke over and over and over again."

Mrs. Parker interrupted by gently suggesting to the girl, "Perhaps he has a one-crack mind."

"Dottie," said Benchley, "you need a refill."

After he was out of earshot, Broun asked Mrs. Parker, "You read Benchley's piece?"

"Somewhat."

"I didn't like it. What should have been as light and fluffy as a meringue crust comes out as heavy and portentous as a first love affair."

"Block that metaphor," said Mrs. Parker.

A man with a heavy beard and mustache shoved his face into Mrs. Parker's. "Aren't you Lillian?" he boomed.

"Oh no. Lillian passed away this morning." The man staggered away, and Mrs. Parker fanned herself with her hand. "The last time I saw a face like his, Tarzan was feeding it bananas."

"Mrs. Parker! How nice to see you again!" It was Florenz Ziegfeld. "And how are you enjoying these Roman revels?"

"About as much as I enjoyed your show last night."

Jacob Singer pushed the girl off his lap and she slid drunkenly to the floor. "Hey!" she yelled, "that's no way to treat a lady!" He stepped over her and pushed his way in search of Mrs. Parker. He overheard Franklin P. Adams asking a young thing, "What part of the South are you from?"

"West Vagina."

"Good evening, Mr. Singer." Singer turned and looked into the smiling face of Lacey Van Weber. "Having a good time?"

"I'm not sure what I'm having," replied Singer. "Mrs. Parker tells me she had quite a time with you today."

"Yes, it was a lovely outing. You must come out and see the estate for yourself."

"I wouldn't mind that at all," said Singer graciously.

Van Weber appeared to be thinking. "Perhaps we can arrange something for this weekend. We might ask Mrs. Parker and Woollcott and a few others. I'm expecting some friends in from Europe. They're sailing into my private dock on their yacht."

"How pretentious."

"They can afford to be. Lord and Lady Wussex. Fred and Elfreda. You must have heard of them."

"Well, I don't travel much in yachting circles, but yeah, I've heard of them. So they'll be docking sometime on Saturday night."

"Wouldn't it be fun to give them a welcoming party?"

"You sure they wouldn't prefer to be welcomed by their own friends?"

"Fred and Elfreda don't care who welcomes them, as long as they're welcomed."

"Well, what the hell?"

"Why not, old sport? Shall we ask the others?"

"Sure, if we can find them. This place is like Madison Square Garden on a Friday night."

"Stop trying to insult Broun," Mrs. Parker was saying to Benchley after he returned with fresh drinks for them. "It's like throwing spitballs at an elephant." Past Broun's imposing figure which did indeed resemble an unkempt mastodon, Mrs. Parker saw Lily Robson huddled by herself against a wall. "I see somebody I know. Don't wait for me to come back." She left them abruptly, elbowing her way toward the Robson girl.

"Hi," said an oily voice that belonged to the unctuous George Raft, "remember me?"

"The way I remember the Alamo."

"I hear you were out visiting my old buddy Lacey's place."

"My, a girl's virtue just ain't safe any place." Mrs. Parker lacked a wad of chewing gum to make her impersonation of a shopgirl perfection. "Just about how old an old buddy of yours is Lacey?"

Raft's face reddened. He'd done it again. Just a few words, but he'd said too much. "You know what I mean when I say old buddy. I always say old buddy when I talk about a chance acquaintance."

"Lacey's no chance acquaintance. He's a real old buddy."

"Oh, yeah?" Raft tried to laugh it off. "You know something I don't know?"

"Mr. Raft, a child of three knows something you don't know." She pushed her way past him, missing the snarl forming around his mouth.

Franklin P. Adams was reciting a new poem to a group he had captured. Benchley listened for a minute and then asked stentoriously, "Anyone for Tennyson?"

A man elbowed his way in front of Mrs. Parker. She recognized him. He was Carl Van Vechten, the tall, willowy novelist and photographer. "Oh, dear, Mrs. Parker, it's you," he simpered, "I didn't mean to jostle my way ahead of you."

"Go right ahead, Mr. Van Vechten," said Mrs. Parker politely with a gracious wave of her hand, "effete first."

Lily Robson saw Mrs. Parker approaching and smiled with recognition. "Honest to God," gasped Mrs. Parker when she reached the girl, "Peary must have made better time to the South Pole than I did crossing this room. How are you, dear, not alone, are you?"

"Mr. Connelly brought me, but I've lost him."

"Let's hope your luck holds out. How are you feeling?"

"A hell of a lot better, let me tell you."

Mrs. Parker bent her head conspiratorially, causing the taller woman to bend slightly in order to hear her. "The pill was innocent. That wasn't what made you sick."

"Gee, thanks for telling me. My nerves are so shot I've been tempted to swallow some all day."

"They're also useless."

"What do you mean?"

"They're like candy. Tasty but meaningless."

"You mean Horathy's been conning me?"

"It's hard to guess what the bad doctor is up to, he's such a shadowy figure. I'd stay away from him in the future, if I were you."

"You don't have to tell me twice. Believe me, it's the last time he's seen my back going out his door. Damn it, Texas is waving at me."

"Wave back."

"She's with somebody she wants me to meet."

"It's Horace Liveright. He's my publisher."

"Is he nice?"

"I used to think so."

"Whaddya mean?"

Mrs. Parker told her about Liveright's orgies.

"Why, that's not nice!" said Lily.

"Dear, are you always given to such understatement?" Mrs. Parker clucked her tongue. "He draws most of his female participants from Polly Adler's seraglio, but he likes to pump in some fresh blood every now and then. Be very careful."

"Thanks for the warning. I'll see you later."

"Oh, I'll be here." God help me, she was thinking, I'll most certainly be here.

"We've been looking all over the place for you." She'd been found by Van Weber and Singer.

"Believe me, I haven't been hiding. Let's move over near the window. I'm suffocating." At the window, Van Weber repeated his invitation for Saturday. Singer looked like the cat that swallowed the canary.

"Has anyone asked Woollcott?" she asked, beginning to feel a bit faint.

"I'm sure he'll want to come," said Singer with the assurance of a hangman about to release the trapdoor.

"You're sure *who'll* want to come and *where?*" Woollcott's arrival was fortuitous. He was mopping his brow with a paper napkin. Van Weber repeated his invitation. "Lord and Lady Wussex? Fred and Elfreda? They have a *yacht?* Where the hell did *they* get a yacht? When seen in the South of France last summer, they were absolutely penurious! Why, it seemed to be just a few steps for them from their *pension* to the poorhouse! Isn't it astonishing how the wheel of misfortune can sometimes reverse itself!" Woollcott was off and running, waxing eloquent like a soapbox orator who had recaptured a lost audience.

"Isn't it nice that you know them?" said Van Weber smoothly. Then to Singer, "So there'll be at least one old friend there to greet them."

"Who says I'll be there to greet them? They're perfectly dreadful people. She has cracked brown teeth and lisps and he suffers from the gout and a deviated septum."

Singer interrupted. "Van Weber says they're bringing with them a crowd of celebrities."

"There, Alec. Isn't that an enticement?" Mrs. Parker explained to Van Weber, "Alec dotes on crowds of celebrities. Look how he's thriving here tonight. Does this picture of jovial good humor look like a man who almost lost his life today?"

"I'm glad you admire my performance," said Woollcott, drawing himself up regally. "It's incredibly difficult to sustain." He favored Van Weber with a vague smile. "I'd be delighted to be among your coterie on Saturday. I presume there will be limousines to transport us to and fro?"

"With liveried chauffeurs," added Mrs. Parker, "if we play our cards right." From the phonograph she could hear "Poor Butterfly" and it made her feel sad. She was happy that Jacob Singer asked her to dance and, once away from Van Weber and Woollcott, told him of Van Weber's offer of elopement, commenting, "My cup runneth over and I just might drown in the spillage."

"Isn't that rather sudden?"

"Exactly what I said."

"Something's up. It's the yacht."

"From what Woollcott said, the Wussexes sound like they'd make anybody decide to head out of town."

"The yacht's a camouflage. I can predict what will be found in the hold."

"Bootleg booze?" asked Mrs. Parker brightly.

"And more. Kilos of morphine. Cocaine. The works. We've been tipped that someone was planning to come in with the biggest haul to date."

"And we're invited there to witness it?"

"We're invited there to witness it and never report it."

"You mean we're to be killed? Lacey couldn't be that angry with me for stalling him!"

"We're insurance. If there's a slip-up, we're out there

and in the line of fire. That's when Van Weber and his boys make their getaway. The yacht's probably equipped with souped-up engines and can outrun the Coast Guard."

"Mr. Singer, I just remembered a sewing bee I promised to attend on Saturday night."

"You ain't chickening out on me now, Mrs. Parker. You don't think I'd let us walk into a beehive like that unprotected, do you?"

"No, I don't. But on the other hand, bravery and self-sacrifice have never been my strong points."

"Think of the fun we'll have."

"I can't wait to see the look on Alec's face when you break it to him."

"I'm not going to break it to him."

"I had an idea you were going to say that. The music's stopped." "Poor Butterfly" gave way to "Bambalina."

Mrs. Parker heard Florenz Ziegfeld asking a buxom, overrouged, overjeweled middle-aged woman, "And how's your husband?"

"My husband?" She shrieked with laughter. "Why, he went down on the *Titanic!* Irving was always thoughtful."

Mrs. Parker and Singer rejoined Woollcott and Van Weber. Woollcott announced, "The cars will call for us promptly at six P.M. Saturday evening. Dress will be informal."

"I'm planning to ask a few others," said Van Weber and then favored Mrs. Parker, "Any preferences?"

"Buffalo Bill and General Pershing." Van Weber laughed. Woollcott squinted. Singer resisted an urge to pinch her as a warning. "I need a drink," said Mrs. Parker, "a very large drink." Van Weber offered to escort her to the kitchen. As they walked away from the others, Mrs. Parker asked, "Isn't this a bit strange, Lacey?"

"I always do things on the spur of the moment. I'm hoping on Saturday night your answer will be 'yes.' This gives you plenty of time to think it over."

"Oh, yes. I'll just be wallowing in time."

On the steps, a young couple were necking outrageously. "Who's them?" Charlotte Royce asked George S. Kaufman.

"Oh, that's the Wilmots, married a week and still acting like newlyweds. Do you come here often?"

"I'm with Flo Ziegfeld."

"Oh. Well, he doesn't come very often."

Woollcott had Singer pinned to a wall. "Now what's this plot all about?"

"It's an invitation. Why make a big deal out of it?"

"There are invitations and there are invitations and this is one of the suspect kind. What's that sinister young man up to?"

"Search me. Sounds like fun. I don't often get asked to the playgrounds of the rich."

"It'll probably spoil you rotten. The Wussexes indeed! She was an acrobatic dancer at the Palladium and he's a failed playboy!" Behind him he could hear a group hotly debating Sacco and Vanzetti and whether they deserved to be executed. Singer had his eye on George Raft. While Woollcott considered joining the debate, Singer left him and shoved his way to Raft.

"Hiya, George."

Raft paled upon recognizing the detective. "Oh, hiya yourself, Jake. I didn't know you was here."

"You know now. I been meaning to get in touch with you."

"Oh, yeah? What about?" Raft was perspiring and loosened his collar.

"Oh, this and that, mostly this. You and Valentino went back a long way, right?"

"Like I said, we used to hustle the old broads together."

"That why you took him and Ilona Mercury to Van Weber's party?"

"Well, there was nothing better on so . . ." He caught himself too late. "Actually, it was Ilona who had the invite."

"No, she didn't. I happen to know when she got there she chewed Van Weber out for not inviting her."

"She didn't exactly chew him out, she was kinda funny

about it." He didn't see Texas Guinan, but intuitively he felt her hot eyes on him. Jesus, not another session with the man, not that. God have mercy; nobody else would.

"Van Weber didn't like Valentino."

"Ah, come on, Jake. What's with the hot seat all of a sudden? This is a party, remember?"

"I remember it's a party. There are things I wish you would remember."

"Am I interrupting anything important?" cooed Texas Guinan as she put an arm through one of Raft's. "Baby needs a drink, sweetie pie, why don't you go get me one?" Raft made his escape with alacrity.

"How goes it, Tex?"

"It'll go better when I get my joint reopened. Any new leads on the murders?"

"I might get some if people like you stopped interrupting."

"You mean Georgie? Georgie don't know nothing. He's just a dumb hoofer from Hell's Kitchen."

"Georgie knows. I suspect he's been warned to forget." He looked around the room. "I don't see Dr. Horathy. Now how could he have missed out on a party like this?"

"I don't know. Why don't you phone him and ask him." She walked away to intercept Raft who was returning with her drink. Singer couldn't hear her, but the way her mouth was working, he could tell Raft was going to wake up in the morning with a bad case of charred ears.

"Have you seen Mrs. Parker?" Van Weber was craning his neck.

"Not since you walked off with her," said Singer.

"Mr. Benchley claimed her and that's the last I've seen of her. By the way, I've asked Neysa and her husband for Saturday. She said they'd be delighted if she remembers."

"Oh, that's just great. She's a great gal."

Under the steps leading to the balcony, Mrs. Parker and Robert Benchley found a temporary haven. They shared a tattered loveseat and held hands.

"Will you miss me when I'm gone, Mrs. Parker?"

"I shall miss you very much, Mr. Benchley." They sounded like the end men of a minstrel show, lacking only an interlocutor.

"I should have married you, Mrs. Parker." He squeezed her hand.

"I've considered that occasionally. We weren't destined for marriage, Mr. Benchley. I'm afraid we're doomed forever to be just good friends."

"I do love my wife, but oh you kid." She smiled. "Is this getting serious, this thing between you and Mr. Van Weber?"

"I think he'd like it to be."

"What about you?"

"You know me, Mr. Benchley. I must always have someone."

"I find him totally without distinction."

"Oh, you're wrong there. He's terribly distinct. He's much more interesting than most of my previous conquests."

"Do yourself a favor this time, Mrs. Parker. Think long, hard and seriously before letting yourself be painted into his landscape."

"Why, Mr. Benchley, that's almost poetic."

"There's always been poetry in me, Mrs. Parker; you've just never permitted yourself to recognize it."

She kissed him gently on the cheek. "Don't let them corrupt you out there."

"I'll try hard not to. But when money talks, I listen."

"Who doesn't? It just doesn't often talk in my direction."

They were interrupted by Neysa McMein. "Is the detective here? I can see he's not, unless he's hiding under you."

"What's wrong?" asked Mrs. Parker.

"There's a phone call for him. Some woman who's absolutely hysterical. His precinct told her he was here." They followed her back to the center of bedlam. Mrs. Parker spotted Singer talking to Lily Robson. She waved, trying to draw Singer's attention. Lily Robson saw her and waved back. Mrs. Parker pointed toward Singer. Lily Robson said something to Singer, who turned around and saw Mrs. Parker beckoning him. He elbowed his way through the mob, and Neysa McMein told him there was a phone call for him. The phone was in the kitchen. Singer headed for the kitchen with Mrs. Parker on his tail.

He picked up the phone and said, "Jacob Singer." He listened. "Now calm down, calm down. Where àre you? That's not too far from here." He gave her Mrs. Parker's address. "I'll be waiting for you in the lobby. Okay. Five minutes." He hung up and said to Mrs. Parker. "That was Horathy's nurse, Cora Gallagher. Somebody tried to murder her."

"Oh, my!"

"She almost got pushed off the top balcony in the Paramount Theater."

"Of all places," said Mrs. Parker, and she could feel a bead of cold perspiration trickling slowly down her spine.

14

During the five anxious minutes in which Jacob Singer and Mrs. Parker awaited Cora Gallagher's arrival, they relayed the information of the failed attack on her life to Woollcott. At the same time, a fresh wave of guests came pouring into Neysa's huge apartment. A plaintive wail of "Dottie! Dottie! Dottie!" sent Mrs. Parker to the outstretched arms of Edna St. Vincent Millay. After hugging Mrs. Parker, her eyes swept up to the skylight, and she declaimed melodically, "Oh, look look look at the splendid skyscrapers sodomizing the sky!"

Playwright Robert E. Sherwood was prevailed upon to do his party specialty, and while Marc Connelly glowered from his corner of the room, the Victrola was shut off, Vincent Youmans sat at the tinny upright, and Sherwood robustly tore into "When the Red, Red Robin Comes Bob, Bob, Bobbin' Along." Lily Robson whispered in Neysa's ear that Charlotte Royce was about to take a bath in the gin. With a Pekingese yelp, Neysa plowed her way to the bathroom in time to tackle the nude Miss Royce as she was about to pollute the gin. Lily found Ziegfeld, and they went to Neysa's assistance.

Harold Ross and Jane Grant arrived as Jacob Singer hurried past them to wait for Cora Gallagher in the lobby. He had the key to Mrs. Parker's apartment in his pocket, and he was excited. He hadn't deliberately set up Cora Gallagher as a target by intercepting her on the street where there could have been some likelihood they might have been spotted; he'd needed to talk to her and had caught her on the run because the element of surprise usually worked in his favor. Make an appointment with a witness or a suspect and you give them time to concoct a story phonier than a bastard's claim of parentage. Cora's escape from her assailant was a lucky break for her and for him, and he could feel his fingertips tingling; the bricks needed to construct the solution to a case were falling into place and taking shape. This was the most complex assignment he had ever tackled with a cast of characters out of Rube Goldberg, but he was loving every minute of it. He expected that someday it would pepper up the memoirs he intended to write.

At Neysa's party, Harold Ross had Mrs. Parker cornered. "I've thought about that profile on Lacey Van Weber. I've decided it's not such a bad idea. Do you think he'll cooperate?"

"Well, Harold," said Mrs. Parker. "I'm beginning to wonder if I might not do better tackling Baron Münchhausen."

At the piano, Vincent Youmans was bravely serenading the room with a medley of his own compositions. Horace Liveright was telling George S. Kaufman, "I now carry two million dollars in life insurance. What do you say to that?"

"I say you should hire a food taster," said Kaufman.

Lacey Van Weber could see Ziegfeld and Lily Robson trying to dress Charlotte Royce, who was struggling like a vixen caught in a trap. The look on Van Weber's face suggested he was smelling bad fish. Mrs. Parker was watching him, and when he suddenly caught her eye, he pantomimed blowing her a kiss. She smiled and went in search of Woollcott. She wanted to be with Jacob Singer when he brought Cora Gallagher to her apartment. Then she wanted to be alone to sort out her thoughts, because she had an idea who Lacey Van Weber really was. It had been nagging at her mind for most of the day, a solution she kept piecing together from little droplets of information that escaped from him indirectly, and the reports from the Los Angeles police. She didn't want to discuss it with either Singer or Woollcott until it made complete sense in her own mind, the way she wouldn't submit a poem or a short story until she was certain that every word was where it belonged, precise and crisp. She saw Woollcott and beckoned him.

In the lobby, Jacob Singer was clenching and unclenching his fists. It was almost ten minutes since he had spoken to Cora Gallagher. Taxi after taxi pulled up disgorging either tenants of the building or fresh troops for Neysa's party. The doorman was trying tactfully to handle the complaints coming down to him from Neysa's neighbors. Singer went out into the street as though hoping his presence there would hasten the arrival of Cora Gallagher. He was considering returning upstairs and phoning his precinct to order an all-points bulletin on Cora Gallagher when he spotted her hurrying toward him from Broadway.

"I couldn't get a cab," she gasped as she reached him and he took her arm, hurrying her into the building.

"I was about to send the bloodhounds after you."

At the party, Marc Connelly was telling George S. Kaufman he'd just been propositioned by a peroxided blonde. Kaufman said with professorial assurance, "Never look a gift whore in the mouth. Where are you two going?" Mrs. Parker and Woollcott had been trying to push past him and Connelly.

"It's finally happened," gasped Mrs. Parker. "I'm taking Alec to my apartment where he plans to rape me."

"Oh, wonderful," said Kaufman. "I hope you have a set of blueprints."

Mrs. Parker and Woollcott came into the hallway as Singer and Cora Gallagher got off the elevator. Singer was ready with the key to Mrs. Parker's apartment, and once inside, Mrs. Parker hurried to the windows to draw the curtains.

"What are you doing that for?" asked Woollcott testily. "We'll suffocate!"

"They always draw curtains in gangster movies, isn't that so, Mr. Singer?" Mrs. Parker was now pouring a stiff Scotch for Cora, who was not too unnerved to wonder how anyone could live in such Spartan surroundings. Singer stood looking down at Gallagher, waiting until they all had drinks and said, "You can relax, Cora." He waited while she imbibed a healthy swig of Scotch. Mrs. Parker and Woollcott sat together on the couch.

"I don't know why I'm here," said Cora. "He really almost got me. If it hadn't been for that usher . . ." She shook her head and began trembling.

"Would you like a sedative, dear?" asked Mrs. Parker.

Cora declined. "I'll be okay soon." She took another wallop of Scotch. Mrs. Parker hoped she had enough on hand to keep Cora supplied.

Singer decided to lead her. "Why were you up in the second balcony?"

"Couldn't get a seat anywhere else in the place. It was jammed. You know how it is with a Gloria Swanson movie. If it hadn't been for you collaring me, I'da got to the Paramount when the early show broke, the way I planned. So now I had to wait on line for almost an hour before I could get in. So I'm in the second balcony, the first row, and I'm watching the movie and it's pitch-black. I could see some guy going up and down the aisles, after a while, like he's looking for a seat. There were some singles, I'd seen them when I found my seat, but he didn't seem interested. So I figured he was looking for an unaccompanied woman to sit next to, you know, a masher. I'm sure you've had trouble with mashers, Mrs. Parker."

"Oh, yes. They're so hard on the knees."

"Well, then I notice he's standing in the aisle and looking for a seat in my row. Well, there was none and I heard somebody behind him telling him to sit down or get out. So he goes away. Later I realize he was looking for *me*." She swallowed another mouthful of Scotch.

Singer took a straight-back chair and straddled it. "Who else besides me knew you were going to the Swanson movie?"

Cora's face turned grim. "Horathy. He knew. He saw me checking the time in the newspaper, and when I told him what I was planning to see, he made some kind of crack about Swanson and some rich guy from Boston she's supposed to be having this thing with."

"Go on. How did your assailant attack you?" Singer was leading her gently.

"Well, it got to the part that I had come in on, and it was late and I was hungry and I didn't see any reason to see the rest of the picture again, so I got up to go. When I got into the aisle, I stood with my back to the aisle leading out of the balcony to check in my handbag for my lipstick, when suddenly I'm grabbed from behind and he's pushing me toward the rail. Then I hear the usher yell, 'Hey, what the hell are you doing?' and then I'm laying on the floor screaming and some people are helping me up. At first I thought the guy was trying to grab my bag, but he was trying to push me over. That's what the usher said it looked like to him. And so help me, Mr. Singer, I asked the usher if he could see what the man looked like, but he didn't. He just said he was broad and wore a big hat and was positively trying to shove me over the railing, and oh, My God . . ." She burst into tears. Mrs. Parker crossed to her and put a protective and comforting arm around her shoulder. Cora rummaged in her handbag, found a handkerchief, wiped her eyes, blew her nose and asked for more Scotch. Woollcott saw to the refill and hoped Mrs. Parker had a reserve supply.

"Horathy must have seen us near the subway entrance," said Singer.

"Sure he must have," said Cora, sniffling. "He was ready to leave when I was except he stayed behind to make a fast phone call to one of his patients canceling a Saturday appointment."

"He takes patients on Saturdays?" asked Singer.

"Sure. But this Saturday he's going away for the weekend. He's been making some heavy withdrawals from his bank accounts."

"Why didn't you tell me this before?" asked Singer.

"You didn't ask me." She thought for a moment. "Sayyyyy! Do you suppose he's planning to lam out?"

"Sounds like it to me. You have any idea where he was planning to go this weekend?"

She bit her lip and then spoke. "Out to East Cove. Out to Van Weber's place. He goes there a lot."

Singer said to Mrs. Parker and Woollcott, "There's smart and there's smart and sometimes there's not smart enough. I questioned this lady before for the better part of half an hour and I think I've learned all there is to learn, including names, and now I find I ain't half as smart a cop as I think I am."

"Don't be so hard on yourself, Jacob," chided Woollcott. "The terrain of East Cove only entered the picture for you a few hours ago. Mr. Van Weber's quixotic invitation, which now by the way I'm told includes Kaufman and a host of others, was only tendered us at the party on the spur of the moment."

"Do you want to bet?" countered Singer.

"On what?" asked Woollcott, his eyes blinking rapidly.

"That there was no spur of the moment." He was at the phone calling his precinct. Into the phone he said, "Singer. What matron's on duty tonight? She'll do fine." He gave the desk sergeant Mrs. Parker's address and apartment number. "Send her here on the double and keep it under your hat. I don't want anybody to know where she's been assigned. If this gets out, I'll have your ass, get it?" He hung up and asked Central to connect him with the Royalton Hotel, situated across the street from the Algonquin. When he got his connection, he asked to speak to the night manager. They seemed to know each other quite well. Singer was saying, "I want a double with bath in the name of Gladys Shea, and I want it in a room that's not near a fire exit or the staircase or the elevator or overlooking Forty-fourth Street. I'd prefer it on the second or third floor. I want the room through Sunday. And as usual, I don't want nobody to know about it. Bill me personally. I'll remember you in my prayers. So long, kid." He hung up and crossed back to Cora. "I'm placing you under protective custody."

"Oh, hell," whined Cora.

"You want me to let you loose out there with a killer after you?"

"Oh, hell."

"You're going into the Royalton with one of my best girls, Gladys Shea. She's built like a tank and moves like a gazelle."

Cora's voice was dark and suspicious. "She ain't no lez, is she?"

"Not on duty," replied Singer.

"Oh, God. What do I do about clothes?"

"We'll worry about that later." He turned to Mrs. Parker. "You ought to be getting back to the party. We don't want Lacey Van Weber getting suspicious."

"It's too late for that and you know it," said Mrs. Parker as she stood up. Woollcott sat staring at the sniveling nurse as though she were an arrival from outer space. "He's suspicious, the people behind him are suspicious, and Saturday we're participating in Gethsemane."

"You're free to cancel," said Singer.

"I know I am and you know I won't. The intrepid Mrs. Parker is notorious for treading where angels fear. It's terribly funny; Harold Ross has told me to go ahead with Van Weber's profile."

Woollcott tore his attention away from Cora Gallagher. "He didn't! He didn't mention it at the house tonight!"

"Well, he mentioned it when he arrived at Neysa's. Who knows, maybe I'll get to write it anyway, regardless of what takes place on Saturday night."

"Oh, shit!" All eyes turned to Cora Gallagher. "I get paid tomorrow! What do I do about *that?*" She got to her feet. "And what happens when I don't show up at the office?"

Mrs. Parker said through a sweet smile, "I should think it might have occurred to you by now that your deadly quack doesn't expect you to show up tomorrow."

"Oh, God. Sure. The bastard fingered me. Oh, God." She grabbed Singer's arm. "What happens after Sunday? What makes you think I'll be safe after Sunday?"

"Trust me, lady," said Singer confidently, "just trust me." There was a smart rap on the door. Singer indicated for Mrs. Parker to question it.

"Who is it?" trilled Mrs. Parker.

"Gladys Shea," came the booming reply, and the door shook. Mrs. Parker admitted Gladys Shea and for an instant the cacophony from Neysa's party swept through Mrs. Parker's apartment. Cora Gallagher stared at Gladys Shea and swallowed nervously. Gladys Shea was not quite six feet tall but seemed six feet broad. She was built like an Olympics athlete, and Cora would later learn she excelled at javelin throwing, the shotput and wrestling. She had been a member of the police force for over two years, and Mrs. Parker would later recall she had participated in the raid on Texas Guinan's. Gladys saluted Singer smartly when she entered and listened attentively and with an intelligent face while he briefed her. She wore civilian clothes, a precaution she had taken on her own when the desk sergeant apprised her she was being assigned to a protective custody case. "I borrowed Yudel Sherman's jalopy. It's double-parked downstairs."

"Leave it there," cautioned Singer. "I'll have it picked up later. You walk a couple of blocks and then pick up a cab. Don't go directly to the Royalton. Get out at Forty-fifth and Sixth and walk the rest of the way, you know, a couple of girls coming home from a night on the town."

"Gotcha," said Gladys, "you want me to stagger?"

"Don't overplay it, Gladys."

"Right. Okay, Miss Gallagher. Let's go."

"Wait a minute," said Singer. "We got some customers across the hall I don't want spotting Miss Gallagher." He went to the door, opened it cautiously, saw the coast was clear and waved the ladies on their way. When the elevator door closed behind them, Singer remembered to return her key to Mrs. Parker and advised her and Woollcott to rejoin the party.

"Where are *you* going?" asked Woollcott, not bothering to mask his disappointment.

"Back to the precinct. I got a lot of work to do. There's not much time before now and Saturday. In fact, there's only tomorrow."

"I love Friday," said Mrs. Parker for no good reason at all.

"So did Robinson Crusoe," snapped Woollcott.

Lacey Van Weber saw Mrs. Parker and Woollcott returning and when after much difficulty he joined them, he asked, "What have you two been up to?"

"Why, we've been necking," said Woollcott with a magnificent display of teeth, and then shouted across the room to Harold Ross, "Ross, you trembling fart, I want to talk to you!"

"Is there any more gin left?" Mrs. Parker wondered aloud. Van Weber offered to escort her to the bathroom. "Amusingly enough, Lacey, Harold Ross wants me to go ahead with the profile on you."

"There'll be no time now," replied Van Weber.

"There's always tomorrow."

"I'm driving out to East Cove tomorrow."

"Oh. Of course. Preparations for Saturday."

"Want to come?"

"No. Tomorrow is for thinking. And heavens, I must see if my beautician can squeeze me in. I'll need old magic fingers to mold me into shape for Saturday night. I hear you've invited Neysa and her husband and Kaufman."

"And some others, too," he said with a broad smile. The Victrola was back in operation and squawking "When Francis Dances with Me." Mrs. Parker got her glass of gin. Then, passionately, Van Weber pressed her against the wall. "Say you'll come away with me. Please. I can fly us up to Montreal in the morning and there we can book on a boat to Greece. *Please,* Dottie."

She was having difficulty breathing. His sudden impassioned assault was a surprise attack for which she was unprepared. Benchley rescued her.

"Mrs. Parker, I need your help. I've just been asked a question and I said Mrs. Parker is an authority. How do you get laid in a rumble seat?"

"With difficulty," replied the authority. Van Weber moved away from her. Her face was flushed, and she could feel Van Weber's hot eyes searching hers. When she looked at him, she said, "Until Saturday night, Lacey."

"Of course. I'll let you know the arrangements. I have to go now."

"So soon?" said Benchley. "Why, it's the shank of the evening. And the Marx Brothers haven't arrived yet."

"I have an early morning," said Van Weber. He kissed Mrs. Parker's cheek. "Until Saturday." He didn't wait for a reply, but elbowed his way to the door and left.

"I don't like that man, Mrs. Parker," said Benchley.

"Why is that?" asked Mrs. Parker. "Why don't you like him, Mr. Benchley?"

"He hasn't invited me to his soiree on Saturday night."

"That's because you told him you were taking the *Twentieth Century Limited* to Los Angeles that morning."

"That explains it." He cupped her chin with his hand. "Why are you looking so mournful?"

"Does it show?"

"Had you been thinking of an involvement with Van Weber? Has it gone off the track?"

"Yes, I've thought of an involvement, and yes, it's going off the track."

"Then why go to his place on Saturday?"

"Because I want to be in at the finish."

Kaufman was getting nowhere propositioning Lily Robson. "Young woman, do you realize I've just given you the best ten minutes of my life?"

"Oh, there's Marc!" She waved across the room at Connelly.

"There's always Marc," said Kaufman glumly. "I don't see how you can occupy yourself with someone born out of idle curiosity." But Lily had left him. Morosely, he stared at his wristwatch and started for the exit, where he was intercepted by Woollcott.

"I hear you've agreed to gambol with us peasants Saturday night," said Woollcott.

"Beatrice is taking the kid to the Swopes in Great Neck, so I figured with Van Weber's layout just a hitchhike away, I might as well get a look at Van Weber's El Dorado."

"There's going to be fireworks," said Woollcott meaningfully.

"I dote on fireworks, Alec, you must know that by now. Now let me out of here. All this rampaging joy has me depressed."

A piercing scream knifed through the room, followed by a series of cries of pain, and Mrs. Parker moved to one side as Charlotte Royce and another girl went at each other with the ferocity of Siamese fighting fish. George Raft was standing next to Mrs. Parker and said something revolting about Charlotte's opponent. "What did you say that girl's name was?"

"Lita Young and she's bad news. How the hell did she get to this party anyway?"

"What's the bad news?" asked Mrs. Parker, remembering she had yet to have a heart to heart with the Royce girl.

"She's on junk, that's the bad news. She's been after Ziegfeld all night, and Charlotte don't tolerate no poaching on her territory." Baragwanath and Ziegfeld were trying to pull the girls apart. Raft was goading the girls on. Texas Guinan moved in on Raft's opposite side and jabbed him in the ribs. He howled with pain, clutching his side. Mrs. Parker went in search of Woollcott. Somebody at the piano was playing "The Star-Spangled Banner." The tenants in the adjoining apartment were banging on their radiators. An irate neighbor in the hallway was banging on the door. Mrs. Parker found Woollcott and told him she was deserting the party before the place exploded. Woollcott told her he'd call her in the morning. Then a chair went crashing through a window, and Mrs. Parker found Neysa McMein sitting near the exit, holding a glass of gin and serenely puffing on a cigarette.

"Do you know that girl lacerating Charlotte Royce?" Mrs. Parker asked Neysa.

"I gather she's the missing link from a Vassar daisy chain." Neysa was pie-eyed.

"Her name's Lita Young. Have you any idea who brought her?"

"What does she look like?"

"A shambles. Earlier, she was a peroxide blonde who's a dope addict. George Raft told me."

"Ah, Raft. That's who she said asked her here, in case he could unload Guinan. Where's my husband? Where's Jack?" She struggled to her feet. "Jack!" she shouted. "*Jack!* I want to set fire to this fucking dump!"

Mrs. Parker let herself out and then locked herself into her apartment. She undressed quickly, poured herself the remainder of the Scotch, and sat at the open window waiting for fatigue to overtake her. She could hear guests noisily departing the party and the heartrending sobbing of a woman she assumed to be either Charlotte Royce or Lita Young. Then she blocked the party from her mind in favor of Lacey Van Weber and the appointment for Saturday night. She was beginning to understand the rationale for the party: with so many celebrities on hand, the risk of gunfire, should there be a police raid, would be minimized.

During the festivities, the yacht would be swiftly unloaded and then used for the getaway, probably stranding Lord and Lady Wussex, which would serve them right. She put the glass of Scotch on the windowsill and stared at her wrists. She felt a sudden mordant chill and embraced herself.

Lonely. So deadly lonely. So hungry for love, for a man of her own. Any old man in a storm. But it couldn't be Lacey Van Weber. It couldn't be him. Because as sure as God made little green apples, she was positive Lacey Van Weber was a murderer.

Back at the party, Texas Guinan was furious. "Where's George? Has anyone seen George?" Someone told her he'd been seen leaving with the peroxided spitfire, Lita Young. Guinan's eyes blazed like a forest fire, and she left the party in a hurry.

On the other side of town, George Raft was inserting the key into the lock of his hotel room door, while Lita Young crooned scatalogical lyrics, oblivious of her battered face and disheveled coiffure.

In his office at the precinct, Jacob Singer was diligently plotting his strategy for Saturday night. In the morning he would talk on the phone with his Nassau County counterpart and the captain of the Long Island Coast Guard. He had heard from Gladys Shea, who told him Cora Gallagher was sleeping like a baby, though babies don't snore, and she'd have to order food in from a coffee shop nearby as the Royalton did not provide room service. Singer assured Shea that she and her charge would be well provided for and to get a good night's sleep. He phoned Yudel Sherman, apologizing for waking him at this unseemly hour, but it was an emergency, and Yudel Sherman arrived at the precinct with the first light of dawn, carrying a bag of his wife's homemade apple strudel and several containers of coffee he'd picked up at the Greek's on the corner.

In his library on the third floor of the Ross brownstone Alexander Woollcott, wearing a tattered bathrobe, sat at the desk collecting his thoughts and making notes. After much thinking and rethinking and jotting down and scratching out and referring to his pocket book which contained his notes on the Los Angeles police reports, he deduced, somewhat sadly, because he had a slight admiration for the man, that Lacey Van Weber might very possibly be a murderer.

In her expensive and tacky apartment, Texas Guinan made a phone call, and at the first light of dawn, the beefy man was letting himself into George Raft's hotel room. Raft was asleep nude with his arm across Lita Young's body. The man picked up a pillow from the couch and, within minutes, had snuffed the life out of Lita Young. The man left the room. Raft hadn't heard a thing.

Early Friday morning, a procession left Frank Campbell's funeral parlor, headed for Grand Central Station. The hearse in the vanguard carried Rudolph Valentino's coffin. The limousine following the coffin contained Opal Engri and Valentino's brother Alberto. Between them sat Valentino's former press agent, S. George Ullman. There had been an overwrought service for the dead actor at St. Malachy's Church attended by many dignitaries of the film, theater and political worlds. Nita Naldi had sat in the back row with Jean Acker, Valentino's first wife, trading unkind words about the Polish actress. There had been a rumor that the body in the coffin was not really Valentino's, but a wax effigy, the body having been spirited back to California secretly.

Mrs. Parker spent a fitful night. She awakened earlier than was her custom, regardless of her impressive intake of an assortment of liquors the night before. She had a lot to do, that was for sure. At the top of her list was a meeting with Charlotte Royce, Ilona Mercury's roommate. She would see the girl this morning if she had to plant herself outside the girl's door.

George Raft awoke with a terrible thirst. It was still early in the morning, unusual for him, but there was this terrible thirst. He crawled out of bed with an effort, and in the bathroom, it took four glasses of water to slake his thirst. In the mirror he examined the black-and-blue bruise marks where he'd been beaten the morning before and where Texas Guinan had deliberately jabbed him at the party. The man. That fucking monster of a man. He returned to the bed and noticed the pillow from the couch covering Lita Young's face. He shoved the pillow aside. He'd seen stiffs before, plenty of them, and it didn't take a kick in the behind to alert him that Lita Young had died by suffocation.

He'd been set up. The man had paid a visit. Raft backed away from the bed. He looked at his wristwatch. It was not yet ten o'clock. He phoned Jacob Singer and prayed he'd be put through to the man without a wait, prayed the man was in his office this morning. His prayers were answered.

"What do you want?" asked Singer, a long time hoping for this phone call, if Raft was calling because he was ready to sing.

"I've been set up. There's a stiff in my bed. Lita Young. She's been suffocated."

"All this while your back was turned?"

"You gotta believe me, Jake! I was out cold when the man paid me a visit. He didn't kill me, too, because they're setting me up."

It didn't sound right to Singer. The boys wouldn't set up Raft. Warn him from time to time, but not send him up the river. He was too valuable an errand boy, and errand boys took a long time to train. This had to be Texas Guinan's work. Jealousy could be very unreasonable. He asked Raft, "Texas know you been two-timing her with Young?"

"She'da guessed last night. I took Lita home from the party. She'd had a scrap with that Royce twat." He thought for a moment. "You mean you think Tex set me up?"

"I want information, Georgie, or you're in serious trouble. You got a homicide on your hands."

"But I tell ya I didn't kill her!"

"That's your story, and there ain't that many who'd buy it."

"Jake, you gotta help me!"

"Georgie?"

"What, Jake, what!"

"I've seen you dance, Georgie, now I want to hear you sing."

There was silence, and Singer waited.

"Jake, where can we meet that's safe?"

"You can come here."

"It's not safe."

That's what Jacob Singer was hoping Raft would say.

15

It was a busy Friday morning for a lot of people. There were two funerals that attracted the sob sisters of the morning tabloids with photographers in tow. It was no coincidence that Ilona Mercury, whose body was found in an empty lot in Canarsie, was buried in Canarsie Cemetery, especially since Canarsie Cemetery offered the cheapest interment of all the boneyards canvassed. A modest group assembled at the graveside early that Friday morning, consisting of those hardy souls who could force themselves awake at the ungodly hour usually favored by funerals. About a dozen people gathered to send Ilona Mercury on her way, including one of Ziegfeld's favorite tenors, John Steele, who sang in his reedy voice "A Pretty Girl Is Like a Melody," which he had introduced in the *Follies of 1919*. One of the girls from *No Foolin'* asked if anyone could sing the Hungarian national anthem but found no takers. A local Canarsie priest was under the impression Miss Mercury had been somebody's wife and mother and sent her off with a totally inappropriate service, which won him several snickers and an assortment of muffled guffaws. The priest hoped the photographers were favoring his better profile, and at least three people wondered why Charlotte Royce, Ilona's roommate, had skipped the funeral altogether.

Out on Long Island, Vera DeLee was being laid to rest in a plot reserved for her in Polly Adler's private burial site in Montefiore Cemetery. All of Polly's girls were on hand, carefully drilled by the madam herself as an honor guard. A six-piece orchestra played a medley of current favorites, and there was a groaning board laden with drinks and food. Polly, not too sure of Vera's religious denomination, covered the situation with a Catholic priest, a Protestant minister and a rabbi. The gentlemen took turns eulogizing the late whore, hoping she'd make it safely to whichever afterlife they were endorsing. Polly wept, a genuine emotion on her part, while making a mental note to penalize Horace Liveright for not having the decency to show up and pay his respects. After all, Vera had always shown up and paid *her* respects when Liveright requested her, save for the night her number came up.

After the services, Polly waved everybody to the food and drink, and the orchestra kept its selections to waltzes and ballads. One of Polly's newest acquisitions, a sweet young thing from the Bible Belt, was absolutely awestruck and hoped someday she'd get this kind of a send-off. Polly assured her it was in the cards.

Back in the city, Dorothy Parker was in the lobby of the Wilfred Arms laying siege to the desk clerk. She had phoned the apartment hotel from home several times, each time hearing that Charlotte Royce left instructions she was not to be disturbed. When Jacob Singer phoned to tell her Raft was cracking, Mrs. Parker asked his advice on how to deal with the Royce girl, and he advised her to try and corner her on her own turf. She then tried to enlist Woollcott's company, but he thought she could handle the situation herself. He was fascinated to hear George Raft was daring to pull a double cross on the mob and decided to get the information firsthand from Jacob Singer. He caught Singer as he was about to leave the precinct for his meeting with Raft at the dancer's hotel room, which both he and Raft agreed would be safe, and Singer assured Woollcott he'd hear the whole story later in the day.

Mrs. Parker thought the desk clerk looked like a baby alligator, what with his jutting jaw and threatening teeth. "Miss Royce has been ill," the desk clerk was explaining in a voice that needed oiling. "She needed attention from our house doctor this morning." Mrs. Parker hadn't forgotten the cat fight at Neysa's party between Royce and Lita Young.

"I know she's been ill," lied Mrs. Parker; "I'm her masseuse. I'm here to knead her back into shape. She has a show to do tonight, you know."

"Not the condition she's in, sweetie." He eyed Mrs. Parker suspiciously. "Masseuse, eh? How come I've never seen you around here before?"

"I don't usually do house calls."

"Well, she'd better not call down here and chew me out, let me tell you. She said positively not to disturb her, but oh, what the hell, go on up." He gave Mrs. Parker Royce's room number.

A few minutes later, Mrs. Parker knocked sharply on Charlotte Royce's door. There was no response. She knocked harder. She thought she heard the girl stirring in her room. "Miss Royce? It's Dorothy Parker! I will stay here all day if necessary. I have to talk to you! Miss Royce?" She heard the key turning in the lock, and the door opened a few inches.

"You've got one hell of a nerve," rasped Charlotte Royce.

"I've got to talk to you." Mrs. Parker pushed the door inward and entered the room. On a desk were the remains of a half-eaten breakfast. The shades were partially drawn, leaving the room in semidarkness. The bed was unmade, and Royce's clothes from the previous night were strewn around the room. The second bed in the room, which Mrs.

Parker assumed correctly had been Ilona Mercury's, held an open suitcase. Miss Royce had apparently been caught in the middle of packing. "Leaving town?"

"What's it to you?" snarled Charlotte. She was at the desk pouring herself a cup of lukewarm coffee. A shaft of light from a window caught her face, and Mrs. Parker suppressed a shudder. Charlotte's right eye was black and puffy. Her right cheek was swollen. There were lacerations on her jaw, and Mrs. Parker wondered if Lita Young's retribution had been the result of the beating she'd given this girl.

"I'll be as quick as possible," said Mrs. Parker, taking a seat. "How long had you been rooming with Ilona Mercury?"

"Ever since the show moved up here from Florida. I got hired as understudy out of a club down there. Flo found me, the son of a bitch." She sipped the coffee, grimaced, slammed the cup and saucer down on the tray and lit a cigarette with shaking fingers.

"So you and Ilona became close friends."

"We became roommates because I couldn't afford to live alone and she had a kind heart. Fat lot of good that did her." She had slumped down in a lounging chair, flicking cigarette ash on the floor.

"What was her relationship to Valentino?"

"They knew each other in Hollywood. She used to work clubs out there. You know, she wasn't no spring chicken, lady. I'm nineteen and let me tell you, she had to be least ten years older than me, especially without makeup."

"What about Dr. Horathy?"

"What about him?"

"Didn't she say she'd worked for him in Hollywood?"

"She told me how Valentino laced into him at that party, that much she told me."

"Did she ever tell you about the time she spent in Mexico?"

"I don't know about that neither." She was staring sullenly at the burning cigarette tip. "Though come to think of it, she used to hum 'La Cucaracha' a lot."

"Did you ever hear her mention the name Hans Javor?"

"Oh, for crying out loud, she mentioned lots of names. From the way she talked you'd think she'd met everyone from Aimee Semple McPherson to the Prince of Wales. She was a big mouth, she was, always trying to impress me with her big connections!"

"You mean big connections like Lacey Van Weber?"

"She sure as hell was sore he didn't ask her to his party. I mean she got there because Georgie Raft brung her and Valentino, but she sure was sore she didn't get no invitation of her own. She came home pissed up to her ears that night or I should say morning because it was after five and I had just gotten in myself. First of all she's sore because Raft didn't have no invitation either, he just crashed and brung them along. He sure has brass, that George Raft." He sure has troubles, Mrs. Parker wanted to tell her, but she decided this wasn't the time to drop a bombshell. The girl was talking, and she just might tell her something of importance.

"What else got her sore that night?"

"Valentino, whaddya think? He got sick, didn't he? That killed the evening. They brung him back to his hotel and then Ilona and Raft went on to Tex Guinan's where Ilona had to pick up the tab because Raft's pockets are sewn together with thick thread. He don't lay out for nobody. There she was, laying there"—she indicated the second bed—"cursing her little heart out. Threatening revenge on everybody, especially the bastard she was married to."

Mrs. Parker sat up. This is it, she thought, this is the piece of information I need. "Who was she married to?"

"I don't know who and I don't know where but all she says is if she tells Winchell the son of a bitch is a bigamist . . ."

"Bigamist . . .!"

"Bigamist! Two wives! What's more, the other wife's got a kid. And let me tell you, that's who I think bumped her off! I told that to Flo and he told me to keep my lip buttoned and oh, shit, here I am spilling the beans to you."

"I never betray a confidence," said Mrs. Parker. "I wonder if she married this man in Mexico?"

"I tell you I don't know nothing about Mexico. I don't even know where it is." She moved to the dressing table where she stubbed out the cigarette. "Will you just look at me? Will you just look at what a mess I am! I could kill that Lita Young."

"Somebody did."

Charlotte spun around, genuinely shocked. "What?"

"Jacob Singer, the detective, is a friend of mine. He was at the party last night. You met him at Texas Guinan's." The girl nodded dumbly. "I spoke to him this morning. He told me she was murdered. Suffocated."

"Oh, my God. Oh, my God. I gotta get out of here. I gotta leave town right now." She began flinging clothes into the suitcase. Mrs. Parker went to her and grabbed her wrist. "Leggo! Get outta here! I've told you enough!"

"You've been just dandy. What about Lita Young? Why did you fight last night? Why does her death frighten you?"

Charlotte heaved a series of dry sobs and sat on her bed. "Listen, Mrs. Parker, I tell you the truth. I don't know nothing about anything. Lita is one of Flo's tricks. She crashed the party last night because Flo told her that was where he was taking me. He's cute like that, the son of a bitch."

"She was a dope fiend."

"And mean as hell. She was always needing money. Last night she was real desperate. So she crashes the party to get money from Flo and he won't give it to her so she takes it out on me."

"She left with George Raft."

"Sure. He knows where to get her a fix! Oh, God. I gotta make tracks." She was packing again.

"Where will you go?"

"I don't know." She was mewling like an infant. "I don't know. I don't know where to go."

"What about your family?"

"They threw me out three years ago."

"Don't you have any friends?"

"I don't have anybody. And looking like this, who'd want me?"

"You poor kid," said Mrs. Parker. She jotted down a name and address on a slip of paper and gave it to the girl. "Go to this place, the Barbizon Hotel for Women."

"Only women?"

"In your condition I wouldn't be too choosy. Check yourself in and stay undercover until Sunday."

"What's on Sunday?"

"With any luck, the second coming. Come on, I'll help you finish packing." A thought struck her while Charlotte began carrying clothes from a closet. "By the way, dear, did Ilona ever mention someone named Den? Maybe Denny? Or Dennis?"

The girl replied wearily, "Mrs. Parker. Give me your phone number. If I think of anything else, I'll call you. Now can we please help get me the hell out of here?"

George Raft was a very frightened man. Jacob Singer took his own sweet time in getting to Raft's hotel room; he wanted Raft to sweat and chew his nails and pace the floor and stare at Lita Young's corpse and jump with fear at every sound he heard from the hallway. Singer could envision Raft barricading the door with every available piece of furniture until Singer's arrival. Singer spoke to Mrs. Parker and to Woollcott and to the Nassau County Chief of Police and to a captain of the Coast Guard, and by the time he was ready to make his rendezvous with Raft, he was feeling very satisfied and very eager and tried hard not to act smug and complacent.

By the time Al Cassidy reported to the precinct, Singer and Yudel Sherman had accomplished a day's work. "What's going on around here?" asked Cassidy.

"You sure took your time getting here," snapped Singer. "Where the hell have you been all morning?"

Cassidy looked mournful. "I went to pay my respects to Vera DeLee. They buried her this morning. I got there too late for the services, but the grub and the drink were great. Polly Adler sure sets a swell table."

"I'm sure," said Singer. "Polly's always had this reputation for satisfying any appetite."

"Where you off to?" Cassidy asked Singer, who was strapping on his shoulder holster.

"I have to see a man about a dog."

"What's on tap for me today?" asked Cassidy.

"Just hold the fort till I get back."

Dr. Bela Horathy was having a very busy morning. He was clearing out his files. He had already visited a variety of bank branches, closing accounts and having money transferred to a variety of banking institutions in Europe and South America. This completed the work he had started earlier in the week. It didn't surprise him that Cora Gallagher had not shown up for work this morning. What did surprise him was a telephone call warning him that she was still alive. The doorman phoned to let him know his car and chauffeur had arrived. Horathy told him to send the chauffeur up.

When the chauffeur presented himself at the office, Horathy greeted him brusquely and ordered him to carry down several manageable packing cases that were filled with his private records. The chauffeur seemed surly and was having trouble with his ill-fitting dentures. A part of his right ear was missing. He handled the packing cases as though they were weightless. Horathy was glad the man was on his side.

The detective tailing Mrs. Parker wondered what she was up to now. She had emerged from the hotel with Charlotte Royce, carrying her suitcase, flagged a cab, and sent Charlotte on her way. Then the detective tailed her to a drugstore where she made a phone call. Mrs. Parker was sharing her information with Woollcott. Next she phoned Singer, but he had gone. No, she didn't care to speak to either Cassidy or Sherman and next phoned her beauty parlor. They promised they could squeeze her in around noon. Mrs. Parker came out of the drugstore, walked briskly to the man hovering in the doorway of a flower shop, and said to the detective, "I've got an hour to kill. How's about a cup of coffee?"

Bigamist.

Woollcott penciled the word in carefully in his notes. Ilona Mercury had defected from Hollywood at the time William Desmond Taylor was murdered, according to the report from the Los Angeles police. Why she had to flee was unexplained. Perhaps she went there to get married and the timing with Desmond Taylor's murder was just a coincidence. Had she married Hans Javor, or was Hans Javor really Bela Horathy as Mrs. Parker, dear Jacob and he believed? If she married him, why resurface in Los Angeles as Magda Moreno? Why come back there at all . . . unless . . . unless . . .

He clapped his hands with delight. Of course. It had to be. She had been married *before* escaping to Mexico. And in Mexico, she was probably abandoned by that skunk of a husband who must have admitted he had a first wife (and child) stashed away elsewhere. That's why she took up with Hans Javor and returned with him to Los Angeles where he became Dr. Bela Horathy and she became Magda Moreno because it was still not safe to be Ilona Mercury. He got out of his chair, yawned, stretched and, feeling very pleased with himself, poured himself a healthy beaker of port. He went to the window and looked out into the street. His watchdog, the detective assigned to protect him, was sitting on a stoop reading a newspaper. He looked up and saw Woollcott in the window. Woollcott lifted the port in a silent toast and the detective winked. Woollcott danced back to the desk to wait to hear from Jacob Singer.

"It's me. Singer."

Raft recognized his voice and unbarricaded the door. Singer entered, Raft shutting and locking the door behind him. The windows were wide open, and the electric fan was whirring away the telltale odor of death. Raft asked nervously, "Did you come alone? Is there anybody waiting out there?"

"I'm alone. When you tell me it's not safe at my precinct, you're telling me there's somebody there who'd slit your throat if he saw you coming in." He stared down at the corpse. He saw the track marks on her arms. "This one was really hooked, wasn't she?"

"A madwoman. Maybe you heard how she tore into Charlotte Royce last night."

"Let me warn you in advance, George. I'm still going to have to book you on suspicion of murder."

"Why? Why, for Crissakes? I told you I didn't kill her!"

Singer sat down and shoved his hat back on his head. "George, your word is good to me. But to my senior officer, your word is as good as a Confederate bond. So, George, I'm playing ball with you, and you play ball with me. You don't play ball, I book you right now and you can get yourself a smart mouthpiece. Except I can't think of any real smart mouthpiece who isn't answering to the boys higher up unless it's Clarence Darrow and I hear he's busy elsewhere. So, you see, I'm here, which means I'm interested in a deal, and you know my word is good."

"I know, Jake, I know. I swear to God I know."

"Okay. Stop dancing around, you're making me nervous. And let's do this fast because the stiff is beginning to get a little high and I ain't had my lunch yet. Who is Lacey Van Weber?"

"You gotta believe me, Jake, when I tell you I don't know all that much about him."

"Tell me what you know. Tell me anything you might think I want to hear. Make it worthwhile, George. Sit down, George, over there where we can eyeball each other."

"I met him ten years ago when Rudy and I were taxi dancing. He said he'd just come over from England."

"The war was on there. Was he draft dodging?"

"Maybe he was. I don't know about that. Anyway, he

-251-

shows up at the place and he says he's Dennis Byron only he don't talked refined like he talks today. I mean he had a street sound."

"Probably Cockney."

"Yeah! That's right! Cockney! I remember now, Cockneys are born within the sound of the Bow Bells."

"Gee, George, I didn't know you had any education."

"Aw, come on, I had some!"

"Tell me more about Dennis Byron."

"Ain't you gonna take notes?"

"I got a sharp memory. Dennis Byron."

"He was flat broke. He needed to make a stake to get him to the Coast where he said he had a connection."

"Did he mention the connection's name?"

"It was some relative. No name attached."

"Go on."

"Well, he wasn't too bad on his feet, but some days he did better than Rudy or me, so we think he was whoring on the side. You know, seeing the ladies after the tea dancing was over and picking up an extra twenty."

"Didn't you?"

Raft grinned. "We all did. But Denny was quicker on the draw. We used to call him 'In and Out Byron.' Anyway, after a couple of months of this, he disappears. Next thing you know, it's last summer. I just latched on to Texas and I'm doing my act at her place, the one that was over near Macy's, remember?"

"Sure. Keep going."

"In comes this big party, the kind of suckers Tex goes for, except they ain't no suckers. This is the cream. The big boys. The accents are straight from Sicily. What ain't from Sicily is from Chicago. This I figure is the syndicate, the boys who back Tex and the Broadway shows . . ."

"And the biggest dope-smuggling operation in the world."

"You said it, I didn't."

"Don't horse around, George."

Raft mopped his perspiring brow with a handkerchief.

"In the middle of this bunch, at the head of the table actually, is this Lacey Van Weber. I get his name from Tex because she's puffed up with pride the boys are paying her a visit. Well, Van Weber sees me, and he suddenly looks at me like I'm a head of rotten cabbage. I wonder what the hell's rubbing him wrong. I think and I think and then it hits me. It's Dennis Byron. I mean there's this resemblance there, even though he's changed a lot. I mean physically now he's all filled out. Where once he was a stringbean, now he's got beef and muscles. The face is filled out and real handsome, I mean you seen for yourself, he's a sharp looker. So I wait till I see him making for the head, and I follow him into the toilet and introduce myself. Boy, did he blow it at me. Then we got it straightened out with each other, still old buddies, see, but I keep my trap shut about Dennis Byron . . ."

"Or else."

"The warning didn't come from him. It come from Tex. Well, you know Van Weber's history since. You know about the estate, his office in town, his parties at the penthouse . . ."

"He's a front for the syndicate."

"One of them. They got them all over the world. They groom them. They train them."

"Where?"

"All over, for crying out loud. Europe, South America, Mexico . . . Don't you get it? I was being set up for Hollywood. They were going to make me a star."

"Was Valentino poisoned because he recognized Van Weber?"

"Rudy wasn't murdered. What killed him was genuine."

"I don't believe you."

"I don't blame you. But I don't think Lacey had anything to do with that."

"Valentino could have met him in Hollywood."

"Maybe he did."

"Stop bullshitting me. You crashed that party of Van Weber's. You took Valentino and Ilona Mercury with you. That was a big mistake. Van Weber didn't want any of you at the party, he didn't want you anywhere within a mile of him. That got you into real trouble, didn't it, George?"

"Yeah, yeah, it did, real trouble."

"Did Mercury know Van Weber from Hollywood?"

"I didn't know she'd been out there."

"Don't lie to me."

"I swear to God I don't know."

Singer told Raft about Mercury's relationship to Horathy in Hollywood when she called herself Magda Moreno.

"It's all news to me," insisted Raft, "I swear."

"You swear too much. How deep into the organization is Horathy?"

"He's one of their best mechanics."

"What do you mean?"

"In the lab. He knows how to transform morphine into cocaine." Singer whistled. "The office is just a front. Sure, he shoots up there and gives out prescriptions, but that's small pickings for the organization. They don't want any part of that. Horathy banks that stuff for himself. They let him; you know, it's like slipping a fin to a headwaiter."

"Do you know who murdered Ilona Mercury?"

"I don't think so."

"Vera DeLee?"

"I might know."

"Who do you think suffocated Lita?"

"The same son of a bitch that strongarmed me too often."

"Is he in my precinct?"

"He's yours."

"Don't keep me in suspense, George."

"Al Cassidy."

Singer got to his feet and plunged his hands in his pockets. Al Cassidy. The man with the big hat. The Stetson. Al Cassidy. We have worked together for five years. Me and Al and Yudel. Al Cassidy, a rogue. The man with the handkerchief at his nose. The man who probably killed Vera De-Lee. The man who beat up Raft and the hell knows how many others. The man who attempted to push Cora Gallagher from the second balcony at the Paramount. The man who probably killed Ilona Mercury. Al's wife. Al's two kids. The man who suffocated Lita Young.

"They call him the 'man,'" continued Raft. "He's their troubleshooter. When they need a job done, send for the 'man.'"

The man. Mr. Man. Singer shook his head sadly and exhaled. Now to handle this without causing a scandal. How to spare the department another blemish. There was so much damned corruption in the city, it was almost bigger than an epidemic. How to handle one of his best friends, Al Cassidy. Singer was shaken.

"George, I'm taking you down to the Tombs."

Raft leaped to his feet. "Ah, come on!"

"Now hold your water and calm down. It's for your own protection. Make believe it's like going away for the weekend."

"I never go away for the weekend. Nobody asks me."

"I'm asking you. I'm inviting you down to the Tombs for the weekend starting now. Pack an overnight bag. Take your tap shoes, maybe you can do a show for the boys. I'm putting you on ice until Sunday."

"Tex'll wonder where I am."

"You forget Tex sent the man after you?"

Raft's face twisted into a vengeful snarl. "That motheaten twat."

"Start packing, George. And don't ask any questions. You've done fine. I'm going to need a signed statement from you. I'll take care of all of that downtown. Mind if I use your phone?"

He called the precinct and asked for Yudel Sherman. He asked if Al Cassidy was there. Cassidy had gone out for a sandwich. Singer told Sherman to send some boys and the coroner to Raft's hotel. He was taking Raft into secret custody. Sherman said he'd meet him down at the Tombs in half an hour. No, he would be sure not to tell Cassidy. "Is it something real lousy with Cassidy?" asked Yudel.

"Real lousy . . ." and he couldn't resist adding, "old sport."

Mrs. Parker left the beauty parlor, looking, she decided, no better than she had when she entered, but then, she was always much too modest about herself. She was down-hearted and wondered if Lacey Van Weber had been trying to reach her. She flagged a cab, looked around to make sure her protection had flagged one, too, and headed home.

There, she phoned the Barbizon to make sure Charlotte Royce was comfortable. Charlotte thanked her for her concern. She called the precinct and was told Singer was unavailable for the rest of the day, but he'd said that if she called, he'd left word with Mr. Woollcott. She phoned Woollcott, who snapped, "Well, it's about time! Where the hell have you been?"

"I've been to the beauty parlor because it was necessary for tomorrow. Now what's been going on?"

"Jacob Singer wants us to have dinner with him tonight."

"Please, not Chinese again."

"No, he suggested Tony's where we ate after the theater, which is quite fine by me. I've heard from Lacey Van Weber."

Her heart flip-flopped. Damn me and damn him. I care, I care, and I mustn't care. My lover could be my killer. My killer. Oh, dear, oh, dear. "Yes? What are the arrangements?"

"Our limousine will pick us up at six and six-ten respectively. You're six. Be prompt, will you, lotus blossom?" His voice was unusually kind and tender. He recognized she was in one of her frequent states of emotional fragility.

"I'll be prompt. After all, I'm to be queen of the prom."

"That's the way I like to hear you! See you at Tony's at seven."

That would give her time to soak in the tub. She hung up and sat at her dressing table. You're thirty-three years old and today you look it. That's not so old, really. That's not old like Edna Ferber. I'll bet Neysa's older. Neysa! My God, I haven't checked in with her. How did she survive the night? She hurried across the hall, but on the McMein's door in huge block letters was a sign that read DO NOT DISTURB. She returned to her apartment and ran her bath. Drops of water were falling into the tub, and Mrs. Parker looked up to see if there was a leak in the ceiling. The ceiling was perfectly fine. Mrs. Parker wasn't. She was crying.

There wasn't much of a crowd at Tony's, and the head-waiter almost fractured his skull bowing and scraping Mrs. Parker to the table where Jacob Singer and Alexander Woollcott had awaited her arrival for over fifteen minutes. She ordered a Jack Rose on the rocks and told them both how fine they looked. She told them about her morning with Charlotte Royce.

"Bigamist," said Singer. "I wonder who he was."

"Is," said Mrs. Parker. "I'm pretty sure he's still alive."

Jacob Singer told them about his day with George Raft. Lita Young was in the morgue where an autopsy would be performed the next morning. Her murder had been withheld from the newspapers and would not be released until Sunday in time for the Sunday evening editions. He told them he was holding Raft in the Tombs for his own protection.

"I've put Miss Royce into the Barbizon Hotel for Women," said Mrs. Parker. "Did I do the right thing?"

"You did fine," Singer assured her. The waiter who was hovering nearby wondered if they were ready to order dinner, but none of the three seemed to have an appetite. They told him to come back later, but first to conjure up another round of drinks.

"I don't mind telling you," said Mrs. Parker, "I'm terribly nervous about tomorrow."

"I'm not," said Woollcott stoically. "I expect to have a perfectly marvelous time and the makings of a superb essay on deceit, fraud and international crime."

"Everything'll be just fine," said Singer, hoping neither of them noticed his fingers were crossed. "I have a heavy Sunday ahead of me. Very sad."

"Somebody dead?" asked Woollcott.

"Yup. One of my partners. Suicide. Killed himself in one of our cells. Deeply depressed. Al Cassidy."

"Oh, my, how sad," said Mrs. Parker. "When did he do it?"

Singer looked at his wristwatch. "Any minute now."

16

Mrs. Parker was aghast. "You mean you know he's going to commit suicide and you're doing nothing to prevent it?"

"Mrs. Parker, he was a bad apple," said Singer unhappily. "He was one of my best friends and he betrayed me. He betrayed the force. He betrayed his family." He stared into his gin. "He betrayed himself. He was on morphine. He admitted it to me. Oh, my God, what an awful scene that was. Me and him and Yudel in my office, the three musketeers, me laying Al out to filth, confronting him with everything Raft told me."

"You trust that leech?" asked Woollcott.

"I trust anybody who makes a positive ident. Raft was scared. He was set up. Tex fixed it for Cassidy to suffocate Lita Young in Raft's bed. She'll have some answering to do."

"Are you arresting her?" asked Mrs. Parker.

"I'll let her do her answering to the big boys. That was Cassidy's big mistake, doing Tex a favor in return for a C-note." He leaned back in his chair and sighed, "Imagine. Cassidy, a two-shot-a-day doper, and we never guessed. But I should have recognized his modus operandi. He was a genius at getting in and out of places unheard and undetected. The man with the handkerchief to his nose. The man who tried to kill Cora Gallagher. An hour ago, this big beefy menace was sitting on the floor of my office slobbering like a kid who lost his bike. It was awful. And poor Yudel. I mean those two were like brothers. They come up in the force together. At one point I catch Yudel eying me like maybe I could also be tainted. And I don't blame him. Who do you trust if you can't trust a guy who was more than a brother to you? Who do you trust, Mrs. Parker?"

"In my circle, that's not easy," she replied wryly.

"You trust *me*," blustered Woollcott.

"On a clear day," replied Mrs. Parker. "So Mr. Cassidy was in their employ. How do they do it? How do they get to a man like that?"

"In his case, it was the dope. In somebody else's case, it's greed."

"There's somebody else?" asked Mrs. Parker.

"Probably. Nobody I know, but probably. Anyway, Cassidy's a write-off. Let's get on to more important matters."

Mrs. Parker was astonished at the way the detective could switch his emotions. Cassidy's a write-off. Let's get on to more important matters. Let's have another cup of coffee and let's have another piece of pie. She caught Woollcott's eye. It was telling her to accept Cassidy as an entry in the debit side of the ledger and get on to other things. Singer was talking while crumbling a breadstick. He was repeating Raft's rendition of his earliest acquaintance with Lacey Van Weber.

"Dennis Byron. How poetic," said Mrs. Parker. "Of course Lord Byron was also a shit."

"He was mad, bad and dangerous to know," recited Woollcott mellifluously. "And if you're wondering where that dreadful line originated, I am quoting a contemporary of Lord Byron's whose name thankfully escapes me."

"Gentlemen, I have a theory." Mrs. Parker sounded like an auctioneer about to knock down an expensive lot. "I must admit a lot of it is inspired by Charlotte Royce's revelations about Ilona Mercury having married a bigamist. A marriage, I'm prone to believe, that took place in Mexico."

"If it took place," said Woollcott.

"It took place. The Mercury girl didn't sound to me like someone who noised about her fantasies. If she was married, then she was married. You see, Alec, you have never roomed with a girlfriend."

Woollcott looked as though a platoon of deadly comebacks was assembling at the tip of his tongue, but happily, he kept his peace.

"Girlfriends get to let their hair down rather frequently. In the wee hours of the morning, especially when liquor has played havoc with caution and one is brushing her hair and the other is wondering why she was sent home alone. Are you all right, Mr. Singer?"

"Don't I look okay?"

"You look sad. We need more drink." Woollcott barked at a waiter. Mrs. Parker returned to her theory. "I must remind you of the Los Angeles police report. Ilona and several others thought it prudent to escape to Mexico when William Desmond Taylor was murdered. I think Desmond Taylor was a set-up, much like Lacey Van Weber is now. I think he was the front through whom drugs were disseminated in Hollywood. Undoubtedly he displeased his people for one reason or another. I personally think he wanted out because he was genuinely in love with one of his little stars, possibly Mary Miles Minter, and because he was becoming a major name in the directorial field. Desmond Taylor had a brother, we have learned. We have learned Taylor's real name was William Deane Tanner. Isn't that clever? Same initials. Now the brother. The suspicion was that Sands, Taylor's butler, who was among those who disappeared, might well have been that brother. The brother's name was Dennis Deane Tanner. I think that's Dennis Byron, also known as Lacey Van Weber. And he married Ilona Mercury somewhere along the line." The replenishment arrived, and Mrs. Parker was terribly pleased with herself. "Is my deduction so staggering? You're both so quiet. Alec? Rebuttal?"

"I think the marriage took place before they left for Mexico," said Woollcott, bringing his notes from his pocket.

"I've been working on this all day. It mostly dovetails with your theory, Dottie, but now listen to this."

Singer was feeling better. He was proud of his students. Mrs. Parker didn't miss the superior look that had developed on the detective's face. How easily he controls his emotions. Why can't that be infectious, like some virus, so he can pass it on to me, she thought.

"Miss Repulsive! You are not listening!" raged Woollcott.

"Believe me, Alec, the center ring is all yours." She dabbed at her nose with a handkerchief, looking about as demure as an ax murderess.

"Mercury married Dennis in Hollywood. A quiet ceremony, I should think, wouldn't you, Dottie?"

"Probably not to disturb the neighbors." She sipped her Jack Rose and made a mental note to offer up a prayer later for bootleggers.

"Desmond Taylor probably didn't know about this marriage, because he was aware there was a wife somewhere back in the boondocks and might have cried foul. After Desmond Taylor's murder, it was politic, to say the least, for Dennis to disappear. He knew too much. He musn't fall into the hands of the police. If they interrogated him, the jig, as they say in certain circles, would be up. So he was sent off."

"Sent off?" Singer was leaning on the table. "What do you mean 'sent off'?"

"I think he was offered the job of replacing his brother in the organization's favor. They offered to groom him into the person we know today. The offer, of course, was irresistible to a man who'd had to whore his way across a continent and then accept the subservient position offered by his sibling. Imagine asking your brother to be your butler."

"It's worth considering," said Mrs. Parker. Woollcott flashed her a nasty look.

"Having accepted their offer, he is off to Mexico to lie low for a while. But now he has a problem. He has Ilona Mercury on his hands. He makes a deal with her to fade into the background in return for certain future monetary favors, which she accepts with alacrity, because I think by this time Hans Javor, later to become Bela Horathy, has attracted her eye. It was probably Mercury, when she assumed the alias of Magda Moreno, who realized Horathy's talents far exceeded his chiropracticing or whatever it was he did, and brought his superior talents for rendering morphine into cocaine to Van Weber's attention. Tight little circle, don't you think, my friends?"

"So are we," commented Mrs. Parker as she sipped her drink.

"Horathy appeared on the local scene long before Van Weber," said Singer.

"The advance guard," said Woollcott, looking very pleased with himself. "Everything awaiting him but rose petals strewn in his path. He sets up his office, Mercury is set up with Ziegfeld, and soon there's heavy traffic in dope addicts. So who killed Ilona Mercury?"

"Lacey Van Weber," said Mrs. Parker, so softly they had to strain to hear her. "Miss Mercury, as it has been impressed upon us by Charlotte Royce among others, is no longer a seller's market. She's over the hill. The body's still good, but the looks are starting to go. She wanted a bigger share of whatever she was getting with which to feather the nest I assume she was planning for herself, oh, probably in the South of France, someplace like that, where they favor fading beauties. Maxine Elliot and Pearl White have settled there."

"And Somerset Maugham," added Woollcott.

"Don't be bitchy on an empty stomach, Alec." Mrs. Parker turned to Singer. "Lacey's probably regretted not shedding himself of Miss Mercury in Mexico, but I suppose at the time his mind was hypnotized with promises of future glory. So typical of Miss Mercury with her kind of ego to select George's pied-à-terre for the scene of her shakedown. It sort of insinuates itself subtly that she, too, enjoys the company of man of distinction and power. "

"Kaufman has the power of a kitten's fart," snorted Woollcott.

"You haven't noticed Mr. Van Weber's hands. They're long and sinewy, very powerful; I know, I've felt them." She was making Jacob Singer uncomfortable. Woollcott's lips were pursed, and he was looking for a sign of the invisible torch he was positive Mrs. Parker was carrying. "I don't mind telling you, I feel very depressed and very unhappy about my feelings about him. I mean, I'm sure somebody had to love Jack the Ripper. You realize, of course, Miss Mercury was not his first victim. It was he who murdered his brother. Isn't it all so terribly Nietzschean?"

Woollcott sighed. "Nietzsche come, Nietzsche go."

Singer folded his arms and said, "Now all we have to do is prove this."

"We'll do that tomorrow," said Mrs. Parker firmly. "He has asked me to run away with him. If the offer still holds, I shall tell him I'm going."

"Don't you dare!" spumed Woollcott.

"Oh, shut up, Alec, and drink your drink. Of course I'm not going. I just plan to lull him into a false sense of security. As we go about preparing to decamp, I shall gaily ask my beloved why he murdered Miss Mercury and his brother and God knows how many others."

"At which point," said Woollcott, "if he has any brains at all, he murders you."

"I know," said Mrs. Parker, "and Mr. Singer will be there to protect me, won't you, Mr. Singer? Alec, you're such an innocent. We've been set up just the way George Raft was set up. We're the cheese in the mousetrap. That's why we're participating in what I presume is to be an incredibly bizarre adventure tomorrow night. Mr. Singer is out to score the biggest victory of his career, and nothing must interfere. Anyone else and everyone else is expendable. Mr. Singer is an ambitious man, so ambitious, it's Shakespearean. He cultivates the cultured, and when he stumbles upon an opportunity to capitalize on heroics, score that big score, he seizes it with both hands. Mr. Cassidy almost blew the deal for Mr. Singer, but the gods proved to be on Mr. Singer's side, and well they should be. He's honest and upright and deserving, and Mr. Cassidy is a write-off."

"Lady," asked Singer, "are you condemning me for having raised my sights?"

"Oh, no, Mr. Singer. I am jealous. I shrink from ambition. I don't want to make history, I just want to make love. I meet others every so often who want to make love, too, but only every now and then, never permanently. So you probably don't understand how I can feel this emotional about a liar, a cheat, a murderer. It's because for a brief moment I saw the other side of the moon, what might have been, and what might have been, might have been just perfectly lovely."

Woollcott announced grandly, "We have just heard a brief discourse from Pollyanna, the Glad Girl."

"Oh, I'm a very glad girl, Alec. Very glad to be a part of this experience. It's new, it's refreshing . . ."

"And it's dangerous," growled Woollcott.

"You wouldn't miss it for the world and neither would I. We're looking forward to dining out on it for months. And believe it or not, I'm getting hungry and drunk, in no particular order. I'm assuming, Alec, that Mr. Singer has made elaborate preparations for tomorrow night. We'll be up to our hips in guardian angels and saviors, won't we, Mr. Singer?"

"You're going to have a perfectly wonderful time," Singer assured her. He saw Yudel Sherman crossing the room toward them. "Here's one of my associates," said Singer, and introduced Yudel. Yudel sat down.

"Excuse the interruption, Jake, but I got bad news." Singer waited. "Al Cassidy shot himself to death. Through the heart."

"Did he leave a note?" asked Singer.

"Yeah," replied Yudel, refraining from adding, exactly the way you dictated it, Jake. "He was depressed and not feeling good."

"You tell his wife?"

"Yeah. She handled it okay. She said he ain't been acting right for a long time."

"He sure ain't been," agreed Singer. "That's real bad news. Real sad. When's the funeral?"

"Sunday, just like you figured." Singer's face reddened. Yudel stifled a gasp at his slip-up.

"It's okay, Yudel," said Singer as he signaled the waiter to bring a round of drinks, "the folks are in on it. You know, Mrs. Parker, when the drinks get here, I want to propose a toast to Al Cassidy. The toast is for the Al Cassidy we used to know, not what he turned in to. I'll always love him for what he used to be." Sherman quickly left the table and looked for the men's room. Mrs. Parker put her hand over Singer's.

"Ain't life just awful?" said Mrs. Parker.

The drinks arrived when Yudel Sherman returned, his face freshly washed. Mrs. Parker was deep in thought, and Woollcott offered a penny for them. "Believe it or not, I was thinking about George Raft. Last night at Neysa's party, he made some crack about not knowing what Lita Young was doing there, when all the time he knew exactly what she was doing there." She was bristling. "I wish you'd keep him locked up in the Tombs forever."

"Unfortunately, Mrs. Parker, that would be against the law." Singer got the waiter's eye. "I think we should eat."

On Saturday morning, shortly before noon, Mrs. Parker was awakened by the telephone. It was Robert Benchley calling from Grand Central Station. "I expected you to see me off, arms laden with lilies and other acceptable assorted flora."

"You're really going?" she asked sleepily.

"That's what the wife asked, except she sounded suspiciously gleeful. I'm sorry to miss the party tonight."

"You'll be hearing about it in detail for the rest of your life. What's the weather like out there?" Mrs. Parker's drapes were drawn against the day and against reality.

"In the stygian depths of Grand Central, it's very somber and very gloomy and my what a pretty thing just passed by carrying a hatbox."

"Hatboxes in Grand Central usually contain a severed head."

"They're announcing my train." He sounded sad. "Goodbye, Mrs. Parker. I shall try to remember to send you pretty postcards. Be a good girl. Stay away from foolish involvements."

"The trouble with that, Mr. Benchley, is I never know an involvement is foolish until I'm too deeply involved." There was a rapping at her door. "There's someone at the door."

"It's me! Neysa!"

"It's Neysa," relayed Mrs. Parker.

"That's mighty Neysa her," said Mr. Benchley, and hung up. Mrs. Parker got out of bed, struggled into a negligee, unlocked the door and admitted Neysa, who was carrying a piping hot pot of coffee.

"This place looks like the inside of a tomb," commented Neysa.

"When were you ever inside a tomb?" asked Mrs. Parker while drawing open the drapes on both windows.

Neysa ignored the question. Having set the coffee pot on the table she was now foraging in the kitchen for cups and saucers. "Jack and I are in your section of the caravan tonight. So's George Kaufman." Mrs. Parker was in the bathroom brushing her teeth. "Your Mr. Van Weber phoned last night with these fresh instructions. I have an idea he's invited so many people, he's running low on limousines."

"If he's running low on limousines," said Mrs. Parker, heading for a cup of coffee, "we'll have to drop him."

"Where were you last night? Van Weber was looking for you."

"He should have thought of trying Tony's. He was the one who first recommended it to us."

"Who were you with?"

"Woollcott and Jacob Singer. Then we were joined by another detective, Yudel Sherman." She was sitting now and enjoying the aroma of the fresh brew.

"Were they mourning their associate?"

"How do you know about Al Cassidy?"

"It's in the morning *World*. Small item at the bottom of the front page. You know I always read the small print on everything."

Small item, thought Mrs. Parker. Small item for big treachery. "Yes, it was a kind of a wake last night, but by the fourteenth round of booze we were feeling ever so gay."

"How's your head?"

"I'm not sure. Is it still there?"

"What are you wearing tonight?"

"I was thinking of this spiffy little number I picked up in Paris at a discount, thanks to Sara Murphy. It's a little trifle Worth dreamed up, flesh-colored *peau de soie*."

"Whatever that means."

"And what are you wearing?"

"I was thinking of a middy blouse and gym bloomers. Not sexy, but practical."

"That sounds like a nice epitaph. The coffee's nice."

"It's laced."

"I know."

"Are you planning to go off with Lacey Van Weber?"

Mrs. Parker lowered her coffee cup. "Where'd you hear that?"

"He mentioned that he'd asked you last night when he called."

"A girl isn't safe any place these days. Well, what do you think? Should I go off with him?"

"Have you been to bed with him?"

"Yes."

"Good performer?"

"Top of the bill."

"That helps. He's terribly good-looking and so marvelously urbane and so terribly wealthy."

"Why, yes, my dear," agreed Mrs. Parker, then inquiring archly, "but is that *enough?*"

They enjoyed a laugh together, but Neysa's question hung disconsolately in the air, unanswered.

"What are you thinking?" Neysa asked.

"I'm wishing."

"What are you wishing?"

"I'm wishing this was Sunday."

At ten minutes to six that evening, George S. Kaufman telephoned Mrs. Parker to tell her the transportation was waiting for him downstairs, and they would be soon picking up her group. Mrs. Parker assured him that she and the Baragwanaths were ready. She then phoned Woollcott to relay the message.

"Nervous?" he asked.

"Isn't everyone on opening night?"

Their transportation was impressive. It was an Isotta-Fraschini town car. Mrs. Parker recognized the chauffeur. He had a scar on his right cheek running from his ear to his mouth. After they picked up Woollcott and were headed for the bridge that would lead them to Long Island, Woollcott asked Mrs. Parker with a wicked look on his face, "No overnight bag, dear?"

"Why, no, Alec, Mr. Van Weber has everything one needs out there, should one care to need it." She wished somebody would raise the window that would separate them from the chauffeur. It wasn't snobbery; it was precaution.

Woollcott was wondering if Jacob Singer was already out there, somewhere in the vicinity of the estate. He had been under the impression that Van Weber had extended an invitation to Singer at Neysa's party. Singer probably preferred the use of his own vehicle to one provided by his host. He'd read penny dreadfuls where town cars such as this were rigged up to suffocate the passengers with poison gas, and subconsciously, Woollcott began sniffing the air.

"Alec," said Kaufman, "are you longing for a fire hydrant?"

"No, you leper's buttock, I thought I smelt something peculiar."

"Jack," Neysa leaned forward to her husband, "are you wearing that awful hair tonic?"

"No, dear," he said affably, "just a trace of chicken fat."

The man at the wheel was an incredibly good driver. They made it to East Cove in under an hour.

"Alec?" It was Neysa again. "Are you promising to be on your best behavior? I know how violent you can get in the midst of rampant ostentation."

"I was thinking I might spend the evening striking poses."

"He has an airplane," said Mrs. Parker. "Maybe he'll take you for a ride." She could envision the difficulty the portly Woollcott would have settling into the cockpit.

Woollcott said contemptuously, "Nobody's going to take me for a ride." Mrs. Parker saw the chauffeur's face in the rear-view mirror and didn't like his expression one bit.

Once on the road leading to the main house, Mrs. Parker said, "Welcome to Abaddon."

"Is that what he calls this place?" asked Baragwanath.

"Abaddon," explained Kaufman, "is the name of the biblical netherworld."

"George, you're so knowledgeable," said Mrs. Parker.

"I know," agreed the playwright, "but I'm not clever."

The trees along the driveway were prettily festooned with Japanese lanterns. The branches were intertwined with dazzling varieties of fairy lights. As they approached, they could hear the music of an orchestra, and in the distance, the lighthouse was aglow with what Mrs. Parker felt was an unusual incandescence. They could see guests wandering about the front lawn with maids and waiters carrying trays of food and drink.

"Some small gathering on the spur of the moment," muttered Mrs. Parker. "I wonder what he'd accomplish if given a decent amount of time."

"What are you thinking, George?" asked Woollcott.

"I'm thinking Mr. Van Weber is just a big show-off."

"Hush, dear," cautioned Mrs. Parker, "chauffeurs have ears." She wondered where was the thug who was missing part of his right ear. Probably at target practice, she decided. "Neysa, what's that strange expression on your face?"

"I'm rehearsing being decorous and aloof. It's bad taste to be impressed by other people's wealth, especially when other people have bad taste."

The town car pulled up in front of the mansion. "All right, you aardvarks," snapped Woollcott, "tidy up your minds and into the fray we go."

Lacey Van Weber saw the car arriving through a window of the dining room. He hurried outside to greet them. He came down the stairs of the veranda and put his arm around Mrs. Parker. "Don't you look glorious."

"It was wise of you to say that," responded Mrs. Parker, "because flattery might get you everywhere."

"Are you hinting you have good news for me?" He squeezed her shoulder gently, and she wished he hadn't. There was something not genuine about his gesture. There was something false about his greeting and his haste in directing her to the subject. He's rehearsed this, she decided, and I have to improvise my role in this comedy.

She looked up into his matinee idol face with a smile she remembered using the night she decided to sacrifice her virginity. "If it's good news you want, you've got it. But this isn't the time to discuss it."

"We have to discuss it soon." The urgency in his voice alarmed her.

"Are you suggesting you're planning to abandon your guests before the evening's out?"

Woollcott interrupted them. "Have you no kind words of welcome for us?" They followed him up the stairs into the house, Woollcott examining the decor of the grand hallway through his pince-nez, which he held in his right hand about an inch above the crown of his nose. "What an unusual decor!" Van Weber found a smile. "Who designed this dump, Count Dracula?"

A flunky was hurrying to Lacey Van Weber. He said

something they couldn't hear. Van Weber announced, "The Wussexes' yacht is entering the bay. They'll be docking in a few minutes."

"Oh, goodie. Dear old Fred and Elfreda," said Woollcott with undisguised venom.

"Are you a friend of Fred's?" asked Kaufman.

"Most of Fred's friends are either dead or dishonored."

Van Weber was leading them on the long walk to the rear of the house which would bring them into the terraced gardens leading down to the dock where the yacht would moor.

"The last mile," said Woollcott in an aside to Mrs. Parker.

"He's planning to blow the party early," she said hastily, hoping she wasn't overheard.

"I see. Maybe he's foreseen his little plot just might backfire."

"There was an item about Cassidy's suicide in one of the papers this morning. That might have triggered their change of plans."

"*Might* have triggered?" Woollcott didn't disguise his dismay.

Neysa asked breathlessly, "Have you looked in the dining room? He's got chairs by Marcel Breuer!"

"Neysa, stop looking like the little match girl." Kaufman's face was a perfect portrait of utter contempt and loathing. "When the hell do we get to the end of this tour?"

Van Weber had led them to the rear terraces where a six-piece orchestra was bouncily offering "It Ain't Gonna Rain No Mo'." Somehow Baragwanath managed to capture a waiter, and they were given drinks. It was like a replay of the Thursday night party at Neysa's. Mrs. Parker recognized almost everyone, except that Florenz Ziegfeld was now accompanied by his wife, the glorious, redheaded Billie Burke. She wore a brilliantly shimmering dress which reminded Mrs. Parker of a magnificent chandelier she'd seen at Versailles.

"My God!" exclaimed Woollcott, "is that an airplane

hangar I see in the distance?"

"That's what it is," said Mrs. Parker. "Maybe Lacey will take you up in his Jenny."

"Who is Jenny?" inquired Woollcott.

"That's Lacey's plane, isn't that right, Lacey?"

"It's ready for a takeoff," said Van Weber to Mrs. Parker, and the hint didn't escape her.

"What a lovely orchestra," commented Neysa. "Were the musicians just recently introduced to each other?"

Van Weber replied, "They're a local group. The best I could do on short notice."

"I think they're lovely," said Neysa, "especially the violinist. I wish somebody would tell him his rug is slipping." The musician's toupee was indeed moving slowly toward his eyebrows, as though propelled by an invisible hand.

Mrs. Parker saw the man who was missing a part of his ear. He was dressed as a butler and seemed to be looking for somebody. She wondered where Bela Horathy was hiding. Singer was positive he had fled to this haven. I wonder if he's in the laboratory, she wondered, creating one last batch of cocaine, like a diligent moonshiner waiting for the revenuers to raid his still. Missing Ear disappeared behind a perfectly trimmed hedge.

The orchestra had struck up "God Save the King." The yacht was docking and being secured to the pier by the crew assembled to complete the operation.

"Not exactly the *Aquitania*," said Mrs. Parker, "but I suppose it'll do."

Van Weber hissed in her ear. "We have to *talk*. Meet me in the gazebo in fifteen minutes." He hurried off to greet his arriving guests, now gathering on deck waiting for the gangplank to be lowered.

"He seems a bit unnerved," Woollcott commented to Mrs. Parker.

"He's rushing me. He wants me to meet him in the gazebo in fifteen minutes. I don't like this. I don't like it at all."

"Where's the gazebo?"

"It's en route to the hangar."

"Ah. And the plane is ready for a takeoff. I shall accompany you to the gazebo."

"You mustn't be seen by Van Weber."

"I won't be, my dearest mudlark." He patted his ample chest. "I've remembered to bring along my old army service revolver."

"I hope it's working better than you are."

"Freshly greased and cleaned this morning. Ah! Well, will you lookie yonder over there! Coming out from behind that beautifully clipped hedge."

With relief, Mrs. Parker recognized Jacob Singer. And then she remembered. The man with the missing ear had disappeared behind that very hedge. Supposing he had had a rendezvous. But with Jacob Singer?

Singer saw them and hurried to join them. He looked anxious and nervous. "Things are moving faster than I thought they would. They know Cassidy's dead and they're not buying the suicide rap."

"How do you know?" asked Mrs. Parker.

"A little birdie just told me."

Mrs. Parker felt a surge of relief. The man with part of his ear missing, he was one of the good guys, he worked for Singer. It had to be that. She told Singer about Van Weber's insistence she meet him at the gazebo. It worried Singer.

"I have to meet him," insisted Mrs. Parker. "I have to get the truth out of him."

"You're so sure he'll confess?"

"I have all the confidence in the world."

Woollcott stuck his head between them. "What's bothering you, Jacob? Is something going wrong?"

"It's like I said, it's moving too fast. I hope to Christ my people are prepared for it. I didn't expect the action this early. Look what's going on at the dock. They're starting to unload and the action's accelerating. Damn it, where's the Coast Guard?"

"Oh, God," groaned Woollcott, "will you look at Fred and Elfreda coming down the gangplank! Don't they look freshly disinterred? Yoo-hoo! Fred! Elfreda! This way to the mausoleum, darlings!"

17

Yudel Sherman and three members of the Nassau County police force were posted near the laboratory. He was nervous and anxious for action. The Nassau County boys looked like Boy Scouts, and he was feeling old enough to be their den mother. From a distance he had heard "God Save the King," followed by "Land of Hope and Glory," and was thinking it was a shame Van Weber couldn't have lined up the kind of snappy bunch who had played at his nephew's bar mitzvah. He stifled a yawn caused by his nervousness, a response usually reserved for the long wait while watching his wife undress. He couldn't believe anyone was having any fun tonight. "Give My Regards to Broadway." That old chestnut. He stifled another yawn.

Woollcott was enjoying himself enormously. He wasn't sure if either Fred or Elfreda remembered him; it had been so many years since he had last insulted them. "Elfreda, darling, you look like your old self again," he cooed. "What's gone wrong?" Mrs. Parker was appalled by the woman's cracked teeth and wondered if her hobby was smelting ore. She wondered if they had traveled alone and soon realized they hadn't. She recognized the two women coming down the gangplank, the repulsively fat one in the lead yodeling greetings to what appeared to be dozens of her most intimate friends.

"My evening's complete," she said sotto voce to Jacob Singer, who was watching the cargo being unloaded. "The two arriving now are Elsa Maxwell and her better half, Dorothy Fellows-Gordon with a hyphen. Dorothy is more familiarly known as 'Dickie.' They go down better if you treat them as characters invented by Gilbert and Sullivan."

"Yoo-hoo, Alec! You old Sherman tank! It's me! Marie!"

The next passenger to disembark was Marie Dressler. She was a tall and imposing figure carrying more weight than she should, and with an unfortunate face that had served to make her popular in her younger days as a music hall comedienne. Woollcott met her at the foot of the gangplank and planted a kiss on her cheek. "What are you doing with this bunch?"

"Hitchhiking, baby, the same as Maxwell and her bitter half. Such fights the past five days." She spread her hands in a lavish gesture. "I'm broke! Stone flat broke! Poverty stricken! The only way I could get out of Europe was to beg passage with Methuselah and his bride. It's not very appetizing watching people decaying before your eyes. Every morning when they came out of their suite, it was like the opening of King Tut's tomb. How do I look? Be honest, tell the truth. I haven't looked in a mirror in years. I can't stand being lied to." She charged ahead without waiting for him to answer. "What's all this festive guck about? How come we're not going through customs? Who's the Barrymore type greeting their majesties or whatever the hell you're supposed to call them?"

"I always called them 'it' and 'that,'" said Woollcott caustically. "As to what's going on here, my dear, you've landed yourself in a hornet's nest."

"Oh? Oh? Give! What's up?" Woollcott explained as much as he could in less than a minute. He knew the old trouper could be trusted. She grunted, groaned and then shrugged her imposing shoulders. "Point me to a dugout and I'll take shelter."

"Well, I'll be damned," muttered Mrs. Parker, "look what's coming down the gangplank." Woollcott moved to Mrs. Parker as Miss Dressler was led to the mansion by a footman.

"Perfect casting for our little adventure," commented Woollcott, as Jacob Singer thought he recognized a beautiful celebrity.

"Is that Jeanne Eagels?" he asked.

"That is indeed Miss Eagels," said Woollcott, his voice lyrical, "the original Sadie Thompson of *Rain*. She doesn't look too bad, does she, Dottie?"

"Not bad at all, considering her spiritual home is a cesspool." She said to Singer, "Miss Eagels is a notorious user of dope."

"I know," said Singer, "she's had some narrow escapes arranged by Judge Crater."

"Dottie, Dottie, and dear Alec. How sweet of you both to be here to meet me." Her hands were outstretched and Woollcott took both. "Where are we?"

"America," said Mrs. Parker.

"But where in America?"

"You're in East Cove, Long Island. Mr. Lacey Van Weber's estate," explained Woollcott.

"Oh, yes. Where's Elsa? She's supposed to be looking after me. Dottie, how charming you look. Is that a Worth?"

"It's a worth plenty," replied Mrs. Parker. Jacob Singer had moved away from them. He had sighted something on the horizon entering Van Weber's bay. He thought he saw boats reflected in the incandescence emanating from the lighthouse. Sons of bitches, he was thinking, it's about time. So much for "Let's synchronize watches."

Miss Eagels was saying, "I saw Tallulah in London. She's doing so nicely in *They Knew What They Wanted*. Maugham wouldn't let her do *Rain*. She thought I put him up to it. Would I do anything as vile as that?"

"Yes," said Mrs. Parker. Woollcott hastily deposited the actress with a footman who was standing by patiently. The orchestra was sawing away at "Yes, Sir, That's My Baby" and Mrs. Parker saw Van Weber hurrying in the direction of the gazebo. She ran to Singer and told him she was going off to keep her appointment with Van Weber. As she hurried after Van Weber, Singer shouted after her to wait for Woollcott.

The piercing wail of a siren shattered the noise of the festivities. It was coming from the lighthouse. The crew unloading the cargo were armed and drew their weapons. Woollcott had seen Mrs. Parker's flight and went in pursuit of her.

Yudel Sherman and his men were deployed in positions to cover the laboratory's back and front doors. He warned his men to avoid hitting the interior of the building if it was necessary to fire their weapons. The laboratory equipment would be highly sophisticated and could explode and incinerate on impact.

Van Weber, in the gazebo, could hear the Jenny warming up. In the hangar, the man with the scar running from his ear to his mouth had finished his task and, with revolver in hand, left the building on the double.

Van Weber could see Mrs. Parker approaching, silhouetted against the lights coming from the party. She entered the gazebo, out of breath. She could hear the siren joined by other sirens marking the arrival of Nassau County patrol wagons. She could hear gunfire and people shouting and screaming, and she couldn't believe Lacey Van Weber was smiling as though he had just been complimented. He took her hand and said, "We've no time to lose. The plane's ready to take off!" She pulled her hand away and backed off until she could feel a railing behind her.

"Will we be married?" She had found her breath and, partially hidden by the shadows as she was, she looked like a wraith with a disembodied voice.

"Of course we will, darling."

"What about your wife?" She heard his intake of breath.

"How did you find out about her?" She didn't recognize his voice. It was harsh and ugly. It wasn't Lacey Van Weber. It was Dennis Deane Tanner.

"Lacey, I have found out many things about you that need explaining." She was surprised at how calm and collected she was, not in the least bit frightened of this man who was quite capable of murdering her at any moment.

"I thought you loved me." He still didn't sound right. Mrs. Parker wondered if Woollcott and his trusty army surplus weapon were within aiming distance.

"A part of me will always love you."

"You had no intention of going away with me."

"I might have gone away with Lacey Van Weber, but Lacey Van Weber doesn't really exist. Lacey Van Weber is a pale imitation of Jay Gatsby, a lovely idea, but here it is backfiring. Yet it's Lacey Van Weber I love, not Dennis Deane Tanner." He said nothing. "You shot your brother. You strangled Ilona Mercury."

"That's two," he said. "I'm superstitious. Things have to come in threes." He took a snubnosed automatic from his pocket and aimed it at her. For a reason she would never understand, Mrs. Parker took a few steps toward him, emerging from the shadows, making it easier for him to kill her.

"Don't be a damned fool. You can't run forever."

He raised the weapon. A shot rang out. The weapon dropped from his hand. He clutched his shoulder, turned around and fled toward the hangar. Woollcott reached Mrs. Parker, holding the smoking revolver.

"Thank you, Alec, thank you very much."

"Are you all right? Weak at the knees or feeling faint?"

"I'm quite all right. You heard him? He didn't deny anything." They saw the plane taxiing out onto the runway. "He's getting away. That's not in the scenario, is it? Villains aren't supposed to get away."

The explosion was of such frightening intensity, it rocked the gazebo. Woollcott threw his arms around Mrs. Parker shouting, "Earthquake!"

On the dock, the explosion interrupted the exchange of gunfire between Singer and his men and their adversaries on the dock and on the yacht. Two Coast Guard boats had been placed strategically in the bay, making any hope of escape for the yacht impossible. Singer cursed and hoped Yudel Sherman wasn't a victim of the detonation.

Yudel Sherman huddled behind a large oak cursing the damn fool who couldn't shoot straight. The flames shot up like a holocaust in hell's inferno and incinerated the tree-tops. A wind from the bay was carrying flames and burning ashes toward the house. In the mansion, Elsa Maxwell was shouting for Dickie, and Marie Dressler, undaunted by impending disaster, stood at the buffet table gnawing at a turkey leg. Jeanne Eagels gathered up her overnight case which contained her cosmetics, her passport, her cash and her drugs, and hurried out of her boudoir into the hall. George S. Kaufman sat in a lawn chair with his arms folded while the undaunted orchestra struck up "Nearer My God to Thee" and Neysa and John Baragwanath waltzed on the lawn. In their suite, Lord Wussex suffered a heart attack and collapsed on the bed while his wife remained riveted to the dressing table, adjusting her wig. Florenz Ziegfeld and his wife threaded their way to their limousine while hearing the ugly rat-a-tat of .45-caliber tommy guns.

Mrs. Parker and Woollcott stood in the light of the moon watching the Jenny as it gained altitude. Woollcott's arm was around her shoulder, and he felt her body quiver as they both heard the Jenny's motor begin to sputter and fail. Mrs. Parker's hands flew to her mouth. Somewhere on the lawn, the man with the scar on his cheek heard the motor fail and smiled. Then he felt a gun being poked in his back, and the smile disappeared, somewhat slowly, like the Cheshire cat's. The man with part of his ear missing said, "Okay, killer, start walking and no tricks." The prey recognized the voice of the captor and cursed. A cop. He should have guessed.

Lacey Van Weber fought to control the foundering plane. There was no parachute. He had told that scarred fool to be sure to pack a parachute, and then he realized what was happening. Once he did, a calmness settled over him. His death had been arranged. He should have known there would be no escape. They had told his brother there was no escape, why did he dare think it would be otherwise for himself? Mrs. Parker. My dear Mrs. Parker. How wisely you chose not to accompany me, but what marvelous headlines we would have made. The plane plunged downward in a spiral. He sat back with his eyes closed. He hoped it would be quick.

The plane struck the top of the lighthouse and ignited.

The plane and the body it contained fell slowly to the ground.

"Oh, look," said George S. Kaufman, "fireworks."

18

The raid on Lacey Van Weber's estate and its attending tragedies made headlines the next night and all day Monday. On Tuesday the headlines were displaced by a brutal sex murder that took place in a midtown hotel.

Woollcott would never forget that horrible night, how Mrs. Parker screamed and how bitterly she wept and Woollcott and Singer doing their best to comfort her. Ruefully, Singer realized that if he predeceased Mrs. Parker, there would be no screaming or bitter tears, probably the gentle clucking of her tongue, a wistful shake of her head, followed by a devastating wisecrack. Reluctantly, he left the grieving woman to Woollcott, who seemed in his element as a mother hen comforting her chickadee.

Singer remembered standing still as a sudden quiet overtook the estate. The mansion had caught fire and nobody was doing anything to rescue it. At the laboratory site, Yudel Sherman was ill. There were four charred corpses lying on the grass, so badly burned they would have to be identified by dental charts, if any existed. He knew one was Bela Horathy. He had seen him earlier through a window and recognized him. He didn't recognize him now.

On Sunday, Jacob Singer and Yudel Sherman dutifully attended Al Cassidy's funeral. Sherman wept openly, and Singer was anxious to get back to the precinct and tie up all the strings still dangling from the previous night's raid.

George Raft was released from the Tombs, went back to his hotel and demanded a better room. They couldn't expect him to continue housekeeping in a place where a stiff had been found.

Texas Guinan suddenly found it necessary to book passage on the *Mauretania* for London on the pretext of urgent business. She left the management of her reopened speakeasy to her brother, Tommy, with strict instructions not to skim too much off the top of the profits or she'd have all ten of his fingers broken.

Horace Liveright secretly entered a hospital to attend to a rash that had appeared on his body that weekend. His doctor had sternly cautioned him that there could be a dangerous infection, and Liveright was horrified at the thought of possible blindness or brain deterioration. He demanded and got a prettier nurse with voluptuous breasts.

George S. Kaufman was being driven to Ring Lardner's Great Neck estate by an accommodating Florenz Ziegfeld. At the estate, Mr. Kaufman dutifully kissed Lardner's wife and daughter and when asked by his host what had gone on at Lacey Van Weber's party, Kaufman laconically replied, "Nothing much."

When Gladys Shea told Cora Gallagher they were free to leave the Royalton and that Bela Horathy was deceased, the ladies packed, checked out of the hotel, and on Monday morning bought a *New York Times* and went in search of a modestly priced apartment they wanted to rent together, hopefully, for the rest of their lives.

Lily Robson spoke to Marc Connelly on the phone Monday morning, and the playwright was saddened to hear that the luscious redhead had had her fill of Texas Guinan, mobs and New York, and was accepting an engagement at a nightclub in Chicago run by a charming young Italian she had met the previous night at a party. His name was Al Capone, and she truly believed him when he said he'd take care of her. Connelly's writing block was ended, and he went back to his typewriter.

Stella Crater read the account of the raid on the Van Weber estate and then sternly regarded her husband, the judge, across the breakfast table. "I know what you're thinking, Joseph Crater, and let me tell you don't you dare harbor any plans for disappearing!"

In Hollywood, Robert Benchley lay in bed staring out a window at a ratty palm tree. He had read and reread the accounts of the raid. There was nothing about Mrs. Parker. He supposed she'd had a lot of fun and would make capital of the event for weeks to come. He got up, got dressed, ate breakfast and called a cab to take him to the studio. He didn't plan to remain in Hollywood any longer than necessary.

Jacob Singer sat at the desk in his office remembering Mrs. Parker's dissertation on his single-minded ambitions. He was surprised it had been all that obvious, especially to her. He didn't think he mattered that much to her or to anybody else. He knew that was what was missing in his life, being of importance to another person. But that had its drawbacks. It would mean burdening himself with the responsibility of sharing a deep emotion, and he recognized from past experience it was a burden he didn't relish. He travels fastest who travels alone, right, Singer? Right.

On Monday, shortly before noon, Mrs. Parker sat by the window. The sky was overcast and so was her heart. She had been sequestered in her studio since returning from East Cove Saturday night, eating little, drinking a lot. Neysa McMein had grown hoarse from her entreaties in the hallway and finally listened to her husband and decided it was best after all to leave Mrs. Parker to sort herself out. Woollcott phoned.

"I've been on this phone all day yesterday and all this morning, and in my free moments I've been typing up my notes. Meet me for lunch and we'll work out a schedule for our collaboration. We've got to get to work before the story grows cold. Pussywillow, are you there?"

"I'm thinking about my husband."

"You mean your brain's a blank?"

"What was nice about being married to Ed was not having to think."

"Now listen, you," said Woollcott, bristling with impatience, "I know you've been through a traumatic experience and I'm more than sympathetic. But it's as plain as the nose on anybody's face, even if he wasn't a fraud and a murderer, there was no future in a relationship with Lacey Van Weber."

"Alec, do you think he'll be buried in an unmarked grave? Who's to claim his body?"

"Science, certainly not you. Now put on one of your pretty little frocks and meet me at the Algonquin. I promise to let you have equal time. Dottie?" Silence. "Dorothy?" Silence. "Mrs. Parker!" he roared.

"Goodbye, Alec," she said wistfully, and hung up the phone.

Woollcott slammed the receiver down on the hook and started to struggle out of his tattered bathrobe. He'd made a date with Polly Adler to go to her place for a game of backgammon after lunch. Mrs. Adler expressed pleasure at the tragic turn of events. But she also advised Woollcott that there would soon be another Lacey Van Weber showing up in the city. "Those boys have a manufacturing exclusive on his kind of patsy. There's always a demand. And where there's a demand, they supply." Her throat rasped as though being attacked by sandpaper.

"Well, I hope to hell whoever he is never comes within blinking distance of Dottie. She's absolutely unqualified to cope with this sort of thing. Would you believe she had hysterics when the bastard's plane crashed?"

"Alec," said Polly Adler knowledgeably, "a woman's heart is a very peculiar organ. It takes special understanding. Believe me, you're talking to a lady who's suffered her share of hysterics. I know just how she feels. I'd call and tell her, but at a time like this, you leave the lady alone. She'll get it settled in her mind soon enough."

"That's what you think! You don't know our Dottie the way I know our Dottie. She's probably eying that straightedge razor she harbors with a hunger peculiar only to her!"

Now Woollcott stared at himself in the mirror as he knotted his tie. His words to Mrs. Adler had come back to haunt him. Straightedge razor. Peculiar hunger.

"Hell fire and damnation!" shouted Woollcott as he grabbed his jacket off the back of a chair and went hurrying out of his room.

Mrs. Parker sat in the bathroom, the razor poised over one of her wrists, her eyes and soul damp with tears. She pressed the razor against the outline of the previous slashing.

She would wait to be rescued.